CROWN
OF
BRIARS

R.L. PEREZ

CROWN OF BRIARS

A BEAUTY AND THE BEAST RETELLING

CROWNS OF THE FAE

To all the readers who were disappointed when the beast transformed into a human.

Varius, in all his monstrous glory, was written for you.

Lunar Court
Winter Court
Star Court
Fire Court
Wind Court
Autumn Court
Summer Court
Sea Court
Spring Court
Earthen Court
Sun Court
Shadow Court
THE TWELVE FAE COURTS OF VALORA

SPRING COURT
EARTHEN COURT
DELLONA MOUNTAINS
TERRONA CASTLE
SHADOW COURT
PERN DISTRICT
AGNARR CASTLE
NOXEN FOREST
THE SOUTHEASTERN REGION

AUTHOR'S NOTE

This novel contains content that may be triggering. Rape and sexual assault (not between the main couple) are mentioned in reference to events that occurred in the past, but nothing graphic is described on the page. There are also scenes with attempted sexual assault.

In addition, the story includes graphic violence and graphic sexual content (consensual).

Please be mindful of your triggers and mental health before you read.

THE BEAST

Tremors wracked my body as the curse took hold, digging its claws deeper into my very soul. I groaned, the sound more like an animalistic growl, as my claws elongated and my barbed tail curled on the gravel where I lay. The skin along my back split open to make way for my wings, and I roared in agony. My claws slashed through the stone ground, adding to the grooves already there from years of the pain taking hold of me.

I clamped my teeth down hard enough for my lower fangs to dig into my top lip, drawing blood. My temples throbbed as the massive horns stretched, growing in height and casting an eerie shadow on the cave wall.

I was monstrous. And every full moon, the curse worsened, making my features even more horrifying. Making me become more of a savage beast.

Shuffling footsteps sounded nearby, and my predator senses homed in on the scent of a fae male coming my way. A growl built in my throat, until I recognized the smell. It was Clermont, my steward.

My claws dug deeper into the ground, a rumbling snarl escaping my lips.

Clermont panted when he reached the mouth of the cave. "My lord?"

"I thought I was clear I was *never* to be disturbed here," I bit out.

"I understand, but… it's the shadows. They've breached the lower towns."

My head snapped up, my nostrils flaring as I scented that horribly familiar smell. The poisons had encroached on the city.

Another ripple of pain quivered up my body. I jerked, my form twitching as I released an echoing shout. My arms and legs stretched as if I could outrun the pain. I writhed on the ground, rocks digging into my bare skin. Mother of Shade, it was unbearable.

"Varius," Clermont said, his voice laced with urgency. He rarely called me by my given name, which meant we were in far worse danger than I feared.

"I—I can't—" I groaned. "The pain…" I broke off with a sharp gasp as my skin split further, and one wing curled outward. The toughened skin of the wing was a deep bloodred, just like the rest of me. Sharpened talons were at the tips of the wing, and I knew firsthand how deeply those could slice. "Clermont, I will *slaughter* my people if I emerge like this." It was taking all my effort not to lunge at him; I couldn't fathom having to face a crowd of innocent fae.

The beast within me would destroy them all.

"I'm not saying you go to them," Clermont said. "I'm saying it's time to call on the Earthen Court."

I stiffened, my arms shaking as I braced them on the ground. Bloodred rage coursed through me, and I was seized by the sudden need to tear skin and bone, to bury my claws into someone's flesh. Violent nausea swelled within me, and I bit back a cry as I stifled the bloodlust, shoving it deep inside me.

But I knew it would resurface. It always did.

My shoulder-length black hair hung like a curtain in front of my face. But through the damp strands, I could make out Clermont's olive green skin and two sets of curled horns. His form was tall and lanky, with a small set of wings atop his shoulders.

"I am… in no condition… to visit the human royals," I rasped, barely able to contain my rage. If Clermont didn't leave the cave soon, I would rip him to shreds.

"Not you," Clermont said. "*Me.* I can go in your place."

"It isn't proper to—"

"To hell with propriety," Clermont snapped. "Our people are under attack, and with the full moon, you cannot make the journey. We must do what is necessary, my lord."

I let my head sink to the ground, succumbing to the chills trembling through my body. My wing curled around me, trying to provide warmth that would never come. Soon, the skin of my left shoulder blade would split wider, and my second wing would unfurl. This would continue well into the night.

"It's… not good, is it?" I asked in a defeated voice.

Clermont had been here for far longer than I had. He had seen my father and grandfather die. Only he knew how severe my condition would become and how much longer I had left before the curse claimed me.

The kings from before had died from the curse. Some had succumbed to the injuries inflicted by the curse's transformation. Others had become so wild and ferocious that they had to be killed before they slaughtered the entire kingdom.

I wondered which would be my fate.

"My time… is almost up," I whispered. "Isn't it?"

I heard Clermont swallow hard. His breathing turned ragged. After a moment, he said, "Yes. This was as far as your father got before the curse killed him." His voice was solemn.

I closed my eyes, trying not to think of my father. Memories of him only reminded me of my shortcomings and the grievous ways I had failed my people, as Father had often told me.

And soon, I would be joining him in the After.

Bile crept up my throat, and I resisted the urge to retch. I only had one more chance to end this. I did not want to leave this world without putting in every effort to save my kingdom.

With the last of my strength, I lifted my head to look straight into Clermont's yellow eyes. My voice was low as I said, "Bring me the human princess."

THE BEAUTY

CHARCOAL COATED MY FINGERTIPS AS I CROUCHED TO THE ground, brushing pebbles and dirt away from my specimen. Squinting, I tried to make out the color of the sheen glinting in the pale sunlight shimmering through the cavern ceiling. Underneath the rocks was a gemstone, but I couldn't tell what mineral it was.

I brought my free hand to the amber necklace at my throat. Immediately, the voice of Azure, my dragon, resonated in my head.

"Another quartz, perhaps?"

I shook my head. "No, this is too dark."

"There are darker forms of quartz."

My mouth twisted as I tried to dig my fingernails further into the rocks, but they wouldn't budge. "Damn it. I can't get to it."

"Mind if I try? My talons are much sharper than your frail human claws."

I rolled my eyes. "They aren't claws. If they *were*, you can bet they'd be sharper."

Azure's long, serpentine form appeared by my side, her pale blue scales glinting in the faint light. Her talons scraped against the rocks on the ground, making a loud crackling sound.

"Step aside, feeble human." The humor in Azure's voice drew a

smile from my lips despite her teasing. This was a frequent debate between us: which of us was the superior species? Azure argued that with her wings, size, and talons, she was clearly stronger. But with my royal connections, fae magic, and wit, I claimed I could best her.

So far, neither of us had won the argument. But, as I watched her sharp talons effortlessly cut through the impenetrable rock, I had to concede she had bested me this round.

I crossed my arms and clicked my tongue. "Stones, you are such a show-off."

Azure let out a low huff, which I interpreted as a chuckle. Sometimes, even when I wasn't touching the amber stone at my throat, she could still understand me. Perhaps it was the tone of my voice. Or perhaps it was because she knew me so well.

Ordinarily, my fae magic could only work when I was directly touching the gemstone that granted me power. In this case, the amber stone was the only way I could communicate with my dragon. She wore a collar with a matching amber stone embedded in it.

But sometimes I wondered how much we actually needed the amber at all. I had a feeling that, if I lost my supply of amber, we would still be able to read each other quite well.

Azure let out a low rumbling sound, and I immediately pressed a hand to my amber necklace.

"Interesting," she mused. *"It looks like a dark form of quartz, but I can tell it's something different. It's a stone I've never encountered before."*

My eyes flared wide at that. Azure was the only being I knew who was more familiar with gemstones than I was. It was what originally brought us together. As a child, I found her wandering our deepest caves in search of the same minerals I was looking for. When we both stumbled upon a trove of amber embedded into the cavern walls, we thought it was a sign from Fate, guiding us toward a lifetime of companionship.

I frowned, waiting for the dust to settle from her digging.

"It does look like black quartz," I said. "You're sure it's not?"

"I am quite sure." Her tone was haughty, as though offended that I even asked.

With a chuckle, I stretched a dirt-crusted hand to run the pad of my thumb over the rocks surrounding the gem, careful not to let my fingers touch the black stone. Then I glanced at the geology reference book lying open a few feet away. The worn leather tome had been our most useful resource guide during our explorations. "Onyx perhaps?"

"I have encountered onyx before as well. It does not smell like this."

"What does this one smell like to you?" I asked. As a dragon, Azure had access to sharpened senses that I could only dream of. Even if I were full-blooded fae instead of half human, my fae senses still would have paled in comparison.

Azure's wide nostrils flared, and her eyes closed. Another low hum escaped her snout. *"Shadows and poison."*

I jerked my hand back as if the rocks had burned me. "Shit."

"Relax, human. If it were dangerous, I would know."

"Oh, really?" I challenged, climbing to my feet and backing away from the stone. "You just said you had never encountered it before. How are you supposed to know if it's dangerous or not?"

"I can smell the magic on it. The Blue Amethyst blood within me calls to enchantments. This one is harmless."

Despite her words, a chill skittered down my body, and I rubbed my arms. "I don't want to risk it. Anything connected to those dark shadows is asking for trouble. Come on, we should leave."

I turned to the cave entrance, but Azure didn't move.

Pausing, I glanced over my shoulder. "Az?"

"Do you know how rare it is for me to see a stone like this?" she asked. *"I would like to keep this one."*

I swallowed hard. My skin pebbled from the cool cave air, and my heart was racing. "I'm not touching that stone."

Azure snorted, twisting her large blue head around to look at me through half-lidded eyes. *"Coward."*

I lifted my chin, offended. "I am *not* a coward. I'm just… being cautious."

"Aren't you meant to go to the Shadow Court soon? What are you so afraid of? Before long, you'll be surrounded by those toxic shadows anyway."

I closed my eyes, and bile crept up my throat. "Don't remind me."

"Sybelle."

At the sound of my name, my eyes opened and fixed on hers. They gleamed with understanding and sympathy, erasing all signs of her earlier teasing.

"You have a plan, remember?" she said. *"You will not be alone in that horrible place. I promise you."*

I nodded. "I know. I'm not afraid. Well, I'm afraid of the shadows I cannot control. But I'm not afraid of the Wraith King."

Azure tilted her head, studying me. *"What if this stone provides a way to control the shadows?"*

I chewed on the inside of my lip, considering this. I had encountered dangerous gemstones before: an explosive form of tanzanite and a rare moon garnet, both of which had emitted a shocking burst of electricity that nearly burned my hair off. With my abilities, I knew danger was a risk anytime I unearthed a new jewel.

"What if it brings the shadows closer?" I whispered, tucking a lock of chestnut hair behind my ear. The Wraith King's shadows were already on our doorstep. Father had increased the patrol and the watchmen, ordering them to alert him the moment the shadows crossed our borders. They could already be seen from our watchtowers, and the eerie mist was ever so slowly creeping closer every day.

Every generation, a princess from the royal family was given to the Wraith King to marry. After the arrangement, the shadows always receded some, as if our gift of a human bride appeased him and he felt merciful enough to withdraw his shadows.

No one knew why the Wraith King hadn't come for his bride yet. From what I'd heard, the shadows had never gotten this close before.

"Place it in the amethyst bag," Azure suggested. *"I can dig it out the rest of the way, and if you can capture it inside the bag without touching it, you'll be safe."*

My heart lurched. The bag—or rather, pouch—was made from Azure's steely blue scales, which warded it from any magical influence. Once a gem was inside the bag, I couldn't use it to fuel my powers.

I set down my pack and dug through it until I found the tiny blue drawstring bag. Azure got to work digging the stone out. I slid the bag open, and when she nudged the loose gem with her talon, it rolled into the bag. I sealed it shut.

"Nice work," I told her.

"You will let me study that later, right?"

Half my mouth quirked into a smile as I slid the bag into my pack and shouldered it. "We'll see."

Terrona Castle was nestled in a large cavity between two jagged mountains. As a child, I had grown up yearning for the dreamy princess castles I'd read about in fairy tales, with lush fields, sparkling rivers, and ornate metal towers that gleamed in the sunlight.

Our palace was forged from the strongest steel in the realm.

Its square structure looked more like a gloomy fortress than a castle. It was built for practicality, not beauty. The impenetrable metal not only blended in with the rocky surroundings, but it also protected us from invaders.

Unfortunately, nothing could protect against the Wraith King's shadows. But Father often reminded me that we were lucky we only had one enemy to face: the Shadow Court. Other courts were often at odds with two or three kingdoms at a time. And, since our court was populated mostly by humans, it made us an easy target.

I wasn't so sure, though. Perhaps it was our impressive fortress that frightened other kingdoms away, but I had a sneaking suspicion most of them were wary of our close proximity to the Shadow Court. If I lived in a different court, I certainly wouldn't be eager to seize a kingdom soon to be overtaken by deadly shadows. It would seem like a lost cause.

Azure and I navigated our way out of the tunnels, using her claw marks on the cavern walls as a guide. Over the years, we had explored so many places that it was easy to get lost along the way.

When we reached the mouth of the cave that opened up to the winding pebbled path leading to the castle, I turned to Azure and brushed my hand along her lengthy snout. I pressed my fingers to my amber necklace and whispered, "Be safe. You know how to reach me."

"Can I take that black stone with me?"

I snorted. "Not a chance. I want to be there when you experiment with it. Let me do some research first, to see if I can dig up any information about it."

Azure huffed in dismay. *"You wanted nothing to do with it earlier."*

"No, I just didn't want to touch it. I'm still curious, and I want to know more." Already, I was itching to search the books in the library, my favorite place in the castle. I found nothing more relaxing than curling up by the fireplace with an enthralling read, surrounded by the smell of ink and parchment. Alone and unbothered. Just how I liked it.

Azure's eyes flared wider, and I could have sworn she was rolling them at me. *"Fine. It will be easy to steal that bag away from you anyway. I'll give you the day to research and then snatch it tomorrow."*

I laughed, knowing it was an empty threat. The cinched opening of the bag was too small for her talons to pry apart. "We can inspect the stone together. I promise. But I've been away for too long. Father has probably already sent guards to look for me."

My father knew about my fae ability, but he didn't know I often snuck around caves in search of new gemstones. If he knew, he would have me locked in my bedroom. He wouldn't risk anything getting in the way of my lessons, not when they would help prepare me for becoming the Wraith King's bride.

"Don't forget to write to our mutual friend about this discovery," Azure reminded me.

I nodded. She was referring to Eira, the princess of the Winter Court. I had met her at a ball in the Fire Court years ago. Like me, Eira was half fae, but in a court of mostly fae nobles, she was looked down upon because of her human bloodline. Azure had spent some time in the Winter Court before settling in my court, so she was acquainted with the Winter Princess, too.

Already, a smile tugged at my lips at the thought of how I would compose my next letter to her. Eira and I often wrote to each other in vague references that only the two of us would understand, in case our letters were intercepted.

"I won't forget," I promised, playfully flicking Azure's ear. I wrapped my arms around her, burying my face in her scaly neck. "I mean it—be safe."

When I withdrew, she fixed her wide blue eyes on me. I

touched my amber stone, and she murmured, *"Don't worry, Sybelle. I am always careful."*

I offered a small smile before I started down the gravel path. When I glanced behind me, Azure had already disappeared into the caves.

My heart sank just a fraction. Oh, how I longed to bring her home with me. But it was too dangerous. For centuries, the dragons belonged solely to the Summer Court. But over the last decade or so, the creatures had been spreading out, finding homes in other courts. Azure was young when I first found her, and I was too afraid someone would cage her or kill her. So, I kept her to myself. And even now, with her large size and ability to defend herself, I loved her too much to risk it. Father would weaponize her and try to use her against the Shadow Court, even at the expense of her life.

No, Azure was much safer kept away from the politics of my family.

So, with a heavy heart, I left her to the safety of the caves as I made my way back to the palace.

As expected, Gerard, the captain of the guards, was pacing in front of the outer gate. Four other soldiers patrolled alongside him. He scrubbed a hand down his clean-shaven chin, his expression agitated.

At my approach, his dark eyebrows drew together, a muscle feathering in his jaw. His blue eyes swept over my form, taking in my dirty tunic and stained hands.

"Again?" Gerard muttered, running a hand through his bronze hair. "My lady..."

"I know," I said with a sigh. "I'll go inside and get cleaned up."

Gerard leaned closer to me, glaring as he hissed, "Protecting this kingdom is hard enough without wayward princesses to chase after. You would do better to stay within the palace walls where you're meant to be. The king has already made inquiries into your absences."

I narrowed my eyes at him before taking a step back, putting more distance between us. "How about you mind your own damn business, Gerard?"

His lips flattened with irritation, but he said nothing else before waving me through the gate.

Despite my barbed retort, my heart thrummed with anxiety. If Father was suspicious of my frequent outings, he might start investigating. He could discover my trove of gemstones. Or worse, he might find out about Azure.

Shit. If Father was already looking for me, then the library would have to wait. I needed to face him to smooth things over.

But first, I had to change. I was filthy from my time in the caves.

Perhaps Gerard was right. Perhaps I needed to stay away from the caves for the next few days, just until Father's temper cooled.

But I promised Azure we would study the new stone together. And what if it ended up helping us with our plans to take down the Shadow Court?

I hurried through the outer bailey and took the back entrance toward the inner gate. Keeping to the rear side of the castle, I entered through the servants' quarters. It was the longer way to my chambers, but it ensured I wouldn't encounter my father or my sister.

Four corridors and three flights of stairs later, my legs were throbbing. My face and neck were coated in sweat as I finally reached my bedchamber. Gasping for breath, I stumbled inside, then leaned against the closed door, shutting my eyes for a moment while waiting for my pulse to slow.

A low chuckle drew my attention, and I stiffened. "I can't believe I beat you here. You took the servants' route again, didn't you?"

I sank against the door in relief as a figure stepped out of the shadows, drawing closer to smirk at me.

"After your *dire warning*, can you blame me?" I teased.

Gerard's smile widened as he closed the distance between us. His hands went to my waist as he pinned me to the door, making the frame rattle. "Nice deflection, by the way, snapping at me like that."

"We wouldn't want your men suspecting anything, would we?"

"Certainly not." His hips ground into me as he brought his mouth to mine.

I moaned, arching against him as his tongue ravished mine. I was filthy, and he reeked of sweat, but I didn't care. The moment his hands were on me, my body ached for that sweet release.

Gerard seemed to be thinking the same thing. In a swift movement, he tugged at my trousers until they were down to my knees. Then, he flipped me around with my chest against the door. I heard the rattle of a buckle as he loosened his belt, then felt his hard length press between my legs.

Without preamble, he plunged inside me, and I gasped at the suddenness of that singular hard thrust. His hips jerked as he drove into me further, and my eyes closed, my body quivering from the friction of his movements. He pumped again and again, each thrust more wild and feral than the last. His grunts became more strained, and I found myself clenching around him as I drew closer to that edge, closer to tumbling off the cliff...

He let out a loud, hoarse groan as he came, and I gasped, following after, the pleasure firing down my body in violent waves. For a long moment, he held himself there, still inside me, allowing our bodies to settle.

Ever so slowly, he withdrew, turned me back around, and buckled his belt again. Sweaty locks of hair clung to his forehead as he offered me a roguish grin, his face flushed.

"I would offer to pull your trousers back up, but I think you need a wash," he teased, still breathless from our intercourse.

I shoved his arm playfully. "You ass."

Truth be told, if I hadn't been worried about my father, I would have invited him to share a bath with me. Lately, my appetite had become more insatiable, and I found myself wanting more than the few minutes of bliss Gerard offered.

I probably shouldn't have even paused for this quick shag with him, but my muscles were so tight with apprehension that I had been desperate for a diversion. This had been exactly what I needed to calm my nerves before facing the king.

"You should leave before Ramia catches you," I said, sliding out of my trousers and stepping away from the door. My maid had an uncanny sense of when to intrude on us. I had a feeling she already knew about my relationship with Gerard, but she was mercifully discreet about it.

Gerard grunted in agreement, smoothing back his hair. "I wanted to see if you'd found any new gemstones."

I cut him a sharp glance. "Perhaps," I hedged. I didn't want to share about the mysterious dark stone Azure and I had found. Not until I knew for sure what it could do. I didn't want to get Gerard's hopes up. "Any news on the shadows?"

"Four men were found dead at the border."

"The border?" My stomach dropped. "You mean they didn't even cross over before the shadows infected them?"

Gerard shook his head, his expression grim. "The shadows are now close enough that the border is too dangerous to patrol. We had to pull our soldiers back to ensure they are a safe distance away."

A knot formed in my throat, and I closed my eyes to ward off the grief that threatened to drown me. If humans inhaled the toxic shadows for more than ten minutes, the poisons festered inside their bodies, killing them almost instantly.

My kingdom would endure the same fate, if the shadows got much closer.

Now, we couldn't even reach the borders of our own lands without the risk of death.

"You know the Wraith King could come for you any day now," Gerard said, his voice strained.

"I know that," I snapped, opening my eyes to glare at him.

"Do you really think your diamond dagger will be enough?"

"Yes, I do." Diamonds were hard to come by, but the few I had experimented with gave me the strength of five fae soldiers when wielded properly. I was confident my dagger with diamonds fused into the hilt would be enough to kill the Wraith King.

"Have you tested it on an unseelie fae before?" Gerard prompted.

"Of course not! Even if I *could* find an unseelie to try it out on, I'm not so heartless as to take the life of an innocent stranger."

"The unseelie aren't innocent," he said darkly. "Half a dozen of them were spotted attacking the village of Pruitt yesterday. They are a scourge that should be purged from the realm."

I resisted the urge to roll my eyes, even as my insides tightened at the thought of more unseelie creatures attacking my people. Gerard said *unseelie*, but I knew he meant *fae.* Even though I was technically seelie, I knew my magic made him uncomfortable. His blatant distaste for all things fae often raised my hackles. The very magic he despised ran through my veins.

But it was also the key to saving our people. Even he couldn't argue against that.

"I have more than just Wraith Killer," I said, using my name for the diamond dagger. "There's also the enchanted rose. If I find that, I can cut off the source of his power."

Gerard gave me a flat look. "Stones, I still can't believe you put your stock in that fable."

"All fables came from somewhere. And all magic has a source."

"I only trust what I can see. And I've seen what your dagger can do, so I'll put my trust in that."

I shook my head, unwilling to argue with him about this. I had studied the ways of the Shadow Fae much more than he had. My entire life had been spent preparing for the day the Wraith King would come for me, so my schedule was packed with combat training, history lessons, instruction in the ways of the unseelie fae, and linguistics studies. I had read every text available on the history of their people and how the poisonous shadows had come to fruition.

Father was hopeful it would prepare me to survive whatever brutal conditions the Wraith King had in store for me. But my studies had revealed the key to the Wraith King's power: the enchanted rose. Legend told of a garden within the Shadow Court that had sprouted a lush rosebush. Within the rosebuds had blossomed a kernel of power. Once touched by the unseelie, shadows had erupted from it, coating the earth and spreading like wildfire. It had consumed the garden, causing it to decay and rot, leaving nothing but a lone rose in its wake. The stories claimed that one remaining rose was the source of the king's shadows. As long as it lived, so did the magic that threatened my kingdom.

If I could cut off the source of his magic, not only could I destroy his shadows for good, but I could end his life, too. And then my people and my land would be free.

As unpleasant as it would be to live in the Shadow Court as the Wraith King's bride, I would endure it to save my people. I would do anything to protect my home.

"You really should go," I said as I removed my tunic. "They'll be looking for you. At least until I face my father."

Gerard's hungry gaze roved over me once more. Despite my dirt-stained skin and the band over my breasts, I was revealing an awful lot of skin to him. His eyes darkened with lust, but he nodded before opening the door.

"Don't forget our goal, love," he said before shutting it.

I sighed as he left. How could I forget? My entire life had been devoted to this cause.

If I failed, my kingdom was doomed. I was our only chance of survival.

With that bleak thought, I removed the rest of my clothes and headed toward the bathing chamber, dreading the looming confrontation with my father.

THE BEAUTY

Today, I encountered a dark one, similar to Onyx. It was unfamiliar. Might be connected to the surly fellow we discussed previously.

A smile spread across my face, my quill poised in the air as I considered my next words to Eira. I had already bathed and dressed in my shift. I knew I should be continuing to get ready, but I wanted to write to my friend before I forgot. In our previous letters, we had joked about how the Wraith King was likely a surly old codger who liked to complain about everything.

Somehow, it made things easier, imagining him to be old and on the edge of death. Even if, deep down, I knew fae were immortal.

Blue wants to investigate right away. But I'm nervous. What do you think? I don't want to dabble in anything related to the old codger.

Blue was our nickname for Azure. Already, I could picture Eira writing me back, hastily listing out all manner of ridiculous ideas for what the new stone could do. Once, she'd suggested a gem could grant me the power to squawk like a crow, realistic enough to fool even the smartest of birds.

I snorted at the memory. Eira never ceased to make me laugh.

I had barely finished my letter when Ramia, my maid, burst into my rooms carrying a bundle of crimson fabric. Her graying brown hair was unusually frazzled, and I assumed her haggard state had something to do with my father's mood.

I straightened, setting down my quill. "Is it bad?"

Ramia pursed her lips, her eyes flashing with a warning. After she laid the red dress on my bed, she said, "It's certainly not one of his finer days, my lady."

"Does he—" I broke off with a hard swallow. Ramia had never outright asked me about my cavern exploits, but she was too shrewd not to notice my charcoal-stained skin and clothes.

"As far as I can tell, he only suspects insubordination and youthful recklessness," Ramia said, her eyes softening just a fraction. "Nothing more."

I nodded, and she fastened the corset around me. I sucked in a breath as she tightened the strings. The boning tugged against my chest and rib cage, and in her haste, Ramia's efforts were enough to squeeze the air right out of me.

"No time to do your hair properly," she muttered before twisting the wet locks into an elegant knot and pinning it in place at the top of my head. When my hair was dry, it was a warm chestnut, but right now it looked almost black, standing out starkly against my pale skin.

After giving me a pair of ruby earrings to match my dress, along with my usual amber necklace, Ramia nodded tersely before stepping to the side to let me exit my chambers. Before I left, I grabbed my diamond dagger and strapped it to my thigh. Ramia pursed her lips in disapproval but said nothing.

I felt more at ease with my dagger on me. And she was accustomed to this.

I made my way to the door, but she gripped my arm tightly, her gray eyes widening.

"Take care with him, my lady," she murmured. "He's barking at *everyone* today."

I wasn't sure there was anything I could do that would improve his mood, but I nodded appreciatively just the same. After leaving my rooms, I hiked up my skirts and ran down the hall, practically flying down the staircase to get to the throne room as soon as possible. Father was likely already waiting for me, but the faster I could get there, the sooner I could rectify whatever damage my absence had caused.

When I reached the throne room doors, I found my sister, Orla, lingering in the hall. Her dark blonde hair fell in tight ringlets around her heart-shaped face. Her cold blue eyes surveyed me with savage smugness. It always delighted her when I disobeyed Father.

I paused for a moment to catch my breath, intending to ignore her.

"You've really done it now, Sybelle," she said, amusement lacing her voice. "You would think, after so many years, you would learn."

I glared at her. "Is that really why you're here? To *gloat*?"

"Well, your constant failures are far too amusing for me to pass up the opportunity." She chuckled.

"Don't you have something better to do than stand here, taunting me? You're the future queen of this kingdom. You should probably start acting like it."

Her smile slipped off her face, and her eyes sharpened. "Don't you dare tell me what to do, you half-breed scum. You are nothing to me. And once the Wraith King comes for you, I won't spare you a single thought. I hope his shadows choke the life out of you."

Orla turned and stormed off, but not before I shouted after her, "If the shadows take me, they're coming for you next!"

Her posture stiffened, but she said nothing before leaving the hall.

I took a few deep breaths, trying to calm my racing heart. The last thing I needed was for Father to reprimand me for panting and sweating, both of which were improper for a lady of my standing.

After a moment, I lifted my chin and strode into the throne room. My back was straight, my arms stiff at my sides, and my chin lifted, all with perfect poise as I glided toward the center of the room, directly across from where my father sat. Slowly, I sank into a perfect curtsy, and then rose, waiting for Father to address me.

He was perched on the throne, eyebrows drawn together and mouth puckered in a scowl so fierce that even his dark beard seemed to sag with displeasure. He said nothing at my entrance, and the double doors slammed shut, sealing me inside.

Twenty minutes passed by with me standing there as still as a marble statue, waiting for him to acknowledge my presence. But I was accustomed to this. It was a mark of his fury that he forced me to stand for that long. Once, when he was particu-larly enraged with me, he made me wait for an hour.

Another five minutes passed, but I refused to break. A bead of sweat trickled down the back of my neck and between my shoulder blades, but still, I did not move. My expression of stoic apathy remained fixed on my face.

After an eternity, Father exhaled deeply and said, "I am very disappointed in you, Sybelle."

I said nothing. I did not move. His words meant he was ready to speak with me, but it did not mean I was allowed to reply. Not yet.

"I sent for you an hour ago," he went on. "You were nowhere to be found. Your tutor had to reschedule your history lessons, and I told him you were more than happy to accommodate his schedule. Now you have not only inconvenienced him, but I have had to rearrange my budget meetings as well. What kind of king am I if I cannot even command my own unruly daughter to do my bidding?"

I bit the inside of my cheek to keep from lashing out at the implication that I was an ornery toddler who needed a firm hand. All because I had not been obediently doing needlework in the sitting room, merely waiting to be summoned like a servant. Of all my grievances, Father was most upset with the fact that I'd had better things to do than wait around for him to give me orders.

"Where were you?" Father demanded.

A question. Now, I could finally respond.

Because of the fae blood running through my veins, I could not directly lie to him. Thankfully, I'd had plenty of practice with this.

"I was in the caves," I said. "The men have been complaining about tunnels caving in as of late. I was curious about which ones were giving them trouble."

None of these statements were lies. I *had* been curious about the cave-ins, but only to determine how many gems I could unearth from them.

Father rubbed his temples with a weary sigh. "And you thought it best to investigate by yourself? Without any supervision?"

I bristled at that. "I am not a child in need of a nanny."

"Do not talk back to me!" Father barked. "Your foolishness suggests otherwise. What if the tunnel had caved in on *you*? No one knew where you were. And all those years of training you to meet the Wraith King would have been wasted."

I frowned. No regrets over my imaginary death. He was only lamenting the *training* he'd wasted.

Slowly, Father rose from the throne, his golden robes

swishing behind him as he stepped closer to me. His slick brown hair gleamed in the light of the chandelier.

"Do you know how tirelessly I have worked these twenty-five years to ensure our kingdom's success?" he asked, his voice soft. "I sullied myself with fae concubines just to produce a child with fae gifts who could one day overpower the Wraith King. I have spent all our gold on the finest tutors and weapons masters. For years, I have only sought the best for you. I have sacrificed *everything* for you and for what you can do for this kingdom. And this is how you repay me? If you want me to stop treating you like a child, then stop acting like one."

My hands balled into fists at my sides, and my arms shook with anger. How dare he? How dare he lecture me on what *he* had sacrificed for this kingdom? I had been bred as a weapon to be used against the Wraith King. From birth, that was all I was: a tool. Nothing more. I had one singular purpose, and beyond that, I was nobody. Father didn't care if I had hopes and dreams. He didn't care if I suffered. All he cared about was for me to be perfectly obedient and prove I could perform the assignment I had been born to fulfill: destroy the Shadow Court.

"Father, I only wanted—" I began, but he interrupted me, his voice booming.

"You *wanted?*" His eyes burned with fury. "What makes you think that I care at all about what you *want?*"

My stomach twisted as if he had shoved a dagger into my gut.

But Father wasn't finished. "You are the eldest. And, just as my older sister was taken, so, too, will you. It is your sacred duty. We all make sacrifices for our people, and this is yours. Right now, the only thing that matters is your responsibility to the Earthen Court. Do your duty. Take down the Shadow Court. Then you can live your life as freely as you wish." He waved his hand idly in the air. "Wander the caves. Roam about the grounds. Whatever you choose to do, I do not care."

He leaned closer, his eyes steely. "But for right now, your wants and desires do not matter. You are nothing and no one, at least not until you fulfill your task. The sooner you accept this, the happier you'll be."

I could only stare at him in blank horror as my chest filled with knots.

Father despised my fae blood, just like Gerard. He hated that he *needed* me to possess fae magic in order to defeat the Wraith King.

But I was not as monstrous as those unseelie beasts. I had feelings and emotions. I could feel pain.

And Father was essentially sending me off to my death.

Did he feel nothing for me? Would he feel any regret at all once I was gone?

In a way, he was right. The most important thing was protecting my home and my people. Even if I hadn't been trained for it my entire life, I would gladly walk into the shadow-infested lands to spare my people any more pain and suffering.

But, just once, I wanted Father to act as if it bothered him to send me off to the Shadow Court. Just once, I wanted to see some emotion—regret, worry, concern, *anything*.

Something besides this cool detachment.

Clearly done with our conversation, Father turned to leave the throne room. Before he left, he said to the guards standing by the doors, "Keep the Lady Sybelle confined to her rooms. Her meals will be brought to her for the next week."

My heart sank to my stomach like a stone in a river. *Confined to her rooms.*

An entire week.

Stones, how was I going to survive without Azure? Without my gems?

A pair of soldiers suddenly burst into the throne room, gasping for breath. I stilled, pulse thundering in alarm.

Father stiffened, his eyes blazing. "What is it?" he barked.

"It's the Wraith King," said one of the soldiers. "He's here."

My heart seized with dread.

He's here.

It's time.

Father's face drained of color, and for a moment, he froze, unable to respond. I, too, was rooted to the spot, my thoughts roaring. Panic pulsed in my body, but I was still as a statue.

A soldier cleared his throat, and Father recovered first. "To the outer gates. All of you, now!"

He didn't spare any of us a glance before he fled the room, no doubt to ready himself for the Wraith King's arrival. The guards around me scurried to obey, ignoring me entirely.

I took only a moment to draw in a few deep breaths before the terror could overwhelm me. Then I snapped into action.

Because I knew what was expected of me. I'd spent my whole life preparing for this moment.

I gathered my skirts and hurried out of the throne room, then raced down the steps toward the open entrance doors. Soldiers were already pouring outside to flank the outer gates.

I had just reached the outer bailey when a soldier stepped in my path, and I collided with him with an ungraceful, "Oof!"

The man turned, catching me by the waist before I fell on my ass. I looked up at him, and my heart lodged itself in my throat.

It was Gerard. His face was pale and stricken with horror. Gone was the playful smirk I both loved and loathed. In its place was a sickening dread that matched my own.

His hands steadied me, and I grasped his arm, not caring who saw us. Everyone was so preoccupied with the Wraith King's arrival that no one would care about my feelings for Gerard.

Besides, by this time tomorrow, I could be dead.

"Have you seen him?" I panted.

Gerard shook his head, his jaw tight. "The patrol spotted the carriage a few miles out. It should be here any moment."

I sucked in several panicked breaths, unable to get enough oxygen into my lungs.

Gerard's hands framed my face as he brought his forehead to mine. "Breathe, love. It will be all right. I'll take you away from here."

I jerked away from him in surprise. "What?"

He was shaking his head, his mouth twisting into a grimace. "I can't do it, Sybelle. I can't watch that monster take you." He grasped my wrist, then hauled me back toward the entrance doors.

I dug my heels in, pulling my arm from his grip. "Gerard!" An incredulous laugh bubbled up my throat. When he grabbed my upper arm instead and continued to drag me, I shoved at his shoulder. The steel armor rattled, but my movements made no difference.

"*Gerard!*" I hissed, finally managing to free my arm. I took three steps back, ensuring a healthy distance separated us. He had never acted like this before. He had never grabbed me tightly enough to bruise. I cast a quick glance around the courtyard, but the soldiers flitting about were too distracted to notice our interaction. "What the hell are you doing? We've been planning this for years. We knew this day would come."

His eyes burned with regret as he strode toward me. "I thought I was strong enough, but I'm not. How can I just stand by and let you go?"

"It's my choice!"

"I don't care. You can hate me all you want, but I'm taking you away from here." His arms gripped my waist again.

The savage determination in his gaze chilled my blood. He was about to hoist me over his shoulder like a sack of grain. In this wretched dress, I couldn't do much. But I'd endured years of training.

Before he could lift me, I hooked my ankle behind his and tugged. He crashed to the ground, the metal of his armor clattering loudly. I drew Wraith Killer, and a surge of supernatural strength filled me. Gerard thrust upward, but I pinned him with my arm, slamming down hard enough for the back of his head to crack against the concrete. He groaned, his eyes going unfocused for a moment. He blinked rapidly until his wide eyes fixed on me.

I brought the blade to his throat, and he froze.

"I will do this for my people," I whispered. "And if you get in my way, I will end you. We both agreed that, for the good of the Earthen Court, I would marry the Wraith King. Do you have so little faith in our plan? Do you honestly believe I will fail?"

"You don't know what waits for you in that hellhole!" he rasped. "It isn't safe, and you can't handle—"

"I can't handle *what?*" I growled.

He licked his lips. "You have not seen war or battle, Sybelle. You have not endured grave injuries or torture before. I fear that whatever awaits you in his kingdom will break you."

"Whatever awaits me is *my* burden to bear and mine alone. And it is still my choice. Not yours. I've made my decision." I withdrew, rising to my feet. A bead of blood trickled down his neck as he glared up at me.

I sheathed my dagger, then turned and hurried down the courtyard to the outer gates. By the time Gerard would be able to climb to his feet in all that armor, I would be among the line of people awaiting the Wraith King's arrival. He wouldn't be able to snatch me with so many witnesses.

Seething, I marched down the steps, finding the gates already wide open with lines of soldiers on each side. My hands formed shaking fists at my sides as I replayed that moment with Gerard over and over.

He had tried to haul me away against my will.

He was no better than the Wraith King.

We had a plan! How had he forgotten?

I remembered the derision with which he'd spoken about the tale of the enchanted rose. My heart sank.

He didn't have faith in me. He thought I would fail.

A knot formed in my throat, and I swallowed hard, shoving away all thoughts of Gerard. He didn't matter. Not right now.

All that mattered was my plan.

THE BEAST

F‌OR THREE DAYS, I LAY CURLED UP ON THE CAVERN FLOOR, quivering in agony as the change ripped through my body. By now, both wings had split through my flesh, carving new scars along my body. Barbs coated my tail, the tender skin still festering from where the sharpened points had pierced it when they had emerged.

Clermont was right. It had never been this severe before.

The curse was growing stronger, and I couldn't stop it.

I should have sent for the human girl sooner, I lamented. Perhaps if I had, I could have done more. Now, I feared I wouldn't even survive her arrival. The pain was so excruciating that I often blacked out, only to awaken several hours later, trembling in cold sweat, with fresh blood dripping down my body from my new wounds.

A loud caw jolted me from my anguished haze, and I blinked incoherently toward the sound. A flutter of wings, and then a large raven appeared, cocking her head at me in curiosity.

"What," I bit out, my voice hoarse from screaming.

Tislora spread her wings wider. Her feathered form stretched and morphed, the wings growing until they eclipsed her entire small body. When she withdrew them, she had shifted into her full unseelie form: a tall, shadowed figure with long, black claws, charcoal skin, and eerie silver eyes. Her raven wings were massive. They fluttered behind her, leaving several black feathers in their wake.

"I thought you'd like to know that Clermont has just left to fetch your human pet," she said, inspecting her lethal claws and flicking a feather off them.

My eyes closed with relief. *Good.* She would be here soon. Perhaps her presence alone would help alleviate the fury of my curse. Though I doubted it would be that easy.

When Tislora only continued to stand there watching me, I snapped, "Anything else?"

She hesitated before replying. "Do you wish for me to extract her blood upon her arrival?"

I growled, the sound low and menacing in my throat. Behind me, my wings flared with my anger, despite the festering cuts along my back that throbbed from the movement. "No," I said through gritted teeth. "You should know better than to ask."

"What I know is that you are a step away from death," Tislora countered. "Your temper doesn't frighten me, Varius. I will do what it takes to keep our sovereign alive, even if your own stupidity gets in the way."

"I... can manage," I rasped, "without her blood."

"I don't believe you."

My strength was failing. Darkness crept into the corners of my eyes. I was in danger of blacking out again. I didn't have the energy to argue with her. As a fae, I couldn't lie, but Tislora knew that if I *believed* the statement, then I could still utter the words.

I believed I could survive without human blood. But Tislora did not.

Tislora knelt to the ground, her black cloak spreading around her like an ink stain. Her silver eyes flashed like orbs. "If you do not emerge from this cave by tomorrow, I will extract her blood. Better to risk her ire than to lose you."

I looked up at her, trying to glare, but my head was spinning, and all I could do was rest my head on the rocky ground with a ragged exhale.

"That's what I thought." Tislora stood, her wings quivering as if preparing to take flight.

"Lor," I called out.

She turned to face me, a single eyebrow raised.

"Do not harm her."

She rolled her eyes. "I can't take her blood without injuring her, Varius."

"I mean…" I swallowed, my mouth parched, then tried again, "Do not use excessive force. Do not frighten her more than is necessary. Understand?"

Her lips tightened, and I couldn't tell if it was amusement or irritation that flickered across her features. "Fine."

Without another word, her wings spread wide, and with a *whoosh*, she left the cave. A burst of magic indicated she had shifted to a raven once more, and her echoing caw was the last I heard before I succumbed to unconsciousness once more.

THE BEAUTY

My heart was hammering in my chest as I raced toward the outer gates. Just before I got there, I brought my fingers to the amber stone at my throat. "The Wraith King is here," I whispered to Azure. "You know what to do."

By now, my dragon had likely sensed the commotion and drawn closer to the castle in case I needed her. Sure enough, her voice sounded in my head.

"I will follow the carriage. Don't worry, Sybelle, I know your scent better than anyone's. I will not leave you alone."

Relief and warmth filled my chest. At least there was still one friend I could count on.

I would not be alone.

My chin lifted as I strode through the gates. Father and Orla were already standing with the guards, backs straight and expressions grim as they waited for the carriage to draw closer.

With a deep breath, I positioned myself on Father's left side, my eyes fixed on the valley that curved between the twin mountains. In the distance, I could hear horse hooves crunching along the gravel path.

My heart thundered a riotous rhythm, and my pulse quickened as the sounds drew closer.

Then, a black carriage appeared, rounding the curve of the valley. My chest constricted at the sight. It was twice as big as our largest carriage. An eerie gray fog billowed behind it, an echo of the shadows waiting for me in the Wraith King's court. The horses were not horses at all but massive skeletal beasts with gleaming red eyes. Their thin, membranous, black skin barely covered their bones, revealing rib cages and muscle. It wasn't until the carriage was a few paces away that I realized the dark shapes along the beasts' backs were wings that had been tucked in.

Wings.

These creatures could *fly*.

Stones, what am I getting myself into? I didn't want to know what hellish realm these creatures came from.

But that realm was going to be my home. Bile crept up my throat, my stomach churning with unease.

Shadows swirled as the carriage stopped and the doors opened of their own volition. I had a wild thought that perhaps the carriage was alive before I noticed the spindly creature hanging on the door handle, holding it open for the occupant. I blanched, realizing the scaly beast had blended into its surroundings like a chameleon. It wore no clothes and had a long tail that flicked behind it.

I swallowed hard, trying to maintain my composure.

From within the carriage, a large figure emerged. My heart galloped in my chest at the sight of him. He had olive green skin, also like a reptile. His gleaming yellow eyes seemed to glow like lamplights as he surveyed the entourage awaiting him. Two sets of white curled horns rested atop his head, and a pair of leathery green wings was perched atop his shoulders. They were so small, though, that I doubted they would be able to hold him up at all, which made me wonder what their purpose was.

The unseelie fae gracefully stepped down from the carriage. He wore an immaculate mauve suit with a fine-trimmed waistcoat. A long, thin tail extended from his rear and slithered along the pebbled road behind him as he approached.

Stones, was this the Wraith King? His form was much more diminutive than I would have expected. He couldn't have been more than a few inches taller than I was, and he was rather scrawny, too. Certainly not the formidable hellish beast I'd heard whispers of.

Beside me, Father stiffened, his eyes narrowing with distaste. "What is this?" he barked. "Where is the king?"

My mouth went dry. This wasn't the Wraith King?

"King Maddox." The green-skinned fae bowed deeply before replying. "My lord sends his deepest apologies. He is detained at the moment and sent me in his stead to fetch his human bride."

"I will not sacrifice my oldest daughter to anyone less than the husband promised to her," Father snapped. "I will certainly not hand her over to some unseelie creature I've never seen before."

I barely refrained from rolling my eyes. Father had no qualms with giving me over to a stranger. He was only offended the king hadn't deigned to grace us with his presence.

The fae bowed again. "Forgive me. My name is Clermont. I am the king's steward. I assure you, your daughter is safe with me."

"How am I to believe you? The moment she is out of sight, perhaps you intend to devour her like some cobra."

"Father, the fae cannot lie," I said without thinking.

Father's eyes flashed as he cut a glare at me. "Be silent, daughter," he growled.

My mouth clamped shut, and I bowed my head in submission, but Clermont only chuckled.

"She is correct," he said. "I cannot lie to you. Rest assured, my king would be here if he could. He would not have sent me in his place if the matter were not urgent. Your daughter is needed as soon as possible."

My eyebrows lifted. "Why?" As far as I knew, the Wraith King demanded a human bride every generation as a show of good faith between our kingdoms. In exchange, he kept his shadows from invading our kingdom. But perhaps there was more to it than that. Perhaps there was another reason he required a human princess.

"*Sybelle*," Father ground out, gripping my arm tightly enough to bruise.

"If I am to be handed off to this stranger, I deserve to know why!" I said, my temper flaring.

"The king will explain more to you once you arrive," Clermont assured me. His gaze shifted to my father, then back to me. I wondered if the Wraith King had forbidden him to give more information before taking me.

Or perhaps he didn't trust my father with the entire truth. I couldn't exactly blame him.

"Please gather what you need for the journey," Clermont said, his gentle and soothing voice in contrast to his reptilian appearance. "But I have been instructed not to return without you." He stood straighter, arms behind his back, as if to show he would not be moved until I joined him in the carriage.

A tense silence fell between us. I could practically smell the fumes of rage seeping from my father. His grip on my arm tightened.

"Our agreement was for the king himself to come and claim his bride," Father said tightly.

"Actually," Clermont said, withdrawing a worn scroll from his breast coat pocket, "I have the contract right here. It says nothing of the Wraith King coming himself. It only says the Earthen Court supplies its eldest daughter to wed him upon his request."

Father's lips became so thin they almost disappeared into his face. "May I inspect the document, please?"

"Of course." Clermont extended the scroll. A soldier took it and brought it to my father, who immediately opened it and began reading. "Please be aware that is a replica of the original agreement, which is in the care of my king."

Father huffed, but I couldn't tell if it was out of annoyance or frustration. Was he hoping it was the original document? I would have been tempted to try to burn the contract if it had been in my hands. I wondered if Father was thinking the same thing.

The shadows are almost here, I reminded myself. Without this contract, we had no way of protecting our kingdom.

Grumbling under his breath, Father rolled up the scroll and handed it back to the soldier. "Regardless of the terms," he said, "this is highly improper."

"I understand, and I apologize again. But it is essential the princess come with me, per the terms of our bargain."

More silence fell. Sweat beaded along my brow. Part of me wanted to bolt—to flee from the scene and escape with my freedom—while the other part wanted to stride confidently toward the carriage to accept my fate.

When Father continued to say nothing, I inhaled deeply and turned to look at him. "We have prepared for this, Father. I am ready."

He fixed a stony look at me, his expression unreadable. A muscle worked in his jaw, and his nostrils flared. After a long moment, he nodded tersely, then snapped at a nearby soldier. "Send for the Lady Sybelle's things at once."

The soldier bowed and scurried away. I watched him leave, then tensed when my father's arms came around me. The motion was stiff and unfeeling. I wasn't sure if he had ever held me in my entire life.

But it was only for show. When I was pulled to his chest, he whispered in my ear, "Do not forget your purpose, daughter. My men know to pack your daggers with your belongings. I trust you will not fail me."

When he withdrew, he plastered a warm smile on his face

that did not reach his beady black eyes. His gaze flashed with a warning—and a threat—as he released me.

I curtsied to him. "Farewell, Father." I was only able to nod at my sister. My nerves were too tightly wound to manage a proper goodbye. It was already taking all my effort to remain upright.

Orla's expression was cold and unfeeling as she surveyed me with cool detachment, as if these proceedings meant nothing to her. She almost seemed bored.

Each step toward the carriage seemed to take an eternity. More sweat slid down my neck and between my shoulder blades. I fixed my gaze on the billowing shadows that drifted behind the carriage like a cape flapping in the wind. My brow furrowed.

"Are those dangerous?" I pointed to the shadows.

I heard my father swear softly behind me, but Clermont followed my gesture with curious interest.

"No, my lady," he supplied. "You will find in our kingdom that there are different types of shadows. This is the Umbra Mist that follows us when we leave our court. It is harmless to both fae and humans."

Fascinated, I inspected the shadows with more scrutiny. Now that I thought about it, the mist did look thinner and more transparent than the thick, rolling shadows I'd spotted from the castle towers.

Just before I reached Clermont, footsteps sounded on the gravel behind me. I turned to find Ramia, my maid, marching purposefully toward me, a traveling bag in her hand. Her graying brown hair was tied into a tight bun, and her mouth was pinched in that disapproving look she often gave me.

I frowned at her. "Ramia, what are you—"

"You cannot present yourself to the king without a lady's maid," she said in a clipped tone. "I am coming with you."

The blood drained from my face. I wet my lips and leaned close to my maid. "Ramia, you *can't*," I said in an undertone.

"I have been charged with caring for you since you were barely old enough to stand," Ramia said, something in her brusque tone softening as she looked at me. "That's not about to change now. I am coming with you, my lady. You cannot stop me."

To prove her point, she stepped around me, handing her bag to Clermont with a brief curtsy before climbing into the carriage.

I looked at Clermont, who seemed unperturbed. He offered me a pleasant smile, as if to reassure me. I sighed before following after Ramia, my feet unsteady on the steps leading to the carriage. In a flash, Clermont was there, his green hand on mine to steady me. I resisted the urge to snatch my hand away, expecting his skin to feel slimy. But it was surprisingly smooth and dry.

Darkness pressed in on me the moment I stepped inside. The curtains were drawn, blocking out all light. As my eyes adjusted, I made out Ramia sitting off to one side, her hands folded in her lap. I took a seat next to her, marveling at how spacious the carriage was on the inside. It was large enough to comfortably fit six people, at least.

After the servants returned with my trunk and tethered it to the carriage, Clermont climbed in, sitting across from me and Ramia. He was still wearing that strange smile on his face, as if he didn't have any other expression to offer. He rapped his knuckles on the roof of the carriage, and the driver urged the skeletal beasts into movement. The carriage jostled, and I couldn't stop myself from peeling back the thick curtain to gaze at the mountains and castle one last time. A lump formed in my throat as we made our way down the gravel road.

No more late nights in the library.

No more trysts with Gerard.

No more cave adventures with Azure.

The lump in my throat tightened, making it difficult to breathe. But I continued to stare at the stone-and-steel fortress that was once my home, trying to memorize every angle of it before it faded from view. When we rounded the curve, the mountains swallowed up the palace, much like the Shadow Court was swallowing up my life.

A heaviness filled my heart, and I closed my eyes, unable to contain the hot tears as they streaked down my face.

From this point on, my life was not my own. I was at the complete mercy of the Wraith King.

Within minutes, Ramia had fallen asleep, her head propped up on the wall of the carriage as we jostled down the road. But I couldn't possibly sleep. My mind was spinning, my body warring between nausea and panic.

Too late, I realized I had never sent my letter to Princess Eira. And I hadn't had time to tell her I'd be leaving for the Shadow Court.

It had all happened so quickly. Would I even be allowed to send letters, once I was in the clutches of the Wraith King?

"What is the Wraith King like?" I asked Clermont, trying to distract myself from my nerves.

Clermont winced, his face twisting into a pained grimace. "I would advise you not to refer to him as that. It was a name given by those who claim his appearance to be 'demonic,' and it's rather offensive to our unseelie kind."

My eyes grew wide, and I felt the blood drain from my face. *Shit.* "I'm so terribly sorry. I had no idea." Stones, would he tell the king what I'd said? Would I be imprisoned the moment I entered the Shadow Court?

Clermont waved a green hand. "Don't fret, my dear. You

were raised by humans. It's hardly your fault what you were taught about our kind. But please be aware that we take pride in our unseelie forms, and to insult them is the gravest offense."

I swallowed hard, committing this piece of information to memory. "Do you—I mean, do the Shadow Fae have seelie forms as well?" From what I'd studied, there were two kinds of fae: seelie and unseelie, or civilized and wild. My mother had been seelie, so she had only had one form. But the unseelie had two forms and could appear as either seelie—ordinary fae—or unseelie, which was often more beastly and animalistic. I shifted uncomfortably in my seat, trying to stifle my anxiety at the thought of encountering so many monstrous creatures.

But, if some of them had seelie forms, perhaps it wouldn't be too terrible.

Clermont was silent for a long moment, his gaze shifting to the window. Sorrow and longing filled his yellow eyes. "We did, once."

I waited for him to elaborate, but he said nothing more of seelie forms. Instead, he answered my first question. "King Varius is a strong and powerful leader. He is seen as ruthless and callous by some, but he does what is best for his people. No one has sacrificed more for our court than he has. He does have a bit of a temper, though." He chuckled to himself as if this were an amusing tidbit and not something that terrified me to my core.

I had many other questions. Would he harm me in any way? Would he take me to his bed by force? Would he have other wives or concubines? But all of these questions would be far too inappropriate to voice, so instead, I looked out the window again. The ground had transformed into a stony gray expanse, all foliage and plant life now gone thanks to the shadows. Mist filled the air, swirling around us as we traveled, and I shrank against the back of my seat.

"Fear not," Clermont said. "The shadows cannot reach us in here."

"Why not?"

"The Umbra Mist protects us."

My brows drew together. It was hard to reconcile the idea of *good shadows* and *bad shadows*. To me, they were all evil. But, according to Clermont, one type of shadow protected us from the other. It was quite confusing.

"Brace yourself," Clermont warned.

I tensed, alarm racing through me as I expected some kind of attack. But there was a slight bump, which jostled the carriage. And suddenly, from outside the window, smoke engulfed us, masking everything from view.

Beside me, Ramia started with a yelp, her head jerking as she woke. With bloodshot eyes, she frantically looked around in confusion.

"We are now in the Shadow Court," Clermont explained.

In spite of my fear, I leaned forward to gaze out the window, fascinated by the way the shadows moved like they were alive. Thick plumes churned as if coming from the ground like a geyser. Some coiled in faint wisps, while others made great sweeping motions in the air. They almost looked like they were dancing.

"I should warn you," Clermont said suddenly, "that Agnarr Castle has certain magical properties that might alarm you."

My gaze snapped to his, my blood chilling. "What does that mean?" My voice was sharper than I'd intended. Beside me, Ramia went stiff as a board.

"It is difficult to explain," Clermont hedged. "It is best to show you in person."

"Will it harm us?" I asked quickly. Surely, he could give us that much information.

"Not unless you intend to inflict harm on someone in the castle."

My stomach turned liquid at that. *Shit, shit, shit.* Would this magical castle somehow know of my intention to kill the king?

"We are human," Ramia said, a panicked edge to her voice. "I—I don't know if we can survive living in a castle that's surrounded by fae magic."

"You can," Clermont said, his voice steady and reassuring. "I know this because the human princesses from before survived it as well."

"Did they?" I challenged. The words slipped from my mouth before I could stop them. "Or did the castle end up killing them? I truly have no idea what fate befell the brides who came before me. Like my aunt, for instance."

Clermont's easy smile slipped from his face, his expression turning cold. "As you are already aware, humans do not have as long a lifespan as fae do. I can assure you the previous brides were *not* killed by the castle, nor were their deaths the result of nefarious means. Some humans simply die of old age or illness. Did you ever wonder why a human bride is collected every generation?" He lifted his eyebrows as if this answered all my questions.

Because the Wraith King got hungry and had run out of human flesh to devour. The thought came to me unbidden, prompted by my nightmares and the frightening stories I'd heard as a child.

I made no response. It was only after the sun started setting, darkening the mist around us, that I realized Clermont never outright stated that Varius did not kill his brides.

He also never said the shadows didn't kill them, either.

Years of manipulating truths because of my fae bloodline made me acutely aware of the way words could be phrased. Clermont *implied* that human brides were collected because they died of old age every generation. But he did not explicitly say this.

Nausea swirled in my gut. It was painfully clear this fae was harboring secrets about his king and the Shadow Court—particularly why they needed me so badly.

Breathe, Sybelle, I told myself, my hand automatically going to the amber stone at my throat. My finger ran over the smooth surface and chiseled edges, seeking comfort in the familiar feel of it. Azure's voice was silent, but I knew she was there. She had to be.

I prayed she could fly high enough to steer clear of the shadows.

Still holding my pendant, I asked, "Is the castle close?"

Clermont looked at me, his face softening into that bland smile again. "Yes. We will arrive shortly."

I smiled, but my question hadn't been for him. After a moment, Azure's voice appeared in my mind.

"I'm flying above the carriage, keeping you in my sights. The castle is less than a mile away."

I released a long breath of relief. She was here. She was following me.

If King Varius tried to eat me or destroy me with his shadows, he would have to get through my dragon first.

A few minutes later, the carriage passed under the portcullis surrounding the castle of the Shadow Court. I sat up straighter and squared my shoulders, trying to emulate confidence.

"The staff are expecting you," Clermont said. "But please be mindful that our customs are quite different from yours. And they will be in their unseelie forms."

I closed my eyes and nodded, trying to picture all manner of beastly figures. Barbed tails, large snouts, several pairs of eyes and limbs... I needed to prepare myself so I could remain composed.

"Will the king be there as well?" I asked, my eyes opening and scanning the scene outside the window. But it was pitch black now. I couldn't even make out the shadows.

"No. You will not see him until the wedding ceremony."

I frowned and glanced at Clermont, but he averted his gaze. Another secret he was keeping. Was the king avoiding me? Or was he just as repulsed by our union as I was?

Far too soon, the carriage came to a stop, and I steeled myself with several deep breaths. Clermont opened the door and slid out, then extended a clawed hand to me.

I forced myself to take his hand, carefully avoiding those formidable talons. Relying on his steady grip, I eased out of the carriage, taking the steps slowly until I emerged in a wide courtyard. Several white lanterns lit the space, illuminating a crowd of fae forming an aisle leading from the carriage to the steps of the castle. I craned my neck to drink in the massive edifice before me. Steel columns and beams glinted in the moonlight, towering high above me. Towers and balconies and winding staircases surrounded even the highest levels. I was so accustomed to my dull block-shaped home that I found myself overwhelmed by the intricate details of this palace. Ornately carved statues. Intricate lattice work. Stained glass windows. Stones, it was *magnificent*. Certainly nothing at all like the prison-like dungeon I'd pictured.

Clermont cleared his throat, and I hastily stepped forward, my legs like lead from the lack of movement. He guided me a few steps closer to the other fae, then turned to assist Ramia out of the carriage. Unlike me, she refused his hand and clambered down the steps with ease.

I eyed the Shadow Fae before us, quickly glancing over each one before I could focus on their features. I didn't want to stare or appear rude, especially after what Clermont said about causing offense. But the sight of each fae only made my stomach churn more violently.

Horns. Fangs. All-black eyes. Flesh with barbs sticking out. Long, forked tongues. Some with crimson skin, others with violet. One fae even had gray skin mottled with amber spots, as if he were sickly. Some had long, thin tails like Clermont's. Others had wide, short tails that looked more like a third leg.

All of them wore servant finery, but the clothing did not cover nearly as much skin as I was accustomed. Some of the male fae had their shirts open at the chest. Some females revealed a scandalous amount of cleavage, or their tunics came up, exposing their bellies. To my surprise, some of the females wore trousers like the males.

None of them were smiling. But I curtsied low, inclining my head as a sign of respect.

In return, they all pressed a fist to their hearts with a loud *thump* that echoed in the night.

I stilled, unsure of how to respond to this. Clermont leaned close to me and murmured, "To our kind, this is a sign of respect. We do not bow or curtsy."

I looked at him in alarm. "Is it—was it wrong for me to do so?"

"Of course not. It is a sign of respect for *your* people, so of course you are right to do it." He smiled again, and for the first time, it felt genuine and kind.

I nodded appreciatively, then turned to face the aisle of fae. I wanted to say something, but I assumed many, if not all of them, would not be able to understand Terrish, the language of the Earthen Court. And I wasn't quite ready to reveal my knowledge of Agnarrish.

"Enzira will show you to your rooms," Clermont said, gesturing to the fae in front. She had wrinkled violet skin that practically blended into the darkness around us. Her hair was in dozens of black braids around her face, and a long pair of fangs protruded from her teeth. "She will see to all your needs within the castle."

Enzira stepped forward and once more pressed a fist to her chest. In a thick accent, she spoke in Terrish. "Welcome to the

Shadow Court." She gestured to the steps leading to the entrance doors. "Come."

THE BEAUTY

Ramia and I followed Enzira up the castle steps, trying not to trod on the long, gliding purple tail that swished behind her. I felt the eyes of all the Shadow Fae boring into the back of my head as I passed, but I resisted the urge to turn and look at them. It was probably just as alarming for them to see a human as it was for me to see them.

Once we passed through the doors, darkness pressed in on us, lit only by the tiny blobs of white light from the lanterns along the wall. I squinted, peering up at the ceiling to see how high it went. With a gasp, I jerked backward, my hand locking onto Ramia's arm.

"What?" she hissed.

I pointed toward the ceiling, and she stiffened beside me.

The lantern light just barely illuminated the wispy smoke coiling overhead, completely masking the ceiling from view. If the shadows descended lower, they would consume us all.

A warm, scaly hand pressed against my arm, and I jerked around to see Enzira looking at me with wide eyes.

"Safe," she said softly. "No danger." She pointed up at the shadows, then said, *"Tirsh."*

I blinked at the Agnarrish word. *Tirsh* meant *Umbra.*

The shadows above us must belong to the Umbra Mist Clermont had spoken of.

Slowly, I nodded, choosing to trust her. I offered Ramia a reassuring pat on her hand, but she grumbled something about *careless fae* and *weak humans*.

From my studies, I knew the Shadow Fae had excellent night vision, like many nocturnal predators. This was made abundantly clear as we made our way through the castle. The strange white orbs barely lit up the hall. I could only just make out the crimson carpet at my feet and Enzira's purple tail, but not much else. When I stretched my arms out on either side of me, they met nothing but air, which meant the hallways were likely built to be wide enough for all manner of enormous unseelie creatures.

Enzira led us up a winding staircase that seemed to climb so high we might have reached the stars. I paused often to catch my breath, and Ramia even more so. But Enzira was patient and waited for us without complaint before continuing onward.

When we reached the top, I couldn't help myself. I gasped, craning my neck as I took in the dome-shaped window at the top. We were so high up that this tower must have pierced through the shadows coating the outside of the castle. Nothing but a wide expanse of gleaming stars could be seen from the window, each one sparkling. The midnight-blue void stretched on and on, reminding me that there was a world beyond these deadly shadows. There was so much more to see than what my tiny existence offered.

"Wow," I whispered, awestruck, then looked around, wondering where the Umbra Mist was. Then, I noticed puffs of it collected in dark corners of the ceiling, as if they were hiding from the stars.

Frowning, I looked at Enzira, who had followed my gaze. She nodded vigorously. "Light," she said, gesturing to the stars. Then, she shook her head, her braids flicking around her when she pointed to the Umbra Mist. "No *tirsh*."

"The... The Umbra Mist doesn't like light?" I asked.

"*Dach.*" That meant *yes.*

I tucked this useful information away for future use, realizing this offered an advantage during the nighttime. But what about the daytime, when the sun was out? Without the Umbra Mist, how could I protect myself against the deadlier shadows?

Also, Clermont had mentioned the Umbra Mist had followed the carriage into my court when he'd come to collect me. But if it hid from the light, how was that possible?

I presumed Enzira didn't understand enough Terrish to answer these questions, so I made a mental note to ask Clermont or someone else later on. Perhaps the library would hold the information I needed.

"Come," Enzira prompted, waving her hand.

I followed her down the hall, which was carpeted in amber, making the floor feel soft and plush even through my shoes. The Umbra Mist was thinner up here, but it still swirled above me as if welcoming me to my new home. The more I looked at the translucent puffs of smoke, the less frightening they seemed.

A few paces down the hall, Enzira stopped and gestured to a closed door. "Your room." She then grabbed Ramia's hand, guiding her to the door on the opposite side of the hall. "And your room."

"I—what—" Ramia sputtered, trying and failing to jerk free of the fae's grip. Enzira was much taller and bulkier than her, so Ramia's feeble attempts were useless. "I—I don't sleep up here!" Ramia protested. "Where do the servants live? That's where I should be."

But Enzira only shook her head more adamantly. For a moment, the two struggled, arguing with each other in their own language until Ramia's shrill voice echoed around us, bouncing off the walls. I finally drew closer to her and grabbed her shoulder, shushing her.

"It's fine," I assured her. "Perhaps that's their custom here. Besides, it might be better if you're close by."

Ramia swallowed, her lips growing thin. Then, she nodded, still looking deeply uncomfortable.

Enzira glanced between us. "Food?"

Ramia looked at me, eyebrows raised questioningly.

I hesitated. "What food do you have?" I asked Enzira.

"*Pesha.*" Enzira brought her clawed hands together and wriggled them like a fish.

Ramia wrinkled her nose. "Is it cooked?"

Enzira only frowned, shaking her head to indicate she didn't understand.

"*Furgish?*" I asked, using my hands to mime a fish swimming, just like she had. Then I pretended to skewer the fish on an invisible rod, and held it over my other hand, wiggling my fingers to make it look like fire.

"Ah!" Enzira said, comprehension dawning. "*Dach. Furgish.*"

I smiled. "That would be wonderful. Yes, we would both like some *pesha* please."

Enzira smiled widely, revealing not one but *two* rows of fangs. Ramia uttered a soft gasp beside me, but I forced myself to keep a calm expression, knowing Enzira did not mean us harm. She was only excited that we understood each other.

Surely, revealing I knew *one* Agnarrish word wouldn't cause alarm.

I moved to open my door, but Enzira made a noise of protest and stepped in front of me before turning the ornate silver handle herself. Slowly, the door eased open, and she peered through the crack, nodding once. She stood back to let me pass.

I looked at her in confusion, and she said, "*Das lochen es brignok.*" She moved her fingers through the air, wiggling them as if she were sprinkling glitter in the air.

My blood chilled. *The castle is enchanted.* I remembered Clermont giving me a similar warning. What would have happened if I'd opened the door without Enzira here? Would something in the room have attacked me?

I shuddered at the thought.

"Safe?" I asked, pointing to the open door.

Enzira nodded. "Yes. Is safe. But no..." She swung the door as if to close it. *"Non mur das pursh."*

Don't close the door.

A shiver of awareness rippled down my spine. I was torn between terror and curiosity. How did the magic work? Did it apply to all the rooms, or only mine? Was it because I was human?

Biting my lip, I nodded, gazing apprehensively at my open door. Enzira shuffled to the other side and cracked open Ramia's door as well. All the while, my maid looked on with narrowed eyes, her face full of displeasure and apprehension.

Enzira pressed a fist to her heart, then gestured down the hall where we'd come. "Food."

With that, she turned and left us. The darkness swallowed her form almost instantly, leaving only the soft padding of her footsteps until they, too, faded completely.

I turned to Ramia and whispered, "Don't close any doors."

She huffed a frustrated sigh. "I gathered as much, my lady." She cut a sharp glance at me. "You were right to keep your knowledge of their language a secret. Who knows what important information you might come across if they speak freely in front of you?"

I certainly understood the advantage, but it didn't mean I liked it. Right now, I would clearly get more information by speaking plainly in Agnarrish instead of pretending I couldn't. But Ramia was right. Once I met the king, there was no telling what conversations I might overhear.

"I think I should go in with you," Ramia said, pointing to my open door. "Just to be safe."

I was perfectly fine with this. Slowly, I pushed the door open the rest of the way. Lanterns immediately came to life, the same eerie white orbs that lined the hallways.

As my eyes adjusted, I made out a massive bed taking up one-half of the room. It was easily twice the size of my bed in the Earthen Court. I presumed the mattresses here were much bigger to accommodate various unseelie forms. Delicate lavender drapes hung across the bed, and it was littered with plush pillows that made me want to dive in and bury myself in the softness.

An armoire made of hand-carved mahogany rested on the opposite end of the room. Next to it was what looked like a giant black hole. My eyes widened as I took it in. I edged closer, but Ramia grabbed my arm.

"Careful, my lady," she hissed.

I nodded, peering closer. It was certainly a hole. All I could make out was darkness from within, but it smelled strangely sulfuric, and the air surrounding it was warmer than the rest of the room. Curiosity wriggled within me, but I wasn't daft enough to move any closer.

My gaze roved over the room once more, and I frowned. "No bathing chamber?"

"I can send for a tub for you later, if you need it," Ramia offered.

I shook my head. "I'm exhausted. I'll just go to sleep and bathe in the morning."

"Very well, my lady." Ramia reached into her bag and withdrew a familiar pouch made of blue scales, then dropped it into my open hand. "This is yours. And I'll leave your books on the stand over there."

I offered her a warm smile. "You are too kind, Ramia. You think of everything."

She returned the smile. "My duty is to you, my lady." She strode toward the door, then paused. "It makes me nervous, leaving the doors open like this. Anyone could come in."

I swallowed. "I think I'm more afraid of what the castle will do to us if we disobey Enzira's warning."

Ramia grimaced. "I suppose you're right. Well, if you need anything—and I mean *anything*, my lady—please come and fetch me."

"I will. Thank you, Ramia. And..." I paused, emotion welling in my throat. "Thank you for coming here with me. I feel terrible, dragging you into this when—"

She raised a hand to stop me. "None of that, my lady. I would feel wretched if I had abandoned you to this fate when my sole duty has been to look after you. You should not go through this alone. And every queen needs her handmaid." She offered me another smile, this time with a gleam in her eye.

When she turned to leave the room, that word hung in the air: *queen.*

I was going to be Queen of the Shadow Court.

With a shaky exhale, I sank to the edge of the bed, wringing my hands together on my lap. It was almost too much to swallow. I had been preparing for this my entire life, but now that I was here... Well, it was all a bit surreal.

To keep my panicked thoughts at bay, I mentally ran through the positive things. For starters, I was alive. I hadn't been attacked or thrown in a dungeon. And the unseelie fae were far more accommodating than I'd expected.

Within a few minutes, Enzira returned with a steaming plate of food. She gestured to my clothes in an offer to help me undress, but I politely declined. I really just wanted to be alone.

Once she left, I drew closer to the food, my stomach growling. A large gray fish lay on the plate, covered in a creamy brown sauce and a plethora of seasonings. My stomach churned as I realized the fish hadn't been gutted at all. Its lifeless eyes seemed to stare straight through me.

But I couldn't deny how delicious it smelled.

I picked up the fork, only to realize it was more like a small dagger. With a grimace, I clutched it gingerly, then dug it into the soft flesh of the fish. It came apart easily, the meat sliding off the bone. With great care, I speared a piece of meat, then brought it to my mouth, careful not to cut my tongue in the process.

An explosion of flavor burst in my mouth, and I groaned with pleasure. The meat was soft and succulent, warm and juicy as it slid down my throat. The creamy sauce added just the right amount of moisture and spices.

In only a few minutes, I had torn apart my fish, leaving the eyes, bones, and much of the more disgusting-looking guts that I couldn't bring myself to consume. The meal settled in my belly, making me feel satisfied and a bit sleepy.

I tugged at the strings of my dress to loosen them, but it was too difficult to remove it entirely without the help of a maid. I didn't want to bother Ramia or Enzira, so I simply shifted the fabric as best I could to allow me more room to breathe.

My hand went to the necklace at my throat, and I ran my thumb along the hard edges of the amber stone. "Azure? Are you there?" I whispered in the darkened room.

A beat of silence. Then came my dragon's voice: *"What has taken you so long? I've been trying to speak with you."*

"Sorry. This is the first time I've been alone since I got here. Are you all right? Are you safe from the shadows?"

"The shadows do not affect me."

I paused, then blinked. "They don't? Are you sure?"

"Quite sure. I noticed other creatures roaming about, heedless of the shadows. At first I thought they were Shadow Fae, but not all of them are. Some aren't even sentient, and they are not bothered by them."

I frowned. "So the shadows only affect humans? How does the Wraith King manage that? It must be a very specific type of magic."

"And powerful," Azure agreed.

Perfect. The Wraith King already had an advantage over me, being an unseelie fae. But now his shadows had more power than I thought, too. How could I ever manage to kill him when he possessed such strong magic?

"Where are you?" I asked her, my eyes flicking to the window. Moonlight shone from high in the sky, filtering into the room. She had to be close by; otherwise, we wouldn't be able to speak.

"Just outside the stables. These strange skeletal beasts can smell me, but they are not threatened."

I suppressed a shudder as I remembered the lethal creatures that had drawn the carriage. "Be careful around them, Az."

"Just because a creature appears frightening does not mean it is dangerous. I think I am proof of that."

I huffed a laugh. "True." I thought of Enzira and the fangs that gleamed when she smiled. She, too, had seemed quite harmless, after the initial shock of seeing her for the first time. In fact, I'd been pleasantly surprised by her desire to be helpful.

Not everything here was as it appeared.

"Do you need me to find you?" Azure asked. *"It shouldn't be hard to locate your window."*

Tempting as it was to have my dragon here beside me, I couldn't risk it. My door was open, and I had no idea who lurked in the hallway. "Not yet," I said. "Let me get acquainted with the castle first. Once I figure out the best way to sneak you in here, we can locate the enchanted rose together."

"As you wish. But, for the record, I could easily smash my way into the castle with or without your help. I thought it prudent to remind you of how much more powerful I am than you, tiny human."

I chuckled and sat back, resting against the mountain of pillows behind me. With Azure's soothing voice in my head, my initial alarm faded, and I felt safer. My dragon often had that effect on me; I knew no harm would come to me when she was near.

"What can you sense about the magic here?" I asked. Azure was a Blue Amethyst, which meant she had magic in her blood. She was able to sense powerful enchantments and spells, although she was still practicing how to identify specific elements of them. She knew earth magic quite well, but I was curious to know how shadow magic differed.

"Everything here is... clouded," she began, her voice contemplative. *"And I don't mean that in reference to the shadows. The magic itself is shrouded in something, like it has been cloaked. It's so powerful that even I cannot penetrate it."*

My eyes began closing, but my brow furrowed at her description. "Is it the Wraith King?"

"I'm not sure. But I doubt even a king holds enough power to blanket the entire court. I sensed it the moment we crossed the border."

"Well, he *is* unseelie. And he's powerful enough to send his poisonous shadows to other lands. It wouldn't surprise me if he's powerful enough to contain his own kingdom in a sort of shield."

"Perhaps." Azure's tone sounded doubtful.

"What else do you notice?"

"All manner of strange creatures. Nothing like what we've seen back home. I came across a two-headed stag. And also a winged fox. It's almost delightful, the possibilities that exist here."

"You aren't afraid?" I mumbled, stifling a yawn.

"So far, I've been the largest creature I've seen. But I'm sure I'll encounter more dangerous species later on. And yes, I will be careful."

As I slipped into unconsciousness, her voice began to fade. And in my mind, I saw winged horses and skeletal demons that danced around my thoughts with laughter and mockery.

A loud pounding jolted me awake. With a startled cry, I jerked upright, blinking blearily at the warm sunlight that illuminated my room. My chestnut hair stuck up all around me, and the sheets had tangled around my legs. Several of the plush pillows had wound up on the floor.

Someone knocked again, this time more urgently.

"I'm awake," I mumbled. Then, more loudly, I said, "Come in!"

"The door is already open," said a rich, feminine voice. "But I thought it polite to knock all the same."

Slowly, the door opened, and a creature shrouded in darkness entered the room. The first thing I noticed about her were her great wings, folded tightly behind her. But even folded, a single wing was as wide as her slender figure, and nearly as tall. The points of the wings almost dragged on the floor behind her. Her skin was the color of charcoal. The only light parts of her body were her silver eyes, which gleamed with an otherworldly glow. One look from her made me feel as if she could peer into the depths of my soul.

I unconsciously drew the sheets up to my chin in trepidation.

The beautiful fae's eyebrows lifted, her crimson-painted lips curling into a smirk. "I am impressed, human. Most of your kind either weeps or shits themselves at the sight of me."

"I... I..." It took a few tries before I could find my voice. "I am growing accustomed to the unique forms of the unseelie."

She chuckled, the sound just as musical as her voice. It almost sounded like a smooth purr. "Just wait until you meet Varius."

Varius. This fae was on a first-name basis with the king?

I cleared my throat, clutching the sheets more tightly around myself. I had been expecting Enzira or Ramia to come to my rooms, not this beautiful and terrifying being. "Is there... something I can help you with?"

She pressed a hand to her chest, and I noted the long, black claws protruding from her fingers. "Forgive my manners. My name is Tislora. I am the sorceress of the Shadow Court."

My blood ran cold. *Sorceress.* Stones, why had she come to see *me*? Was she going to curse me? Bind my fate so that I could inflict no harm on the Wraith King?

Tislora laughed, tossing her sheet of shiny black hair over her shoulder. "Fear not, little human. I mean you no harm. I only wish to collect a vial of your blood."

My brows knitted together. "My blood?"

"Yes. For the marriage ceremony tomorrow."

My head jerked back, panic coursing through me in violent waves. "*Tomorrow*? I—I am marrying the king tomorrow?"

She cocked her head at me, scrutinizing me in such a way that reminded me of a bird of prey. "Isn't that what you came here to do?"

"Well, yes, but... I didn't think—" I broke off, my face burning as I realized how foolish I sounded. *Of course* I came here to marry the Wraith King. I wasn't an idiot. But I had thought—or rather, *hoped*—that I would have a few days to settle in, to explore the castle, and, perhaps, to locate the enchanted rose that was linked to the Wraith King's power.

And, if I was being perfectly honest, a small, foolish part of me hoped I would find it right away. Then I could end the Wraith King before having to suffer through a marriage ceremony and a wedding night with him.

"I'm sorry," I said with a quick shake of my head. "I only just arrived, and I am still adjusting. That's all." I frowned at her. "But why do you need my blood now? I thought the blood vows would be exchanged at the ceremony."

"You are correct." Tislora lifted a hand and began cleaning her sharp claws. The sound of the talons scraping together rang out in the room, reminding me of how easily she could slice open my throat. If she wanted my blood, she could take it by force. To ask was a courtesy I should be grateful for. "But I would like to inspect your blood first. The more potent and untainted the blood is, the easier it will be to bond with the king."

My mouth went completely dry, and my stomach tumbled painfully within me. *Inspect your blood.*

I did *not* want this sorceress scrutinizing my blood. She would almost certainly discover I was part fae.

And what did it mean to *bond* with the king? Would these vows ensure I would be unable to cause him harm?

Fear and terror washed over me like a tidal wave of icy water. My pulse quickened, my heartbeat thundering loudly in my ears.

Tislora dropped her hands and cast me a bemused look. "I can hear your pulse, human. There is no need to be afraid. The blood exchange is simple, and it will not cause you any severe harm. It's merely a cut across your palm. You share it with Varius. And you utter the vows."

"Will—Will the words physically bind me?" I knew how fae bargains worked. With my fae blood, I would literally be bound by whatever words I swore to the king.

"Yes," Tislora said, her tone serious. "But as I said, it will not cause you harm."

"But will it... will *he*... be able to control me?" My words came out as barely more than a whisper. "Will it make me become someone else? Or something else?"

Tislora's eyebrows lifted. She almost looked impressed that I would ask such questions. "It is wise of you to be wary of fae bargains. But I can assure you, the vows are only uttered to ensure the safety of the Shadow Court."

This did nothing to alleviate my concerns. Too late, I realized Tislora would notice that my pulse was still racing.

Her eyes narrowed. "This does not reassure you?"

"I—what about *my* court?" I asked.

Tislora pursed her lips. "Ah yes. The *Earthen* Court." She

sneered at the word, and I stiffened. Clearly, she detested my court as much as my people detested the Shadow Fae.

"It's my home," I said coldly. "You don't have to like it to respect that I am loyal to it."

Tislora's gleaming eyes sharpened as they fixed on me with predatory intensity. "If it pleases you, human, I will add to the vows that your precious human wasteland will be protected as well. Does this appease you?"

I took a moment to consider my words. Technically, I was not *appeased*—I was still concerned that something would happen to me during the vows, since I intended to destroy the Shadow Court. If the vows were meant to protect this kingdom, then I feared what that magic might do to me. Speaking carefully, I said, "I appreciate the addition. The change is acceptable to me."

"Good." Tislora drew closer to the bed. "Which arm should I take your blood from?"

I lifted my left arm, which was my non-dominant hand. I forced myself to hold her gaze, not even flinching when her sharp claws sliced into my wrist. With supernatural speed, she drew a glass vial from her black cloak and lifted it, catching every single drop of blood as it spilled from my arm. When the vial was full, she closed her fingers around the wound and whispered, "*Belech.*"

Warmth seared into my skin, and I almost jerked my hand back in alarm. A searing red glow surrounded my flesh, and when she removed her hand, the wound was gone. Not even a scar marred my skin.

I stared at my wrist, turning my arm over in awe. Her magic was flawless. There was no evidence at all that she'd taken my blood.

Tislora lifted the vial of blood, peering through the glass as if she could ascertain everything about me with a single look. Perhaps, with the magnitude of her power, she could.

Her eyes met mine, and she said, "I'll see you at the cere-mony tomorrow, human."

Before she could sweep from the room, I said loudly, "My name is Sybelle, by the way. Not *human*."

She paused but did not look back before exiting the room. From the hall, I could have sworn I heard a flutter of wings and an echoing caw.

THE BEAST

Feverish nightmares claimed me, my head spinning with the delirium of the wretched curse. My father's face swam into view, his eyes all black as he summoned his shadows around himself like a cloak. The shadows swelled, rising higher and higher until they drowned him completely. His anguished cry echoed even long after the darkness had swallowed him whole.

I saw Tislora's face, then Clermont's, as the curse consumed them, too. Their tortured screams echoed in my mind, reverberating into my skull. My bones quivered from the intensity of it, my stomach curdling. I had already expelled what little food and drink I'd managed to take in during my stay in the cave. But even so, the nausea rose up until bile crept into my mouth.

So many lives lost because of me. Because of my incompetence. My powerlessness.

I couldn't break the curse. I couldn't save them.

They were dying because of *me*. Women and children, sobbing in the street as the dark mist took them, washing them away from existence.

"No," I moaned, back arching as I tried to rid myself of the visions. "No, *please*."

"Varius."

"No," I pleaded, tears streaming from my eyes. "I beg of you. *Stop*."

"Varius!"

Hands shook me, jolting me from my sickly haze. I blinked blearily, and the blurry form of Tislora came into view. I must have been a frightening sight indeed, for I *never* saw this much concern in her eyes. Her dark brows were drawn together, her crimson lips turned down in a frown. Her eyes flared wide as she shook me more violently.

"Snap out of it, Varius," she commanded me. "You are stronger than this."

I struggled to draw breath, afraid I might vomit on her. I swallowed hard, then inhaled shakily. As air filled my lungs, my vision cleared, and the swarming visions faded from my mind.

"I have the blood for you," Tislora said. "Are you strong enough for me to perform the spell?"

I shifted, trying to prop myself up on one elbow. But Mother of Shade, the throbbing in my skull only intensified. I gritted my teeth so hard that my fangs pierced my upper lip, drawing blood. The pain sharpened my senses, and I glared up at Tislora. "Do what you must."

Something sharp sliced into my forearm, and I couldn't hold back a growl as Tislora dragged her claw along my flesh, drawing blood. She held a vial, already half full of blood, to capture the black drops of my own. One thing I admired about Tislora was her ability to do what needed to be done. Others saw her as cruel and calloused, but in this case, it was efficient. She didn't coddle me. She didn't patronize me.

When the vial was full, my own darker blood mixing with the human's, Tislora pressed her palm against my wound and murmured, "*Belech.*" Warmth surrounded the wound, and I felt my flesh begin to knit itself back together.

She then cupped the vial between her two hands and closed her eyes. "*Et brusha das brignok.*"

The combined blood began to swirl and churn of its own accord. A golden glow emitted from within, bright enough to illuminate the dark cavern. I squinted against the intensity of it, resisting the urge to shield my eyes. If I could endure days of torment, I could certainly bear to witness Tislora's spell.

Gradually, the light faded, and she handed the vial to me. "It's ready for you."

I took the vial, which was still warm from her magic. Without hesitating, I poured the contents into my mouth, letting the thick blood slide down my throat. The metallic, coppery taste burned my tongue, and I coughed. Human blood was so foul.

Tislora's fingers brushed against my various wounds as she murmured, "*Belech,*" over each one, healing them one at a time. I hissed as heat burned through each injury, followed by the soothing relief of her magic.

When she was finished, Tislora straightened, smoothing her hands along her black cloak. "It should take effect soon. Don't rest too long. Clermont is expecting you in your chambers soon to prepare you for your *wedding.*" Her tone held a touch of mockery.

I shot her a glare, already feeling strength in my limbs. "Jealousy is unbecoming of you."

Her eyebrows lifted, her eyes turning steely. "I'm hardly jealous. Need I remind you that it was *me* who ended things between us?"

"So, nothing has changed then? You still feel this way?"

"I have told you before that I do not share. Whoever I bed must choose me and me alone."

"I did not *choose* this," I hissed.

"But it is still your fate." Her expression remained somber.

We'd had this argument time and time again. It would end the same way it always did.

"She is hotheaded," Tislora said. "Your bride, I mean. And a bit fragile." She chuckled. "I worry you might break her, Varius."

Anger flared, and I bared my fangs at her. "Get out."

Another chuckle echoed, but before I could bark another order, her wings swept wide, and she shifted to her raven form before darting out of the cave.

Tislora was right; within minutes, the pain had receded, but my body still ached from the ordeal and needed rest. I slept fitfully for a few hours. When I woke, I was able to tuck my giant wings against my back, and my skull no longer throbbed. My stomach growled loud enough for the sound to bounce off the cavern walls.

I needed something to eat. It wouldn't do for the groom's growling stomach to scare off the bride before the vows were even exchanged.

With a sigh, I climbed to my feet, my legs shaking slightly. I was covered in dried sweat, dirt, and blood. Aside from a pulsing headache, I felt fine, albeit drained and exhausted.

I emerged from the cave, then spread my wings, using them to glide downhill toward the rear of the castle. The wind carried me, and I landed on the second-floor balcony, gasping for breath. My wings were powerful, but they were only good for gliding. I couldn't pump them or lift myself any higher.

But this was fine. I could make it to my chambers from here.

I gathered my shadows around me, shrouding myself from view. The interior of the castle was already so cloaked in darkness that it would be easy to blend in.

I skirted down the hall, dodging a few servants as they swept past me. My steps were careful and silent as I made my way up the stairs toward the king's chambers.

Voices stopped me in my tracks, and I froze.

"Are you sure this is necessary?" asked a loud voice. It rang through the hall with shrill authority.

Mother of Shade. Was this my bride-to-be?

Revulsion stirred in my gut, and my curiosity got the best of me. I had to see her, even just to get a glimpse of my future wife.

More voices joined with the first, mingling so I couldn't

distinguish one from the other. I inched closer, ensuring my shadows still concealed me from view. When I reached the end of the hall, I hovered by the open door where the voices were coming from.

"It—It's too scandalous!" said the shrill voice. "Her breasts are practically spilling out of the dress."

I nearly choked, giving myself away.

Whoever was speaking was *not* the human princess. Her maid, perhaps?

But now, I simply had to see this supposedly *appalling* dress that the human maid was griping about.

I drew closer to the cracked door, my shadows swirling as I peered inside.

Three figures stood in the room, one wearing the traditional black gown the unseelie females wore for wedding ceremonies. The female next to her was a servant I recognized—Enzira— and the other was a short human with graying hair and a severe scowl on her face.

"Ramia, it's fine," said the figure in the middle, smoothing her hands along the silk fabric of her skirt. "If this is their custom wedding gown, then I'll wear it."

My eyes fixed on the human princess. She stood before a mirror, gazing at her reflection with a pensive look in her warm brown eyes. Her full lips had been painted red, and her chestnut hair was loose down her back. Her skin was quite pale, but perhaps that was the standard complexion of human flesh. The black gown did indeed reveal a stark amount of her skin, barely concealing her breasts. But it certainly wasn't *scandalous*. It was common for unseelie females to dress in such a way, especially for sacred ceremonies.

It only looked jarring on the human because her skin was sickly and wan.

As far as humans went, she wasn't... *unpleasant* to look at.

But she seemed so frail and feeble. My shadows alone could easily snap her in two.

I continued to gaze at her, wondering what she was thinking as she stared at her reflection. Her expression gave nothing away, save for the slight pull of her eyebrows indicating she was concentrating on something.

In a flash, her gaze snapped to mine, and I froze.

My shadows are hiding me, I reminded myself. *She cannot see me.*

Her mouth puckered into a slight frown, and she turned to face the door, her eyes flicking over my shadows.

Shit. Slowly and carefully, I withdrew from the door, sweeping my shadows away one tendril at a time.

I had lingered here for too long. The human princess's voice murmured something, but I was already retreating down the hall, worried she might emerge and investigate. Regardless of how well my shadows concealed me, if the princess noticed a large mass of darkness creeping toward her, it would surely terrify her, perhaps send her running.

And I couldn't afford to delay the wedding ceremony.

I edged down the hall to my own chambers, my stomach growling again. The smell of cooked fish wafted from my rooms, and I smiled. Clermont had sent for food.

Of course he had. My steward never failed to anticipate my needs.

Before I could step into my room, the door was thrown open, and Clermont appeared, his wide eyes taking in my shadows.

He exhaled in a relieved sigh. "Thank the gods. I feared the pain had claimed you again, my lord. Come in, please. Your wedding is in a few hours, and there is much to be done."

Don't remind me. I wanted to retch at the thought. The idea of marrying that tiny, pathetic human was almost as dreadful as the torment I'd endured these past few days.

Almost.

If it were only my life hanging in the balance, I would gladly endure the repercussions of the curse myself. But it was not just me. Tislora, Clermont, and the entire castle staff would be at the mercy of the deadly shadows if I did not do this.

So, begrudgingly, I entered the room and let my staff tend to me. A few of them had brought in buckets of steaming water. After removing the filthy pair of trousers that clung to my legs, two servants began scrubbing me from head to foot with rough loofas that chafed my already tender skin. I was filthy, but there wasn't time for me to soak in our hot springs. This would have to do.

Once I was clean, two more attendants rushed forward to dress me in my violet ceremonial jerkin. The tunic was open at the chest, revealing a large expanse of my crimson flesh. A thick, black leather belt encircled my waist, the golden buckle shined to perfection. The black kilt hung from my hips, with thick leather strips of battle armor reaching down to my thighs. Underneath the kilt, I wore fighting leathers. It was all ceremonial, of course; no battle was to be expected. But for generations, my people had worn this attire to show that our commitment to our marriage vows was as sacred as our loyalty on the battlefield.

The thought made me feel ill all over again. I would be exchanging vows with a stranger. And I would feel no loyalty toward her. Nothing but spite and bitterness.

We did not know each other. I had seen her once, but I still knew nothing about her. And I did not want to. She was nothing to me. Nothing but a means of saving my people. That was all.

The fuchsia rays of dusk filtered in through the window, reminding me that our time was limited. Clermont looked me over, his face full of scrutiny, then nodded once. "Yes. Very fine indeed, my lord."

I gave a grunt that was neither denial nor agreement. Behind Clermont, the row of servants watched me expectantly, some with reverent expressions on their faces.

With a sigh, I ran a hand down my face. "Thank you, Clermont. And thanks to all of you for your efforts." I looked each servant in the eye and nodded my gratitude. A few stood up straighter, their faces full of pride.

"We pledge to follow you, my lord," Clermont said, his chin lifting. "What you do serves this entire court. We will not forget it."

His words made my stomach knot and didn't bring me an ounce of relief. It only reminded me of the curse, my failure to break it, and my fruitless efforts to save my people.

This is the first step, I reminded myself. *You cannot break the enchantment without doing this first. After this, you can see to the rest of your plan.*

With this thought, I squared my shoulders and faced the door. "I'm ready."

Clermont ordered the servants to return to their stations, then escorted me from the room. I walked with him, somber and silent, as I made my way toward a fate I dreaded more than anything.

THE BEAUTY

I COULD HAVE SWORN THE SHADOWS BY THE DOOR WERE watching me.

But when I looked closer through the crack, they vanished. A shiver of unease rippled over me, but I shook it off and turned back to the mirror to prepare myself for the ceremony.

The wedding garment was certainly the most revealing thing I'd ever worn in my life. Two swaths of black silk were draped over my torso, barely covering my breasts. They came together at my waist, with two identical pieces of fabric at my front and backside that covered the space between my legs. While the silk reached all the way down to my ankles, it left the sides of my legs and buttocks completely exposed. Not to mention if I turned a certain way, one would get a full view of my breasts.

I kept wringing my hands together, feeling restless and anxious, until Enzira took one of my hands in hers to still me. She gestured to my chest with a clawed hand. "Is fine."

I swallowed, still feeling uncomfortable.

Enzira seemed to sense my distress. Her dark brows drew together as she tried to form the right words. "For Shadow Fae… is fine. Dress is… like this." She pointed to my garment again.

I nodded, but this did nothing to loosen the tight knots in

my stomach. If a loose and revealing garment was customary for the Shadow Fae, that must mean I would be expected to wear things like this all the time.

Would the Wraith King wear something similar, too? Panic flared in my chest at the thought.

Enzira seated me at the vanity so she could do my hair. Her hands went to the amber necklace at my throat, and I quickly stopped her, my fingers catching hers.

"Please," I said quietly. I wasn't sure how to convey to her the importance of such a thing without giving too much away.

But Enzira was more perceptive than I gave her credit for. She scanned my eyes, then nodded once with a gentle smile. She dug inside a drawer of the vanity, and I caught sight of sapphires and diamonds that made my eyes go wide. She found a matching pair of amber earrings and placed them on my earlobes.

My fingers itched to sift through the gemstones in the vanity to see what powers they would grant me, but that would have to wait. Would these gems work differently because they were in a different court? The diamonds alone would provide a huge advantage. To wear diamond jewelry was one thing—it granted me boldness and bravery, but not physical strength. However, if I wielded a *weapon* made with diamonds, then my body was granted the endurance and agility of five fae warriors. Like with my amber necklace, there were certain caveats in order for my magic to work to the fullest extent.

What if I could find a way to embed these diamonds into the hilts of other blades? Then I would have a whole arsenal of Wraith Killers.

"Do you know the king well?" I asked.

Enzira's brow furrowed again, her fingers busy weaving through my hair. "King Varius?"

"Yes. Do you know him?"

She pressed her lips together, her eyes flicking to the ceiling as she considered how to respond. "King Varius is strong. And good. He is saving Shadow Fae."

I licked my lips. "And what about humans? Does he hate them?"

Enzira was quiet for a long moment as she continued working, pinning sections of my hair into small knots in the back of my head. Then she said, "Not hate."

Well, that wasn't very comforting.

When she finished, she tugged a few strands of hair loose so they framed my face, highlighting its heart shape. She gripped my shoulders tightly and looked in my eyes.

"King Varius not hurt you," she said firmly. "He is *good.*"

I blinked at this unexpected conviction. When she continued looking at me as if expecting a response, I stammered, "O-Okay."

I wasn't sure I believed her. Varius could be the most benevolent king in the world, but if he detested humans as much as my people detested the unseelie, then none of that benevolence would apply to me.

"I found it!" Ramia chirped from my doorway. She bustled in, nudging past Enzira to face me. In her hands was a gleaming diamond tiara, which she arranged neatly in my hair.

My breath caught in my throat. It was stunning. A row of sparkling diamonds spread across the length of the tiara, and in the center was one of the largest diamonds I had ever seen. I sucked in a sharp breath as my blood warmed. A strange energy and boldness took hold, blotting out all fear and uncertainty.

Ramia bent close to me and whispered, "To give you strength."

My gaze cut to hers. I didn't like that look of shrewd understanding in her eyes. Did she know what diamonds could do? Did she know the full extent of my power?

I gazed at my reflection in the mirror. Between the scandalous black dress—which made Ramia purse her lips on multiple occasions—to the dark kohl lining my eyes, I looked unrecognizable. Truth be told, if I looked like this in the Earthen Court, people would expect me to work in a brothel.

But with the tiara and other jewels, plus Enzira's insistence that this was the custom in her court, I could envision myself through new eyes. I'd seen Shadow Fae before, though it was mostly castle attendants. They did dress differently. And they embraced the beast that was a part of themselves.

In a sense, I was doing the same. I might not have had horns or fangs or a tail, but that didn't mean I couldn't proudly display the body that belonged to me.

I sat up straighter, the diamond tiara making me feel more confident. This was what I had been born to do. I had known from the beginning that this was my fate. And I would accept it with all the courage and grace I could muster.

I stood, smoothing my palms along my skirt, and turned to find Enzira handing me a small ceremonial dagger. Rubies and sapphires glittered from the hilt. My breath hitched as I recognized the glint of diamond as well.

"I—what is this for?" I asked breathlessly. Did Enzira realize what a dagger like this could do, if I were to wield it?

"For blood," Enzira said. "King Varius has knife. You have knife. It is fine."

I was learning that when Enzira said *fine*, she meant it was customary to her people. My throat knotted, and I swallowed hard before accepting the dagger. As soon as my fingers wrapped around the hilt, power swelled within me, making me gasp.

Enzira took a hesitant step back, assessing me with concern in her eyes. "Is good?" she asked uncertainly.

I nodded quickly, my breaths sharper and faster now. My body felt empowered, like I could run for miles and not tire. "I am well. It's just—it's so beautiful." I lifted the blade to better inspect the gemstones. Along with the diamond, I recognized rubies and sapphires. Rubies allowed me to see across vast distances, and sapphires gave me the gift of music. Neither of these powers would be helpful to me today.

Enzira brought a leather strap with a sheath that blended in with my dress. She tied it around my waist, then gestured for me to tuck the dagger inside.

I didn't want to part from it. I wanted *more*. But as Enzira watched me expectantly, I knew I couldn't hold onto it without arousing suspicion. My hand shook as I slid it into the sheath, then released my grip on it.

Immediately, the energy left me, and I almost wilted from the exhaustion that took its place. In an instant, Ramia was at my side, lacing my arm through hers. I made a mental note to ask her exactly how much she knew about my powers, but in this moment, I couldn't be mad about it.

"Shall we?" Ramia asked, patting my hand.

Enzira offered a wide smile, then led us out of the bedchamber. To my surprise, she only strode two steps down the hall before reaching for the first door on the right and pushing it open.

I frowned. The hall for the wedding ceremony was located in the guest suite?

But when the door swung open all the way, I gasped. Light filtered in, but it wasn't the dull gleam of the white orbs I was accustomed to in the castle. This was outdoor light. Pinks and purples and reds from the setting sun cast a warm glow on me as I stepped forward, entranced.

Through the doorway was a courtyard surrounded by several burning braziers. A square fire pit stood in the center, within which burned an ethereal violet flame. Mighty pillars supported a dome-shaped pavilion that provided shade for the entire square, and directly across from my doorway was a decorative archway made of stone. Intricate designs had been carved on every inch of it, and I yearned to draw closer and inspect it with greater scrutiny.

The courtyard was full of unseelie fae, most of them castle staff I recognized from my arrival. They were flitting about, arranging flowers, painting what looked like runes in crimson paint on each of the pillars, and tending to the roaring fire in the center.

I stared at the scene before me, transfixed. "Is this—is this real?" I wanted to reach through the doorway and try to touch it, expecting the image to ripple like water. Was I looking into a magical portal? We were in the highest level of the castle, and yet, this door led to an outdoor courtyard.

"Go," Enzira said, nodding her head. "Is fine."

There was that word again. *Fine.* I inched closer, trusting her, but Ramia gripped my arm, her face stricken with terror.

"We are human," she said to Enzira, her voice a touch too loud. "Will this harm us?"

Enzira pointed to the courtyard. "Safe," she assured us. Then, she gestured to the doorframe. "Magic. The door knows."

The door knows. It sounded rather cryptic. But I recalled her admonishment to keep all doors open, and I wondered if this was why. If the doors closed, did that mean they somehow became portals to other places? I was torn between curiosity and fear. The idea that these doors could *think* was terrifying. What if they could read my mind? What if they knew of my plan to kill the king?

Ramia's fingernails dug into my arm. It was clear she wouldn't let me step through the doorway.

Enzira seemed to notice this. She sighed, then drew forward, walking over the threshold and emerging into the amber light of the courtyard. Sunlight illuminated her form immediately until she stepped underneath the pavilion cover for shade. A few servants muttered something in Agnarrish as they jostled past her, one of them bumping her shoulder.

She was there. She was *actually* there in the courtyard.

"It's fine, Ramia," I whispered.

She shot me a dubious look but loosened her hold on me. Her hand was still clamped around my arm, so I linked our elbows and walked us both through the portal.

The effect was instantaneous. One moment we were standing in the hall of the castle, our surroundings dark and chilled. The next, warmth and light engulfed us, a stark contrast to the confinements of the castle. Even with the shade of the pavilion, the area was so *open*. A wide expanse of forest surrounded the courtyard, and the sky seemed to stretch on for an eternity. In the distance, I could make out the mountains of the Earthen Court.

A wide smile of amazement spread across my face. I turned around completely, facing the way we'd come, and found the open door. The frame was built into a stone wall, and as I looked beyond it, I made out the turrets and towers of the castle. It was much farther away than before—perhaps a quarter of a mile.

How did we get transported so far? What kind of magic was this?

I turned to Ramia to share my wonderment with her, but I found her face pale and her eyes wide as saucers. The sheer horror on her face was so different from my excited curiosity that my exclamation died on my lips.

For her, this was just a reminder that we were in a strange land with a strange magic that could easily destroy us if we weren't careful.

Someone nudged my shoulder, and I turned to find Enzira beaming at me, a pot of crimson paint in her hand. "I paint you now," she said.

I nodded, holding perfectly still as she painted runes along my arms and shoulders, then one on each of my cheeks. They were similar to the runes being painted on the pillars, and I wondered what they meant.

Before I could ask Enzira, she had finished painting and was ushering me toward the stone archway. I gladly obeyed, moving close enough to gaze at the carvings on the arch. At the bottom was a large cloud next to a lightning bolt. Above that was a figure with horns and a tail with a crown atop his head. As my eyes moved over the carvings, I became more and more enthralled. They seemed to be telling a story of a king's demise. I saw a woman with a mighty scepter, and several people with anguished expressions on their faces.

My heart lurched in my throat when I reached the other side of the arch and found a single rose etched into the stone. My pulse quickened, and I glanced around, worried someone was watching me. I looked back at the rose, running my fingers along the grooves of the carving.

What did this mean? Could these carvings tell me where I could find the enchanted rose?

"Enzira…" I began, turning to find her, hoping to coax some words out of her. But when I looked behind me, I found the castle staff parting, scurrying like frightened ants until they formed an aisle between them. When they were in position, they went perfectly still, chins lifted and backs straight.

Shadows poured down the aisle between the servants, curling and coiling like smoke. I flinched, ducking my head to avoid the toxic fumes that would almost certainly kill me.

But when the chilled tendrils of shadow brushed against my arms, raising the tiny hairs on the back of my neck, I realized they weren't poisonous. The air was clean. In fact, the faintest smell of dark spices and heavy rainfall reached my nose. Far more pleasant than the putrid scent I envisioned.

I had never encountered shadows like this before.

I extended a hand, and the shadows twisted around my

finger. It was colder than the air around me, and slightly moist, like a cloud.

Before I could inspect it further, every single servant fell to their knees, heads bowed. I stiffened, glancing around to find a dark figure making its way down the aisle, moving slowly toward me.

The Wraith King had arrived.

THE BEAUTY

Shadows continued spilling down the aisle, coating the ground until I could no longer see my feet. The air felt misty and cool, making my skin pebble. I wished I'd worn a wrap or a shawl.

But what chilled me the most was the dark figure gliding toward me like a haunting specter. I was rooted to the spot, frozen as it loomed ever closer. I couldn't make out its eyes, but somehow I knew it was watching me. My heart stilled, and my hands began to shake.

It was a mark of how potent my fear was that it managed to bleed through the courage the diamonds gave me. If I hadn't been wearing the tiara, I probably would have pissed myself.

Years of training and education and preparation had led me to this moment. But now that I was finally faced with looking upon the Wraith King for the first time, I discovered something that threw an unexpected wrench in my plans: I was a coward.

Here and now, watching that darkened shape approach, I was rendered immobile like a prey caught in a predator's trap. Faintly, I remembered the dagger sheathed at my hip. But I couldn't even reach for it if I wanted to. More and more shadows rolled forward, and the air was so thick with them that the setting sun was blotted out.

Nothing but darkness and fear remained.

Shadows coiled and twisted like serpents snaking toward me. The mass of darkness was drawing ever closer. Close enough to suffocate me. Close enough to devour me.

My heart lodged itself in my throat, and my pulse quickened. Sweat formed along my brow and the back of my neck, trickling down my skin in spite of the cool air. My breathing came in short spurts, and I worried I might faint.

Get ahold of yourself, Sybelle, I ordered myself. *You knew he was monstrous. You knew he was a demon. Shove aside your fear and do what needs to be done!*

I internally screamed at myself to move, to shift, just to prove I could overcome this mind-numbing terror. With great effort, I flexed a few fingers, shaking off the cold horror that had frozen me. I took a deep breath, then lifted my hand to my amber necklace, running my fingers over those familiar grooves.

"Give me strength," I whispered, not caring that the supernatural fae senses meant everyone present could likely hear me.

It didn't matter. I needed Azure's soothing voice in my head. This was the moment I needed my dragon the most.

"I am here, Sybelle," came her warm voice.

I closed my eyes, letting her friendly and familiar presence wash over me.

"So many shadows," Azure said. *"I can even see them from here. It is the Wraith King, isn't it?"*

I said nothing. My eyes opened, and the dark shape was only a few paces away from me now. The darkness was so massive that it blotted out a large portion of the light behind it, dimming my surroundings. I focused on controlling my breathing and reminded myself that Azure was close by. She was close enough to see the shadows.

She would not let harm come to me.

"You can do this," Azure said. *"You may be nothing more than a*

pitiful human, but I know you are capable of facing this wretched monster. If you can tolerate me, you can certainly tolerate him."

The corners of my mouth twitched at her weak attempt at humor. She was trying to ease my fears by goading me. I was tempted to tell her it wasn't working, but that would have been a lie. Already my heart was lighter, and the ghost of a smile on my face lifted my spirits.

Az was on my side. And she always would be.

I *could* do this.

At long last, the mass of shadows reached me. The king appeared as a shapeless form made only of darkness and mist. It churned and roiled more intensely than the rest of the shadows, as if the king's silhouette was strengthened by his body heat. I could make out faint outlines of his arms and legs, and two large shapes near the top of his head led me to believe he had horns.

But the darkness obscured everything else, rippling like a pool of ink. I couldn't even make out his eyes, though I felt them scrutinizing me.

With the echoes of Azure's voice still in my head, I found my strength and lifted my chin to gaze directly into what I thought was the Wraith King's face. I would not cower before him.

Slowly, my legs bent in a curtsy, but I did not bow my head. I kept my eyes on him the whole time. I held the curtsy and then straightened once more. Unlike his subjects, I was not his subordinate. In this moment, we were equals. And once the marriage ceremony was over, I refused to entertain the idea that I was an object to be commanded.

He would not rule me with fear. Not like he ruled everyone else.

Another figure approached from the opposite end of the courtyard. It didn't take me long to recognize her. The great black wings folded behind her were impossible to forget. With a saccharine smile on her face, Tislora drew closer until she stood before us, directly underneath the archway.

In Agnarrish, she said to the king, "Are you ready?"

Grateful I'd kept my knowledge of their language a secret, I stared at the shadows swarming around the Wraith King, waiting for him to speak.

A single Agnarrish word: *"Dach." Yes.*

His voice was deep and much smoother than I'd expected. I had prepared myself for a rough and gravelly sound, the voice of a true monster, a voice that grated against my ears. But instead, it was low and sultry and washed over me like a warm caress.

This was completely at odds with my mental picture of the Wraith King.

Tislora nodded, then looked at me. In Terrish, she said loudly, "We are here to unite these two in the binding ceremony of vows and blood."

I shot a glance over my shoulder, frowning at the crowd behind us. They had all been here moments before, setting up for the ceremony. Now they were wedding guests? Where were the nobles and courtiers? I had to admit, I had expected more fanfare and a much bigger crowd. This almost seemed like a small, intimate affair. Not at all what I pictured for the wedding of the King of the Shadow Court.

"Sybelle of the Earthen Court," Tislora continued, "do you vow to bind yourself in body and blood to the Shadow King? To serve this court to the best of your ability, provided that the Earthen Court is not at risk?"

Beside me, the Wraith King stiffened, and I wondered if Tislora failed to mention to him her promise to include the protection of my home in the marriage vows.

I held my breath, waiting for him to object, but he said nothing. After a moment, I realized Tislora was waiting for my response, so I quickly said, "I do."

In an undertone, Tislora whispered, "You must say, *I solemnly vow.*"

Clearing my throat, I said firmly, "I solemnly vow."

Sudden warmth whispered across my skin, and the dagger at my hip burned hot from the presence of magic in the air.

Tislora turned to the shadows swirling around the Wraith King. In Agnarrish, she said, "Do you, King Varius, vow to bind yourself in body and blood to the Earthen Princess? To serve the Shadow Court and make your sacrifice to the curse that cages us?"

I frowned. What curse? But as Tislora's eyes flicked to mine, I quickly arranged my features into what I hoped was a neutral expression. I didn't want her to know I understood what she was saying.

With his deep, melodious voice, the king said in Agnarrish, "I solemnly vow."

Magic hissed in the air, and my skin prickled. The runes painted on my arms and cheeks began to burn, and I resisted the urge to scratch at them.

"Now pledge your vows in blood," Tislora said.

My stomach knotted, and I looked at her in alarm. But she was watching the Wraith King. A metallic sound rang out as he drew his blade, still obscured by his shadows. Black droplets of blood oozed from a wound I could not see. I stared at the inky liquid pooling on the ground, mesmerized by it.

"I, King Varius, vow to bind myself in body and blood to the Earthen Princess, and to serve the Shadow Court and make my sacrifice to the curse that cages them. I pledge this vow with my own blood."

My insides were frozen with terror as warmth seared into my skin once more. The runes burned hotter than before, making my skin sizzle as if I had been branded.

Tislora looked at me and smirked. In my own language, she said, "Your turn, human."

I scowled at her, then withdrew the dagger at my hip. Immediately, a flood of awareness rushed over me, and I stifled a gasp of alarm. Energy and courage swelled in my chest, blotting out all fear.

"Repeat after me," Tislora said. "I, Sybelle of the Earthen Court, vow to bind myself in body and blood to the Shadow King..."

Dragging the tip of the blade along the center of my palm, I repeated the words.

"...and to serve this court to the best of my ability," said Tislora.

My breath trembled as I spoke the words.

"...provided that the Earthen Court is not at risk," said Tislora.

"...provided that the Earthen Court *or its inhabitants* are not at risk," I said with emphasis. The gemstones from the dagger were making me feel bold, but I did not care.

Tislora's silver eyes flashed. Clearly, she had noticed my altered wording of the vow. But I refused to recount it. The Wraith King could easily kidnap a member of my court, drag them to the Shadow Court, and hold them hostage, all while claiming the Earthen Court was not in any danger. I wanted to ensure that not only the land of my home was protected but also the people within it.

My own crimson blood dripped to the ground, mingling with the black blood of the king's. I expected Tislora to insist I repeat the vow with the proper wording. But she didn't.

"Bring your hands together," Tislora instructed.

Though she spoke in my language, the king still understood. His shadows shifted, and a hand emerged. My eyes flared wide, and a surge of horror rose up inside me. His hand was covered in scarred skin that was the exact shade of my blood. Long, black claws extended from his fingernails. A narrow gash still bled freely from the center of his palm.

I felt Tislora watching me, so I forced myself to inch forward, reaching for the king's hand. I paused a few inches away from those sharp talons, revulsion and unease churning in my gut. With my other hand, I gripped the dagger hilt more tightly, relying on the diamonds for strength, then placed my palm against the king's.

His skin was smoother than I expected. I was anticipating his flesh to be rough and scaly, like a reptile's. But it was as soft as my own, and warm as well. His sticky blood mingled with my own as our hands clasped together, his fingers interlacing with mine. I flinched, waiting for his claws to slice into me, but they didn't. In fact, he seemed to be taking extra care to ensure they did not touch me at all. They were extended in the air, hovering away from my hand, his fingers taut and outstretched.

Between our palms, the combined blood began to sizzle and burn. I hissed in pain, shutting my eyes as the smell of charred flesh swelled around me.

Tislora murmured a few words I did not recognize and waved her hands in the air, forming a circle between myself and the king. White sparks ignited from her fingertips, and the air hummed with power. I stiffened, my back arching as the heat of our blood seemed to boil right through my body. I gritted my teeth so hard my head began to throb. Surely my skin was melting away. Surely when I withdrew my hand it would be a blackened husk.

In Agnarrish, Tislora said, "The vow is complete."

King Varius immediately dropped my hand, withdrawing his own into the safety of his shadows. With a gasp, I sheathed my dagger so I could cradle my hand and inspect the injury. To my utter shock, the skin was clean and unmarred. Only an echo of the warmth from earlier remained. Even the cut had been healed.

Mouth agape, I looked up at Tislora, who had a glint in her eyes that told me she enjoyed my bewilderment. She lifted her chin, and, her voice echoing in the courtyard around us, proclaimed in Agnarrish, "Behold, the King of the Shadow Court and his new bride!"

Behind us, cheers erupted, and the people chanted a single Agnarrish word: *"Benedor."*

Freedom.

Slowly, I turned to face the crowd, my eyes wide as I took in the joy and excitement on their faces. Were they truly so happy about this union? I was a stranger to them.

Freedom. Some of the fae had tears in their eyes as they clapped their hands together.

A knot formed in my throat. What did this ceremony mean to them? What did *I* mean to them?

I turned to look at the Wraith King, wondering what he thought of all this, but his shadows were moving away from me. Gradually, the king made his way back up the aisle, pausing occasionally to grip the hands of his subjects. I caught a glimpse of those red fingertips as they emerged from the shadows, only to be swallowed up once more after he moved on.

I stood there, feeling like a complete fool as my husband abandoned me and disappeared through the door built into the wall. My body was frozen, rooted to the spot, unable to move. What was I to do? I was the queen… Or was I? I hadn't been officially coronated. And this was all very unorthodox. Generally, the husband and wife joined hands and addressed their people as a united front. Oftentimes, there was a celebratory ball afterward.

And, of course, the consummation.

At the thought, I felt the blood drain from my face. For years, my father had instructed me on how to properly tend to my husband's carnal needs. *You are to please him as often as he desires of you,* he had told me. *You are never to complain and never to refuse. Use your body to satisfy his demands so he does not detect your duplicity. Do whatever it takes to make him happy so he does not suspect what you are up to.*

Stomach churning, I turned to look at Tislora, unable to hide my panicked expression. "What happens now?" I whispered.

I wasn't sure if I could handle it. I knew how important my mission was, but Stones, I didn't know if I could bed him. Not now, with my nerves so wound up.

The gleam from Tislora's eyes was gone. She gazed at me with a solemness that made me wonder if she guessed where my thoughts had turned. "Now, you are free to return to your rooms."

I blinked. "That's it?"

She smiled. "Yes. That's it. For now."

For now. What exactly was in store for me from here on out? Nothing about this was clear. I didn't even know what the expectations were for the queen of this court.

Ramia appeared by my side, her expression stony as if we had attended a funeral instead of a wedding. She linked her arm with mine, and I sensed she could tell I was on the verge of fainting. I was tempted to grab hold of my dagger, just for strength, but I didn't want to alarm anyone.

"Are you well, my lady?" Ramia whispered.

Weakly, I nodded, leaning into her. She was stronger than she looked and was able to bear my weight as we made our way up the aisle. "I just need to rest."

Vaguely, I wondered if Tislora's magic had done something to me. Had she siphoned the energy from my body? Were the unseelie fae some sort of soul-sucking vampires?

I supposed there wasn't anything I could do about it if they were. Even with my half-fae blood, I was no match for them, and I was drastically outnumbered. If they wanted to feast on my flesh, nothing was stopping them.

I stared at the door where the king had disappeared. A servant stood next to it and opened it for us. The hallway of the guest suite waited for us on the other side. I nodded my thanks to the fae, and Ramia and I stepped through.

Once the door closed, all the sounds and smells of the court-yard vanished, leaving only the darkened corridor leading to our rooms. It was almost a relief, to blot out the cheers and voices of the crowd. The silence was a comfort to me.

I heaved a sigh, closing my eyes for a moment. As Ramia helped me into my room, her deft hands able to transition me from my wedding gown to my shift with minimal effort, my thoughts turned to the Wraith King. He had vanished so quickly. I couldn't blame him if he resented this union; I certainly didn't have fond thoughts of it.

But he hadn't uttered a single word to me. And he had just left me standing there like a fool.

When I was dressed for bed, Ramia bid me good night and left the door cracked open. I sank into my bed, surrounding myself with pillows, and I couldn't help scowling into the dark-ness, thinking of the Wraith King's cold, aloof behavior. It shouldn't have been at all surprising. In fact, this kind of behavior was exactly what I had expected of him. It only made it easier to bring about his demise. And, now that we were married, I could begin my search for the enchanted rose so I could finally destroy him and free my people from the threat of his shadows.

THE BEAST

I COULD STILL SMELL THE HUMAN'S FEAR LONG AFTER I'D STEPPED through the door, which transported me back to my chambers. The moment the door snapped shut behind me, I shed my shadow shield and began pacing the wide length of my room, fingers curled into fists.

I had thought I could do this. I had thought her disgust and horror would not bother me.

My eyes closed as I ran a hand down my face, biting back a growl of frustration. A fire crackled in the hearth in front of me, and I slowly approached, my gaze fixed on the rippling flames as I waited for my pulse to slow.

Behind me, a knock sounded, and my eyes shut again. "Do not disturb me."

"Your Highness, please." Clermont's voice was agitated.

I gritted my teeth but twisted my wrist, flicking my fingers toward the door behind me. A tendril of shadow curled forward, tugging on the door handle to let Clermont in. Once he was inside, my shadows pressed against the door so it shut loudly behind him.

I could sense Clermont flinching, even without looking at him.

"What," I bit out, keeping my eyes on the fire. If I looked at Clermont directly, I feared my shadows might inadvertently strangle him. Which was exactly why I had told him not to disturb me.

"Is this really wise?" His usual formal demeanor was gone, which meant he was addressing me as a friend and not as my steward.

"Is *what* wise?"

"Storming off like that. Refusing to show your face. Avoiding the consummation. Varius, this is not—"

"Not what a normal king should do?" I spat. "Tell me, Clermont, what about my situation is *normal*?" I huffed a bitter laugh and shook my head before bracing my arms against the walls, flattening my palms against the black marble. "Every second I stood alongside that human, her putrid fear stung my nose. I couldn't stand it. And my shadow shield was necessary. You saw how terrified she was, even with my shield in place. I imagine she would have shit all over herself if she'd seen my true form."

"You don't know that."

"What I *do* know is how many brides tried to flee." I slowly turned to face Clermont, unable to hide the torment from my gaze. "How many of them screamed and fought, even at the altar. I refused to let that happen again. She might have feared me and my shadow shield, but at least she didn't try to run. If I am to break this curse, I need at least *some* hope that she will look on me with anything but disgust."

Clermont sighed, his yellow eyes sharp as they appraised me. "And the consummation? You cannot put it off forever. It is a necessary step."

I clenched my teeth. Mother of Shade, if the human bride was afraid *now*, then she really *would* shit herself if I took her to bed.

Shadows pooled on the floor around me, spreading across my room until they obscured the floor from view. With a sharp jerk of my head, they receded back into me, my body absorbing them. My temper was a constant weakness I needed to control. My shadows often reacted to it, and this was no exception.

"No," I said at last. "I refuse to force myself on anyone. Even a human. We will consummate when she is ready."

"And what if she is *never* ready?" Clermont challenged. "Will you make our people wait, make them suffer, all because of this girl you don't know? This is what's *done*, Varius. Royals do not marry for love. She is expecting this. She may not like it, but it is her responsibility as your wife."

I cut him a lethal look, my nostrils flaring. Each word was sharp and forceful as I repeated, "I will not force myself on her."

Clermont's lips thinned. "And what of an heir? If you die, the kingdom will have no leader. The curse—"

"I refuse," I seethed. If I had a child, the curse would pass to them as soon as I died. Just as my father had passed the curse on to me.

But I would not allow it. It would end with me.

"I refuse to burden an innocent child with this wretched curse," I said. "And I will *not* force anyone into my bed just to prolong a curse that will doom our people again and again."

Clermont's face paled. "But Varius, if you die..." He trailed off, unable to finish.

"Generations of kings have failed to break the curse," I said. "If I can't do it, then... it's likely it can *never* be broken. If I die, then it means our people must abandon this land in search of a new home. The council can rule without me."

"Varius, you *can't*. Your father—"

"I am not my father," I snarled, stepping toward him. Shadows exploded from my body, darkening the room and coiling around Clermont. To his credit, he staggered backward, eyes flared wide. "Do not compare me to him. His methods failed, and the curse claimed him, too. So do not dare to question me again, Clermont. Now leave me before my shadows choke the life out of you."

Clermont's eyes flashed, and for a moment, he looked as if he might argue. But my shadows darkened until they were black as night, swarming and twisting until they clouded the room, blocking the light of the moon from the windows. With my fae sight, I could still make out Clermont's form before me, but it was faint.

His voice was low and calm as he said, "Yes, my lord." He had returned to my dutiful servant. My friend was gone.

Had my shadows chased him away? Or my temper? Perhaps it was both. Either way, I could only watch as he left the room. As soon as the door closed, my shadows vanished, leaving me feeling cold and empty.

Clermont did not deserve that. But I was spent. My body was still recovering from the events of the full moon, and my emotions were chaotic since meeting the human bride.

Sybelle.

That was her name.

As far as humans went, she was certainly quite lovely. Long, wavy chestnut hair, warm caramel-colored eyes, and a proud chin that spoke of the stubbornness that often came with royalty. Her skin had been a sickly pale color, and her diminutive stature made me fear she would break at any moment, leaving us doomed to the fate of the curse.

But there had been moments when I'd sensed fire in her spirit. A fire that drowned out any fear or disgust on her face. A fire that spoke of strength and a willpower stronger than most humans.

Hope rose within my chest, but I slammed my fist against the wall and shoved it away. This meant nothing. All it meant was that she would fight me, just as the other human brides had fought. It did not mean she was the key to ending our suffering.

Hope was almost more dangerous than my temper.

With a weary sigh, I ran my fingers through my dark curls and shed my waistcoat. Clermont and his staff had taken such care to dress me in the ceremonial attire, and it had all been for nothing. I hadn't decided until the moment I appeared in the courtyard to summon my shadow shield. I had seen the back of Sybelle's head, and I had just *known* she would scream when she saw me.

Why does it matter? I asked myself. *You are indeed a monster. It is better that she sees who you truly are from the beginning.*

It didn't matter if I terrified Sybelle or not. What mattered was if she possessed the strength to overcome that fear, to be the savior our people needed.

All that mattered was breaking the curse.

She didn't need to love me. Hell, she didn't even need to like me. Those weren't required to break the curse. I could endure her horror and loathing for now, as long as, eventually, she could overcome it and save my kingdom.

I stared into the fire once more, my heart rate slowing and my breathing becoming steadier. "I will conquer this," I vowed to the flames. "Even if it kills me, I will find a way to end this."

THE BEAUTY

I didn't sleep much. My exhaustion from the wedding ceremony was cured after about an hour of sleep. From then on, I was either wide awake or tossing and turning. Half the night was plagued by nightmares of the Wraith King's shadow form with his red-skinned arm extending toward me, while the other half was spent in sheer terror that he would come to my rooms to consummate our union.

I was fidgeting constantly in my bed, my sheets tangled and half the pillows on the floor. Every few seconds, I whirled to look toward the door, thinking I had heard a creak or a scuffle.

After hours of trying and failing to sleep, I finally gave up, shoving off the blankets and sitting up. My hair clung to my sweaty neck in sticky chunks, and I peeled it off my body and tied it into a loose braid. The sky was still pitch black outside, reminding me of the darkness of the Wraith King's shadows. Suppressing a shudder, I slid off the bed and wrapped a shawl around myself, then ran my fingers over the amber stone at my throat.

"Azure? Are you there?" My voice was soft, but it still seemed to echo around me, and I feared it would draw someone's attention. After all, my door was left open.

But now that I knew the doors were portals, I was more keen on experimenting with them.

"I am here, Sybelle," came Azure's warm voice. *"How was the wedding?"*

Amusement laced her tone, but I refused to be baited.

"Fine," I said in a clipped voice. "Well, rather unusual, to be honest. Are you close?"

"Yes. I have found your window, and I'm resting on the balcony adjacent to yours."

Alarm jolted through me, and my heart lodged in my throat. "Stones, Az! Are you crazy? What if you're caught?"

"It's just another guest wing. I checked, and all the rooms are unoccupied. Don't worry, human. My dragon senses are far superior to yours, and I will hear if anyone approaches."

I flinched at her usage of the word *human*. For her, it was a shared joke between us. But for me, it served as a reminder of Tislora and the powerful spells she could wield.

"I want to try to explore the castle," I whispered. "Maybe I can find the enchanted rose."

"Now?" Azure sounded uncertain.

I frowned. "Do you have something better to do?"

I could almost hear her rolling her eyes at me. *"Are you sure wandering a bewitched castle in the middle of the night is wise? It might be better to wait until the daytime, when there are staff members about who can assist you. You are to be their queen, after all. It would not be suspicious if they saw you acquainting yourself with your new home."*

The idea of thrashing around in my bed for a few more hours was about as appealing as eating rocks. I couldn't possibly sit here and do nothing all night. "Look, if you're afraid of the dark, I can just go on my own." I strode for the open door.

"You are impossible," Azure said with a sigh. *"I will be right there."*

Fighting back a smile at my small victory, I moved to the balcony doors and eased them open. The cool midnight air nipped at my arms, and I tugged my shawl more tightly around myself. After a moment, the beating of wings reached my ears, and a dark shape loomed closer. Azure blended in so well with the midnight sky that I couldn't fully see her until she was right in front of me. Her blue scales could lighten or darken depending on her surroundings, allowing her the benefit of camouflaging her appearance. However, she could not change color; if she was surrounded by desert sand, even if she appeared the palest of blues, she would still be visible.

Azure gracefully landed on the concrete balcony before me, her icy blue eyes appraising me. She looked me up and down, as if assessing for injuries.

"I'm fine," I assured her.

"You look paler than normal," she observed. Her tone was sincere, as if she were genuinely concerned instead of poking fun at me.

"I'm *fine*," I insisted. "Have you uncovered anything useful about the magic here?"

"Only that it's inconsistent. It feels like the rules of the magic are fluctuating. It's hard to keep up."

"How so?"

"The Umbra Mist keeps changing. Sometimes it is thick and powerful; other times it is thin and feeble. I have been watching the guardsmen and how they react to it. When it is thin, they arm themselves and draw closer to the keep. The outer shadows are poisonous, from what I can gather. That's what they are afraid of. The Umbra Mist keeps those shadows at bay, but not all the time."

My brow furrowed. "Why are they afraid of their own shadows?"

"Perhaps they are not immune to them."

"But they come from their king!" I argued. "Do you think he is intentionally trying to frighten his people? Or has his magic become so volatile that he has no control over it?"

"I don't know."

I turned toward the balcony doors. "Well, come on, then. Let's see how much of this castle we can uncover."

"I hardly think a creature of my size will be able to sneak around this place easily."

I glanced at her over my shoulder, arching an eyebrow. "Have you seen this place? It's enormous. They are clearly catering to the largest of unseelie beasts. Besides, it's very poorly lit. Just darken your scales a bit, and you'll be fine."

Azure huffed loudly. *"You humans are so impatient."* But she lumbered forward, her talons clicking along the stone floor. I had to push open both doors to let her into my room. She was right; she was rather large, easily taking up half the space of my bedchamber. However, because she had just flown in, her wings were half out. With them folded against her back, I was confident she would be able to fit in the hall. I once poked fun at her rather serpentine shape when her wings were completely tucked in; her body appeared much longer and narrower that way, like a snake's.

I hastily belted the jeweled dagger on my waist. It felt silly to wear it over my loose nightgown, but I didn't care. My fingers itched to wrap around the hilt, just to feel the effects of the diamonds once again. Already, I felt more secure. More comfortable.

Azure's eyes roved over me, and she made a low, throaty sound.

When I touched the amber stone, she said, *"You look ridiculous."*

"I don't care. I'm armed, so I already feel safer."

I inched closer to my bedroom door, which was slightly ajar, and pressed my ear to the gap to determine if anyone was in the hall.

Nothing but silence.

I looked back at Azure. "Follow me," I whispered. "And tell me if you sense any fae magic nearby."

"You mean besides your own?" Azure asked jokingly.

"Very funny," I muttered. With a deep breath, I inched the door open all the way and crept into the hall.

Silence blared against my ears, making each step and thump of my heart sound like an avalanche. The cold stone floor bit at my bare feet, and I deeply regretted not grabbing a pair of slippers from my room. Behind me, the clicking of Azure's talons rang out in the hall, making me wince.

I knew it was foolish, creeping around the castle in the middle of the night with a rare and unique dragon accompanying me. What if we encountered someone?

But the terror seeping into me was too intense, and I couldn't do this alone. I needed my friend with me.

Besides, if we came across any fae who gave us trouble, I knew Azure wouldn't hesitate to rip them to pieces.

My steps were slow and steady, and it seemed to take an eternity to reach the end of the hallway. But when we did, nothing but a dead end awaited us.

Frowning, I glanced behind me. Azure blinked slowly at me, her blue eyes seeming to glow in the darkness.

Touching my amber necklace, I whispered, "I definitely remember there being a staircase at the end of the hall."

A moment passed. Then, Azure replied, *"Well, clearly, you were mistaken."*

Biting back a growl, I turned and walked toward the other end of the hallway. We passed my room and Ramia's, then continued onward.

This, too, led to a dead end.

I curled my hands into fists in frustration. Azure nudged my leg with her snout to get my attention, and I clutched the amber stone again.

"I smell magic."

My heart stilled, and I looked around, sweat beading along my brow. "Who's there?" I whispered.

"It's not a who. But a what."

I shook my head. "Explain, please."

"It's the castle."

My throat went dry as I recalled Enzira telling me the castle was enchanted. But I had believed this only applied to the opening and closing of doors.

How foolish of me to assume that magic worked according to a strict set of rules. If the castle was enchanted, there was no reason why that enchantment shouldn't affect everything and anything contained within these walls.

Which meant I was trapped inside a prison that could deter me from my mission over and over again.

I chewed on my lower lip, wracking my brain for a way around this. Could the castle sense my intentions? Did it know I planned to kill the king? Or did it only know I was a stranger who had just arrived here only yesterday?

"Okay," I muttered, thinking fast. "We have to try opening a door."

"We do?" Azure sounded uneasy.

"Yes. We won't know what we're up against unless we take the first step and see where the castle wants us to go." My voice sounded more sure than I felt.

"If you say so."

I glanced at Azure, arching an eyebrow. "Do you disagree? Can you sense any… foul magic afoot?"

Azure inhaled deeply, then angled her head slightly. *"It's magic I've never encountered before. But I don't sense any ill intent with this enchantment. Only… curiosity."*

Interesting. So the castle was… *curious* about me?

I sighed. "Okay then. Let's give this a try." I turned and faced the door in front of me. It looked like all the others, its brass handle gleaming in the low bobbing lights along the walls.

Steeling myself, I turned the handle and swung it open.

On the other side was a low burning fire that cast an amber

glow on a thick, black fur rug that looked like it had come straight off the hide of a bear. The room was dark, lit only by the dying embers of the flames. On either side of the walls were shelves of what looked like old books.

Immediately, my body hummed with anticipation as I itched to run my fingers along the spines of those tomes. What secrets did they hold?

But fear stayed my hand, making me pause on the threshold of the door.

From within the room, something creaked loudly, and soft footsteps approached. My heart jolted painfully in my chest, and, on instinct, I abruptly slammed the door shut. My pulse roared in my ears, my heart seizing with unease.

Azure bumped the back of my leg with her snout, and I jumped, yelping as I turned to face her. She stared at me with concern in her bright eyes.

I clutched my amber necklace, struggling to steady my breathing. "I'm fine. It's all right. I just... heard something. Come on, let's try a different door." I was eager to put space between myself and this door in case whoever was on the other side was curious enough to try to find me.

It's likely just a member of the staff, I told myself. *That's all.*

I stepped farther down the hallway and turned the handle of the next door.

The same fireplace greeted me, the smell of charcoal and burning wood tickling my nose. My eyes flared wide, and I slammed the door shut again.

Azure huffed, but I couldn't tell if it was out of amusement or frustration.

The next door yielded the same results. And the next. And the next. I tried every single door in the hallway, save for my own and Ramia's, which both remained open. Each door only showed me that same room with the fireplace and the black fur rug.

I ran my hands through my hair in frustration. There was no way out of this hall, and the enchanted castle *clearly* wanted me to go into that room.

But why? Who or what was waiting for me in there? If this castle wanted me to go in there, then I had to assume danger lurked on the other side.

My head was reeling, and I staggered back a few steps. My back met the wall, and I leaned my head against it, breathing heavily. I felt Azure draw closer to me, pressing her nose into my side and humming gently, trying to soothe me. Absently, I stroked her snout, already comforted by the warmth her body offered.

My fingers pressed into the amber stone. Before I could speak, Azure's voice was in my head.

"I could go into the room with you and face whatever is there," Azure offered.

"No," I said quickly. "What if it's something dangerous? You aren't even supposed to be here. If they find out, they might…" I couldn't finish that sentence. I had no idea what these unseelie fae would do if they encountered a dragon. I hadn't been bold enough to tell my father or even Gerard about Azure.

"Leave the door slightly ajar. Just in case."

I shot her a stern look. "Don't you dare come after me."

"If your life is in danger, I certainly will. You cannot stop me, human."

I rolled my eyes, knowing it was useless arguing with her. I wouldn't deny it, but her insistence filled me with a modicum of comfort. At least some being in this world would mourn if I met my demise at the hands of a bloodthirsty unseelie fae.

"All right, castle, I'm trusting you," I muttered before turning the handle and opening the door once more.

Just as before, the fireplace greeted me. The flames were even weaker than before, providing hardly any light at all. A few stray embers floated from the ashes within.

I paused at the threshold, running my fingers along the leather strap at my hip, reminding myself the weapon was there. Then, I strode inside. My foot caught the door before it snapped shut, leaving it open just a fraction, as Azure requested.

When I stepped fully into the room, I squinted into the darkness, hardly able to make out any details around me. With the fire nearly gone, the room, or whatever it was, was nearly swallowed in darkness.

A soft ticking noise echoed. The reverberations of the sound led me to believe the room was quite large. Frowning, I turned my head, trying to figure out where it was coming from.

Another loud creak sounded from behind me, and I whirled, heart thundering in my chest. My hand immediately went to the dagger at my hip, fingers brushing the hilt. A surge of strength and power flooded me. Emboldened, I said loudly, "Who's there?"

Two silhouettes sat before me. It took a moment for me to realize they were a pair of matching wing-backed chairs.

One of them was occupied.

Slowly, the figure sitting in the chair stood. I could only make out a large pair of horns and a tall, muscular frame before a mass of shadows swarmed him like a cloud, blocking him from my scrutiny.

My heart sank with dread as I realized who it was even before he spoke.

"What are you doing here, human?" asked the Wraith King.

The Beast

My chambers became too stifling the more I paced, so I made my way to the library, which was my favorite room in the castle. My thoughts blurred as I stared into the fire, remaining in my chair long after the embers had died.

I had come here to be alone. To gather my thoughts. To escape.

So, naturally, my wife decided to intrude.

My fae hearing picked up on the slight creak of the door opening. Her sickly sweet human scent assaulted me almost immediately. Still, I waited. Perhaps she would leave me be.

The door closed. Then opened again.

This repeated for quite some time. I massaged my temples, my head throbbing. I knew exactly what was happening; she was trying different doors. The castle was toying with her.

"Enough," I growled.

But the castle didn't listen. It never did.

At long last, she entered the room, and I had to admire her courage. The sensible thing to do would be to give up, to retire for the night. After all, she was a weak and frail human who needed far more sleep than I did.

She faced me, brown eyes squinting. I had to remind myself that human sight was abysmal, and she likely couldn't see me properly.

I sensed her fear the moment she realized I was sitting before her. Her pulse quickened, and her heart stuttered. I chose this moment to rise, then cloaked myself in my shadow shield for good measure. I was in no mood to watch her run screaming from my presence. Not tonight.

"What are you doing here, human?" I asked in her tongue. I despised Terrish. It felt rough on my lips, and the syllables were harsh and jarring compared to my own language. But it was the only thing she understood, and if it would get her to leave me more quickly, I would speak it.

The human—*Sybelle*—stood straighter, her eyes flashing. She wore nothing but a transparent shift and a thin shawl. My eyes dipped to the leather belt around her waist that held the ceremonial dagger from earlier. Her hand was wrapped around the hilt. My eyes narrowed at the sight. Was she truly so terrified that I might harm her? The idea sent a bolt of anger rushing through me.

She thought we were savages. All of us. That we couldn't keep our hands off the humans for even a moment.

"You might be more suited to answer that question," Sybelle said. Her voice was level and held a hint of ire. What right did she have to be angry with me?

"I beg your pardon?" I snapped.

"Why am I here?" she repeated. "Why did your steward send for me so urgently? Why has your kingdom taken human brides all this time? Do you feed them to some four-headed demon hiding in the dungeon? Do you sacrifice them to the moon gods? Do you feast on their flesh? Please, enlighten me."

Each of her questions was uttered in a bored and unaffected tone, as if these horrifying options did not bother her in the slightest.

My brows drew together as I stared at her. Her eyes were fixed on me—or rather, where she presumed my face to be. But she held no ounce of fear. The quickened pulse was still there, but I could scent nothing but anger from her.

Interesting.

"You are here to fulfill your end of the bargain between our kingdoms," I supplied.

"Yes, but *why*? Why stipulate that as part of your demands? What purpose does it serve?"

She was not the first human bride to ask this question. I had to be careful with how I responded, since I could not lie. "There are certain shadows here that even my magic cannot fight. For some reason, the presence of a human will keep them at bay."

Her jaw went slack, revealing several of her abnormally square teeth. Mother of Shade, she didn't even have fangs. What were those teeth good for? Could they slice or cut at all?

"*That's* why you've asked for human brides?" She shook her head. "But I don't understand. How am I supposed to stop the shadows? I don't—I can't—" Her mouth clamped shut, as she was clearly at a loss for words.

"You have no magic," I finished for her. "Yes, I know. But I can't explain it, either. Over the years, we have tried many things. The only thing that seems to work is your kind."

"So, what am I supposed to do?"

My eyebrows lifted. "For now? Return to your rooms and rest."

Her nostrils flared. "I'm a bit too preoccupied to sleep."

"Try harder."

I turned away from her, prepared to leave the room, if she insisted on staying. I didn't want to be in her presence another moment.

"Why the shadows?" she called after me.

Slowly, I turned back to face her. Her chin was lifted, revealing that spirit I had sensed in her before.

"You will have to be more specific," I said tightly.

She gestured to my form. "Why conceal yourself with shadows?"

"Because I want to," I snapped. "Isn't that reason enough?"

"What exactly are you hiding? It isn't quite fair, as *I* do not possess the ability to shroud myself in terrifying shadows. It's only fitting I should get to look upon the face of my beloved husband."

I bristled at the words, disgusted with the way she described me. *Beloved husband.* It was revolting.

"This is my home, and I will don my shadow shield as I see fit," I said, struggling to keep my temper in check. "I do not need to answer to you, human."

"Sybelle," she said.

"What?"

"My name is *Sybelle*. Not *human*."

"I don't care!" I barked, and my shadows flared. "I don't care what your name is. I don't care if my shadows bother you. Now leave me be."

I expected her to shudder from my outburst, to stumble backward in alarm. But, to my surprise, she inched closer to me, her eyes full of interest as she examined my shadows. "How do you do that?" Her voice was full of curiosity.

I was slightly taken aback by this response, and my anger ebbed. "Do what?"

She wiggled her fingers through the air. "Make your shadows move."

I wasn't sure what to say. No human had ever asked me that before.

"You just told me you summon your shadow shield at will," she went on. "But when you raised your voice just now, they... swelled. Was that intentional?"

I had the strangest desire to fidget under her scrutiny. Which was ridiculous. I could do as I damn well pleased, regardless of who was watching. And I certainly shouldn't care about the opinion of this lowly human.

But there was no malice on her face. Nothing but intrigue.

She was not afraid or disgusted or horrified. She was inquisitive.

"No," I said at last. "They are bound to me and often respond to my… emotions."

Something dark crossed her face. Something I couldn't read. "So you have no control over your magic." Her voice shifted, becoming flat and full of accusation.

My anger returned, heating my bones and boiling my blood. "I never said that. I can control them just fine; otherwise, I wouldn't be able to maintain the shield around the castle that protects it during the daytime when the Umbra Mist is thinnest. My shadows merely change forms depending on my mood. They are not dangerous. If they were, you would have suffocated by now."

She snorted loudly, and my head reared back at the ghastly sound. "*Not dangerous*," she repeated. "By whose standards? Yours? Those of the unseelie fae, whose bodies are indestructible? Well, sure, I would wager that with fangs and talons and tough, scaly skin, you can withstand toxic shadows easily. But my people can't. And, thanks to your little temper tantrums, my kingdom is about to get wiped out by these *not-so-dangerous* shadows."

Rage and indignation roared within my chest, and my shadows spread, creeping along the floor until they slithered toward Sybelle. They wrapped around her ankles, snaking up her legs.

She stiffened but was otherwise unfazed by the closeness of my shadows, her venomous gaze still fixed on me.

I had to give her credit for her bravery.

"You think you know everything, *human*," I spat. "But you don't know me, and you know nothing of my magic. I've been alive longer than your grandparents. Don't come in here and fling accusations at me as if you understand anything. You don't know what secrets lie behind the walls of your own home. Now, go back to your rooms before I lock you in there myself. I'm sure your father is eagerly awaiting a letter from you spilling all my secrets. Sorry to have to disappoint you both."

Her cheeks flushed, and her eyes burned with hatred. Her breaths came in short spurts as she struggled to think of a response. Her hand tightened around the jeweled dagger, and I chuckled.

"Are you going to fight me with that pathetic weapon? Is that why you're here? To kill me?"

Her eyes widened, and her face suddenly drained of color. "I'm not—I wouldn't—"

My chuckles turned into full-blown laughter as I envisioned her swinging that dagger wildly, like a toddler. The idea that this feeble creature would try to challenge me was simply hilarious.

"Go back to sleep before you injure yourself," I said, still amused by this. "Or worse, *embarrass* yourself. I wouldn't want to damage that fragile ego of yours."

Once more, I turned away, but she wasn't finished with me. "You are vile!" she shouted, her voice echoing in the vast space.

I wanted to laugh again, but I was interested to see what she would do next. So I stilled, waiting for her to finish.

"I don't want to be here any more than you want me here," she went on. "Neither of us asked for this. The least you could do is be accommodating and forthcoming and *kind*. Is that so much to ask for? Instead, you mock and insult me, you don't even bother to show your face to me, and you laugh at the notion that I might fear for my life in this place, when you have given me no reason at all to feel safe."

Mother of Shade, I had had *enough* of this human. Unable to contain my fury, I dropped my shadow shield, allowing my magic to withdraw completely as it receded into my body. Slowly, I turned to face her, exposing my true form. With my shadows gone, the dying embers cast a glow on my crimson skin, revealing every detail to her.

I waited for her to scream. For her to draw her weapon and fling it at me. For her to run from the room. Perhaps she would cry or beg for mercy, as the previous human brides had.

But once again, this human surprised me. Sybelle did not even flinch. She stared at me with that calculating gaze, with that same look in her eye when she had asked about my shadows. With deliberate slowness, her gaze dipped to my bare feet with black claws, then traveled up my legs, taking in my black kilt and fighting leathers, and the violet tunic that revealed a significant amount of my bare chest. I still hadn't disrobed from the ceremony, but perhaps that was fitting. She wanted to look upon her husband, so here I was, still dressed in my wedding attire.

Her eyes continued making their way upward, noting my lower set of fangs, my thick, curly black hair, and my ibex horns. My long, barbed tail flicked to my right, and her eyes snagged on that, too.

Not once did terror strike her features like I expected it to. She merely observed me as a scientist would, taking in all the details. Even so, I could feel her pulse thrumming, her heart racing, and her breath hitching. I wasn't sure what caused it, but it certainly wasn't fear.

At long last, she spoke. "If that's supposed to terrify me, you'll have to try harder."

I almost laughed again. She was surprising me over and over, and I was honestly finding it quite delightful.

"And what, precisely, *would* terrify you?" I asked, unable to keep the amusement from my voice.

She chewed on her lower lip as she considered this. Then,

with a slight smile, she said, "An excessively affectionate husband."

I couldn't help it. I threw my head back and roared with laughter, the sound reverberating against the walls and echoing all around us. Sybelle joined in, her giggles lighter and shriller, but no less vibrant. Together, our voices mingled, creating a cacophony of sounds that collided and twisted together until they formed something unique and unrecognizable.

A human and an unseelie fae laughing together. Who would have thought it?

"You are an enigma, *Sybelle*," I said when my laughter had finally subsided.

She arched an eyebrow at me. "I'm not sure if that's a compliment."

"It's the most you'll get from me this evening." I pressed my fist to my heart. "I bid you good night."

She returned the gesture. "Good night, husband."

I flinched, and she chuckled again, as if she'd known how much I would despise the word. As I turned away from her, I wondered whether this bold, unexpected creature would continue to amuse me, or frustrate me to no end.

THE BEAUTY

The Wraith King was terrifying. No doubt about it.

But the first thing I noted were his bare, clawed feet. The talons were black, gleaming like onyx in the dying firelight.

It reminded me of Azure. The talons on her tail legs were the same color.

From there, I could only see similarities to my best friend. The claws. The sharpened teeth. His set of fangs along the bottom were so large they protruded from his mouth even when his lips were closed. And every single tooth that showed when he spoke was sharpened like the point of a dagger.

Azure's teeth were the same. She often mocked me for my dull, rectangular teeth, claiming they couldn't possibly tear meat properly.

There were, of course, several major differences between King Varius and Azure. For instance, his two rather large black horns that added several inches to his already impressive height. His eyes were jet black. The bare chest visible from his open tunic was firm and muscular, along with his powerful arms. I was certain he could crush my windpipe with one hand.

His thin, barbed tail curled behind him, and I noticed the jagged edges were long and sharp, slightly different from Azure's shorter and wider barbs.

If Azure stood in this room with us, the Wraith King would look quite normal alongside her. *I* would be the odd one out.

The notion calmed my racing heart and helped me see Varius with new eyes.

He's a dragon, I thought. *Nothing more.*

My grip on the jeweled dagger tightened, and a renewed sense of boldness took over me. I had ascertained that the Wraith King liked to be surprised, which was why I told him an excessively affectionate husband would have terrified me the most.

It wasn't a lie. If someone like the Wraith King *had* insisted on remaining by my side, touching me constantly, and taking me to his bed every night, my circumstances would have been a lot more horrifying.

After bidding me good night, the king turned and strode from the room. My eyes bulged at the sight of his massive red wings tucked against his back. I hadn't noticed them before. They weren't quite as big as Tislora's, but I imagined that, when they were open wide, they were just as long as his body height.

As soon as the door slammed shut from Varius's departure, lanterns in the walls flared to life, as if his shadows had intentionally kept the room dim while he was here. The pearly white orbs I recognized from all over the castle burned to life against the wall, one by one, making my jaw drop as I took in the vast space.

It was a library. And it was ten times the size of the library I was accustomed to in the Earthen Court. The massive space stretched three levels high with a dome-shaped window on the ceiling that revealed the starry night sky. Spiral staircases were in each corner of the room, leading up to the next two levels of shelves. In front of the fireplace were the two wing-backed chairs I had noticed earlier.

And *Stones*, there were so many books! From floor to ceiling, the walls were covered in shelves of books. Now that I was aware of it, the familiar smell of old parchment filled my nose. How had I not noticed it before? Azure would have commented on my weak human senses if she were here. Rows and rows of leather volumes and ancient tomes were stacked neatly along the shelves, with tiny labels underneath that were most likely in Agnarrish.

Already, I itched to run my hands along the books, to see what knowledge I could glean from them. Were they *all* in Agnarrish? Were there some in other languages I had never heard of before?

Maybe there was something about the enchanted rose here.

I strode forward, determination fueling me as I squinted at the spines closest to me. Yes, they were certainly in Agnarrish. But they didn't make any sense. One was a cookbook for cultural delicacies in the Shadow Court. And the one right beside it was an encyclopedia on winged fae.

Frowning, I glanced over the next few volumes. *A History of Unseelie Warfare*, *The Traveler's Comprehensive Guide to Foliage*, and *The Family Tree of King Farabor IV*.

This organization system made no sense. There was nothing in common between these volumes. Was there something I was missing?

I glanced at the guide to foliage again. "Maybe this has information about roses," I muttered aloud, stretching my hand to remove it from the shelf.

Before I could, a faint rumbling sound echoed around me. I stilled, my heart racing as I whirled around, expecting to find an unseelie fae about to charge toward me.

But I was alone in the room.

The rumbling grew louder until the books on the shelves began to tremble. My hands flew outward to steady myself as I waited for the earthquake to rend the ground in two or for the walls to come crashing down.

A loud *thump* next to me elicited a shriek of alarm. I jerked backward, nearly colliding with the bookshelf as I tried to avoid whatever had landed in the center of the room. Pulse skittering, I looked around, only to find it was a book.

A *book* had seemingly fallen from the ceiling and landed in the center of the library.

I remained frozen for a full minute, waiting for the book to spring legs or grow fangs or do *something*. Clearly it was enchanted; otherwise, how had it magically appeared there? Was it safe? Would this book attack me if I drew nearer?

Another minute passed, and my curiosity got the better of me. Slowly, I approached the book, each step cautious and hesitant. The book didn't move. I continued until I stood directly above it, my brow furrowing as I inspected the burgundy leather cover.

I crouched down, hands hovering close to the book, waiting for it to move. When it didn't, I held my breath and grabbed it, my hands closing over the soft cover.

Nothing happened. It felt like... an ordinary book. It wasn't warm or trembling or alive. I turned it over in my hands, marveling at how unexceptional it appeared. For all I knew, this book could have come from my own shelf back in the Earthen Court. I ran my fingers over the embossed title etched into the spine: *How to Grow and Nurture Rosebushes.*

My heart stuttered in my chest, and I looked around the room once more, searching for eavesdroppers. Had someone heard me talking about roses? With so many unseelie fae around, it wouldn't have been hard to overhear my mutterings.

But the room still seemed eerily empty.

Even so, perhaps someone had some sort of invisibility magic I didn't know about. It wouldn't be *that* far-fetched.

Swallowing hard, I cradled the book to my chest, trying not to let my fear rule me. It wasn't lost on me that an empty library frightened me more than the beastly appearance of the Wraith King.

But it was always the unknown that terrified me. Which was one of the reasons why, when the king had dispersed his shadows, he had seemed *less* frightening. Oftentimes, my imagination conjured the worst scenarios imaginable, so removing that unknown factor was almost a relief. I had pictured a four-headed beast with a scorpion tail and four sets of eyes, with fangs that dripped venom. So, naturally, the king's true appearance had been a relief.

"Where are you?" I murmured, inching backward, my eyes still roving over the expansive library. Surely *someone* must be hiding nearby.

A faint, low growl sounded from afar, and a chill raced down my spine. The growl came again, and I frowned, recognizing it.

"Az?" I muttered, then quickly touched my amber necklace.

"Where the hell have you been?" Azure snapped. *"I was about to burst in there and rescue you."*

I laughed because Azure only swore when she was truly in distress. "I'm sorry, I'm sorry," I said quickly. "I got distracted. You can come in."

I would have said, *I'm alone*, but I wasn't sure if that was true.

The door across from the fireplace creaked open, and my dragon's hulking blue form appeared. In the cathedral-sized library, she almost looked minuscule, and I happily noted how fitting this space would be for her, provided we could keep it hidden from the castle staff.

Azure's blue eyes surveyed the spacious room with suspicion and distrust as she padded toward me, talons clicking along the stone floor. When she finally reached me, she inhaled deeply.

"It smells like the magic from before," she said. *"That same curious feeling."*

"The castle?" I asked, confused. "I thought that magic was only associated with the doors."

"A castle consists of more than just doors, *human,"* she said in a bored voice.

I rolled my eyes. "I know that, *dragon*. But I thought the *magic* only extended to the doors. Obviously, I was wrong."

I gazed at the book in my left hand, trying to puzzle it out. "Castle," I said slowly, feeling ridiculous, "if you can understand me, could you please send me a book about trolls?"

Azure snorted. *"You are insane."*

I shushed her as that same rumbling sound overtook the room. I spun, my gaze flicking over the shelves as I realized the *books* were shaking. A hesitant smile spread across my face, and when the book fell from the ceiling, I was ready for it.

"Oof!" I grunted, catching the book in my arms. The force of it was so intense it knocked me on my rear, and I ended up dropping both books. Beside me, Azure wheezed with laughter.

"Shut up," I muttered, stumbling to my feet and picking the books off the floor. The newest one had a forest green cover and was titled, *Tilly the Troll Voyages Across the Realm*. I flipped through the pages, noting the detailed illustrations. It looked to be a children's tale.

My smile widened. "The castle controls the library. It hears my requests."

Azure stilled beside me. When I shot her a triumphant grin, she only blinked at me warily.

My smile faded. "What?"

"Be careful, Sybelle. I worry this place can discern more than just thoughts that are voiced."

The joy in my heart shriveled, dissolving into ash as I realized what she implied. Could the castle read my thoughts? And, if it couldn't, what was stopping it from acquiring such a power? What if, the longer I was here, the more this place could creep into my mind?

My diamond dagger.

My plans to locate the enchanted rose.

The plot to destroy the king and his shadows.

Icy cold dread filled my chest, and I abruptly set the books down on the table between the wing-backed chairs. "We should go," I whispered.

"Agreed," said Azure, already heading for the door, which was still ajar. I followed, stepping over the threshold. I cast one more longing look over the library, wishing I could stay and unravel its secrets.

But that magic could go both ways. If I could explore this library, then it could explore me as well. Already, it could be reporting everything it had learned about me to the Wraith King.

Which meant he would know about Azure.

I hurried into the hallway, letting the door close behind me. Panting, I turned to Azure. "You need to leave," I hissed. *"Now."*

"Let me see you to your rooms first," she insisted. *"I don't trust this place."*

"Me neither."

Azure led me down the hall, and I swallowed around a knot of emotions, trying not to panic. Just when I feared all the doors had been closed, we reached the set of open ones—mine and Ramia's. My breath left me with a relieved exhale as we darted inside. The balcony doors were still open, and Azure made her way toward them, wings folded against her back. She angled her head toward me, eyes intent.

"Be careful, Sybelle. I won't be far."

I nodded. "Stay hidden. Don't do anything stupid."

"That's your *habit, remember?"*

I chuckled as she leapt off the balcony and took off into the sky. The silhouette of her great form, wings spread wide, shone against the moonlit sky. With each flap of her wings, my heart settled into a steady rhythm. Still, I kept my fingers wrapped around my amber stone, just in case.

When Azure finally faded from view, and all was quiet once more, I could finally breathe easily.

THE BEAST

"The elixir is ready."

I looked up from my desk, my head throbbing from trying—and failing—to come up with a solution to the riots breaking out in the lower towns. I was attempting to write a missive to my general with instructions on how to quell the unrest.

My people were suffering. The deadly shadows were drawing closer, and I had no way to protect them. I couldn't blame them for panicking.

Tislora stood at my open door, arms folded across her chest. "I used all the human's blood. You'll need to get more."

"Why can't *you* get it?" I growled, running a hand through my dark curls.

"If you're going to be cantankerous, you can make your own damn elixir," she said.

I groaned, sitting back in my seat. The chair creaked loudly as I massaged my temples. "I apologize. This is my problem. Not yours."

"Varius."

I gave her a weary look. Her silver orb-like eyes seemed to peer into my soul.

"You have to tell her," she said. "It's the only way."

"I can't lie, Lor. I'm not exactly ready to tell her that this curse will kill her. If I start to tell her the truth, she will ask questions. This one is… curious. *Too* curious."

Tislora leaned against the doorframe, her lips forming a thin line. "You knew this wouldn't be easy. And she is only *one human*. The fate of your kingdom is at stake."

"I *know*," I snapped. "You think I don't know that?"

"I think that bleeding heart of yours is going to get you into trouble. Who gives a shit if the human has a comfortable life or not? She was born to be a pawn in this game those human royals play. She doesn't matter. But your people do."

I clenched my teeth to refrain from snapping at her again. I knew all this. Truly, I did.

But I also knew that the elixir would be the most powerful if I allowed the bond between Sybelle and myself to strengthen first. It had only been one day since the wedding ceremony. I didn't think that was enough time to make a strong enough connection between our blood.

A darker part of my mind registered that consummation was the surest way to solidify a blood bond between husband and wife.

Tislora was right. My people were more important than one mortal woman's discomfort.

If I had to bed her, I would.

If I had to bleed her dry, I would.

But that didn't mean I wouldn't look for every alternative before resorting to those measures.

"Leave the elixir on my desk," I said, my voice tired. When Tislora didn't move, I added, "Please."

She strode into my room, her cloak swishing with each lithe movement, before placing the tiny vial atop my oak desk. "You cannot fix every problem, Varius," she whispered. "That's not on you. Your ancestors couldn't break this curse, either."

"That doesn't mean I have accepted my fate," I said through gritted teeth.

When Tislora continued to stand there, watching me, I said, "I will figure something out. I promise."

"Very well." She turned to leave, then paused at the threshold to face me once more. "I have spells available, if you need them. Spells to help make humans more… compliant."

Icy horror chilled me to the bone at her implication, and I fixed a hard stare on her. Not a hint of remorse marred her expression. She only blinked at me with cool apathy.

My nostrils flared, and I bared my teeth at her. She smirked, understanding my refusal of her offer, before turning and leaving, the clicking of her boots echoing down the hall.

Long after she retreated, I took the small vial in my hands, turning it over. The mixture was inky black, even darker than my blood. And it was made with the last few drops of Sybelle's blood.

After this, I would either need to extract her blood by force… or coerce her into giving it willingly. The former was how my predecessors would have done it, out of desperation and impatience. But the latter was the safest way to gain her trust and, hopefully, steer her in the direction of breaking the curse for me.

But time was not on my side. Even if I *did* gain her trust, there was no guarantee she would fulfill all the steps required to break this curse.

Which was the better choice—to prolong the inevitable and grant my people a bit more time, while torturing a human in the process… or to allow my people to keep suffering while I attempted to woo the human?

With a growl, I uncorked the vial and downed the contents, smacking my lips at the foul, bitter taste. I shuddered, and my wings twitched as the elixir swept through me. My blood boiled, and I groaned, slumping over on the desk. It was an echo of the torment I endured in that cave, but it was better than having to go through it all again.

This tiny vial of liquid granted me another full moon of freedom. But after that, I was doomed. There was nothing left to save me.

Except Sybelle.

I thought of Clermont's words: *This is what's done.*

My father would have done what was necessary.

My clawed fingers curled into fists atop my desk. Rage arose within me, thick and volatile, as I thought of that murderous bastard. He had crossed every line in his desperate attempts to free himself from the curse. From the moment I had witnessed him choking the life out of one of his concubines, I vowed to *never* be like him.

Was this a sign? If my father would have taken blood from the human by force, was it my fate to do the opposite?

Or was I destined to follow in his footsteps no matter what?

I rose to my feet, my chair groaning against the stone floor as I made my way to the door. It still stood ajar after Tislora's visit. Frowning, I swung the door shut and waited for the magic to take effect. Then, I said softly, "Show me what you want from me."

I opened the door and found myself facing... the kitchens. Servants and staff bustled about, and the smell of spiced vegetables reached my nose.

My brow furrowed. What was this? Was the castle mocking me? It wouldn't have been the first time. The sentient place seemed to have a mischievous sense of humor.

I closed the door, then reopened it. The same scene awaited me. A servant carrying a tray of buttered bread paused to stare, wide-eyed, at me, his face paling.

"Damn it all," I muttered before striding into the kitchens.

The entire space fell silent at my entrance. Fae went completely still, eyes fixed on me in shock and fear.

I waved a hand. "Go about your business. I'm just... observing."

After a moment, a few fae started moving again, and the bustling resumed. I lingered against the wall, arms crossed as I surveyed the spacious kitchen. The chef was barking orders at his attendants. To the left, steam rose from a fresh pot of stew. The pounding of a blade against a chopping board rang out in the room.

What is it you want me to see? I wondered. *Why am I here?*

Most fae, my father included, discounted the enchanted castle as a side effect of the curse. But I knew it to be more than that. This place was the heart of the sorceress's spell. It held more secrets and answers than any of us.

And it was more stubborn than any creature I had ever met.

A loud crash sounded from the next room over, and I straightened, tensing with apprehension. A flurry of motion followed as servants rushed toward the source of the commotion. Loud voices rang out, followed by one I immediately recognized.

"I'm so terribly sorry!" Sybelle said. "Please, let me help you clean this up."

In Agnarrish, a servant said hastily, "No, no, don't trouble yourself, my lady. Please return to your rooms. We will send someone to see to your needs."

I suppressed a groan. What the hell was she doing in the kitchens, of all places?

"I just need…" Sybelle broke off with a noise of frustration. Curious, I edged closer to the next room, careful not to reveal my presence. From the corridor that led to the dining hall, I remained in the shadows as I peered around the corner.

Sybelle was in the medicine room, surrounded by broken glass, as servants scrambled around her trying to clean up her mess. Her cheeks were flushed, and her eyes were wide with panic. Her wavy chestnut hair hung loose and frayed around her, and she wore a simple blue dress that was stained with various potion ingredients.

My scowl deepened. What was she doing poking around our medicine room?

Then, she said something that made me freeze.

"*Gerra modi.* Do you have any? I need *gerra modi.*"

The servants around her stilled as well, recognition dawning on their faces. One of them nodded and started shuffling through the mess of jars.

She was asking for birch root, which was a medicinal herb for the fae beasts who had cracked talons or split claws. It helped numb the area so the healer could mend the creature. It was the only thing strong enough to affect the toughened flesh of unseelie beasts.

Why did this weak, fragile human need such a thing?

And how did she know the word for it in my language?

Suspicion crept through me, and I silently thanked the castle for leading me here. Perhaps there were more secrets to my human bride than I originally thought.

I remained hidden in the corridor as Sybelle clumsily helped the servants clean up. When a kitchen maid appeared with a jar of birch root, Sybelle accepted it and murmured, "*Garsha.*"

Thank you.

Now that I was focused on it, I realized her accent and pronunciation were flawless. She uttered the word like a native.

The staff began ushering her from the room, eager to have her removed from the kitchens. Sybelle stumbled over more apologies and thanks as she hurried from the room. I followed her down the corridor, keeping a safe distance as she made her way up the spiral staircase that led to the ground level of the castle.

I smirked. She didn't realize there was a door waiting for her at the top of the stairs. Any number of unseelie fae would know all they needed to do was open a door—any door. She should have merely strode down the hall of the kitchens and opened the same door I'd come through.

But of course she didn't know any better.

And if the castle was still in a mischievous mood, it might take advantage of her ignorance.

When Sybelle reached the top of the stairs, she uttered a soft, "Shit."

I had to refrain from chuckling.

The door creaked open, and blinding sunlight illuminated the darkened stairwell. I shrank against the walls, afraid the brilliant light would alert her to the beast lurking behind her. She lifted a hand, shielding her eyes as she slammed the door shut. With another whispered curse, she shook her hands two times, then tried again.

More sunlight. The smell of oak trees and fresh grass filled my nose.

The training yard. The castle was trying to send her to the training yard.

I wanted to laugh.

Sybelle groaned and shut the door. "Could you take me to my rooms? Please?"

She opened the door again, but nothing changed.

"What about the library? You tried so hard to get me there the other night."

She opened it again, and it was still the training yard.

"*Damn it all!*" she hissed, stomping her foot in frustration.

I couldn't keep hiding like this. Clearing my throat, I murmured, "It doesn't quite work like that."

Sybelle jumped and let out a soft squeak of surprise, her hand covering her mouth as she stared at me with wide eyes. "*Stones*, how long have you been standing there?"

"Long enough to know the castle is toying with you." I leaned against the stone wall and flashed her a grin. "You are making it too easy."

"I—I just—" She sighed and let her hand fall against her

thigh. "I just want to get back to my rooms. Why is it making it difficult for me?"

Ignoring her question, I gestured to the jar in her hand. Her eyes fell to my long, black claws, and I sensed her pulse quickening. "Why do you need that?"

If it weren't for my fae senses, I might have missed the faint blush that crept across her cheeks. "Birch root is known to cure severe headaches."

My eyebrows lifted at the obvious lie. "Is it, now?"

"Yes. My people have been using it for centuries. Is that a problem?"

I cocked my head, assessing her. Her free hand fisted her skirts, and she kept biting her bottom lip. "Do you have a headache, wife?"

She swallowed. "I haven't been sleeping well."

I smirked at that, remembering our midnight rendezvous in the library. There was something odd about the way she was speaking, but I couldn't quite figure out what it was. "If you need better accommodations, all you have to do is ask. In fact, it's probably time to move you over to the queen's suite. Right next to mine."

Her face drained of color. "N-No. That won't be necessary. I'm quite comfortable in the guest quarters."

I took a step up so that we were practically at eye level. Her breath hitched at the nearness, but she did not flinch away from me.

"But you are not a *guest* any longer, Sybelle. You are my wife."

Her breathing was sharp and ragged now. Fear emanated from her in thick waves, and I marveled at this. When I revealed my true nature and yelled at her in the library, she did not fear me. But now, she did. Why?

Was it the prospect of sleeping in a room that shared a wall with mine?

"I will not touch you," I vowed to her. "I swear it. Not unless you invite me to. You will still have your privacy."

She let out a huff that sounded somewhere between a cough and a laugh.

My eyes narrowed. Did she not believe me? "What is your objection to this? Does it disgust you to be so close to a creature like me?"

Her jaw slackened, and indignation flashed in her eyes. "Of course not!"

"Then, what is the issue?"

"I don't—" She took a breath and tried again. "You're right. I do like my privacy. And I have... appreciated how secluded the guest wing is."

Yes, so you can wander about as you please, I thought. What had she been looking for when she'd stumbled into the library that night?

"Your maid, of course, is free to move to the east wing as well," I added. "And I will see that Enzira will come, too."

"You know Enzira's name?" she asked in surprise.

I frowned. "Why wouldn't I?"

"Aren't there hundreds of servants in this castle?"

I chuckled. "The minds of you humans are so fragile. We live for thousands of years, dear wife, and so it is not as easy for us to forget our people's names."

Her brows knitted together, and something akin to disappointment crossed her face. But I couldn't fathom why.

"Come." I swept past her and grasped the door handle. When I opened it, the training yard greeted us once more. *Stubborn castle,* I thought. If it wanted us to go here, there was no fighting it. I had learned that long ago.

"The best way out is forward," I said, stepping through the doorway and extending my hand to Sybelle. She eyed it for a long moment before taking it, her tiny fingers interlacing with mine. When she stiffened, I wondered if she thought my claws would tear her soft flesh to ribbons.

These humans always thought us nothing more than savage, feral beasts with no control. If we were intelligent enough to possess magic, we were certainly nimble enough to keep our claws from slicing open poor, defenseless humans.

Sybelle's eyes darted from my crimson fingers to my face and back again, as if she were utterly shocked. Was my skin hotter than she anticipated? Were the claws too terrifying?

But none of those seemed to suit the curiosity burning in her gaze. She lifted our entwined fingers so she could better scrutinize my hand.

"Does your skin… change color?" she asked. Her voice was full of awe. Not a hint of disgust or horror.

I cleared my throat, unsure of why such a close inspection made me feel uncomfortable. "Sometimes. It is not all one color, but I cannot change it at will. It often gets darker in the winter and lighter in the summer, though."

A small smile lit her face as she turned my hand over, her eyes traveling from my knuckles to my wrist and back down again. It felt oddly… intimate. As I followed the path of her gaze, I realized what she was seeing. The skin on my hand ranged from bright cherry to dark burgundy, creating an ombre of colors. When I looked at the contrast of her pale fingers, I realized human skin was not like this; it was one uniform shade.

Interesting.

"Your Highness?"

I started, turning to find Murvo, my captain of the guards, standing in the grass, sword drawn as he looked at us with curiosity and confusion. He was tall and bulky with amber skin and two large sets of wings folded at his back. Behind him stood a row of soldiers, also holding swords.

We had obviously interrupted a training exercise. I heard

Sybelle suck in a sharp breath beside me, but I kept her hand clamped in mine.

"Forgive us, Murvo," I said in Agnarrish. "You know how the castle is. We'll just be going."

Murvo's dark gaze flicked from me to Sybelle. Something flashed in his gaze when he looked at the human, but it was gone in an instant. He nodded, turning back to face the soldiers as I guided Sybelle toward the east side of the castle.

"What are they training for?" Sybelle asked, her voice tight.

I glanced at her. Her eyes were hard, and her mouth formed a thin line. "They are soldiers," I said slowly. "They train to defend our home against outside threats."

"Or perhaps they train to invade other lands," she said.

Rage simmered in my blood at the accusation in her tone. I abruptly dropped her hand and stopped walking so I could face her fully. "Go ahead and say what you mean, human. Don't mince words."

She squared her shoulders, inhaling deeply. Her chin lifted, but she still only reached my collarbone. She didn't seem to notice; her eyes were full of venom as she looked up at me.

"Those are the very soldiers who have been slaughtering my people for years," she said, her voice trembling with rage. "Are you saying that *we* pose a threat to your home? Or do you simply not have any control over your men?"

My rage deepened into an all-consuming fury that rocked violently through my body. I felt my wings spread behind me, and my claws elongated. Sybelle's eyes flared wide as she noticed it, too.

I loomed over her, teeth bared as I growled, "So you believe your people are completely innocent? That they are not invading *my* lands and plundering *my* villages first?"

"Why would they do that?" she demanded.

"Why indeed," I hissed. "It must be easy, to be human. You can lie and tell your people there are good reasons for attacking the horrid unseelie demons across the border. But *I* cannot lie, human. And I have seen firsthand *your* soldiers stealing from innocent civilians, beating women and children, and burning down homes all for their own amusement. So perhaps you should be interrogating your own people before throwing accusations at me."

It wasn't until Sybelle gasped that I realized black shadows had pooled at my feet, surrounding us both. They continued to inch upward, reacting to my anger.

I took a step back, and the shadows receded slightly. I was breathing heavily, my heart thundering in my chest. "I'll have Enzira move you to the east wing as soon as possible," I said, unable to look her in the eye. "If you'll excuse me, I have important matters to attend to."

I strode past her, sensing her watching me as I made my way back to the castle. I would place her next to my rooms so I could watch her and uncover her secrets. She was the key to breaking the curse, and she could not do that unless I steered her in the right direction.

But that did not mean I had to enjoy the situation, nor did it mean I had to like her in any way. She had proven her prejudices against my kind spoke more loudly to her than common sense. If that was how she wanted to live and think, then fine.

For now, I needed to put as much distance between myself and my human bride as possible, before my shadows choked the life out of her.

The Beauty

My head was still spinning with rage and confusion from Varius's words. *Perhaps you should be interrogating your own people before throwing accusations at me.*

How dare he? As if he knew *anything* about what my people had suffered at the hands of the unseelie fae.

My hands curled into shaking fists as I tried to follow Varius into the castle, but he had vanished so quickly that I wondered if his shadows had swallowed him up. At any rate, he walked directly through a line of soldiers practicing archery, and I wasn't quite bold enough to step in their line of fire.

The training yard was a maze of wooden beams, shooting targets, and massive climbing walls. Everything was so huge I could hardly make out the castle turrets that I knew were somewhere behind the training yard.

High in the sky, dark shadows swirled. They were thicker and denser than the Umbra Mist I was accustomed to. Then I remembered what Enzira had told me about the Umbra Mist—it recoiled from light. Right now, with the sun high in the sky, the usual thin and transparent layer of Umbra Mist was gone.

I frowned, glancing upward again. Clearly, I was in no danger; if the soldiers could train here without issue, then *something* was keeping the dark shadows at bay.

I recalled Varius's words from the library: *I maintain the shield around the castle that protects it during the daytime when the Umbra Mist is thinnest.*

Squinting, I peered closer at the shadows in the sky, raising a hand to block the brilliance of the sun so I could see better.

Sure enough, an almost invisible pearly white fog hovered just in front of the darkness, like a ghostly barrier.

That had to be Varius's magic.

Satisfied with my assessment, I lowered my gaze and watched the soldiers train for a while, curious of their method. The drills were very unlike what I was accustomed to with my own training; Gerard often had the men run laps, then spar one-on-one to improve their technique.

The fae soldiers all fought in one massive group. After watching for a few minutes, I realized why: they were learning how to battle multiple opponents and threats at once. And, with unseelie creatures who possessed tails and wings and other appendages that could be used in battle, this was a valuable technique to learn. One fae used his barbed tail to take down a soldier at his back, then slashed at an opponent with his claws while striking another with his sword.

And the leather armor the soldiers wore was quite flimsy. Claws and blades easily pierced through it, and several men were bleeding profusely by the end of the exercise. I watched them leave the training yard, some limping and others needing to be dragged out. I could only hope they were on their way to a healer.

Then I realized that healer likely resided in the castle, so I hurried across the grass after them, hoping they would lead me out of the chaotic training yard. I needed to get back to my rooms to help Azure. She had gotten a massive splinter that had cracked one of her talons when she'd landed last night. She had only just told me this morning, after enduring a sleepless night of agony. The birch root tucked in the folds of my skirts would help her heal, and I was anxious to remove the splinter for her.

The injured soldiers climbed a steep hill, and on the other side was a covered walkway that led to the rear side of the palace.

A breath of relief whooshed out of me as I trailed after them—but I stopped short when an unfamiliar soldier stepped in my path.

I offered a nervous smile and tried to step around him.

He blocked me again.

"Excuse me," I said in Agnarrish.

The soldier only smiled. I looked him over, noting his muscular frame that towered over me. He had a pair of black horns and strange, mismatched eyes, one gold and one silver. His skin was a pale blue.

"Where are you off to, human?" he asked in my language. "You seemed so interested in our training earlier."

"I was only curious," I said. "And a bit lost. This castle is confusing, and I'm trying to find my way back."

Once more, I stepped to the left, trying to get past him, but he matched my movements. Anger prickled underneath my skin, and I glared up at him. "Do you mind?"

He cocked his head at me and flashed a smug smile. The king often canted his head a certain way when he looked at me, but this was nothing like that. Varius did it to scrutinize me. But this soldier was looking at me like I was his next meal.

And I didn't like it one bit.

My hand clamped around the hilt of the dagger hidden in my skirts, and the strength of the diamonds flooded my veins, filling me with boldness and clarity. "Let me pass," I ordered, trying to put as much authority in my voice as possible.

"Perhaps you should linger for a while longer," the soldier said, unfazed by my demands. "The squadron hasn't had a good hunt in a long while. It would be exciting for them."

My blood chilled. Surely this stranger wasn't suggesting the trained soldiers would *hunt* me for sport.

I thought of the unseelie creatures terrorizing the villagers in my kingdom. Bile crept up my throat.

But I refused to let this fae's threats cow me. I drew my dagger and aimed it for his chest. "Step aside," I said in a low voice, "or I will run you through."

The soldier looked at my dagger and laughed. "You think you can harm me, human? Have they not educated you in those tiny schools of yours? Mortals cannot kill us."

I did know this. Only weapons of iron could truly kill a fae.

Which was why I could not wield an iron blade, as it would harm me just to touch the hilt.

But I also knew that the diamonds infused in this dagger granted me the strength of five fae soldiers. It wouldn't take much to sever this bastard's head from his body. And *that* would certainly kill him.

I drew closer to him, letting the tip of my dagger press against his leather tunic. "Would you like to test my blade, soldier?"

His smile only widened, as if he enjoyed the threat.

I shoved harder, letting the blade slice through his tunic and graze his flesh.

His smile vanished in an instant as I drew blood. A black droplet oozed from the wound, trickling down his tunic. He hissed in pain, jerking away from me, his eyes darting to the dagger.

I only offered a smug grin. With the dagger still poised and ready to strike, I moved forward. He slid out of my path, letting me pass. My steps quickened as I raced across the grass, my heart pounding, until I reached the covered walkway. I glanced over my shoulder to find the soldier standing where I'd left him, watching me with a curious expression on his face.

Stones, I did not like that fae.

I kept a tight grip on my dagger as I hurried down the walkway, anxious to put as much distance between myself and the fae soldier as possible.

155

I kept a tight grip on my dagger as I hurried down the walkway, anxious to put as much distance between myself and the fae soldier as possible.

THE BEAUTY

The next day, I stood in the hallway, my stomach in knots as Enzira finished moving my things into the queen's chambers. It was fairly easy; I had only been in the Shadow Court for a few days, so most of my things were still in my trunk. I had quickly extracted my dagger, Wraith Killer, as well as my pouch of gemstones and the vial of birch root, then shoved them in my bodice before anyone noticed. With the chaos of servants moving my things to the queen's chambers, there hadn't been a moment for me to visit Azure and use the birch root to remove her splinter.

Now I couldn't even risk seeing her because the king was suspicious of me. Why else would he insist on putting me in the rooms adjacent to his? It was clear he held no affection for me, and I was only his wife because of some part I had to play to keep the toxic shadows at bay—a part I knew nothing about.

And with Varius's brutish behavior yesterday, I didn't expect him to be very forthcoming. He had completely dismissed my accusation that his men had terrorized my people—which I had seen firsthand, regardless of his claims—and instead turned the accusation on me.

But, despite the fire raging in my chest, it *did* make me wonder how much of what he said was true. I had only witnessed unseelie creatures attacking my people *once*. Every other time had been a report from my father or someone like Gerard.

Someone who could easily have been lying, or had been fed lies by others.

I thought of Gerard's blatant hatred for all things fae—seelie or unseelie. I recalled how much he despised the magic in my blood. It didn't matter that he cared for me or trusted me. He would never trust the power thrumming inside my veins.

Was I as blind as he was? Was I so poisoned against the unseelie that I would immediately assume the worst about them?

That isn't fair, I told myself. *It is natural to trust your own people over these strangers.*

But then I thought of the kind face of Enzira, who, regardless of her appearance, seemed like she wouldn't harm a fly. I thought of all the other servants I had encountered throughout the castle, and how helpful and polite they had been.

Not beastly or monstrous at all. Not like I was taught.

"Are you sure about this?" Ramia whispered, jerking me from my thoughts. We stood in the hall outside the queen's chambers, overseeing the staff as they readied the rooms for us. "I feel uneasy about your rooms being so close to his."

"This is what I came here to do, remember?" I whispered. "I'm meant to be the queen here, and this is the first step."

"We don't know anything about the king," Ramia whispered, though I was sure the fae could still hear her words. "For all we know, he'll wait for you to fall asleep and then feast on your flesh."

"*Ramia,*" I hissed in warning, glancing nervously at a smiling Enzira who passed by us. "Even if this *were* true, which I'm sure it's not, how exactly do you think you would be able to stop him?"

Ramia glanced at me, her expression falling.

"Like it or not, we are at the mercy of the Shadow King," I said. "We will need to trust him."

Even if he seems untrustworthy, I wanted to add.

"Right," Ramia agreed, nodding as if to reassure herself more than me. "For the good of our people."

My mouth twisted in a grimace, because I wasn't sure *what* good this alliance was actually doing. It was meant to keep the shadows at bay, but Varius implied *I* had to do something first. I just didn't know what.

And either Varius was blind to what his soldiers were doing, or he was telling the truth and my people *weren't* being attacked by the unseelie. Neither scenario was very comforting. If my father was lying about the attacks, what did he hope to gain? What was he covering up? I knew Father was slimy and unpleasant, and he saw me as nothing more than a weapon to wield, but he cared about his people. It didn't seem like him to craft lies in order to incite terror and panic.

None of this made any sense. And I had no idea who to believe. I couldn't trust anyone—except maybe Azure.

Enzira appeared again and pressed a fist to her chest. "Room ready, my lady." Her eyes gleamed with pride.

I offered a small smile. She seemed positively thrilled that I had married Varius. Many of the fae—Varius included—looked at me with distrust in their eyes, but Enzira had been nothing but kind and supportive from the moment I arrived.

The thought warmed my chest, loosening some of the tension there, and I drew closer to her, taking her clawed hands in mine. Her eyes widened in alarm, but she didn't step away from me.

"Thank you, Enzira," I said quietly. "For everything. *Garsha.*"

She blinked, then nodded uncertainly.

I sighed, dropping the pretense for a moment. In Agnarrish, I whispered, "You are a kind soul, and I greatly appreciate you."

Her mouth fell open, revealing her fangs. In her native

tongue, she whispered, "I—thank you, my queen." She swallowed, her gaze darting around the hall as if looking to see if anyone else had heard me speak Agnarrish so fluently. After a moment, she withdrew her hands from mine, smoothed them on her skirts, and shuffled away.

Perhaps it was foolish to reveal that secret. But given all the others I was keeping, it seemed the least dangerous.

Besides, Enzira didn't deserve to suffer because of my duplicity. If she went and told the king I knew their language, then so be it.

I turned and found Ramia scowling at me.

"That was unwise, my lady," she muttered.

I waved a hand. "It would have come out eventually. Besides, I learned the language for a reason. I'd prefer to use it, instead of acting the ignorant fool."

Ramia leaned close to me and said in a low voice, "Just be sure to keep certain *other* things to yourself, will you?"

My eyes narrowed, but she turned away before I could question her further. I suspected she knew about my gemstone magic, and that was what she was referring to. Ramia was very observant.

But right now, with the king asking questions about the birch root, it made me wonder who *else* might know about Azure. Had I not been as careful as I should have? Was she in danger?

I shook my head to rid myself of this paranoia, then strode into my new chambers. A gasp burst from me, and I stumbled back a step at the grandeur of the room. It was twice the size of my guest chamber, which had already been massive. In one corner of the room was a small nook with several bookshelves and a comfortable-looking armchair. Next to it was the largest fireplace I had ever seen. And on the other end was a mahogany writing desk. The massive bed took up most of the space on the opposite end of the room. A small armoire was next to the bed, along with a tiny breakfast table, upon which rested a tray of fruits and cheeses.

Floor-to-ceiling windows lined the wall, boasting a sunny view of the Dellona Mountains, which looked like two jagged spears in the distance. Somewhere between them was my castle. My home. My father was probably lording over his free time now that he no longer had to train me to be the Shadow Queen. And Orla, my sister, was likely gloating over my absence and making her plans to become the Earthen Queen.

Gerard had probably found another lover by now. But, to my surprise, this didn't spark any jealousy in me. He had only been a means for me to escape my trapped world. Nothing more.

A pang of longing filled me as I thought of the home I'd once had. I didn't necessarily miss Father or Orla, but I missed the caves. I missed exploring them with Azure.

I missed the comfort of a land and a castle that I knew well. I felt safe there.

Wringing my hands together, I turned away from the window and peered into the bathing chamber. I took in the massive black hole built into the center of the floor, just like in my previous room. I frowned. Ramia and I had never figured out *what* this hole was.

Well, now that Enzira knew I could speak her language, perhaps I could ask her. I was tired of playing games.

I found myself moving toward the desk without realizing it. I still hadn't written to my friend Eira in the Winter Court. She would be appalled that I'd moved to the Shadow Court *and* gotten married without informing her.

After a quick search through the drawers, I found an inkwell, a quill, and a few rolls of parchment. I hastily began writing.

· · ·

I have a new home now. It's quite dark and misty. And my husband is far worse than a mean old codger.

"I see you've gotten settled," said a voice from behind me.

I yelped and whirled to find King Varius standing at an open door I hadn't noticed before. It was nestled between the armoire and the bed, and, now that I focused on it, I realized it must lead to *his* chambers.

His bed. His *room*. Directly next to mine.

My throat knotted, and I found I couldn't speak. My shaking hands hastened to stuff the parchment behind me and into one of the drawers.

The last thing I needed was for him to see the words *mean old codger*.

Varius tilted his head at me. He did that often, I noticed. It made him look more predatory. "Is everything to your liking?" His gaze flicked to the desk behind me.

"What is that?" I asked, desperate to distract him before he discovered my letter. My voice was far too loud, so I cleared my throat and gestured to the bathing chamber. "That hole in there. What is it?"

"You haven't used it yet?" His eyes roved over me, his brows knitting together. "Do humans not… bathe as often as the fae do?"

My cheeks flushed, and my jaw went slack. "It's… it's a *bathtub?*"

"A hot spring. There are caves below ground with rivers of heated mineral water. Part of the magic of the castle is that the springs can flow through our pipes, no matter what level our rooms are on."

"Hot springs," I repeated, feeling remarkably stupid for not figuring that out. The hole had just looked so *dark* that the idea of climbing inside seemed undeniably insane.

"It's quite relaxing. I highly recommend it." He leaned casually on the doorframe, his arms crossing to accentuate the thick muscles of his biceps. Today he wore a sleeveless tunic open at the chest, which, I gathered, was the style for the male royals. His trousers came just past his knees, clinging to his toned legs, and, once more, he was barefoot.

I realized my mouth was still open, so I clamped it shut and jerked my gaze back to his face. A smirk played on his lips as if he'd noticed I'd been staring.

He seemed so... at ease. As if our conversation yesterday hadn't happened at all.

"For the record," I said in a clipped tone, "I *have* bathed since arriving. Enzira and I... Well, there was a communication issue, and she ended up bringing me buckets of water for bathing. Which was fine, of course. I just... didn't know there was an alternative."

"Why didn't you just ask her?"

My mouth formed a thin line. "It is... difficult to ask for things. I am still a stranger here, surrounded by strange creatures."

"And do you think one of us will harm you if you ask a simple question?" His voice turned sharp, and thin shadows appeared at his feet, revealing his anger.

"No," I snapped. "I only mean I am a stranger here and don't quite feel comfortable bothering everyone with my confusion and my needs. Do you honestly expect me to become acclimated to this infuriating enchanted castle after only a few days?"

"Of course not."

"Glad we are in agreement, then," I muttered sarcastically, turning away from him to close the desk drawer, hiding my incriminating letter from view. Then I busied myself with opening my trunk at the foot of my bed. I sifted through several garments until I found a clean shift, then straightened and found the king staring at me, his expression inscrutable.

My eyebrows lifted. Why was he still here? "Well, I'll just be testing out the hot springs." I gestured to the bathing chamber.

He arched a single eyebrow, half his mouth curling in a smirk. Too late, I realized my statement sounded an awful lot like an invitation. My face heated. "I mean—I don't—what I *meant* was, I'd like some privacy. So, please tell me why you're in my rooms, or get out so I can bathe in peace."

His smirk vanished, and his nostrils flared. "You dare speak to your king in such a manner?"

"You aren't *my* king."

He stepped farther into my room, shadows swelling behind him. "You are my wife and a resident of the Shadow Court. *My* court. So yes, I *am* your king."

My chin lifted at the sharp tone in his voice. "But I am not your subordinate. You hold no power over me."

His lips curled into a sneer. "Bold words, coming from a human whose spine I could snap like a twig."

Fear twisted in my gut, but I forced myself to stand up straighter, looking him directly in the eye. "Go ahead and kill me, Wraith King. See how well you do with those shadows if I'm dead."

It was a bluff; I actually had no idea what my presence did for the shadows. But he had alluded enough for me to infer that I was important.

At least important enough not to kill.

He bared his teeth at me, fangs gleaming as a low growl built in his throat. It seemed to rumble from the very floor beneath my feet, and it took all my willpower not to stagger back a step. The shadows behind him darkened as if made of ink, spreading and thickening until almost all the sunlight from the windows was blocked out.

Still, I held my ground, hands forming fists at my sides. I

would not be cowed. I would not falter. Varius was a bully and nothing more.

He wouldn't hurt me.

At least, I told myself he wouldn't.

"Watch yourself, human," he said, his voice low and dangerous. "There are worse things than death."

"My name is *Sybelle*," I snapped. "Not human."

"And I am no *wraith*," Varius spat. His shadows darkened further, and I gasped as his eyes shifted to all black, leaving no traces of white.

He looked all animal now. Nothing but a deadly predator.

"Fine," I said, my voice slightly higher than normal as I tried to force a bravado I did not feel. "I'll call you Varius, and you'll call me Sybelle. Agreed?"

Varius blinked at me, the darkness in his eyes receding until they looked normal once more. Still coal black, but the whites of his eyes made him seem less monstrous. His shadows curled inward, the darkness thinning and allowing light from the windows to seep through.

A long, tense moment passed between us. I stood there, rigid and waiting for him to advance on me. He pinned me with his loathsome stare, fangs still bared.

At last, he said gruffly, "Agreed." He turned away, then said over his shoulder, "Sybelle."

He went through the door connecting our rooms, and it closed shut after his departure. I let out a long exhale, my frame sagging and my pulse racing. For a moment, I sank to the edge of my mattress, pressing a hand to my chest as I waited for my heartbeat to slow.

I still wasn't sure why Varius had come to my rooms at all. Had he only wanted to fling accusations at me? Or was there something else?

Either way, I was regretting moving to the queen's chambers. He was a brute, and every encounter only revealed how loathsome he was.

Shaking my head, I moved to the writing desk and scribbled out the *mean old codger* part. Next to it, I wrote, *He is exactly as we thought he would be. Only more frightening.*

After penning the rest of my letter, using vague references to our past conversations, I sealed it up and put Eira's name on it, hoping Enzira would be able to mail it for me.

I honestly wasn't sure if I would ever get to see my friend again. But it would be nice to know that we could still correspond with one another.

I grabbed my shift and made my way to the bathing chamber. After glancing behind me to ensure Varius hadn't returned, I removed my clothing and approached the gaping hole with trepidation.

I was trusting in Varius's inability to lie; if this weren't actually a hot spring, he wouldn't have been able to tell me so.

But despite the logic behind this, my heart still hammered painfully in my chest at the prospect of stepping into a large, black abyss.

With a shaky breath, I sank to the ground, sitting with my bare bottom on the stone floor. It was warmer than I expected.

I frowned, scooting forward until my legs dangled over the edge of the hole. Steam and heat swirled around me, making the skin on my thighs pebble. I inched closer to the edge, and my toes met bubbling hot water. I gasped at the contact, jerking my feet back. After a moment, I eased them back in, then sighed with pleasure. It was hot, but not painfully so, and the water was close enough to the edge of the floor that I knew I would be able to climb back out with ease.

Assuming the bottom wasn't too deep. If this place was suited for large unseelie creatures, would a tiny human like me be able to stand?

Only one way to find out, I thought before sliding all the way in.

The jolt of sudden heat around my body made me stiffen and gasp, my legs flailing and my skin burning. I scrambled for purchase, my head going underwater for a few seconds before my feet met solid ground. I came up for air, choking and sputtering, then swam toward one end of the cavern. I hit the wall, and my feet bumped against a thin ledge that had been built into the ground, almost like a small step for the fae to climb out of the springs.

Relief spread through me as I put my weight on that ledge, allowing me to stand up high enough for the water to rest just below my chin.

I could make this work.

I lifted my arms, barely able to see them in the darkness of the hole. Bubbles continued churning around me, tickling my skin and making my stomach rumble. A small smile spread across my lips, and I flicked the water, then dove underneath once more, allowing the heat to rush over me.

When I emerged once more, a laugh burst from me, echoing in the small cavern.

Varius might have been an ass, but he was right about one thing: The hot springs were delightful.

THE BEAST

STILL FUMING FROM MY ENCOUNTER WITH SYBELLE, I PACED THE length of my room, my shadows swirling chaotically around me as I waited for my temper to cool.

The nerve of her… To order *me* around, like her servant? And then to act affronted when I reminded her I was her king?

A low growl rumbled from within me, and my shadows thickened, darkening the room.

I had planned to ask her for a vial of her blood. Perhaps if I implied Tislora needed it for a spell, she would comply. But after our conversation, I was doubtful Sybelle would do anything if it did not benefit herself.

I ran my hands through my curly hair, biting back a snarl. How was I to convince her to help me and my court if she despised us so much?

My thoughts turned to my conversation with Tislora. *Who gives a shit if the human has a comfortable life or not?*

Sybelle had been endearing when I'd met her in the library. Now she was downright insufferable.

But if I took Tislora's approach, and extracted the human's blood by force, that made me exactly the type of monster Sybelle accused me of being. In the library, she had called me vile. She had all but stated she feared for her life among my people.

Forcing her to comply with the curse's demands would only strengthen her belief that we were the enemy. We were the beasts to be feared.

A knock sounded at my door, and I bit back a snarl of rage. "What?" I barked.

"My lord, they are ready for you," came Clermont's curt voice.

I groaned and rubbed my temples. Of course. I'd forgotten about the council with the generals. Mother of Shade, this was not what I needed right now.

Realizing Clermont was waiting for an answer, I said, "I'll be right there."

His steps retreated, and I closed my eyes, willing my temper to abate so I could face this problem.

I changed my clothes and splashed cool water on my face before opening the door, finding myself facing the throne room. Silently thanking the castle for being compliant this time, I strode inside. The six generals were already seated at the round table, muttering among themselves. All wore grim expressions, and I couldn't blame them. The riots were getting out of control, and the shadows had already reached the lower towns.

We were out of time.

The generals all stood as I made my way to the table, seating myself between Generals Vexon and Salyut.

Once everyone was seated, I cleared my throat. "What's the report?"

"Six dead from riots," said General Forsenn, who sat directly across from me. The fae had forest green skin and piercing blue eyes. His webbed hands came together atop the table as he spoke. "Two infected by Necro Shadows. One still lives, but he is fading. The other we could not save."

I exhaled slowly, my chest tightening from the loss. Until now, the shadows had only skirted the boundaries of the city. I had hoped that drinking the elixir would hold them off for a bit longer.

Clearly, I was wrong.

"Sire, the human is here," said General Olectus, a large fae with antlers and violet skin. His silver eyes were full of accusation as he stared at me from across the table. "The shadows should have slowed by now."

A few other generals murmured their agreement.

"I understand your frustration and your concerns," I said. "But as you know, the bond between myself and the human takes time to strengthen. We have only been married a few days."

"We don't have time for you to woo your human bride," Olectus snarled, his nostrils flaring. "People are *dying*."

I slammed my hands on the table, making it rattle. Shadows oozed from my body, encircling the table in black mist.

Everyone fell silent, their eyes wide as they fixed on me.

"Remember your place, Olectus," I growled. "I am your king. Show some damn respect."

Beside me, Vexon sucked in a sharp breath, and Salyut went completely rigid. I let my shadows linger for a moment longer, driving home the point, before I collected them once more and took a steadying breath.

"I am doing what I can," I said slowly. "I have taken an elixir. I will extract more blood from her. But you all need to understand that the potion is far more potent if the human bride is *willing*. That is the goal."

"It doesn't matter if she is *willing* if our people are all dead," Olectus said. His voice was more subdued, but there was no denying the anger in his eyes.

He was furious with me.

I let my mouth curl into a smirk. Let him rage. I could certainly use a good fight. "Unlike you, I am looking for a permanent solution to this problem," I said. "If I take the blood from her by force, it will strengthen the animosity between our people. It may buy us time for now, but later on, we will pay the price. The Necro Shadows will grow closer no matter what, and the elixir is only a temporary fix. For now, move the people in the lower towns closer to the city. You can offer up rooms in the castle if you must. I will speak with the human about accessing her blood. If I can convince her, it will grant us more time."

"Will she even want to help?" Forsenn asked softly.

I rubbed my knuckles, considering this. My instincts told me *no*, Sybelle would not want to help. But she had seemed intrigued when I'd told her she was connected to the shadows. If anything, I could tell I had piqued her curiosity. Perhaps I could capitalize on that.

"I'm not sure," I said at last. "But if I help her understand how dire things are, it might help."

Olectus's eyebrows lowered with displeasure. "It won't work. The human will never be able to see things our way."

"That one-sided way of thinking is exactly what is keeping the curse from breaking," Salyut said in a clipped voice.

Olectus leaned forward, bracing both hands on the table as he leered at Salyut. "Be careful, general. You sound awfully sympathetic toward the fragile humans and, dare I say it, the sorceress who started this whole ordeal in the first place."

Salyut paled, his head jerking backward in shock. His fearful eyes met mine, but my gaze was pinned on Olectus.

"Perhaps you are a sympathizer," Olectus continued. "Perhaps we should—"

My rage spilled over. With the flick of my wrist, my shadows wrapped around Olectus, tightening and swirling until they bound his form like thick ropes. Black mist clamped over his mouth, cutting off whatever he had been about to say. He grunted and struggled against them, but my shadows only cinched further, coiling around him like a serpent.

"If you need to spar with someone to work off some frustration, Olectus, you only have to say the word," I growled. "But I will not have this antagonism in my throne room. This is your final warning. Check yourself, or get the hell out of my castle."

Olectus's muffled shouts echoed in the room, but I did not release him from my shadows. I turned to the other generals at the table. "Would anyone else like to challenge the loyalty of this council?"

A few generals, like Salyut, seemed positively terrified. Others looked at Olectus with smug expressions, as if they had been yearning to see the general silenced.

No one said a word.

"Very good," I said, my anger ebbing. As long as Olectus remained tied up, I could keep my emotions in check.

I wasn't sure why I'd kept him on the council for this long. I made a mental note to dismiss him and appoint a different general in his stead. One that wasn't as hotheaded.

"Tell me about the riots," I said to no one in particular.

"They are getting worse," Forsenn said. "The rioters are plundering and burning down buildings, and there is talk of the townspeople storming the castle. We arrested twenty this week alone. The jail cells in the Pern District are at full capacity. We either need to execute them or move them elsewhere."

"How many casualties?" I asked, my voice calm despite the panic churning in my gut.

"Four perished in the fire," Forsenn said. "We executed two rioters on site to keep them from striking down other townsfolk."

My eyes closed for a moment to mourn the loss of such precious lives. The curse hadn't claimed my kingdom yet, but people were still dying. Even if I had time before the curse claimed my life, it still felt like I had lost. I could not fix the broken pieces of my kingdom.

"Destroy the weapons of all the prisoners," I said at last. "Pardon anyone who will make a fae bargain swearing not to bring harm to any buildings or citizens of this court. Anyone who doesn't, execute them in three days' time."

A few generals at the table shifted uncomfortably in their seats, but as I glanced at each of them, they averted their gazes, unwilling to speak up.

I didn't like it, either. But I had very few options to work with.

"I will ensure the human bride cooperates," I said quietly. "You all have my word."

Olectus might be an arrogant bastard, but he had a point. I couldn't tiptoe around this issue. It didn't matter if my demands made Sybelle uncomfortable or not. This was precisely why she was here.

I would ask for her permission. But if she did not give it, I would need to show her firsthand just how awful things were for the Shadow Fae.

When the council ended, I opened the doors of the throne room, hoping the castle would anticipate my needs and take me directly to Sybelle.

Instead, it led me to the grand hall, which was filled with portraits and sculptures of the fae kings from ages past. I frowned as I stepped inside, wondering if Sybelle was here, scrutinizing the art and likely judging each of my forefathers for crimes they did not commit.

Although, I thought bitterly, *most of these kings were despicable enough to warrant her judgment.*

Did that make me the same as them? Did Sybelle see it that way?

I shook the questions from my mind, knowing they would do no good. I could not force Sybelle to respect me, and I shouldn't care what she thought of me anyway.

I wandered the length of the hall, but the vast space easily showed me I was alone here.

With a sigh, I turned left toward the open archway that led to the spiral staircase, thinking perhaps the castle was playing a joke on me again. If I could maneuver my way around other doors, perhaps I could find Sybelle myself.

Instead, I nearly bumped into two figures deep in conversation, standing just underneath the archway. They started when they saw me, and I blinked, glancing between them. It was Murvo, my captain of the guards, and a soldier I did not recognize. Both stared at me, wide-eyed.

I frowned, then nodded politely at Murvo. "Captain."

"My king." He pressed a fist to his chest. But as he shot a fleeting look at the soldier beside him, I sensed something was wrong.

"What is it?" I asked.

The soldier's lips pressed together in a thin line, and he shook his head mutely. I looked at Murvo, whose mouth opened and closed before he said in a strained voice, "It's… the human."

My eyebrows lowered. Shit, what had Sybelle done now? "What about the human?" My voice was almost a growl.

"She's been wandering around the training yard," Murvo said. The lilt to his voice led me to believe there was more to the story.

"And?" I prompted, impatience rising.

"It's distracting the men," Murvo said with a pleading expression, his eyebrows drawing together.

I tilted my head at him, eyes narrowing. "Distracting them *how?*"

"Well, many of us don't feel comfortable being around humans," Murvo said, dropping his gaze and rubbing the back of his neck. "They make us feel nervous."

My rage emerged again like a feral beast hungry to strike.

Gritting my teeth, I said, "Was my wife threatening you or your men?"

"Well, no, but—"

"Was she doing anything dangerous or suspicious?"

"No, but—"

"Did she directly interfere with any training exercises?" My voice rose in volume, and Murvo flinched.

"No," he said firmly, avoiding my furious gaze. "But she was *watching* us, Your Highness. In a very calculating way."

I knew exactly what he was referring to. Sybelle got a certain gleam in her eyes when she was scrutinizing something. She had looked at *me* that way, and I could admit, it was unsettling.

But what Murvo was implying was outrageous. He expected me to believe that an entire *squadron* of soldiers felt threatened by one tiny, weak human?

"Are you suggesting my wife is not allowed to look at you? Or anyone, for that matter?" My voice was icy and low.

Murvo's eyes flared wide. "Your Highness, I would never—"

I raised a hand to silence him, ready to be finished with this absurd conversation. "Let me make one thing clear. If you ever insinuate that my wife is not free to roam the grounds or *look* at anyone in a certain way, I will carve out your spleen. Is that understood?"

Murvo's face turned ashen. He swallowed, then nodded quickly.

"Your Highness," said the soldier, his voice timid. "Does this mean the human is permitted to go *anywhere* in the castle?"

I inspected the fae for the first time, taking in his polished boots and freshly pressed uniform. He had cerulean skin and a pair of ram horns. One eye gleamed gold, and the other was silver.

His clean attire indicated he was new to the regiment. But there was a confidence in his expression that concerned me.

Ordinarily, new soldiers were nervous and antsy. This one seemed calm and collected. Almost arrogant.

I also didn't like the way he had drawn out the word *anywhere*. It led me to believe he was privy to certain areas of the castle that no soldier should know about.

"Yes," I said tersely. "What's your name, soldier?"

"Warwick, Your Highness," he supplied.

I burned the name into my memory, making a mental note to investigate this soldier further. I trusted Murvo, who had served me for over a decade. But I didn't know this fae at all.

I took a step closer to him, my shadows swelling around me. Warwick's eyes roved over the shadows with interest, but he did not back away or show any sign of fear. He stood a few inches shorter than me, which was an impressive feat, since I normally towered over even the tallest of soldiers.

"Get back to your training before I arrest you for insubordination," I hissed, jerking my head toward the foyer.

Warwick stared at me for a long moment, unmoving. My shadows darkened, spreading around us like thick black ink. Murvo looked terrified enough to shit himself. He tugged on Warwick's arm.

"*Move*, soldier," Murvo snapped when Warwick continued to hold my gaze. At long last, he turned and followed Murvo down the hallway. I watched them pass through the foyer and then the open entrance doors. Afternoon sunlight beat down on them as they descended the steps to the courtyard and veered to the right, toward the training yard and out of sight.

That new soldier seemed far too interested in Sybelle and the goings-on of my castle. I would need to ask Clermont to look into him for me.

Shaking off my unease, I took the hall in the opposite direction in search of my wayward wife.

THE BEAUTY

I FINISHED BATHING AND DRESSED MYSELF IN A PALE GOLD GOWN with a lower neckline than I would have liked. When I was dressed, I glanced at the door leading to Varius's chambers, wondering if I should have told him about my encounter with the soldier in the training yard.

No, I thought. He would only accuse me of harboring prejudices against the unseelie. And I wasn't entirely sure he would believe me, either.

Besides, the fae hadn't actually harmed me. Perhaps he had only uttered empty threats to intimidate me.

As I leaned my head against the wall, I had to admit, the intimidation had worked. And it reminded me that I wasn't entirely welcome here. Varius might claim my presence was needed, but I wasn't sure all the Shadow Fae felt that way.

Shaking my head to rid myself of the lingering anxiety, I withdrew the vial of birch root I'd stowed in the drawer of my armoire, then made my way to the balcony doors. My hand went to my amber necklace, and I asked, "Are you close by?"

"That soldier is an arrogant prick," was Azure's reply.

I smiled, relieved and a bit amused to find she'd been eavesdropping. "I'm glad you didn't interfere. The last thing I need is for these fae to realize I'm hiding a dragon."

"I was very close to incinerating him on the spot. He's lucky."

I chuckled and opened the balcony doors. "Can you come here, please? I have no idea when Varius will intrude." Enzira had told me he had a council meeting to attend to today, but I wasn't sure how long it would last.

"Ah, so now it's Varius? And not the Wraith King?"

I was spared from having to answer by the massive shape of my dragon appearing in the sky. Her scales shimmered in the sunlight, the brilliant blue blending in with the sky. With grace and ease, she landed on the balcony before me, then growled, lifting one foot.

I drew closer, inspecting the split talon. It had gotten worse; the barb that had punctured her claw had wedged itself deeper.

"Damn," I muttered. "I may need some tools to get that out."

"Birch root first," Azure commanded.

"So bossy," I muttered, but I uncorked the vial and poured a few droplets on the affected talon. A deep rumbling sound emanated from her chest, a cross between a sigh and a purr. Slowly, she laid her head down on the stone floor, her eyes closing.

"Better?" I asked with a smirk.

"Just get it over with before the effects wear off."

I sighed, but I couldn't blame her for her grouchy demeanor. She had been enduring the pain of a sliced talon for almost twenty-four hours. I couldn't imagine the agony.

I ducked back into my chambers, heart in my throat as I expected to find Varius at our shared door once more.

But he wasn't there.

I snatched the jeweled dagger and my pouch of gemstones from the armoire. I returned to the balcony, shutting the doors behind me.

"Brace yourself," I said.

Azure tensed but kept her eyes closed. My lips pursed in concentration as I angled the sharpened point of the dagger directly into her split talon.

She growled, jerking away from me, but I urged the blade further in, easing it in the crack.

"Hold still," I warned her. "If you move, I could push it in too deep."

Azure grumbled something unintelligible as I continued shifting the dagger back and forth, trying to wiggle the barb free. It took several minutes, but at long last, the sharpened thorn clattered to the stone floor.

But it wasn't a thorn at all.

Setting the dagger down, I sank to my knees to inspect the spike.

It was longer than I expected; about half the length of my dagger. And it certainly resembled a large thorn from a bush.

But when I held it up to the sun, it gleamed *crimson*.

I had never seen a crimson barb before.

"Please, Sybelle," came Azure's desperate voice.

"Sorry," I muttered, digging through my pouch of gemstones until I found what I was looking for: the white moonstone. This jewel had the power to heal even the most dire of injuries.

I lifted the stone, holding it up to her claw where the barb had protruded from earlier. A white glow emanated from the stone, and warmth burned against my palm.

Within seconds, Azure made a humming sound of satisfaction, and I knew the healing was finished. I placed the moonstone back in the pouch and crouched down to inspect the crimson barb.

My fingers went to my amber necklace again. "Do you sense any magic in this?"

Azure's head was cradled against one of her legs, and she made another low purring sound. *"Perhaps. But I am too tired to focus on it."*

I suppressed a groan, knowing she needed to catch up on sleep. Climbing to my feet, I turned to the balcony doors, then glanced over my shoulder at Azure.

"You can't stay here long," I warned her.

She was already snoozing, her snores rumbling around us.

Biting back a curse, I opened the balcony doors, vowing to come back and poke her awake in an hour if she was still here. Even with the doors and curtains closed, it would be impossible for Varius not to hear her snores.

When I was in my rooms once more, the balcony doors shut and the golden curtains blocking the view of my dragon, I scrutinized the barb more closely. Certain parts of it seemed to gleam, almost like glass.

With a frown, I held it up alongside my dagger. The gemstones glistened in the low light of the sconces, and the barb did the same. When I held the barb up to the rubies in the hilt, it was almost the exact same shade of red.

Was this… made of some kind of *stone*?

I resolved to ask Azure where she had found this. If there were gemstones hidden nearby, I would need to find them. Who knew what rare jewels I might discover here in the Shadow Court? If this *was* from a gemstone, it wasn't big enough to grant me any powers. I had learned from my own experiments that a gemstone had to be at least the width of my thumb in order to give me magic.

A loud knock sounded at my door, and I faltered, nearly dropping the dagger and the barb. After hastily shoving both into the drawer of my armoire, I rushed to the door, hoping to send Ramia or Enzira away before they discovered Azure.

But when I threw the door open, it was Varius waiting for me on the other side.

The Beast

SYBELLE'S CHEEKS WERE FLUSHED, HER EYES WIDE AS SHE STARED at me breathlessly. The fear pulsing in her veins was more potent than I'd ever sensed from her before.

She was downright *terrified*.

I frowned, glancing behind her to see if someone else was with her. My mind was still on that strange encounter with the soldier named Warwick.

"Are you well?" I asked quietly.

"I—yes," Sybelle said with a nervous chuckle, tucking a lock of hair behind her ear. "I—I am surprised to see you at this door." She gestured to the connecting door in the room, which I had used last time.

"Yes, well, it was inappropriate of me to intrude without your permission," I said. "I figured this was more polite."

It was an olive branch, and I was begging her to take it. I needed us to be on good terms for what I was about to ask of her.

She offered a hesitant smile. "Well, I appreciate that. Is there something you needed?"

"Yes, actually. Would you mind if I stepped inside? The matter is… delicate." *To say the least.*

Panic struck her face, her jaw going slack and her eyes

widening further. "I—um—I can't—" She muttered a soft curse and said hastily, "Can we speak in your rooms instead?"

I stared at her in confusion. Why would she want to go to my bedchamber?

"It's just, I have yet to see the king's quarters," she said, her words coming out in a rush. "And I'm curious."

My frown deepened. Something was definitely amiss with her. Once more, I tried looking past her to see if anything strange was in her room, but she refused to open the door any wider.

"Sybelle," I said, my voice barely above a whisper, "are you well?" I enunciated the words, hoping she understood my meaning. *Are you in danger? Is someone threatening you?*

She blinked. "Yes. I am well."

"Because you are acting very strange, and it concerns me."

She sighed, rubbing her forehead. "I am… flustered. Between moving rooms, and me getting lost in the training yard yesterday—"

"I apologize for that," I said quickly. "It was my fault for abandoning you. I should have shown you the way instead of leaving you like that. Please forgive me."

She lifted a hand, shaking her head. "Please don't think anything of it. I enjoy exploring. It just took more energy than I was expecting. Everything here is so *big*. Far bigger than the castle I grew up in."

My eyebrows lifted at that.

"Please, may I see your rooms?" she asked. Her eyes sparked with delight, a look I now recognized as curiosity. She wore it often. "It shouldn't be too scandalous; I am your wife after all."

Heat rushed to my face at her implication. "I see." I folded my arms across my chest. "So my wife wishes me to take her to my bedchamber."

Her face flushed crimson, and her mouth fell open with a startled laugh. "I—that is *not* what I meant."

I chuckled. "Relax, Sybelle. I know what you meant." I stood back, jerking my head toward the hallway.

Her expression brightened, and she followed me, easing the door shut behind her. My gaze flicked over her form, taking in the gold silk that clung to her body and brought out the amber hues in her hair. The low neckline revealed a tantalizing glimpse of the tops of her breasts. Begrudgingly, I had to admit that she looked… quite lovely.

We strode side by side as we made our way across the short distance between our rooms. It was an odd feeling, to be striding alongside this human bride of mine. As if we were equals.

Clearing my throat, I reached the door to my own room, grateful I'd left it ajar. I wasn't in the mood to play the castle's games tonight.

Sybelle reached out to push the door open further, then hesitated, her expression suddenly wary. "Varius, I—"

Mother of Shade, there was something about the way my name fell off her lips that made my insides stir.

I shoved the feeling aside and focused on Sybelle's discomfort. "Is something wrong?"

She looked up at me. "We haven't consummated our marriage."

"I am aware."

"Are you—do you—" She broke off, gritting her teeth in apparent frustration. "Do you plan to change that anytime soon? I would just like to be prepared."

At my side, my fingers curled into fists. She was afraid of me. Afraid of what I might force her to do.

As always, she believed me to be a monster.

"I told you once before that I would not touch you without your permission," I said. "And I meant it."

Her brow creased, as if this was confusing to her. It was bewildering that I would *not* force her to my bed.

It was getting more and more difficult to keep my frustrations at bay. "Why does this shock you?" I hissed, barely leashing my words.

"Because we are married. And, until we consummate, the marriage is not valid. Did you not say my presence here was necessary, that it had something to do with the shadows? If your situation is flexible enough to allow you to avoid consummating, then why bother going through the ceremony with me at all?"

My head reared back at the bluntness of her words. Was she being earnest with me?

"Dear wife," I said, unable to keep the amusement from my voice, "are you *encouraging* me to bed you this evening? Because if that is what you wish, I can certainly make arrangements for it."

She blushed again, her mouth forming a tight line as she glared at me. "*No.* I am merely questioning the validity of our marriage. I came here to wed you. We have not completed the necessary steps to make this lawful."

"Ah." I leaned against the doorframe, thoroughly enjoying watching her squirm. She shifted her weight from one foot to the other, avoiding my gaze. "So you are only concerned with the legality of our union. That is all."

"Yes," she bit out. "That is all."

"And this has nothing at all to do with your curiosity regarding my body?"

She blanched, looking downright horrified. "*No!*"

I grinned. "You aren't the least bit curious?"

"I am familiar with the male anatomy, thank you very much," she said curtly.

I raised my eyebrows. "Are you, now? That's surprising."

Her blush spread to her ears and neck now. What a thoroughly strange thing these human bodies did.

"Besides," I went on, "I am not human. I have wings and a

tail. Does it not interest you what *other* parts of mine might be different?"

Her eyes dipped below my belt, then jerked back up again, as if she hadn't meant to look.

I couldn't help but laugh.

She scowled at me. "Why do you enjoy mocking my embarrassment?"

"Because you make it so easy, *dannahla*."

I hadn't meant to use the term of endearment; it had slipped out on its own. But when Sybelle's eyes widened, I realized my mistake.

Not only that, but she clearly knew what the word meant. This confirmed my suspicions that she understood more of the Agnarrish language than she let on.

Instead of addressing it, I pretended not to notice. If she wanted to play the part of the ignorant human, so be it. No need to draw attention to the fact that I just called her *darling*.

I stretched my hand to the open door. "After you."

She shot me one last look of loathing before striding into my rooms. I trailed after her, surveying the space with a fresh perspective. The fireplace was bigger, and the walls in my room were black marble instead of cream. But overall, it looked much the same as the queen's suite.

Sybelle was eyeing the bookshelves in one corner of the room, her head tilted as she tried to read the spines.

"They are in my language," I supplied, wondering if she would finally admit she knew Agnarrish.

She whirled to look at me, then cleared her throat. "Oh," was her only response. She fingered the orange necklace at her throat, a habit I had seen her do before. I wondered if it meant she was nervous.

I stepped forward. "Sybelle, just to be clear, consummation *is* required to seal our marriage. But I do not intend to force it upon you. Ever. When you are ready to consummate, then we will. That is all."

She blinked at me. "And what if I am never ready?"

I offered a wry smile. Clermont had expressed the same concern. "Let's give it some more time before we make such decisions. But, if you truly do not believe you can stomach being with a creature like me, then perhaps we will discuss nullifying the marriage and sending for a different human bride."

She looked at me with an incredulous expression. "You cannot be serious."

"Much as it might shock you, wife, I have morals. There are lines even a demon like me will not cross."

"Oh, for the last time, I do *not* think you are a demon! Stones, Varius, you are a *stranger* to me. That is all. Why must you judge everything I say and twist it into some kind of prejudice against your kind? I would be having these same feelings even if you were a human."

For the last time. As if she had repeatedly told me so.

She had not, in fact. Not once.

But, assuming she spoke the truth, her words eased some of the tension inside me. Because I realized that, just like her, I was most apprehensive about this entire situation because we were strangers. Setting aside the notion that we were different species, we were merely two royals thrown together in a marriage arrangement that neither of us asked for.

Perhaps we were not so different after all.

"Where I come from, the nobility often marry without love or affection," she said. "It is a business transaction and nothing more. That's what I thought this was. So the idea of consummating is not that unexpected. I have prepared for it. My whole life has been spent training to be your wife. For years, my father taught me to be diligent with my wifely duties, to ensure my husband was satisfied as often as he demanded." Her voice caught on those last words. "It will take more than a few moments to discard the notion that has been drilled into me for so long."

A new sense of anger kindled in my chest, a burning hatred for the man who raised her to be nothing more than an object to be used and discarded. Again, I drew closer to her, noting how she didn't flinch away from me.

"Let me set one thing straight," I said, my voice low. "In my court, things are different. We do not demand that our wives pleasure us even when it sickens them. Many nobles are fae who have never been married. Even the females. And they have just as much freedom as the males."

Sybelle gaped at me. "Truly?"

"Truly. Decades ago, long before—well, before all this started, the court was ruled by females. From queen to queen, the crown was passed down."

"*Stones*," she breathed, pressing a hand to her chest. "To my kind, that's unheard of. Why did it change?"

I smirked. "One queen had all sons."

She laughed, a light but melodious sound that warmed my blood. "Well, I can see why that would alter things a bit."

"The kings before me might have forced their wives to comply," I went on. "I will not pretend that the royals of my family were saints. Many of them were despicable, and the training you underwent was likely in anticipation of such behavior. But I vow to be different from my forefathers. And I promise to you right now, Sybelle, that I *will not* touch you unless you invite me to. I will swear it in blood, if you wish."

I hadn't planned to make such a vow, but I couldn't take it back, even if I wanted to. Clermont would have been affronted at such a declaration, but it felt right. Sybelle needed safety and comfort, and I would give that to her.

If the curse required me to become the type of male who would willingly rape females, then my kingdom had long since been doomed. Nothing and no one would ever make me cross that line.

Sybelle stared at me, eyebrows raised and lips parted. Her breath hitched as she gazed at me, and I wondered what she was thinking. At long last, she spoke, her voice as soft as a caress. "You are not at all what I expected, Varius."

I frowned. Echoing her words from the library, I said, "I'm not sure if that's a compliment."

She laughed again. "It is." Her expression sobered, and she added, "I feel like I should say, though, that I never once thought you were a wraith or a monster. I am more frightened of the unknown than anything else. And right now, I am not frightened of you."

I nodded, grateful for her words. "Thank you for that." I clasped my hands behind my back, dreading my next words. But it could not be avoided. We had dodged it for too long. "I must ask something of you, though."

"Oh?" Curiosity burned in her gaze once more.

I heaved a sigh. "I need your blood."

THE BEAUTY

"You need my blood," I repeated slowly. "Why?"

I should have been afraid. But honestly, I was more intrigued than anything. A week ago, I would have feared the horrible Wraith King wanted to *drink* my blood. But I knew better than that.

"For the shadows," Varius said, his words stilted.

I scrutinized him. His dark eyes were full of caution and concern. His expression was taut, as if he were restraining himself.

Restraining from doing what?

"Can you be more specific?" I asked. "How does my blood affect the shadows?"

"You recall how I told you that the presence of humans keeps the poisonous shadows at bay?"

"Yes."

"The deadly shadows are called Necro Shadows. They are lethal even to my kind. Over the years, we have tried many things to prevent them from spreading. The Umbra Mist is channeled from the earth, but it is only effective at night."

"Except for in my court," I blurted without thinking.

Varius blinked at me. "What?"

"There was Umbra Mist surrounding the carriage when

Clermont arrived," I said, vividly remembering the way it had surrounded the carriage like smoke. "It was daytime."

"Ah, yes. We have discovered that certain toxins in the Necro Shadows are drawn out by sunlight. These specific toxins chase away the Umbra Mist. But since the Necro Shadows are only confined to the Shadow Court, the Umbra Mist is free to roam during the daytime in the Earthen Court."

I fell silent, frowning as I processed this. The Necro Shadows hadn't reached my court… *yet.* But once they did, the Umbra Mist wouldn't be able to help anyone. Not during the day.

Varius went on, "As I was saying, we have tried many things. The Umbra Mist helps, and the Lumen from my own shadow magic is also a deterrent. But the only thing that seems to truly push the shadows back is human blood."

I blinked, finally registering that he had conveniently kept this tidbit to himself when he'd explained why my presence was necessary. Not once did he mention it required *blood.*

Then again, we had only just met. I couldn't blame him for it.

Even now, we were still essentially strangers… despite how much more comfortable I felt in his presence.

"How much blood?" I asked.

Varius rubbed his wrists and lowered his gaze. "Tonight, I only need a vial. Tislora will use it to make an elixir. With her magic, it will push back the shadows."

"Tonight," I repeated. "But you will need more later?"

He grimaced. "I am not sure. It's likely I will need more later, but I will always ask first. I will *never* take your blood without your permission. I swear it."

This did not assure me in the slightest. I swallowed hard, my fear rising up in place of my curiosity. Would he drain me of all my blood? Was this how the previous human brides died?

"Why will you need more, if my blood will help push the

shadows back?" I asked, fingering one of the gold-trimmed curtains to distract myself from the growing terror inside me.

"It is only temporary. Eventually, the shadows creep forward again. But this will buy us enough time to evacuate the people in the lower towns."

My gaze snapped to his. "The shadows have reached the villages?"

He nodded, his mouth set in a thin line.

"And… the shadows are toxic to your people as well?"

Again, he nodded. "Depending on how concentrated the shadows are, they can… leave a certain mark." He slid down the collar of his shirt, exposing his left shoulder.

My breath caught in my throat. A black scorch mark marred his crimson skin, with jagged lines protruding from it like a spiderweb.

"Most of the shadows are poisonous when inhaled," Varius continued, rolling his tunic back into place. "But when they gather enough strength, sometimes they can burn. I barely escaped with my life."

Stones. My pulse quickened, and I found myself staring at that spot on his shoulder, even though it was now covered. I had assumed that, as shadow fae, they were immune—particularly the king. But the unseelie fae were just as helpless as my own people. I remembered the horror of seeing the shadows creep toward the border of the Earthen Court. The soldiers at the border had been killed by getting too close.

I couldn't imagine how awful it would be to have the shadows overtake my own city, destroying my people.

A lump formed in my throat. How could I refuse his request, when I knew innocent people were dying?

I wrung my hands together, suddenly feeling uncomfortable. I was here to kill the king—to eradicate his shadow magic completely.

But speaking with him now, knowing he was trying to

protect his people—that he had even stood in the path of the poisonous shadows—made it extremely difficult. Inwardly, I felt my resolve cracking.

Could I really go through with this?

I cleared my throat. "You said it was temporary. What would be a permanent solution?"

"I—there is—" His mouth clamped shut, and a muscle feathered in his jaw. His nostrils flared as he gave me a frustrated look. "I don't know."

"You don't know?"

"Will you stop repeating what I say?" he snapped.

"I will when you start making sense!"

He pinched the bridge of his nose and expelled a harsh breath. "There are things I cannot tell you, Sybelle. There is magic binding me, preventing me from doing so. I *want* you to know more. But I cannot say."

A cold chill skittered over me, making my bones tremble. I suppressed a shudder and wrapped my arms around my chest. "Is my life in danger?" The words came out in a whisper.

Varius looked at me for a long moment, his expression inscrutable. Finally, he said, "Right now? No."

My eyes closed. "Stones, that is *not* comforting."

"Would you prefer I lie?"

"You can't lie," I said with a snort.

"I am trying to be as forthcoming as I can with you." He spread his hands as if to placate me. "I was hoping to avoid deceiving you by giving you all the information I could. My council… suggested I ignore your wishes and take what I needed, but I refused."

"Am I supposed to show gratitude for that?" I choked on an incredulous laugh. "Oh thank you, kind and magnanimous King Varius, for not tying me to a chair and extracting my blood by force. Thank you for telling me *up front* that I might die to save your people."

"I said nothing of the sort," he growled. "Do not put words in my mouth."

"Do not patronize me by withholding truths!"

"I am telling you all that I can!"

"That's bullshit!" I shouted, hands curled into fists at my side. "Tell me plainly, is it at all possible that giving you my blood to stop these shadows will cost me my life?"

A tense silence fell between us as we stared each other down. His spine was rigid, and dark shadows pooled on the floor by his feet, inching toward me. Fury rippled off him in waves, but I continued to glare at him, waiting.

At long last, he spoke.

"Yes."

I huffed a harsh laugh, turning away from him with one hand on my hip and the other on my forehead. My skull was throbbing from the monumental revelations he had just divulged.

He could not control the shadows.

They were deadly to the unseelie.

Only human blood could stop them.

It was very possible I could die by giving up my blood to save his kingdom.

I had a very strong suspicion that *this* was why the Shadow Court continuously asked for human brides. And when each human's blood ran out, Varius was forced to send for another.

The cycle would continue forever. For hundreds of years, the Earthen Court would be sacrificing princesses all for the sake of appeasing these toxic shadows.

All to save *their* court. For reasons Varius couldn't even tell me.

My hands began to shake as I turned to face him, hatred boiling my blood. "You bastard," I hissed through gritted teeth. "All this time, and *this* is why you demand brides? My people have no idea what they are giving up, or why! You have led us to believe that marrying a princess from my lands is meant to keep peace between our people, but really it is to *save your ass!*"

Shadows darkened the room, clouding the white lights from the sconces. Varius loomed over me, expression lethal. "You know *nothing*, human."

"You're right," I said, unfazed by his show of power. "I know nothing, thanks to you and your deception."

I strode for the door, pushing past him with no regard for the way his dark mist swirled around me.

"Sybelle," he said angrily.

At the door, I turned to look at him once more. "I will have to take some time to consider your request, *Highness*. But if your people die tonight from those shadows, it is on *you*, not me."

I stormed out of his chambers. Fury pounded in my veins as I made my way back to my own rooms, ignoring the black shadows that crept along the floor in my wake, a sign of the king's venomous rage.

THE BEAUTY

Azure was gone from my balcony when I returned to my rooms. I checked in with her through my amber stone, and her talon was healing nicely. She was spending the night behind the stables, as usual.

My relief was short-lived as I once again thought about my argument with Varius, and the true reason behind his contract with my kingdom.

I paced the length of my room, hands balled into fists while I muttered to myself all the hateful things I should have said to his face. By the time Ramia arrived to dress me for bed, my temper had abated, but not by much.

Earlier, I had been hesitant to move forward with my plan to track down the enchanted rose and kill Varius. But now that I knew how many secrets he'd been keeping, and that he had no regard whatsoever for me and my kingdom, I felt differently.

He should have been honest from the beginning. He should have given my people a *choice*. Instead, he used the threat of his shadow magic to coerce them into sacrificing a royal daughter. Every generation.

For hours, I lay awake, staring at the ceiling, my thoughts racing. It was too much to comprehend. There were too many details I didn't know.

I slept restlessly, tossing and turning and dreaming of the Necro Shadows coming for me, suffocating me in my sleep.

I woke before dawn and dressed myself in a simple burgundy gown, tied my hair in a loose braid, and made my way down the hall. Though I wasn't sure where I was headed, I only knew I couldn't keep to my rooms any longer. I couldn't *breathe* in there. Not with Varius and his secrets residing next door.

Out of curiosity, I opened the first door I passed in the hall, just to see where the castle wished for me to go.

On the other side was the vast library where I'd first seen Varius's true form.

I faltered, frozen in place, my gaze sweeping over the large space before me. Was Varius sitting by the fire, like he had been that night? I waited for any sound of movement, any sign that the library was occupied.

Nothing but silence awaited me.

With a deep breath, I stepped over the threshold and let the door shut behind me. I stood next to the pair of wing-backed chairs, expecting Varius to appear from the shadows. A fire crackled in the hearth, indicating a servant had been tending to this room recently. I drew closer, warming my hands by the flames and letting the heat wash over my cold skin. The constant presence of shadows made this place far cooler than my home, and I hadn't yet adjusted to the temperature change.

After my fingers were nice and toasty, I turned to face the bookshelves, remembering how the library had magically provided me with the books I'd asked for. It had been days, and Varius hadn't once mentioned Azure or questioned me about her. Was it possible the castle could keep my secrets?

Perhaps I could start small. Surely there was nothing damning about researching gardening tips.

"Um, castle?" I asked hesitantly. "Could you give me a book on roses?"

The shelves trembled, rattling against the walls. I waited for a book to fall from the ceiling like it had before, but instead, it spontaneously appeared on the table in front of me.

I almost laughed. Clearly, the castle liked to play games. I wondered what other ways it liked to present its books to me. Drawing closer to the table, I fingered the forest green cover of the book labeled, *A Gardener's Guide to Rosebushes*.

I smiled. "Thank you," I murmured before bringing the book to one of the chairs by the fire and settling in for a long read.

An hour later, I knew the best soil properties and sunlight-to-water ratio to produce the most lush roses. I made a mental note to ask Enzira if there were any gardens in the castle. At least I would know the area in which to look for them. A section of the garden that got the most sunlight in the morning would be ideal. And any rosebushes would be planted in the richest loam.

I looked around for a piece of parchment to write on but found nothing. A small *pop* drew my attention to the table where the book had appeared.

There sat a scroll, a quill, and an inkwell. I smiled again. "Thank you for providing for my needs," I said to the castle before dipping the quill in ink and jotting down my notes for later.

I spent most of my day in the library. After the first book, I asked the castle for books on spells, curses, and enchantments, particularly regarding the magic of the Shadow Fae. But I couldn't tie any of the information to an enchanted rose. If anything, the magic of the Shadow Fae seemed more tethered to mist and darkness, not flora. I grew frustrated the more and more I read.

Truth be told, it would make more sense for enchanted roses to exist in *my* kingdom. I had heard of magical gardens throughout the kingdom. The Terrona Castle had a magnificent garden, although since we lived in caves, it wasn't quite as grand as others I'd been to over the years.

I frowned, rubbing my eyes as I returned my sixth book to the table. Stifling a yawn, I asked, "Castle, can you send me a book about relations between the Shadow Court and the Earthen Court?"

I waited for the shelves to rattle like they always did, but nothing happened. Only silence met my request.

My pulse quickened. "Castle?" I called, uncertain.

Still nothing.

Perhaps the magic was spent for the day. Did the library have a limit to how many books it could provide in one day?

"Can you give me a book just about the Earthen Court?" I amended.

The shelves rattled again, and a thick crimson volume appeared on the table.

Strange. So, either this enormous library had no information about relations between my court and Varius's, or the castle was somehow forbidden from providing it.

Interesting.

I gathered up the hefty tome in my hands, wiping dust from the leather-bound cover as I made my way back to the chair. It was clear no one had perused this book in years, but that wasn't all that surprising. Why would anyone from the Shadow Court need to know about the despicable human court?

The thought instantly soured my mood as I thought of Varius and his blatant disregard for my people. Sure, sacrifice as many human brides as was necessary, as long as the precious unseelie remained unharmed. The humans were too stupid to trust with this information anyway. What would they know about breaking curses?

My hands tightened, gripping the book so tightly the edges of the cover dug small grooves into my palms.

"Damn you, Varius," I whispered. He always accused me of harboring prejudices against his people, but he was doing the exact same thing with mine.

I forced myself back to the task at hand, thinking it might be useful to study whatever information the Shadow Court had about my own people. Perhaps that would help me puzzle this all out.

My stomach growled as I read, but I ignored it, my brow furrowing when I came across something about Earthen witches.

Witches? I knew of no witch clans in our lands. I had heard of them in others, though.

The most powerful witch enchantments were anchored to an object or person, which fueled its power, allowing it to survive as long as the object or person remained healthy and intact. Trinkets, coins, heirlooms, and gemstones were commonly used. The rarest of spells were able to harness the power of a witch's lineage in order to fuel the magic.

My eyes snagged on the word *gemstones*, and a chill raced down my spine.

Was it possible that some of the gems I'd collected were anchored to a powerful spell?

I shook my head. This had nothing to do with shadow magic, so I moved on, continuing to read.

The Earthen royals emerged from a bloodline of witches who mated with humans, mingling their blood until nearly all magic was erased from the populous.

I snorted. Well, *that* was untrue. Father would have been horrified to find out this was what other courts thought of us. To have our bloodline tainted by witch magic would have been the worst offense, second only to being tainted by unseelie blood.

But... if the Shadow Fae believed this about my kind, perhaps it could help me understand their magic better.

Another two hours passed, and I had to rise to stretch my legs and roll my shoulders back, my body tense from remaining in the same spot for too long. My stomach continued to growl angrily at me, and when a brief bout of dizziness swept over me, I acknowledged it was time for me to eat something.

I no sooner had the thought than the door opened. I tensed, expecting to see Varius.

Instead, I found Ramia approaching, holding a tray of sliced meat, buttered bread, and fresh fruit.

My mouth watered at the sight, and I smiled gratefully at her. "Thank you, Ramia."

"I figured you might be in here," she said with a wink before easing the tray onto the table next to me. "You never could stay away from the books."

"It's incredible, isn't it?" I bit into a slice of bread, barely restraining a moan of delight at how soft and warm it was.

Ramia's gaze swept over the endless sea of books. "It certainly is." She sat in the chair across from me as I devoured the food she'd brought.

When I was finished, she handed me a handkerchief, which I used to dab at my mouth and fingers.

"I have something for you," she said, and I didn't like the gleam in her eye.

"What?" I eyed her with suspicion as she dug through the pockets of her dress until she withdrew a small envelope. She handed it to me with a smirk.

Frowning, I turned the envelope over, finding my name written in familiar ink.

"Shit," I hissed.

"Language," Ramia snapped. "There's no need for that."

I felt my face drain of color as I looked at her in horror. "Why do you have this?"

"I've been in correspondence with Kendra," Ramia said shortly, although her pink cheeks betrayed her embarrassment.

"Ah." I drew out the word, giving her a knowing look. Kendra was a kitchen maid from the Earthen palace, and I had gotten the sense that she and Ramia were on more than friendly terms at some point.

"Yes, well, she mentioned the captain would like to get this to you," Ramia went on, her blush deepening as she gestured to the letter.

I shook my head, looking over the worn envelope with a mixture of dread and confusion. Why would Gerard risk sending me a letter like this? Not only was it very likely that Kendra or someone else would share this information with my father, but what if Varius's servants had intercepted this? If there was anything incriminating in this letter, I could be executed for treason.

"Gerard, you fool," I muttered, running my fingers over the crinkled paper. I couldn't deny the fresh wave of longing that coursed over me, though. It wasn't Gerard I yearned for, but news of my home. I missed it terribly, and the comfort of that familiarity called to me.

Not to mention the fears and anxieties that kept me on edge often had me yearning for that sweet physical release that Gerard gave me. Here, there was no remedy. Not unless I wanted to invite Varius into my bed.

Which would *not* be happening.

"I'll give you some privacy," Ramia said softly, gathering up the tray and bustling out of the room. I continued to stare at the letter in my hand, trying to gather the courage to open it.

With a deep breath, I broke the seal and read Gerard's message.

My Lady,

I yearn for you. Every moment since you left has been torture for me. Please send word that you are safe. I am going mad not knowing. I miss having you to hold in my arms. I miss the way our bodies fit together.

There is no one like you. And there never will be.

I had to stop reading to close my eyes against the torrent of guilt and anguish. My relationship with Gerard had been casual; a way to escape and release pent-up tension. We had both established this, knowing our dalliances would have to end once the Shadow King came for me. How could Gerard be saying these things to me, knowing I was now married?

Swallowing down my discomfort, I forced myself to keep reading.

But that is not the only reason I write to you. I must also ask if the endeavor we discussed previously has been accomplished yet. If it has, please send word immediately. Our armies intend to cross the border and invade the kingdom if it's clear you have been unsuccessful.

My heart dropped to my stomach, and I re-read the paragraph once more.

Invade the kingdom...

"Father, you cannot be serious," I whispered. How would invading possibly help? The Shadow Court's forces were far more powerful than ours. If I was unsuccessful, it would either be because I got caught, or because killing Varius and destroying the source of his magic did nothing to stop the shadows. And if the shadows could survive without Varius, then we were *all* doomed.

Heart racing, I skimmed the rest of Gerard's letter.

. . .

I am risking my life by sending this to you, but I would never forgive myself if something happened to you because I did not warn you. I am in love with you, my darling, and I would give anything to have you in my arms once more.

Please write back quickly. If you are close to achieving your goal, I can send word and delay the army.

All my love,

G

Nausea churned in my gut as I set the parchment on my lap, struggling to calm my breathing. Stones, this was an utter and complete mess.

I raised my hand to my forehead, my pulse jumping so violently I thought I might faint. If Ramia hadn't brought me food, I most likely would have.

Gerard still wanted me. And Father planned to invade the Shadow Court.

What in the *hell* was he thinking? He was no match for the Shadow Fae. It was why he hadn't been able to do anything all this time. What had changed? I was his secret weapon. All those years and all that time invested in creating the perfect spy... Why would he throw all of that away now? It had only been a week since I had left.

None of this was right. Gerard should not be pining for me. And Father should not be making a move against my husband's kingdom.

Terror seeped into my bones as I stood, pacing the length of the library while I considered what to do. Unfortunately, I was *not* any closer to finding the enchanted rose. It was very possible the flower did not exist at all and Gerard had been right to scoff at me.

But I had to write him back, or else Father would risk the safety of my home by attacking a kingdom he did not have the power to defeat.

Using the quill and parchment on the table, I hastily scrawled a response to Gerard. I begged him to give me more time and told him I had come across some interesting information that might lead me to the rose.

It wasn't a lie, but it wasn't a truth, either. I had uncovered lots of interesting tidbits. But I was no closer to finding the rose.

It was a deception. And it made me even more desperate to find the truth.

Footsteps sounded nearby, and I jumped. With shaking hands, I folded up the two letters and tucked them into my bodice, along with the notes I had taken during my studies. I was terrified someone would walk in and discover the damning evidence of my betrayal.

After smoothing my hands on my skirts a few times, I took a deep breath and left the library, my heart skittering uncontrollably at the thought of my father invading and igniting a war between the two courts.

A war my people would most certainly lose.

THE BEAST

I gripped the reins tightly as Zorben, my alpora, tore through the sky. Wind whipped at my face, stinging my eyes, and making my hair fly wildly behind me.

Alporas were slightly larger than horses, and far faster, even on land. I didn't often use the alporas for flying; the Necro Shadows made them far too skittish to fly that high. But Zorben was fearless, and the urgent missive from General Forsenn could not be ignored. On foot, Zorben would have taken half a day to reach the lower towns.

I couldn't wait that long.

With each beat of Zorben's wings, his muscles flexed underneath my thighs. It was certainly not a comfortable ride. The skeletal beasts had hardly any fat surrounding their bones, which meant I felt every single movement acutely.

The moisture of the clouds tickled my arms, and I kept a careful eye on the Necro Shadows, which hovered close by. Zorben flew lower, giving us more space from those deadly shadows. The Lumen from my own shadow magic only extended as far as the Agnarr Castle. I wasn't powerful enough to stretch beyond that; otherwise, I would use it to protect the entire kingdom.

Zorben unleashed a screech that pierced the air, making my ears throb. I gritted my teeth, tugging on the reins as we made our descent. The alpora's black wings were massive, large enough to span ten soldiers when fully flexed. My own wings were powerful, but I could only glide with them, and using them significantly drained my magic.

I was also keen to ignore just how much the curse had claimed me already. It wasn't long after my father's wings appeared that he lost his life. Some naïve part of me thought that if I used my wings as little as possible, I could slow the effects of the curse.

Foolish indeed.

Zorben arced lower, gliding between the trees and landing just east of a gravel path leading into the village. His hooves hit the ground hard, the muscles of his four legs jostling me as he pumped furiously. I jolted in the saddle and grunted from the impact, but Zorben continued at a gallop, shifting effortlessly from flying to running. Shadows swirled around us, but Zorben recognized it as the Umbra Mist that protected us. Even so, I shot a wary glance toward the sky, noting the darkened mist of the Necro Shadows that floated in the air like storm clouds. They were thicker here, nearly blocking out the sun entirely.

And straight ahead, right where the village rested, was a massive plume of Necro Shadows, swirling like an intense funnel cloud.

With a shout, I jerked on Zorben's reins, bringing him to an abrupt halt. My eyes traveled up the height of the shadow pillar, my heart seizing in my chest.

I had no idea the situation was this dire. I had certainly believed Forsenn when he'd told me the shadows had reached the village.

But *this*? This was volatile and menacing. This was as if the shadows had developed a mind of their own, collecting together to form a unique entity that could swallow the court entirely.

"Mother of Shade help us," I whispered as I stared at the raging tornado in horror. Zorben snorted, huffing in discomfort, his hooves digging into the gravel at his feet. I patted the side of his neck, my fingers meeting the thin black skin that barely covered the bones jutting out from his body.

"It's all right," I murmured to him. "You're safe, old boy." I dug my heels into Zorben's sides, urging him into a cautious trot. I needed to get closer, but if I got too close, the shadows would poison me, or even burn me. The old wound in my shoulder seemed to throb from the memory of the last time I'd gotten too close. Alporas were immune to the toxins of the Necro Shadows, but Zorben was still wary of them. He likely hated the smell.

I couldn't blame him. It smelled like rotten wood, ash, and death itself.

"Easy does it," I urged. We drew close enough for the putrid odor of the poison to sting my nostrils. I wrapped my cloak around my nose and mouth to help block the smell, knowing some people were poisoned just by ingesting the shadows.

As we progressed farther down the road, the roar of the storm grew closer, the wind howling and the trees swaying as if a hurricane had settled right above the village.

I jerked Zorben to a stop, then slid off his back before tying the reins to a nearby tree. He nudged my arm with his snout, his dark eyes full of fear and concern.

"I'll be right back," I promised.

He huffed again as if he didn't believe me.

With a grimace, I turned to face the shadow storm. From within the funnel cloud, lightning flashed, and I staggered backward in shock, my pulse skittering.

I had never seen anything like that before. Shadows, yes, but lightning? How could the magic from the curse produce such a violent storm?

This had never happened. Not in the centuries since the curse had been cast.

A shout echoed from behind me. I whirled to find a figure

atop another alpora, racing toward me. As the figure drew nearer, I recognized him as General Forsenn. He, too, wore a cloth to cover his mouth and nose. He waved me over, arms gesturing wildly.

I nodded and untied Zorben's reins, urging him back toward the captain. The beast moved without complaint, clearly eager to put as much distance between us and the storm as possible.

Forsenn dismounted, his face ashen. "You shouldn't have come this close."

"I had to see how bad it was." My voice was grim as I glanced back at the storm. The tornado was shifting, widening in size as it consumed a cottage, tearing apart the logs as if they were straw.

"Your Highness, we need to know what to do to fight this," Forsenn said, his brows drawing together. "We have never faced a force this strong before."

I nodded. I was at a loss as well.

With a storm this great, it would only gain momentum, devouring everything in its path. How long before it reached Agnarr Castle? Was my Lumen enough to hold it off?

Somehow, I doubted it. Already, the magic of the curse was proving to be stronger than I ever could be.

"Bring as many civilians to the palace grounds as you can," I told Forsenn. "We will provide shelter for them. And with the revel happening this week, hopefully they will be preoccupied."

"Families are already making their way to the castle now," Forsenn said. "But it is a temporary solution, Your Highness. Do you have a plan for how to bring down this monstrosity?" He gestured to the howling storm, which was drawing closer.

I climbed atop Zorben, who was inching backward, looking as if he might bolt at any moment. "When you've finished with the evacuation, meet me at the castle. My sorceress and I will discuss our options. We will figure something out, Forsenn. I won't rest until we do."

He nodded, but his brow only creased further as he stared hard at the raging shadows. I followed his gaze, forcing myself to watch as the storm ripped apart a clock tower, the bell cracking and releasing a sharp, metallic sound that mingled with the screaming wind.

Forsenn urged his alpora into motion, and I finally tore my gaze away and followed suit. Together, we took off down the road, away from the Necro Shadows and the destroyed village.

THE BEAUTY

AFTER SEVERAL DAYS OF SEARCHING IN THE LIBRARY, I STILL HAD no idea where the enchanted rose was or how to stop the Necro Shadows.

Ramia had helpfully offered to include my letters to Gerard and Eira in her response to Kendra, claiming it would be easy for the kitchen maid to deliver them for me in the Earthen Court. At least I wasn't *completely* cut off from the outside world, and Eira would know of my whereabouts. This brought me a modicum of comfort, though I knew the post would take a while to reach the Winter Court.

I hadn't forgotten about Varius's request for my blood. I was still angry with him, but... if his people were dying and he *needed* my blood, then how could I refuse?

But after reading Gerard's letter, it seemed more important to find the enchanted rose. Instead of researching in the library, I decided to change tactics and explore as much of the castle as possible. Perhaps if I could find the enchanted rose on my own and destroy Varius's magic, I could end the shadows for good. Then, he wouldn't need my blood at all, and our courts would not go to war.

But exploring proved more difficult than I thought. Varius had been right: The castle *did* love toying with me.

It seemed to only want to show me places I'd already been to before: the kitchens, the library, even the courtyard where Varius and I had exchanged vows.

Then one day, I finally found myself in an unfamiliar hall, this one lined with silver carpet instead of the amber I was accustomed to by my rooms. My heart jolted with excitement at the prospect of discovering new rooms in the castle.

Strange purple smoke wafted down the hallway. Terror gripped my chest as I assumed it to be Necro Shadows. But upon further inspection, I realized they were fumes. I sniffed the air, which smelled so strongly of peppermint that it stung my nostrils.

Frowning, I followed the scent to an open door halfway down the hall. I peered inside, my curiosity getting the better of me.

The fumes were so thick it took me a moment to see through them. Heat floated around me, and from within the room, a female voice murmured words I didn't recognize. They weren't Terrish or Agnarrish.

I stepped forward, and a floorboard creaked under my foot. My heart leapt in my throat as I eased backward, afraid of getting caught.

In a flash, the door swung open to reveal Tislora, her sparkling silver eyes sweeping over me. Her brows lowered in displeasure.

"Can I help you?" Her tone was clipped.

"I—forgive me. I'm just—" I gestured helplessly toward the hall where I'd come, unable to find the right words.

Tislora scowled, then followed my gaze. She sighed. "The castle deposited you on my doorstep, did it? Well, come in, then."

My eyebrows lifted as she stood back, retreating inside the smoky and hazy room to allow me to enter. The room was not at all what I expected. Nearly as large as the queen's chambers, it was stocked with shelves that wrapped around the entire perimeter of the foggy room. In the center stood a massive, bubbling cauldron, behind which rested a small stand with an open book perched on it.

My eyes widened. "What is this place?"

Tislora shot me a smirk over her shoulder as she moved closer to the cauldron. "Never seen an apothecary before?"

"Not like this," I admitted, wondering why the castle decided to send me here, of all places. Was it possible Tislora could help me locate the enchanted rose?

"You might as well make yourself useful while you're here," Tislora said, flipping through the pages of the large tome on top of the stand. "Can you fetch me the jar of sage? It's on the far right, with green leaves."

I scanned the contents of the shelves, trying to wave the smoke out of my eyes, before I finally laid eyes on it. The jar was small, and it easily fit in the palm of my hand. I gave it to Tislora, who was staring intently at the page of the book. She peered into the cauldron and inhaled deeply. A furrow formed between her brows.

"It still doesn't smell quite right." Her eyes became unfocused for a moment. "Something is... off." She glanced back at the book and turned a few pages. "Human, fetch me some ground demon horn."

I blanched, my stomach twisting with unease. "Demon horn?" I repeated.

She shot me an amused look. "It's not *actually* the horn of a demon. It's the horn of a bakathra, the largest species of fae creature known to our kind. It usually resides in the mountains and is dangerous and volatile when disturbed. The powder is white, and the jar is quite tall. The substance is rare, so do be careful, will you?"

I nodded, turning to the shelves again as I searched for the ground demon horn. I allowed myself to glance over the labels of the other jars and vials while I looked. The worn parchment labels were written in an untidy scrawl, the ink slightly faded, which made it harder to read.

"Mother of Shade, you humans are so *slow*. Have you found it yet?"

I rolled my eyes. "And you fae are so impatient. I don't have to help, you know." I found the white powder, grabbed the jar, and handed it to Tislora. Despite our barbed exchanges, she had a small smile on her face.

Tislora's moon-like eyes swept over my form. "You're not dressed."

"Yes, I am." I glanced down at my violet gown.

Tislora snorted. "I mean for the revel."

"What revel?"

Tislora looked at me again, her shrewd eyes calculating. After a moment, all she said was, "Hmm."

I folded my arms over my chest and watched as she tipped the jar of ground demon horn just enough to let a few white grains trickle into the simmering contents of the cauldron. It hissed, and purple steam billowed from within. I coughed, waving a hand in front of my face.

"What is the revel?" I asked impatiently.

"It's a day of merriment. A tradition for our kind."

I arched an eyebrow. "You want to have a party? While there are deadly shadows surrounding the castle as we speak?"

Tislora's gaze turned cold as she looked at me. "That is exactly why we *should* have it. The people are scared. Would you prefer we have them cowering in their closets every night for the foreseeable future?"

I had no response to that. She was right, of course. And I felt like an idiot. My gaze dropped to the cauldron once more. The steam had now turned fuchsia.

"Will *you* be attending the revel?" I asked her.

"I'll make an appearance," she said vaguely.

When I said nothing, she looked me over, her gaze calculating. "You should come."

I blinked. "To the unseelie revel?"

"Yes. Consider this your formal invitation. Come and see what the unseelie do when we are... *unrestrained*."

I resisted the urge to fidget. Her words sounded more like a threat than an invitation. "I—are you sure it would be appropriate for me to be there?"

She arched an eyebrow at me. "Aren't you Varius's wife? If he's there, you should be, too."

Varius. She was using his given name again. "The king will be in attendance?"

"Of course. He is unseelie, and he must make a point to show the people that even he will make time for them."

My throat went dry as I considered her words. Should I really do it? Attend this unseelie revel? My efforts to explore the castle had been unfruitful. And if Varius was going to be there, I could speak with him and try to dig up some more answers.

My insides squirmed, but I forced myself to say, "Perhaps you're right. If I'm the Queen of the Shadow Court, surely, I should make an appearance."

Tislora laughed again, louder this time. "*Queen of the Shadow Court.* As if that actually means anything."

My cheeks flamed. Who did this fae think she was, to scoff at me like that? "Well, I *am* married to the Shadow King, as you said."

Tislora leveled a hard look at me. "Even if you *had* consummated the marriage, which I'm assuming you haven't, there hasn't been an official coronation. Not to mention the people of this court would never respect you as their queen. You are a stranger, and a feeble human. No one even knows who you are. You may be the Shadow King's wife according to the law, but that does *not* make you the queen of this people or this land. You aren't even willing to give a few drops of your blood for the sake of protecting our people." Now her tone was downright icy.

I went completely rigid, my heart stuttering in my chest. She knew about Varius's need for my blood?

Of course she did. She was the court sorceress.

I swallowed thickly, unable to find my voice.

Tislora's lips curled into a satisfied smile. "Yes, I know about your blood. And I know you have refused Varius's request."

"I did not refuse," I said tightly. "I just… needed to consider it."

"Yes, and while you are taking your precious time to *consider*, those deadly shadows are killing innocent fae." Her steely eyes drilled into me.

I gritted my teeth, trying to ignore the way my chest constricted at her words.

Stones, she was right. I was so selfish. I thought I could solve this myself, but people were *dying*.

I needed to speak with Varius. Sooner rather than later.

Which meant… I would be attending this revel. No matter how much the idea tied my stomach into knots.

I gestured to the cauldron, eager to change the subject. "What are you cooking in there?"

"An elixir," she said shortly. She sniffed the contents again, then frowned. Clearly, something about this potion was bothering her.

I remembered Varius mentioning an elixir when he told me he needed my blood. "What is it for?"

"I'm quite certain that's none of your business, human."

"My name is Sybelle," I snapped.

"I know."

Stones, she was unpleasant. Did Varius let her speak to him this way, too?

My heart dropped as I realized that was not the same thing at all. Tislora was right—I had no authority here.

I smoothed my hands along my skirt, thinking it might be best if I simply left. Before I could turn away, however, a thought occurred to me. I looked at Tislora with newfound curiosity. "Have you ever been to the Earthen Court?"

She flicked a quick glance my way before returning her attention to the cauldron. "A few times. Why?"

"Have you ever heard of Earthen witches?"

Tislora froze in the act of stirring, the ladle going stiff in her grip. Her nostrils flared slightly, and I could have sworn her silver irises gleamed. "That... is an interesting question," she said slowly. Her voice was low and lethal. I sensed I was treading on dangerous grounds.

"I came across a book in the library about the history of my court," I said quickly, "and I'm fairly certain there were no witches in the lineage of my people."

Tislora removed the ladle from the cauldron and set it on the table in front of her, then fixed her steely gaze on me. "And you humans think you know everything that ever happened in the history of your court? Your lifespans are so short. How can you possibly know what happened before your time?"

"Stories were passed down," I said. "Histories and journals and texts."

"Ah. And you believe it's impossible that certain truths were omitted from these texts?"

"Of course not. But surely *someone* would have mentioned witches if they had been around at some point."

"Yes, because you humans *love* to mingle with other species and then tell everyone about it." Tislora rolled her eyes.

I frowned at that, remembering how I'd thought of Father and the way he would have balked at the idea of being descended from witches. Could it be true? If someone like Father had discovered a bloodline of witches in the royal family, he would have covered it up before someone found it out. He would have erased it from every record to ensure the public believed his bloodline was pure.

Nausea roiled in my gut as I realized that, once more, Tislora was right.

"So… so it's true then?" I asked breathlessly. "My people are descended from witches?"

Tislora gave a single slow nod.

"Shit," I whispered, rubbing my forehead. "*Shit.*"

Tislora chuckled again. "Indeed."

I couldn't believe it. I was descended from *witches*? But how? And where were they now? Had they died out? I found that hard to believe. Witches were powerful; far more powerful than humans. So, what happened to them, and how did humans gain control of the court?

"Don't think too hard, human," Tislora teased. "You'll hurt yourself."

"Did you know any witches?" I asked. "From my court?"

Tislora was silent as she hovered over the open book resting on the stand. Her eyes weren't moving, so I knew she wasn't reading. Her mouth grew very thin, and her eyes were guarded.

"That was a long time ago," she murmured, her voice distant. I noticed she did not answer my question.

I stood there, watching her, waiting for her to say something else. Her finger was pressed against the page, but she was utterly frozen, unmoving, her gaze fixed on a faraway point I could not see. What was she thinking about?

Suddenly, her eyes snapped to me, and she straightened, as if jolted from her stupor. "If you're to attend the revel, you need a new dress. Enzira is your maid, right? I'll send for her. She can escort you to your rooms and get you ready."

"No, there's no need—" I started, but Tislora had already crossed the room and pulled a small rope hanging from the ceiling.

A few moments later, an unfamiliar servant appeared, and Tislora said to him, "Send for Enzira, please."

The servant bowed and left.

I sighed. "I can return to my rooms on my own."

"Can you?" Tislora's voice was filled with amusement.

In spite of the situation, my mouth twitched with the hint of a smile. "Well, perhaps not. But I'd wager *everyone* has trouble finding their way in this castle."

"True," Tislora said.

I watched her stir the contents of the cauldron again. The steam had dissipated, but the room was still sweltering. It didn't seem to affect Tislora, who wore her usual black robes that fell down to her wrists and gathered along the floor like the train of a wedding gown.

Enzira appeared in the doorway, and her face paled when she noticed me. "My lady." She pressed a fist to her chest and hurried over to me, gently grasping my elbow. "Your room. Please."

I nodded. "Yes, I'm sorry. I got lost." I let her guide me out the door. Just as we reached the hallway, Tislora's voice floated after us.

"See you at the revel, human."

THE BEAUTY

 We climbed all the way to the top, and only then did I remember my chambers were on the highest level of the castle. I glanced upward at the dome-shaped ceiling, which revealed a fuchsia sky with the setting sun. Already, the Umbra Mist was creeping closer toward the window as if it could sense the light was fading.

Enzira took me down the hall toward the queen's suite, and I said in Agnarrish, "You didn't tell me there was a revel happening tonight."

Enzira cut a gaze at me, her dark eyes wary. "I didn't think I should. Revels can be dangerous and… shameful for humans to witness."

Shameful? I frowned. "But if I'm to live among the unseelie, shouldn't I experience things like this, since it's a part of your culture?"

Enzira's lips pressed together in a thin line, covering up her fangs. "Perhaps," she said, but she sounded uncertain.

We reached my chambers, and Enzira strode inside, then held the door open for me. She eased it almost all the way shut, then turned to face me.

"I'm assuming you've told the king I can speak your language?" I asked, trying to keep the sharpness out of my tone.

It wasn't her fault the king had lied to me, and I couldn't blame her for being loyal to him.

But to my surprise, Enzira shook her head. "No."

My eyes widened. "Why not?"

She shrugged one shoulder. "It was not my place to tell. I am *your* maid. Not his."

I blinked at her, astonished.

She offered me a small smile. "Did you think I was spying on you?"

"A little," I admitted. "And honestly, I wouldn't put it past Varius to spy on me."

Enzira's brows knitted together. "Why do you say that?"

I gave her a cautious look, unwilling to give too much away. How much did she know?

Understanding lit her features. "You mean the Necro Shadows."

My pulse quickened. "What do you know of them?"

"I know that's why you're here. That's why all the humans come."

I let my hands fall against my thighs in frustration. "So I am the *last* one to know the true reason for me being here?"

"Can you blame us for keeping it a secret?" Enzira asked. "If we had told your people why we needed human brides, would they have consented?"

I fell silent at that, because the truth was *no*. My father would have flat-out refused. Shaking my head, I argued, "But it's still deceitful. Varius has led my kingdom to believe he would use his own shadows to slaughter us if we did not comply."

"Does the agreement say that?"

"Of course not. Fae can't lie. But the implication is there."

"But if you don't comply, the shadows *will* destroy your kingdom."

I felt the blood drain from my face. "What do you mean?"

"Didn't the king tell you?"

Slowly, I shook my head again. I thought back to Varius's confession and my own angry retaliation. I had stormed out of the room before he'd been able to continue.

Guilt and shame crept into my chest. *Shit.* What had I done?

I drew closer to Enzira. "Tell me. Please."

"The Necro Shadows are not bound to only our court," Enzira said solemnly. "If left unchecked, they will cross the border to your lands and destroy them, too."

My heart twisted with dread. Stones, how could I have been so foolish? I raised my hands to my forehead, my thoughts spinning. I was torn between utter humiliation from the hateful things I'd said to Varius and horror at the thought of my own kingdom being in peril without anyone knowing.

All this time, the Necro Shadows had been getting closer and closer to my kingdom. But in my mind, there was always that kernel of doubt that they would actually cross the border. A naïve part of me believed the boundaries of our kingdom would keep them away. As if some invisible line between the Earthen and Shadow Courts would ward off the Necro Shadows.

But of course it wasn't that easy.

"Why didn't he *tell* us?" I asked, my voice weak. "We could have joined forces against the shadows."

"We are forbidden from speaking of the dark magic and where it has come from," Enzira said. "The human royals would have asked too many questions."

I stared at her, at the way her eyes were tight with concern and fear. "Were you there?" I asked. "When it all started?"

"I was a child. Too young to remember much. But my mother remembered, and she told me stories. It was… horrible." She shuddered, and I didn't press her for more.

How had this all started? Why was there magic like this in the first place? It had to have come from somewhere. I made a mental note to search the library again for answers. I remembered the silence after I requested a book about relations between the Earthen Court and the Shadow Court. Was the castle also forbidden from leading me to these answers?

Perhaps I could find a way around that.

Enzira clapped her hands together, her expression brightening. "Do you truly wish to attend the revel tonight, my lady?"

The words *my lady* jolted me. I had forgotten, for a moment, that she was my maid. During our conversation, she had felt like a friend instead of a servant. And I preferred it that way. The castle staff in the Earthen Court *never* would have had such a frank conversation with me. It was refreshing. And genuine.

I cleared my throat, still disconcerted about the idea of celebrating despite the horrifying uncertainty of these death shadows. "Can you tell me exactly what goes on during a revel? Will my life be in danger?"

"Most likely, no. But a revel is a time for us to unleash our wildest nature. For some, like me, it only involves excessive drinking of faerie wine." She flashed a grin, showing her fangs.

I barked out a laugh at that. Stones, why hadn't I spoken Agnarrish with Enzira sooner? I was growing to love this new personality that was emerging.

I looked at her, realizing she was including herself in this. "You attend revels?"

She grinned again. "Yes. All the servants do. It is a time to unite our people together, regardless of class or station."

My heart lifted at such a beautiful notion, and I longed for the Earthen Court to do something similar.

"But for many of the Shadow Fae, it is an opportunity to submit to more… carnal urges."

My face heated, and my eyes widened, as I registered her meaning. "Ah. You mean… intimacy?"

She nodded, unfazed. "Although, not quite intimacy, since it is very public."

My blush deepened at the mere thought of engaging in such acts in front of an audience. But I couldn't deny that I was deeply curious. "And, ah, will I be expected to… participate in these festivities?"

"Oh, no, certainly not. Not everyone does it. But please understand that we have no notion of privacy at revels."

I nodded, my face feeling hot. "So, you'll be there tonight?"

"Yes. But only for drinking." She grinned again.

"May I… er, join you? I mean, with the drinking." I laughed again.

To my surprise, Enzira's face paled slightly, and she shook her head. "You should not drink faerie wine, my lady. It isn't safe for humans."

"Is there *anything* that's safe for me there? Will there be normal wine?"

She tapped her chin, considering this. Then, her eyes crinkled with her smile. "I will speak with the kitchen staff and ensure something is prepared for you."

"Oh, you don't have to do that. I don't need to drink anything."

"Nonsense! If you are to adjust to our customs, it is only fitting that we should do the same."

My entire chest warmed at her words, and I found I didn't know what to say. I felt undeserving of the affectionate gesture, and all I could do was mumble a chagrined, "Thank you."

Enzira's smile widened. "Of course." She strode to the armoire and threw open its doors. "Now, we must find you something fitting to wear. I should warn you, the attire for the event tends to be scandalous by your standards."

I snorted. "After your description of the revel, I'm hardly surprised." I shifted my weight from one foot to the other, hoping I wasn't making a terrible mistake in doing this. The dresses and gowns I was accustomed to in the Earthen Court showed a bit of cleavage but nothing too appalling. Already, I noticed the fashions here were quite different and showed far more skin than I was used to.

Enzira pulled out a tiny black strip of fabric, then held it up to where I stood, her eyes calculating. Then, she shook her head. "No, that isn't right." She put the fabric back, and only then did I realize the tiny slip had been a *dress*.

Stones. This was going to be a disaster. The heat in my face had spread to my neck and ears, and it suddenly felt far too hot in this room.

"Ah, this is the one." She pulled out a thin, burgundy dress, the bodice barely held together by an ornate lace design.

I swallowed hard as she approached me, holding up the dress to ensure it was the right size. She nodded with a smile. "It brings out the red in your hair."

I self-consciously touched the waves of my hair. No one had ever said my hair was *red* before. It was brown or chestnut or *mud-colored*, as Orla had once claimed.

Enzira seemed to read the hesitation on my face. "My lady, you do not have to go tonight."

I dropped my hand and lifted my chin. "Will the king be there?"

"Yes."

"Then, I should go." Not only to experience the customs of the unseelie but also... to apologize for my brutish behavior toward Varius earlier. He had not deserved my wrath.

"If you like, I can stay by your side the entire time," Enzira offered.

That strange, warm feeling in my chest burrowed deeper inside me. "Oh, you don't have to do that. You should enjoy yourself with your friends."

Enzira cocked her head at me in genuine confusion. "But, you *are* my friend. Aren't you?"

My chest coiled so tightly I couldn't breathe. The earnestness in her eyes made me want to weep.

"Yes," I said in a strained voice. I took a breath and said more firmly, "Yes. You are definitely my friend."

Enzira smiled, her eyes crinkling again.

A soft knock sounded at the door. For a moment, I turned to the shared door to Varius's room, expecting the king to emerge. Then, I realized the knock came from the door to the hall, and Ramia poked her head in.

My stomach sank. Why had I been hoping for Varius? It must have been my guilt, nagging me to clear the air between us. I didn't like to leave things unresolved.

Ramia frowned as she looked over the scrap of lace in Enzira's hands. "I was about to turn in for the night, but I sense something is going on here?" She almost sounded as if she didn't want to know.

"There is a revel tonight," I said. "It will be an event of unseelie merriment."

As expected, Ramia blanched, her face stricken as if I had just suggested we go on a murderous rampage. "You—You plan on attending this?"

I nodded.

Ramia stepped further into the room and squared her shoulders. "Then, I will, too."

I snorted loudly, then quickly covered my face with my hands as Ramia's eyes bulged. "Sorry," I said. "It's just—Ramia, there will be naked fae. Doing… naked things. Are you sure?"

Her face turned ashen, and her lips thinned. "I—I should be with *you*, my lady."

Enzira, who had been watching our exchange with a slight frown, said in broken Terrish, "I go with her." She gestured to me. "All night, I be with her."

Ramia looked at Enzira for a long moment. I expected my lady's maid to refuse, to insist that the best and only person who could keep me safe was herself.

But Ramia nodded once. "Very good."

I glanced from Ramia to Enzira, my mouth falling open in

surprise. Did that mean Ramia trusted Enzira? Or was she *that* reluctant to attend the revel herself?

"Don't look so shocked," Ramia said to me. "Enzira is quite capable. She's proven as much since we arrived here."

Enzira beamed at the praise, which I thought was well deserved.

"I'll leave you to your… festivities, my lady. Please send for me if you need anything." Ramia bobbed a quick curtsey before leaving the room.

Enzira began digging through the drawers of the armoire. "Would you like any jewelry, my lady?"

"Just my amber necklace." I touched it for reassurance, then paused as an idea came to me. "Actually… what about the diamond tiara from the wedding ceremony?"

In answer, Enzira lifted the gleaming tiara. My eyes fixated on the diamonds glittering around the piece. Just the sight of them gave me a boost of confidence.

If there was any night that I needed courage, it would be tonight.

I smiled. "Perfect."

The Beast

After witnessing the terrifying shadow storm, the last thing I wanted to do was attend a revel.

But with evacuees coming to the castle, the people needed reassurance and comfort. And they needed to know that I was there for them.

The shadow storm could wait.

At least, that was what I told myself.

I stood in my chambers, trying to muster the strength to face my people and pretend like everything was fine. I flexed my fingers twice, then curled them into fists. A deep, cleansing breath whooshed from my lungs.

I wore nothing but a tan cloth that fell halfway down my thighs, as was the custom for the Unseelie King. My wings were on full display against my back, and my hair was loose, curling just above my shoulders.

By unseelie standards, my attire was modest. I knew the majority of unseelie fae preferred to attend revels in the nude as a way of embracing their unseelie forms.

I was not quite so bold.

My eyes closed as I tried to collect my thoughts. But all I could see was that raging funnel cloud roaring as it came toward me, and the decimated homes left in its wake.

Lives destroyed. A village obliterated.

My fault. My fault.

The words rang in my thoughts so loudly I could hear nothing else. With a roar, I slammed my fist into the stone wall, causing it to crack. My hand throbbed, and bloody scrapes lined my knuckles.

But the pain pierced through the haze of my thoughts, bringing me a moment of clarity. With a sigh, I brushed the dust from my hands and strode to the door. When I threw it open, the ballroom awaited me, the smells and sounds of the revel swelling and beckoning me closer. The tart raspberry scent of faerie wine floated in the air, tickling my nostrils, and already the sounds of fae pleasuring each other filled the room, their moans and groans mingling with the music.

I stepped into the room, and only a few fae glanced up at my arrival, inclining their heads politely. The others continued with their merriment.

This was one of the reasons why I loved revels. Here, I was no longer the Shadow King, but an ordinary unseelie fae eager to embrace his nature. We were all one at the revel. No titles. No expectations.

Nothing but freedom.

Already, I felt my body relaxing as I strode deeper into the room. The orbs of light from my Lumen had been dimmed, and all around me, figures were lurking in dark corners or sprawled along the floor. Against the back wall was a long table with faerie wine, chocolate tarts, and some alcoholic drink I didn't recognize. An orchestral tune was playing loudly, but I saw no instruments. I wouldn't have been surprised if some fae were using their magic to conjure the sounds. We tried to allow the revel to proceed without the assistance of staff or servants, so I knew no musicians had been hired for the event.

I strode through the ballroom, sidestepping two naked males groping each other along the floor. To my left, a group of females danced provocatively, laughing and shouting with delight. To my right, a fae male sat on a large cushion with a female on his lap, grinding mercilessly against him. He cupped her breast with one hand while drinking faerie wine with the other.

When I reached the refreshments table, I grabbed a glass of faerie wine and sipped it. The strong fruity flavor assaulted my tongue and burned as it trickled down my throat. I took another sip for good measure, allowing it to settle comfortably within me, bolstering my spirits and loosening something in my chest.

A teal sofa rested next to the table, and I sat on it, crossing my ankle over my knee and smiling contentedly at the laughter echoing around me. I downed my drink, then grabbed another, letting the burning liquid melt away my fears and concerns.

This was worth it. This moment, when I could see my people enjoying themselves and forgetting about the terrors waiting outside these walls, made the revels worth it.

A collective gasp sounded from the other side of the room, and the music faltered for a moment before continuing. Several couples sprang apart, turning to stare at something I couldn't see.

I straightened, setting my glass on the table and frowning at the disruption. What had happened? Was it the Necro Shadows?

I rose to my feet and moved toward the commotion. Fae were whispering to one another in shock and surprise. I followed their gazes, then went rigid when I saw what they were staring at.

Sybelle had entered the room, and she wore nothing but a thin scrap of lacy red fabric that barely contained her breasts. A flimsy skirt floated just below her navel, revealing a wide expanse of pale skin along her thighs. The same amber necklace she often wore rested against her collarbone, and the diamond tiara from our wedding ceremony sparkled atop her head. Her wavy hair was down and fell just past her breasts, and her caramel eyes sparkled in the low light.

I found myself entranced by her. She stepped into the room with confident strides, her chin lifted and her expression regal. She looked at each fae she passed and nodded at them as if she recognized them.

Perhaps she did.

Then, her gaze slid to mine, and she stilled. I saw the moment she realized my attire was just as revealing as hers. A faint blush crept into her cheeks as her eyes dipped to the cloth tied at my waist. She noted the long, barbed tail that swished behind me, and the shadow of my wings visible just past my shoulders.

My nostrils flared, and I gritted my teeth. What was she doing here? This revel was a celebration meant for unseelie fae. Her presence alone could make my people feel uncomfortable just for being themselves.

I had kept my distance from her over the past several days, hoping that once her temper cooled, she would see reason and accept my request for her blood. But this was not the setting where I wished to have that conversation.

I strode toward her, intent on telling her to leave before she ruined the festivities, when a figure appeared beside her— Enzira, Sybelle's maid. The fae was wearing a black dress that hugged her curves and fell just past her knees, with a long slit exposing the side of her thigh. Though the dress covered a bit more than Sybelle's, it still showed off a good deal of her violet skin.

To my surprise, Enzira looped her arm through Sybelle's and laughed at something the human said. Sybelle glanced at someone over Enzira's shoulder and grinned broadly, then waved one of her pale arms in recognition.

A few of the unseelie around her began to move and chatter among themselves, somewhat appeased by this. As Enzira tugged on Sybelle's arm, pulling her forward to dance with another crowd of fae, my shoulders relaxed slightly. After a moment or two, the room settled into normalcy. Couples resumed their lovemaking, and shouts of laughter echoed once more.

I loosed the breath that had tightened in my chest, then glared in Sybelle's direction. Her arms were in the air as she swayed her hips in rhythm to the music. Her smile was so wide it showed off her blocky white teeth.

Everything about her stood out as a testament to why she did not belong here. Her thin and wispy hair, her short and stubby fingernails, even her large doe-like eyes.

She was a stranger, intruding on a moment reserved for the fae. Perhaps she didn't know any better, but I, as her husband, had a duty to educate her about these things.

I made my way over to her as her laughter rang out around me. When I was only a few steps away, Sybelle twirled, then collided straight into me. I gripped her waist to keep her from toppling over, and her hands braced against my chest. Her mouth opened in surprise as she met my furious stare.

"Varius," she said, slightly breathless.

"Sybelle," I bit out.

Our gazes held, and I waited for her to wilt under the wrath of my fearsome scowl. Instead, she swayed her hips again, her body writhing against mine as a sultry smile spread across her face.

"Come to dance with your wife?" she asked.

I could only blink at her. Was this the same human who blushed when I teased her about consummating our marriage?

I gripped her wrists, tugging them away from my chest as I leaned in. "Why are you here, Sybelle?" My voice was a low growl.

"Tislora invited me."

A fresh wave of fury rippled over me. *Of course* Tislora

invited her. She was probably laughing at the idea of this human showing up at a revel and expecting a stuffy human ball.

"You are not unseelie," I said.

"No, but I am your wife, aren't I?"

I closed my eyes for a moment to keep my rage in check. "This event is for the unseelie to be themselves. With you, a human, interrupting that, it defeats the purpose."

Her brows knitted together, and she glanced around the room as if just now noticing she was surrounded by unseelie fae. She frowned slightly, and I waited for her to realize her mistake.

Then, she said, "I don't see anyone's enjoyment being interrupted. Do you?"

Anger swelled in my chest, and my grip on her wrists tightened. "Sybelle," I ground out.

Her eyebrows lifted. "Varius."

I exhaled a breath through my teeth. Mother of Shade, this human would be the death of me.

"It seems the only one distressed by my presence here is *you*, husband," Sybelle said. "Are you going to haul me out of the room by force?"

A few of the fae were watching us curiously. I knew I *could* carry her out of the ballroom, but it would certainly cause a scene. Already, we were attracting attention.

How would it look for the king to treat his wife in such a way?

It was something my father would have done. The thought soured my stomach, ebbing my anger slightly.

I allowed my gaze to sweep over the room, noting the dancing fae and the couples writhing together along the floor. On the opposite side of the room, a naked fae male lay with his arms and legs spread while a crowd of fae groped and licked him.

Sybelle was right. While her entrance had elicited shock

from the fae, as soon as she began participating alongside them, their concerns had melted away. It was as if she wasn't even here.

Sybelle continued to watch me, waiting for my response.

I bit back a curse, then released one of her wrists. She tugged her other arm, but I held fast.

"You are here as my wife, are you not?" I asked.

Her eyes narrowed. "Yes," she said, drawing out the word.

I tugged on her arm, dragging her back toward the sofa I'd been sitting on. She stumbled, then yelped, protesting as she struggled to keep up with my loping strides.

When I reached the sofa, I sat on the cushion, then pulled her onto my lap. I noticed Enzira gaping openly at us, a glass of faerie wine in her hand. She took a few steps toward us as if to intervene, then thought better of it.

"Varius," Sybelle hissed, wriggling as she tried to extricate herself. Her movements did sinful things to me, sending unexpected heat straight between my legs. I stiffened, trying to leash the sudden and feral need sweeping through me.

She went rigid as she no doubt felt it, too. Slowly, she turned to look at me, one eyebrow arched in accusation.

I huffed a laugh. "Don't flatter yourself, human. It's natural to be aroused at a revel, regardless of whoever is draped across my lap."

It didn't help that I'd already had a few drinks.

Still, she looked at me with a smugness that made my blood boil. "I'm not hearing a denial."

I clenched my teeth, my jaw tensing. "Fine. If I were to seek someone out for a moment of pleasure, it would *not* be you. Is that clear enough for you?"

"If that's the case, then kindly remove me from your lap." Once more, she tried sliding off my knee, but I clamped my hand on her waist, pinning her against me. I suppressed a groan as her backside ground directly into my arousal.

"You are the one who is intent on attending this revel," I murmured against her ear. "If you insist on being here as my wife, then it's only fitting that you play the part."

She turned her head to glare at me, her eyes flashing. "Is that what you did with the other human brides—parade them around as your plaything?"

Shock skittered through me at her words. *Other human brides.* "Sybelle," I said slowly, "you are my first and only human wife."

Her head reared back, her jaw dropping.

Mother of Shade, had she really not known this? Had she believed I was an ageless fae demon who abducted her ancestors over hundreds of years?

"But you are the only human foolish enough to attend a revel as if you were an invited guest," I went on, trying to gloss over this startling revelation.

It didn't work. Sybelle continued to gape at me, unabashed. I cleared my throat, looking around the room to see if anyone was eavesdropping. But no one cared. The fae were too distracted by their merriment.

"So you *aren't* the same Wraith King who has come for a human bride from my kingdom every generation?" she asked quietly.

I bit back a growl. "I am no wraith."

"I know that." She stated this so plainly that I almost believed her.

I sighed. "No. I am not the same king that married the other human brides. That would be my father, and his father, and his father before that."

She blinked at me, clearly astonished by this. What was so alarming about this information?

"But... fae are immortal," she said.

I smirked. "I am well aware."

She shook her head. "So..."

"You may be my first human bride, but many kings before me had multiple wives. It is not unheard of."

She swallowed hard, her gaze lowering as she considered this. Her eyes turned calculating, a look I knew well by now.

Her interest was piqued.

"Can we perhaps discuss something else?" I murmured. The curse was the last thing I wanted to talk about, especially since, when I'd previously brought it up, she had yelled at me and stormed out of the room. If anything would disrupt a revel, it was that kind of behavior.

Sybelle blinked as if I'd jolted her from her thoughts. "I wanted to apologize."

I raised my eyebrows, surprised by this. "Oh?"

"Yes. I reacted badly to your request for my blood, and I'm terribly sorry for that. I should have allowed you to explain further. Please forgive me."

An unexpected knot of emotion formed in my throat. I hadn't expected this level of sincerity from her. She had seemed so confident and—dare I say it—arrogant when she'd arrived. I thought for sure she had come to yell at me again.

"Is that why you came to the revel?" I asked, my voice low and soft.

A blush spread along her cheeks. "Partly."

I found myself smirking again. "And the other part?"

Her blush deepened. "I was curious. And, yes, I wanted to embrace my role as your wife, and I can't very well do that by hiding in my chambers every time you host a revel, now, can I?"

My smile widened, showing my fangs. Sybelle's eyes dipped to those incisors, but I scented no fear on her. "Well, that's quite admirable of you, *dannahla*."

"So it's *dannahla* again, is it?"

"You *are* sitting on my lap, wife." I leaned closer, my lips brushing the shell of her ear. Her hair smelled like lilacs. "It is certainly not the most scandalous thing I could call you."

I delighted in the way her skin pebbled as a shudder swept over her. But my victory was short-lived when my own body reacted as well.

Sybelle clearly sensed it, too, because she wriggled against me once again. I clamped my teeth together to keep from groaning.

"You'll want to stop doing that," I murmured in a strained voice.

"Oh?" She tilted her head toward me, her red-tinted lips curling into a smile.

"Do you recall how I warned you about certain *parts* of me being more monstrous than a typical human male?"

She snorted. "Warned me? Or taunted me?"

I grinned. "Both."

"So you want me to *stop* arousing you because your male appendage is monstrous?" Her eyes gleamed. "Now you've made me curious."

Well, damn. I should have expected that. I heaved a sigh. I was flustered enough from her sitting on my lap with no regard for my red skin and clawed fingers. Did nothing affect her?

She leaned closer to me, her lips brushing my jaw. "Can you tell me?"

I suppressed a shiver from the way her breath tickled my face. That lilac scent enveloped me once more, tinged with the barest hint of old parchment and burning incense. "Tell you? Or show you?"

Her cheeks flushed again, but she said nothing.

"This is a revel, after all," I went on, bolstered by her bashfulness. "If I were to disrobe right here, no one would think anything of it."

Her pupils flared, and her lips parted. I felt her breath hitch, and her pulse quickened.

Mother of Shade, was she actually considering this? If she

said, *Yes, Varius, please show me your cock,* then I wasn't sure how I would respond.

Before she could say anything, I explained, "It's barbed."

Her eyes widened. "It is?"

"Well, there are ridges, and, on command, I can summon the barbs."

"Ridges," she repeated.

"Yes. Like… hard bumps."

Her eyes dropped to just below my navel, and that same intrigued gleam sparked in her eyes.

"You want to see it, don't you?" I smirked again.

"I—n—" Her mouth clamped shut, and her blush deepened. She had been about to deny it. A normal human would have. They could lie, after all.

So why hadn't she? Was she so accustomed to being around the unseelie that she did not want to lie?

I chuckled. "You can't lie to me, wife."

She huffed an exasperated breath. "I am merely fascinated by the anatomy of the unseelie fae. Are all males like that, or just you?"

Now it was my turn to feel flustered. "I don't know. I—I don't often *look* at other males' genitalia."

She laughed at that, and I couldn't help but grin in response.

Someone cleared their throat loudly, and we both turned to find Enzira standing awkwardly before us, clutching a glass of deep purple wine. It was different from the mauve color of faerie wine.

"Forgive the interruption," she said in Agnarrish, pressing her free hand to her chest as a sign of respect to me. She turned to Sybelle and said in broken Terrish, "You drink? Is safe."

Sybelle smiled at her, then reached out her hand. "*Garsha,* Enzira." She accepted the flute and sipped from it, then hummed with pleasure. "This is delicious. What is it?"

"Berry wine." Enzira beamed.

Sybelle nodded and took another sip. "Thank you. That is very kind of you."

Enzira inclined her head, then gestured to the group of females dancing behind her. "Dance?"

I found myself smiling as well. It was clear Enzira was providing Sybelle with a way to escape, if she was uncomfortable with me. I felt Sybelle stiffen on my lap, and I wondered if she would take Enzira's offer.

I tried to tell myself I wouldn't be disappointed if she left me. But that would have been a lie.

Sybelle glanced at me, biting on her lower lip. The motion drew my eyes to her full mouth, and that same rumbling need coursed through me with violent fervor.

Mother of Shade, what was wrong with me? She was a human. I was simply aroused and in need of release, that was all. It *had* been far too long.

After a moment, Sybelle said, "No, thank you. I'm content to remain here with my husband."

THE BEAUTY

The power of the diamonds in my tiara gave me far more confidence than I expected. Enough to dance, drink, sit on my husband's lap, and look him in the eye as I felt his arousal for me underneath the far-too-thin cloth he was wearing.

The logical Sybelle, who was cautious and calculating in everything she did, would have balked at my audacity. I could almost feel her screaming against the walls of my mind, begging me to use common sense.

But I couldn't hear her against the adrenaline coursing through me. The heat of Varius's body seeped into mine, drawing me closer. He was firm and large, and he smelled of spice and rain.

And he was not at all as monstrous as he claimed to be.

Here in the darkened ballroom, I couldn't even tell that his skin was a different shade from mine. His black horns blended in with the darkness around him, and his clawed hands were surprisingly gentle as they held me securely on his lap.

Sitting so closely with him reminded me that he was just like any ordinary man. Yes, he had his differences, but his firm chest and muscular biceps and… well, hard arousal… were exactly the same as the human men I'd encountered.

I leaned into his chest, and a rumbling growl vibrated through him.

Well, I amended, *perhaps not* exactly *the same.*

But, to be honest, I was more intrigued by Varius than any human from my own court. Even Gerard.

And I was *far* too interested in how much his body responded to mine. We were different species, after all, and he had made his disgust for my kind clear.

But when I arched into him or leaned closer or writhed against his hardness, he visibly reacted.

Perhaps it was as he said, and it was only a result of the revel.

But the daring side of me, brought out by the diamonds, wanted to test my theory.

I dragged a fingertip between his two pectorals, tracing a path all the way down to his navel. He stiffened, his breath catching as he held perfectly still while I stroked him.

A couple had each other pressed against the wall next to our sofa. The male kissed her neck, and the female's legs wrapped around him as she threw her head back.

They weren't the only ones engaging in such activities. In fact, the entire ballroom was full of such couples. But this one was so close. I could hear the male murmuring something in Agnarrish against her throat as he licked up and down. She cried out, gasping as she tugged on his violet hair.

The male reached up her skirt, his fingers working her, and she moaned loudly. In Agnarrish, she told him, "Don't stop. Oh, *please* don't stop."

Her skirt hitched higher, and the male fumbled with his trousers. She ground against him, and the wall rattled as he slammed her hard against it. She shouted in ecstasy, her legs tightening around him as he thrust inside her. They both grunted from the impact as he drove harder and deeper inside her. Her animalistic sounds rose in pitch and volume until she was screaming. She rode him so hard that she was bouncing on him, and he continued to plunge inside her, growling and snarling, his movements becoming frantic and demanding.

The female's eyes closed, her mouth falling open as she continued her strangled sounds of pleasure.

Varius's voice in my ear made me jump. "Enjoying the show?"

My thighs clenched around his knee as desire turned my insides molten. The way the female was crying out, the look of intense delight on her face…

I said nothing for a long moment, still watching the writhing couple. They only seemed spurred on by their desire, moving faster and harder. But still they did not stop.

"Do—Do the fae have a longer stamina than humans?" My throat was dry.

Varius chuckled. "Yes. We are immortal, after all."

"I—I just mean… how long does it last?" I couldn't tear my eyes away from them. "Won't they finish soon? What will they do afterward?"

Varius was silent for so long that I looked at him. His expression was torn between amusement and confusion. "I thought you said you were familiar with the male body."

My cheeks heated. "I *am*. But… it… well for me, it hasn't lasted very long. Not *this* long."

Varius tilted his head, considering this. "Then whoever is pleasuring you is doing a terrible job. When done *properly*, it can sometimes last for hours. With multiple climaxes."

My heart seized in my chest, and heat pooled in my belly. *Stones, multiple climaxes?* Surely this had to be something unique to the fae. I couldn't even imagine such a thing with Gerard.

My thighs tightened, and I resisted the urge to squirm on Varius's lap.

Something brushed against my arm, and I turned to find Varius's barbed tail coiling toward me. Despite the sharp points, its touch was soft and feather-light. I sucked in a breath as it dragged slowly down my arm, then curled against my calf.

The first time I'd seen his tail, I had perceived it as a weapon.

If he thrashed his tail against an opponent, it could easily tear through flesh.

But this... The movements were delicate enough to tickle my skin, proving that even the prickliest parts of Varius were capable of tenderness.

I sucked in an unsteady breath. "What are you doing?" My voice was as shaky as my breathing.

"Proving to you how much I can make you *feel*... even without my hands on you."

Cool air whispered against my skin, making the hairs on my arms stand on end. I suppressed a shudder, glancing down to find a tendril of Varius's shadows creeping up my leg.

"Don't worry, *dannahla*," Varius murmured in my ear. "I meant what I said before: I won't touch you until you are *begging* me to." He paused, and a shiver of pleasure rippled through me. "But I can't speak for my shadows."

More shadows encircled my legs, then tightened like ropes. I inhaled sharply at the cool contact. The shadows loosened, then warmed slightly, and I wondered if Varius was reading my reactions and making it more... pleasant for me.

Why? Why was he doing this?

I was about to ask him when a thick shadow slid up my skirt and plunged between my legs.

I jerked wildly, unable to keep myself from crying out.

The shadow withdrew, leaving me panting. My legs parted of their own volition, and Varius's shadows inched closer, as if waiting for me to stop him.

I did not.

My body quivered with a need I didn't know I possessed. Could he really do... *this*? With his shadows alone?

The strand of his shadow thickened and solidified until it was almost corporeal. When it met my sensitive flesh again, it was firm and almost *hard*. Just like... just like...

The smoothness burrowed between my thighs. I let my head roll back against Varius's chest, my eyes closing.

"I think, darling wife, that you have been deprived of *true* pleasure." Varius's voice was hot in my ear. His shadows pushed inside me, and I writhed my hips with a low moan. "This is merely a taste of what I can do for you."

The shadows thrust hard, and I bit down on my lip to keep from screaming. My thighs spread wider, urging him onward. The shadows twisted, curling inward, driving into me with relentless intensity.

"Oh, *Stones*," I breathed.

"If you want me to stop, just say the word."

"Don't stop."

His shadows pounded into me, harder and faster. The feel of them, gliding through my body, burrowing deeper than I ever thought possible, made me see stars. Sweat trickled down my neck, and my body seemed to burn with each movement as his shadows claimed me. Again and again.

My arms lifted, needing to touch him. My fingers found his neck and tangled in his hair, which was thicker and more luscious than I imagined. "Varius," I whispered. Tension coursed through me in violent waves, winding tighter and tighter until I couldn't breathe. The sounds and sights before me faded. All I felt—all I *knew*—was the force of that hard strength thrusting into me. He consumed my senses, driving all other thoughts from my mind. I needed more of him. So much more.

All too suddenly, the shadows vanished, leaving the wetness between my legs painfully unsatisfied. Panting, my eyes opened, and I found myself stretched out on Varius's lap, legs wide open and back arched against him like some feral creature.

I swallowed hard, righting myself as I turned to look at him. He offered an infuriating smirk that made my blood boil.

"If I made you come right away, where would be the fun in that?" he taunted.

I gritted my teeth, trying to ignore the restless heat stirring within me, begging to be satiated. "That was cruel."

"That was a mere demonstration. Your pitiful human lovers might bring you a moment of release, but I can make it last for hours, *dannahla*. Just say the words." His dark eyes glittered with a challenge.

I met his stare and lifted my chin. I refused to admit just how much his shadows had affected me. And I would *never* reveal how much I yearned for that release. It would mean that he'd won. "No."

He grinned, showing his fangs. A hungry look sparkled in his eyes. This was a game to him. A dance. He had made the first move.

Now, it was my turn.

"Dance with me," I said.

Varius's eyes narrowed with suspicion. "Why?"

I smiled, feigning innocence. "Because you are my husband and I want to dance."

"You were dancing perfectly well without my help earlier."

My eyebrows lifted. "So, you do not *want* to dance with me?"

"I—you—" A growling sound resonated in his throat.

My smile widened. He couldn't say no; that would be a lie.

I slid off his lap, my movements slow and deliberate as I made sure to drag myself directly over his hardened length. Stones, it was much larger than I expected. And the cloth was so thin that I did indeed feel the raised bumps he'd been referring to.

His eyes shuttered, and he groaned. I yearned to rip off that measly piece of cloth to inspect him myself. And the bolder side of me was itching to know how it would feel to have something like that inside me.

No. I shut out the thought as soon as it appeared. *Don't let him win, Sybelle.*

No good would come from that line of thinking.

When I stood on the floor, I laced my fingers through his and tugged on his arm. "Come and dance with me," I said again.

I waited for him to refuse, or to jerk on my arm and drag me back onto his lap. I wouldn't have minded, really.

But then he would have to address *why* he refused to dance.

He looked at me with a conflicted expression. A muscle worked in his jaw, and his nostrils flared.

"If you don't want to, all you have to do is say so." I stared expectantly at him, but his huff of exasperation told me he saw right through my facade.

"One dance," he said, and I grinned at him again.

He let me steer him toward the crowd of dancers. A few couples were grinding against one another, faces full of rapture. Some fae formed large circles as they danced together with drinks in their hands. I noticed Enzira with a group of her friends, laughing and cheering. It brought a smile to my face to see her enjoying herself.

I twisted to face Varius, then draped my arms over him. He was so much taller than me that my hands could barely reach the back of his neck. I twined my fingers in his dark curls again, delighting in how soft and lush they felt.

My hips swayed as I inched closer to him until our bodies were flush against each other. He stared down at me, lips parted and eyes full of unexpected warmth. But he stood ramrod still, unmoving.

"Are you going to make me do all the work myself?" I teased, placing my hands on his hips and urging him to sway along with me.

He chuckled but obliged, his large body crowding mine. His chest was so warm as it pressed into me, and I let my palms rest against him, tracing small circles just above his nipples.

A low, rumbling sound resonated from his throat. His arm came around my waist, bringing me fully against him so I could feel that delicious hardness once more. I arched into him, and he growled again. His hands splayed along my back, the tips of his claws tickling my bare flesh. I suppressed a shiver, and a small part of me registered he could easily tear me to ribbons.

But I wasn't afraid.

I looked up at him with boldness and desire, realizing there was nothing about him that disgusted me or deterred me from the lust boiling through my body.

"Can I touch you?" I asked, overcome by the confidence swelling inside me.

"Yes." His voice was strained.

I raised my arms and ran my fingers over his full lips, pausing on those large fangs protruding from his mouth. His eyes closed as I traced each one, noting the sharpened points. All of his teeth were like blades, ready to cut and slice open. But they did not hurt me as I brushed my fingertips over them. If anything, the harsh lines of his teeth brought an acute sensation, sending waves of awareness pulsing through my body as they dragged along my skin.

My arms lifted higher, and I had to stand on my tiptoes to reach the curling ibex horns atop his head. I ran my hands over them, feeling their rough firmness. Varius made a strangled sound that hummed through my body.

"Does this hurt?" I asked, withdrawing my hands.

He grabbed my wrist, freezing me in place. "No. Please... keep going."

I blinked at him. His mouth was open, his eyes dark with need and desire. So, I continued my perusal of his horns, running my hands up and down them, teasing the rough edges and bumps.

Fascinating. I could study him all day. And I yearned to do just that.

My hands moved back down his face, gliding along the firm planes and ridges of muscle along his chest. I traced the charred mark on his shoulder where the deadly shadows had burned him, and his breath shuddered. My arms came around his back until my fingers flicked against the barbed points of his tail.

He hissed a sharp breath of surprise.

"Too much?" I whispered.

"Not at all." His voice was low and husky. I had a sense that no one was quite bold enough to explore his body like this. He was the king, after all.

Yes, he's the king, Sybelle! shouted a small voice in my head. *Where is your sense of propriety? Get ahold of yourself!*

I shoved the voice away. My fingers found a section of his tail that wasn't barbed, reminding me of the stem of a rose in between its thorns. I squeezed, feeling hard bone beneath the skin, almost like a spine.

He groaned, dropping his head to my shoulder, his breath shuddering.

I froze. "I'm hurting you." The sound he'd just made was *not* pleasant.

"These... parts of me you are touching," he panted, "are just... quite sensitive. They aren't... often touched like that."

"Should I—?"

"Do *not* stop."

I bit back a smile. So he enjoyed my scrutiny.

"As long as you allow me to return the favor."

I stilled, and heat pooled low in my core. *Stones, what am I getting myself into?*

"It's only fair," he added, "that I inspect your body with just as much care and attention."

"You already did that," I said, my voice a bit strained.

"No. My shadows did. I want to worship your body with my *hands*, wife."

The dark and seductive promise in his words made my toes curl. Part of me wanted to withdraw from him before he undid me completely.

But the more dominant side of me wanted to lean into him

and hold him to that promise, to see just what those clawed fingers could do as they explored every inch of my body.

Warmth clouded my throat, and I found it difficult to breathe. That aching need pulsed through me, making my thighs clench. Varius's body was so close to mine that he felt it.

He chuckled against my ear. "So, I am not the only one," he murmured, his breath tickling me.

I shivered.

"If you wish," he continued, running his claw along the outside of my forearm, "we could continue what we started. I could show you the true meaning of pleasure and fulfill you in every possible way. I guarantee I could make you come at least four times before the night is over."

My eyelids fluttered shut as that building ache between my legs only worsened. Stones, it was almost *painful*.

"Is that the Shadow Queen?" barked a voice nearby.

My eyes snapped open, and Varius's grip around me tightened. I turned my head to see who had spoken, and my blood chilled.

It was the same soldier who had harassed me in the training yard. He stood alongside Murvo, the captain, both of them clutching female fae against their bodies. Murvo's mouth pressed together in a thin line, and when he caught my gaze, he quickly looked away.

But the soldier looked positively gleeful. He pushed the female away from him as he sauntered closer to us.

"Ah, my king, but you don't expect to keep this lovely specimen all to yourself tonight, do you?" the soldier crooned, his eyes still fixed on me. They gleamed with a hunger that made my stomach roil.

All warmth from my dance with Varius fled my body, chilling my blood and icing my bones. Varius gripped my waist tightly and growled, "Yes, I do. Be on your way, Warwick." Inky black shadows pooled at his feet and spread along the floor.

"She is a *human* among the unseelie at our revel. If she is bold enough to participate in our festivities, then we must show her how it's done properly." He started to unfasten his trousers.

A roar burst from Varius's mouth as he moved between us, shielding me behind his large body. I clung to his arms, terror coursing through me like a swift current. Darkness clouded the room, obscuring the lights as his shadows swelled around us both.

"She is *my wife*," Varius snarled. "Now, leave us before I tear out your throat." I gasped as his wings twitched along his back.

Warwick raised his palms, but the smirk remained on his face. "Easy, oh great king. In past revels, the human brides were passed around the crowd for our enjoyment. I only assumed this one would be the same."

Nausea churned in my gut, and my eyes slammed shut. *Oh, Stones...* I found myself backing away from the scene, away from Varius and all these unseelie fae who were now looking at me like I was a snack.

Except for Enzira. Her wide, terrified eyes landed on me. In an instant, she was at my side, her arm linked through mine.

"We should leave," she hissed in my ear.

I nodded, glancing over the faces of the other fae. No one seemed perturbed by Warwick's proposal. If anything, they looked intrigued and even *eager*. A few males were loosening their own belts in anticipation.

Varius reached behind him to grasp my arm. "Sybelle..."

"I'm leaving," I said loudly, but my shaking voice betrayed my fear. "Thank you for the festivities, but I'll leave you all to enjoy the rest of the revel without me."

Before anyone could reply, Enzira steered me from the room. She threw open the first door she found. Perhaps the castle was on our side today, for it immediately showed us my chambers. Enzira and I rushed through, and she shut the door quickly behind us.

THE BEAST

♛

The moment Sybelle and Enzira vanished through the door, I had my hand wrapped around Warwick's throat and pinned him so hard against the wall that the ceiling and chandelier rattled. Around us, the music stopped, and gasps filled the air.

But I only had eyes for Warwick. I bared my teeth at him, allowing the fury roiling inside me to burst free. My fingers wrapped tighter around his neck, my claws drawing blood. My shadows, which had already surrounded us, thickened and roiled like black smoke. The lights were smothered, and it was only thanks to fae sight that anyone could make out what was happening.

But even as the black droplets ran down his throat, Warwick still managed to grin at me, a strained chuckle wheezing past his lips.

"You kill me," he rasped, "and you'll never know the answer."

"To what," I snarled, barely able to leash my temper. I was seconds away from slicing open his throat and watching him bleed out on the floor.

"To ending your curse."

Everything in me went still at his words. Behind me, Murvo said in a warning voice, "Warwick, *don't.*"

I could only stare at this soldier, who had a glint in his eye. He knew he'd won.

Still, I held his throat, keeping him pinned to the wall. I wasn't ready to release him. Not when he'd threatened Sybelle. This bastard had no ounce of remorse.

He would do it again. I was certain of it.

"You're bluffing," I hissed.

"I'm fae," he said with another hoarse laugh. "Can't lie."

"Then say it," I bit out.

"Loosen your grip," he choked out, "and I will."

A growl rumbled in my throat as I glared at him. He gazed calmly back, as if I weren't about to crush his windpipe.

He knew he had the upper hand.

Whispers and murmurs rippled around me. The revel had officially halted, and I was aware of every pair of eyes watching us.

Slowly, I relaxed my hold on him, but I kept my fingers on his throat, just to be safe.

"Talk," I said.

Warwick smirked, his mouth curling in smug satisfaction. "I swear on my life and the fae blood coursing through my veins that I know the key to ending your curse. Something you didn't know about before."

What the hell was he talking about? And how did he know this?

"*Warwick!*" Murvo barked. "That's enough."

I whirled, keeping a firm grip on the soldier while I glared at my captain of the guards. "Who are you to give him orders when his king holds him by the throat?" I roared.

"You are not his king," Murvo said, his voice surprisingly bold. Not once had he ever spoken to me like that.

I froze, my blood chilling. If Warwick was not one of my subjects, then…

Slowly, I turned to look at the soldier, my nostrils flaring. "Who the hell are you? And why are you in my court?"

"Ah, well, those are questions that I can only answer when you aren't threatening my life, good king." Warwick offered a lopsided smile that only fueled my rage.

With my free hand, I rammed my fist into the wall just inches away from Warwick's face. Fae screamed at the crash that echoed in the room. Stone crumbled, and my knuckles throbbed. But Warwick held my gaze, unperturbed.

"Murvo, who the hell is he?" I bellowed, my gaze never straying from Warwick's.

"Remember your bargain, captain," Warwick said loudly.

I scented Murvo's fear, a putrid thing that swirled in the air next to me. "I—I cannot, Your Highness. I am bound by fae laws."

I bit back a curse, resisting the urge to run my claws straight through Murvo's chest.

"Varius," said a soft voice to my right.

I didn't need to look to know it was Clermont, trying to quiet my fury.

But it was far too late for that.

"Varius, you should let him go." Clermont's voice was stronger now. I wasn't sure when he had appeared; perhaps someone had sent for him after Sybelle and I had made a scene.

Mother of Shade. *Sybelle.* Everything changed now that this soldier, this *intruder* was among us and knew about my curse. And with her here, it complicated things.

I couldn't risk her safety.

"If he is from another court, he could be a spy," I ground out. "I should throw him in the dungeons."

"He could also be a nobleman or a royal," Clermont said. "We cannot risk it. We cannot afford a war with another court! Release him, Varius. I am begging you."

I knew him well enough to understand he wasn't ordering

me but pleading. If anyone other than Clermont had been speaking to me in such a way, I would have broken their legs.

"Swear you will not bring harm to Sybelle," I growled, my eyes drilling into Warwick, "and I will release you."

Warwick hummed as if considering this. He leaned forward, drawing my claws deeper into his throat and allowing rivulets of black blood to spill down his shirt. "No."

My shadows exploded, and I unleashed a roar, shoving him to the floor and slashing my claws across his forearm. Blood spurted, soaking the carpet, and several screams rang out.

"*Varius!*" Clermont screamed.

"I don't care who the hell he is. Throw him in the dungeons," I said to no one in particular. "And Clermont—see that Murvo is awaiting me in my chambers."

I didn't wait for anyone to respond before I tore from the room, flinging the door open and stepping into whatever place the castle deemed fitting.

Any room was preferable to this. If I lingered around other fae for much longer, I was bound to kill someone.

I found myself in my own chambers. It was just as well. I needed to be alone to compose myself, but I also wanted to be alert the moment Murvo was brought to me.

That son of a bitch. That lying piece of shit. I didn't know what was going on, but I intended to inflict as much pain as was required for Murvo to give me answers. Fae bargain be damned.

I paced the length of my room, my steps hard and furious, my shadows spilling around me and swirling more violently than a rushing river. My fingers curled and uncurled into tight fists, and I couldn't keep my arms from trembling.

I distracted myself by changing into a loose tunic and trousers, feeling ridiculous wearing my revel attire. When I finished, I found myself pausing at the adjoining door to Sybelle's room. My hand stretched for the doorknob, prepared to open it and see if the castle would take me to her.

Seconds before touching the knob, I froze, my fingers stiff. With a growl, I withdrew and continued my pacing.

I didn't need to be around Sybelle right now. She couldn't see me like this. It would only frighten her further, and she was likely already terrified enough.

Besides, Enzira was with her, and she was quite capable. She seemed to sense when Sybelle needed assistance, and I respected her for that.

Fifteen minutes passed, and my anger only mounted as I considered every past interaction with Murvo. I trusted him. Relied on him. For a decade, he had proven his loyalty to me.

And he was betraying me with Warwick, whoever the hell he was.

When the knock sounded at my door, my shadows had thinned to a subtle mist that coated the floor. But within me, my anger continued to simmer.

I had just gotten better control of it.

Steeling myself with a steady breath, I opened the door and found a bound and gagged Murvo waiting on the other side. Behind him was Clermont, his face rigid and his jaw tense.

"As you requested," my steward said tightly before shoving Murvo toward me. I caught the captain before he collapsed to the floor, then glanced at Clermont. "And Warwick?"

"In the dungeons, as you ordered." Clermont wouldn't meet my eyes.

He was unhappy with this situation. I couldn't blame him. I expected a stern lecture from him later.

But for now, I only nodded once at him before shutting the door with my foot. I shoved Murvo forward, and he landed hard on his elbows with a muffled cry. One of his eyes was swollen and bloody, and a large gash on his shoulder bled freely.

I kicked him for good measure, then crouched before him, bracing my arms on my knees. He was whimpering, muttering something I couldn't make out from behind the gag.

"You know what I am capable of, Murvo," I murmured softly. "You know what my shadows will do to you."

He nodded quickly, tears shining in his eyes. His entire body was shaking.

"So, you will talk?"

Again, he nodded vigorously.

"I will remove your gag. But if you scream, I will slit your throat with my claws. Do you understand?"

Another nod.

"Very good."

Slowly, I slid the gag out of his mouth, and he coughed, then sucked in a ragged breath.

"Now, talk."

I sat back on my rear, arms still resting on my knees, and waited. My insides churned restlessly with rage and violence, but I held my body perfectly still.

"There is little I can s-say," Murvo sputtered, blinking more tears from his eyes. "Because of the b-bargain."

"Then, tell me what you *can* say. When was this bargain struck?"

"T-Two years ago."

"And you cannot say with whom?"

"N-No, Your Highness."

"Can you tell me the terms of your bargain?"

He shook his head.

I let out a frustrated sigh. "What *can* you tell me? Does it involve another court?"

"Yes."

"Can you tell me which court?"

"No."

I mentally ran through my list of enemies. The Earthen Court was high on that list, but they had no associations with the fae. Could it be the Sun Court? They had been quiet for the past decade or so, but Father had had strained relations with them once. Perhaps old grudges had been brought to light.

But with our shadows, who would seek us out? Who would target us? Most courts assumed the shadows belonged to me, and their fear kept them from invading. Anyone else believed a plague or blight to be upon our land and wanted nothing to do with us.

They weren't far from the truth.

"Do you know anything about the curse?" I asked quietly.

Murvo met my gaze, his lip trembling. "I know… that there is more to it… than you think." He gritted his teeth, and a vein flared in his temple. He shook, his face flushing as an anguished cry burst from his throat.

I had seen the effects of breaking fae bargains before. He was close to violating the terms of the agreement.

If the bargain killed him, he would be useless to me.

I gripped his chin with my hand, silencing him. "Don't," I warned.

He shook his head, his breaths coming in sharp wheezes. "He will kill me anyway. After this. It does not matter."

"Murvo," I said. "Do not do this. I can protect you."

He barked a humorless laugh. "No, you can't."

My grip on his face tightened. "*Tell* me what you can. I beg of you. If it can save my people, then…"

"I will tell you," he rasped. "But you must listen carefully, Varius. *Listen to me.*"

I nodded, my eyes intently fixed on him. My heart thrummed in anticipation, and my shadows billowed around us, forming a protective shield should anything or anyone interrupt us.

Murvo took a deep breath, then said in a rush, "Find the original script of the curse. In order to break the curse, you must… you must…"

"A human must willingly give her life for mine," I supplied.

"Yes, but... there are terms outlining the—the—" He broke off with a grunt, then inhaled with a rattling gasp. "There is more... that you must do... to..."

Blood trickled from his nose and mouth.

Shit. The magic was killing him.

"To... end the curse?" I urged.

He nodded, more blood leaking from his nose. "F-For a spell of that magnitude, the witch h-had to... had to... include... terms..."

My mind was working furiously to fill in the gaps for him. "She had to include... certain conditions, or else the spell wouldn't work. Is that right?"

"Yes. But... V-Varius, the most important thing... that you must do... The first condition... With her dead... there is... a..." He coughed, and blood spattered my tunic. But I didn't care. I gripped his collar with my free hand and jerked him closer, our noses almost touching.

"Tell me."

"There is another," he choked out. "Someone... else..." He trailed off, his breath leaving him. Blood now leaked from his eyes, which rolled back. His body started seizing in my arms.

My eyes closed as I cradled him against my chest, trying to soothe him through it. He was too far gone now. I had seen this happen before.

Even with strangers, it was difficult to witness. But I had known Murvo for years. I had trained with him. Regardless of the secrets he had kept from me, I had once trusted him in battle. We had been brothers in arms.

Before today, I had considered him a friend.

Each strangled breath of his seemed to twist a knife deeper into my chest.

All I could do was hold him as the magic claimed him. He continued to thrash, the movements jerky and wild. His blood oozed from every opening of his body, seeping into my clothes. He started gurgling on it, struggling to breathe.

Tears stung my eyes, but I kept them closed, holding him so tightly my hands went numb. It felt like an eternity before his body finally went still.

And as my captain lay dead in my arms, I wept bitterly for him.

The Beauty

The moment we entered my chambers, I removed the diamond tiara from my head and flung it across the room. My hands shook, and as soon as the diamonds were outside my reach, the terror and nausea caught up to me. I fumbled with the balcony doors, threw them open, and vomited over the balustrade. The contents of my stomach hit the stone below with a sickening splat.

I coughed, then wiped my mouth with the back of my hand when I was certain I was done. Slowly, I turned to face Enzira, who stood at the open doors with a look of concern on her face.

"I'm sorry," I muttered. "I took you away from the festivities."

She shook her head. "After a scene like that, you can be certain the king canceled the revel."

I closed my eyes, remembering Varius's fury and the way his shadows had swarmed around me. "Do you think Varius killed that soldier?"

Enzira's lips pressed together. "I don't know."

"Do you know him? Warwick, I think his name was. Do you know anything about him?"

"He's new. I know many of the soldiers here, but I don't recognize him. And the other maids, they compliment his good looks, but they don't know much, either. Not his family name or where he grew up. I didn't think it odd until now. We get soldiers from all over the Shadow Court, some who lived very quiet lives. It wasn't out of the ordinary."

I nodded, my brow furrowing. "But, what does he want with *me*? Why does he keep threatening me? Is it just because I'm human?"

Enzira gave me a pained look.

My gaze slid to hers. "You were here before—when the other human brides were here. Is what he said true? Did—Did the princesses get *passed around* at these revels?" Just saying the words made me want to retch again.

Enzira took a shuddering breath, her eyes shining with tears. "My lady..."

I covered my face with my hands, choking on a sob. "Stones, please tell me it isn't true," I wailed. "Please, *please* say it isn't true."

"My lady, please," Enzira said, her voice thick. I felt her draw closer to me, but I held up a hand to stop her. "I was so young back then. I didn't know... I had only heard stories. I—I'm so terribly sorry."

Deep down, I knew it wasn't her fault. And I knew she hadn't directly been involved in such vile behavior.

But it had happened. My ancestors, my *people* had been tortured and assaulted and raped among these fae beasts. All for their own amusement.

"Leave me," I whispered.

Enzira didn't move.

"Enzira, please let me be alone," I said, my voice firm and sharp. "I cannot look at you right now. Please."

"Lady, it isn't safe."

"Get out!" I shouted, jabbing my finger toward the door. "Now!"

Tears streamed down her face, but she nodded. She pressed her fist to her chest before fleeing the room. The door snapped shut with her departure.

I sank to the cold stone floor of the balcony, curling my body into itself as I continued to weep. The tears would not stop. They flowed down my cheeks, sticky and salty. The cool breeze whipped around me, and the moisture on my face burned from the cold.

I hadn't realized my fingers were touching the amber at my throat until Azure murmured, *"Sybelle, what's happened? Are you hurt?"*

I couldn't even find it in me to speak. I could only shut my eyes, letting the last of my tears trickle down my face.

"You found the stone, didn't you? Please don't be angry with me."

My eyes snapped open at that, and I sat up so quickly that my head spun. "What stone?"

Azure was silent.

"Damn it, Az, *what stone?*"

"Look on your vanity." Azure's voice was dejected and full of an emotion I couldn't place. I had never heard her sound like that before.

It almost felt like… *shame.*

Azure was never ashamed.

Alarm pulsed through me, swift and violent, as I scrambled to my feet. I darted into my room, then rushed over to the vanity. It didn't take me long to find it.

It was the black stone we'd found in the caves just before Clermont had come to collect me. I remembered how Azure had claimed it smelled like the shadows. I had refused to touch it. Stones, it felt like ages ago. An entire lifetime.

I had completely forgotten about this gem.

"What is it doing here?" I asked slowly, drawing closer to inspect it. When Azure didn't respond, I said, "Az! Answer me!"

"I was curious. And impatient. I am sorry, Sybelle."

"What—What did you do?" Fear iced my bones.

"You know I cannot wield the stones as you do."

"But this did not just *appear* on the vanity, Azure. What the hell did you do?"

"There's no need to be rude about it. I will tell you. The bag was open from the last time you sifted through the stones. You must have forgotten to close it."

"That's not true," I snapped. "I *never* forget to close it."

"I'm not lying to you, Sybelle. It was open."

A chill skittered down my spine. Shit, shit, shit… Why had the bag been opened? Had someone been snooping? Enzira? Varius?

Shit!

"What did the bag smell like?" I demanded. "Did you recognize the magic surrounding it?"

"No magic was used to open the bag. And I did not recognize the scent."

I wasn't sure if that information comforted me or not. It meant it likely hadn't been Varius; his shadows were always so potent around him.

"So, you took the black stone out?" I prompted. "Why? What did you learn about it?"

Azure hesitated for a moment. *"There was something familiar about it. I wanted to find out more. When I used my talon to draw it out, I heard a ringing sound. It was shrill and high, and it echoed through my entire body."*

I frowned. "Did that happen before, in the cave?"

"No, it didn't. But I realized I had heard that sound before. When I got the splinter in my claw."

I blinked, remembering the sharp gem-like thorn I had removed. I looked up, then moved over to the armoire, digging underneath a thick red cloak before finding the gleaming thorn I'd hidden there. I lifted it, turning it over in my hands. It was thin and translucent, but it emitted a soft crimson glow.

"Sybelle, the black stone smelled of the same magic as that splinter," Azure said. *"They come from the same power."*

"Can you show me where you got the splinter?" I asked. "Do you remember the location exactly?"

She huffed in annoyance. *"Of course. My memory is impeccable."*

"Save your arrogance for another time. I'm still angry with you."

The fact that she fell silent instead of teasing me with a clever quip showed just how remorseful she was. It dulled the festering rage still simmering in my bones.

"Let me change, and then you can take me there." I dug through the armoire, looking for trousers and boots.

"Sybelle, it's the middle of the night. You need to rest, and I won't be able to see it clearly anyway."

"You got the damn splinter at night, didn't you? You've bragged about your eyesight to me thousands of times. I know you can find it."

"But you won't be able to see."

I muttered a curse under my breath before stomping to the vanity again and pulling out the scaled pouch with my gems. I overturned it on the table, and the stones clattered loudly. My impatience grew as I scanned the jewels for what I was looking for.

There it was. A small, round opal. When I clasped it in my palm, it emitted a brilliant light that burned against my eyes. Squinting against the intensity of it, I dropped it into the pouch, then drew the strings closed.

"There," I snapped at Azure. "I have a light now. Are you satisfied?"

Once more, Azure was silent. I let her stew over my words while I changed into a corseted blue tunic, leather trousers, and the red cloak I'd used to hide the splinter. I had just tucked Wraith Killer into my boot when a knock sounded at my door.

My gaze snapped up, my pulse thundering in my ears. *Shit.* Was that Varius? Or Enzira? Either way, it looked quite damning for me to be in traveling clothes. And my gemstones were sprawled all over the vanity.

I thought about shouting for the intruder to go away. Or opening the door and pushing myself into the hall to hide the contents of my room.

The beating of wings outside the balcony drew my attention. There was Azure, her blue scales gleaming in the moonlight.

In that split second, I made a decision. I swept the rest of the gemstones in the scaled pouch, then tucked it into the pocket of my cloak. With hastened steps, I hurried to the balcony where Azure rested, already crouched low for me to ride. I didn't often do this—her back was quite narrow and bony with her long spine jutting from her scaly body. And without a proper harness, it was quite unsettling. I never felt safe or secure.

But we didn't have a choice right now.

Loud pounding hammered against the door now. It couldn't be Enzira or Ramia.

Which meant it was either Varius... or someone else. Someone like Warwick.

My breaths came in sharp spurts as I seated myself on Azure's back, then leaned forward to wrap my arms as tightly around her as I could. She made a low rumbling sound that I interpreted as a warning before she took off, her great wings beating on either side of me. Within moments, we flew into the sky, and the balcony behind me grew smaller and smaller.

THE BEAUTY

I was grateful I'd donned a cloak before taking off; the brisk wind nipped at my face and stung my cheeks. I clung as tightly as I could to Azure's back, the terrifying weightlessness of the ride making me feel as if I could slide off at any second.

Her descent was smooth and graceful, as if she sensed my panic. She landed with such agility that I didn't even feel a jolt or a bump when she hit the ground. In this moment, when my fear and adrenaline were so poignant, I appreciated that small act of consideration.

I held the opal stone in my freezing fingers, using it to cast a light around us. With the midnight darkness and the Umbra Mist engulfing us, it was hard to make out our surroundings, even with the stone. I squinted, shivering against the evening chill as I gazed up at the crooked trees towering above me.

"What is this place?" I whispered, pressing my free hand to my amber necklace.

"I've heard the fae refer to this as the Noxen Forest," Azure said. *"It's located just behind the training yard of the castle."*

I slid off Azure's back, keeping the opal stone gripped firmly in my hand. I lifted it and stared into the dark abyss of the forest before me.

Suppressing a shudder, I asked Azure, "Is it safe? What about the Necro Shadows?"

"They were not around when I came here."

I hesitated. Perhaps she was immune, but I certainly wasn't.

"These shadows are different, Sybelle. They do not smell like the Necro Shadows."

I frowned at that. "Is it Umbra Mist? Or the king's magic?"

"It is not anything I have scented anywhere else before. This particular kind of shadow is unique to this forest alone, as far as I can tell."

My eyebrows lifted. A new type of shadow that could only be found in this forest? My mind sparked with possibilities.

"Sybelle, no matter how angry you are with me, you must trust that I would never put your life in danger. I would never risk your safety if I did not know for sure."

I nodded immediately. "I know that," I said. Our connection was too strong to be broken over a single heated argument.

She would protect me with her life.

I took a deep breath and exchanged a glance with her. "Lead the way."

She made a low grumbling sound in her throat, then faced the forest and lumbered forward. Leaves and branches crunched under her feet, and I followed her dark shape. The opal stone gleamed, illuminating the shadowed figures of the trees. As we passed under the canopy, the stars and moon suddenly shrouded from view, I held my breath, waiting for the Necro Shadows to devour me.

But they didn't.

It felt much cooler within the forest, and I tugged my cloak more securely around my shoulders. Ahead of me, Azure patiently waited for me to get my bearings before continuing onward.

Even with the opal, the trees still looked black in the dark of the night. They seemed to creep toward me, prepared to swallow me up.

My breath shuddered, and I hurried to Azure's side, not wanting us to become separated.

"Is it much farther?" I whispered.

"We are close," she said. *"I can smell it."*

I nodded, clutching the opal so tightly that the edges dug small grooves into my palm.

A few minutes later, Azure came to a stop, then dragged one talon through the earth at her feet.

"Here," she told me. *"This is where I got the splinter. I was in so much pain that I wasn't able to investigate where it came from. But the ringing started in this spot."*

I drew closer, holding up the opal to inspect the area. All I could see were piles of leaves and twigs. I swung the opal stone left and right, then froze as something glinted from underneath the brush.

Squatting, I held the opal stone closer to the ground. Once more, I swung it like a pendulum, pausing when that gleam caught the light once more. It was shiny like a gemstone, standing out among the foliage.

"What is that?" I hissed.

Azure groaned, her head shaking. *"It's making that sound again."* Her voice was strained.

"I'm sorry. Give me just a moment." I sank to my knees, swiping away leaves and dirt to get a closer look at what was buried underneath. I thought about drawing Wraith Killer to dig into the dirt, but then I noticed a long, narrow spike protruding from the leaves. It was identical to what I had pulled out of Azure's talon. My pulse quickened as I brushed aside more leaves, careful not to skewer my finger on the barb.

A luminous red glow shone from underneath the pile of leaves. I dug deeper into the earth, and the light intensified, casting crimson shadows on Azure and me. With the strange light, I was able to set the opal down and dig with both hands, gathering piles of dirt and scooting it to the side.

At long last, a small hole rested before me, and inside was a gleaming red jewel the size of my head. Sharpened black spikes speared from underneath it, and the jewel was strangely lumpy in shape, like it had multiple layers to it.

It was unlike anything I had ever seen. Bigger than any gemstone I'd found. The coloring was similar to that of a ruby, but a lighter, more vibrant red.

As I stared at it, my eyes wide and my heart thumping painfully in my chest, a searing ringing sound split the air.

I cried out, clapping my hands over my ears as it seemed to pierce through my very skull.

Beside me, Azure grumbled in frustration, as if irritated it had taken me this long to hear the sound. Perhaps, with my human blood, I wasn't affected as easily as she was.

I hovered closer to the red jewel, squinting as I tried to make out the details. A gasp broke from my lips as I realized what it looked like.

It was a rose. The gem was carved into the exact shape of a rose, with layers of curved petals surrounding the bud.

Which meant the barbs *were* indeed thorns. Jeweled thorns.

"Stones, this is incredible," I breathed, still covering my ears to block out the shrill sound. It intensified, growing louder and louder until my ears were throbbing. I had to shut my eyes against the agony pulsing through my brain.

Azure whined beside me, ducking her head, her back bowing. Her ears tucked back, and she shifted her hind legs restlessly.

She was in immense pain. I had to get her out of here.

Vowing to return to this exact place, I tucked the opal stone back in my pocket and climbed on her back. Together, we bounded out of the forest. Once we cleared the trees, she took off into the sky once again.

I was still breathless from my discovery when Azure arced around the castle, heading for my balcony.

I tugged on one of her scales to get her attention, then brought my hand to the amber stone. "Not my chambers. Can you take me to Ramia's?" I still wasn't sure who'd been pounding on my door earlier, but I didn't want to find out. I felt safer staying with my maid.

"*Of course*," was Azure's response.

Her wings shifted, and I felt the strong muscles move on either side of me. She veered to the left, circling around the other side of the castle and landing on a smaller balcony than the one outside my rooms. I didn't ask how she knew where Ramia's balcony was, but it didn't surprise me that she did.

Azure was always prepared, and she always knew more than I gave her credit for.

I cast a nervous glance toward the closed balcony doors. The curtains were drawn, blocking Ramia's room from view. She was likely sleeping.

With careful movements, I slid off Azure's back, then turned to face her. Her wide blue eyes blinked at me, full of sorrow and anguish.

I sighed, drawing closer and pressing my head to hers. She was warm and safe. She was *home* to me.

I touched my necklace and murmured, "I'm not angry with you, Az. But if you want to study the gems, all you have to do is ask."

"*I know. I am sorry. My curiosity got the better of me.*"

I chuckled. "We have that in common."

She nuzzled my neck with her snout, and I laughed again, stroking her head affectionately.

"*I'll be sleeping a few levels down. There's an empty guest suite with a big enough balcony for me to use.*"

"All right. Please be careful."

"*I'm always careful, human.*" Her voice was laced with that same amusement I knew so well. I smiled, grateful to have an echo of our usual banter.

I stood back to let her take off. She dove off the edge of the balcony, wings spread to slow her descent. I peered over the edge, watching as she settled onto a large stone platform a few levels below me. The sight of her so close to me, ready to come to my aid if needed, soothed some of the chaotic emotions roiling within me.

I took a deep breath and moved closer to the doors before tapping lightly on the glass. When Ramia didn't respond, I knocked louder, the pane rattling. I flinched, hoping there were no fae nearby who would hear.

A muffled exclamation sounded from within the chamber. An orange light indicated Ramia had lit a lantern. Within seconds, she was fumbling with the balcony doors. When they flew open, I offered a hesitant smile.

Ramia's graying hair was down, falling nearly halfway down her back. She wore a loose white sleeping gown and blinked blearily at me, as if she thought I was a specter come to visit in her dreams.

"I'm sorry for the intrusion," I said quickly. "But I don't feel safe in my rooms. Can I stay with you?"

Ramia uttered a soft gasp, then stepped forward to grab my elbow. "Of course, my lady."

I exhaled, relieved she didn't ask questions. I would have to tell her what happened sooner or later. But, as she guided me into her rooms and closed the balcony doors, I decided it could wait. I felt too emotionally exhausted to sift through the memories of tonight—the diamond tiara, my bold behavior with the king, Warwick's threats, the strange black stone, and my discovery with Azure in the Noxen Forest.

Not to mention whoever had been urgently trying to get into my rooms.

Ramia offered me her bed, but I immediately curled up on the sofa on the opposite end of her room, tucking my cloak around me. Wordlessly, she draped a large fur blanket over me and offered a gentle smile before she blew out the lantern and returned to bed.

When my eyes shut, I saw that same glowing red gem. It beckoned to me, as if calling me to return.

And I swore that I would. Soon.

THE BEAST

I summoned Clermont to take care of Murvo's body. My mind kept sifting through Murvo's last words to me, trying to make sense of them.

Find the original script of the curse.

There is more that you must do.

With her dead, there is another... Someone else...

Another what? What had he been about to tell me?

As for the original script, I had no idea where to find it. Journals had been passed down through the years, but all accounts of the sorceress's curse were from my bloodline. There was no way to know if the words documented had been an exact transcription of the curse or not. Even the alteration of one word could make a monumental difference.

I sat in the library, running a hand down my face for the hundredth time as I stared into the fire. No matter how many times I mentally ran over my interrogation with Murvo, it still didn't make any sense.

I needed to speak with Tislora. She knew ancient magic like this and might be able to shed some light on it.

But I didn't move from my chair. I couldn't bring myself to just yet.

Tislora knew everything about the curse. There had been a

time when we had shared everything together. When my father had been king, I had held nothing back.

But then, once he'd died, everything had changed. I had inherited the curse, and, from there, my life was not my own.

Tislora was clever and intelligent, and her resources were invaluable. I knew she could be of assistance.

But... she cared little for Sybelle. If I told her about Warwick, I knew exactly what she would say: *Who cares if the little human gets attacked?*

I gritted my teeth as I glared at the flames in the hearth. Much to my surprise and irritation, *I* cared what happened to Sybelle. I didn't want to. Hell, I had tried my damnedest not to.

But I couldn't stand by and allow her to be hurt, especially by a bastard like Warwick. She was my wife. Regardless of where she came from or how despicable her people were, she did not deserve to be left at the mercy of a fae like Warwick.

"Your Highness?"

I jolted, then turned in my chair to see Clermont standing at an open door, back rigid and hands clasped in front of him. Ever the waiting servant.

Only the cold detachment of his gaze indicated his displeasure with me.

I sighed. "Yes?"

"The task you requested of me is finished."

So Murvo's body was gone. A hollow feeling settled in my chest. "Thank you, Clermont."

He didn't move. He just continued to stare at me.

I did not have the energy for this. But my friend deserved an apology. "I'm sorry, Clermont. For putting you in this position. And for overreacting at the revel. I understand if you are irate with me."

Clermont remained perfectly poised and rigid, unresponsive to my apology. I watched him, waiting, unsure if I had the energy for anything more than that. But I waited for the inevitable lecture that was to come.

After a long moment, Clermont exhaled loudly, his frame drooping. He rubbed the back of his neck. "Varius, I am more concerned about your behavior and what our enemies can learn from it."

I frowned. "I do not know what you mean."

"I know what Warwick said to you. And what he implied about his loyalties."

I nodded, urging him to go on.

"When you reacted like that to him... it told him all he needed to know about how to manipulate you."

My head throbbed as I tried to understand what Clermont was insinuating. "Please speak plainly, Clermont."

He let his arms fall against his thighs in exasperation. "He threatened the human. And you practically skewered him with your claws. That kind of reaction is more telling than anything else. Now he *knows* he can use Sybelle to get to you."

My blood chilled, and a roaring sound filled my ears. Mother of Shade, how had I not considered this? With Murvo's death and Warwick's threat ringing in my mind, I hadn't considered...

"Shit," I hissed, rising to my feet. My shadows pooled around me, spilling over the carpet.

Clermont only gave me a somber look in response.

Damn it, I had been so foolish. I should have sought out my steward immediately. He was always better at thinking critically in these situations than I was.

And here I was, dreading a *lecture*.

Warwick was in the dungeons, but he hadn't been acting alone. Murvo had been proof of that.

There could be others.

I lunged for the door. Before I could reach it, a figure appeared on the threshold, gasping for breath. It took me a moment to see through the haze of my panic. Alarm coursed through me when I recognized Enzira. She clutched the doorframe, breathless, as if she had sprinted here. I wondered how many doors she'd had to step through before the castle had brought her here.

"What's wrong?" I asked, my voice sharp.

"It's my lady—Sybelle. She—She isn't in her rooms. I can't find her anywhere."

I stepped forward, but Clermont gripped my elbow, his jaw tight. His eyes were fixed on Enzira.

"What else?" Clermont said. "There's more, isn't there?"

I glanced at Enzira, noting the terror in her eyes. She nodded, then swallowed. "Her room has been ransacked. I—I don't know who was in there, but someone tore the place apart, searching for something."

I sprinted for the door, and this time, no one stopped me. Enzira darted out of the way as I barreled through, my shadows swirling around me like gusts of wind.

The open door led me to the hall of the queen's chambers. Several other doors were open along the wall, indicating Enzira had searched them all before finding me. I peered into each one, thinking perhaps Sybelle might have shown up after Enzira left.

But each door only revealed the same location: the training yard.

I stilled, staring at the fourth door that opened to that same location. The same place where Warwick had first noticed Sybelle.

My mouth fell open. Mother of Shade, the castle had been trying to warn us. Why else would it have led us there? Why else was it showing me this place right now?

The castle hadn't been toying with us at all. And, once again, I was a bloody fool.

I grabbed the door handle and slammed it shut, then took a

deep breath. "Please show me Sybelle's room. I need to search for clues. Please."

I threw open the door, and blinked as Sybelle's chambers greeted me. But they were almost unrecognizable. Bookshelves had been toppled over, leaving the tomes strewn all over the floor. Some had pages torn clean off. The armoire sat open, and several silk dresses were crumpled on the floor. The vanity's drawer had been removed and its contents scattered.

My arms shook, the room darkening as my shadows thickened. Rage clouded my mind, roaring and screaming. I blinked through the haze, and my eyes shifted to Sybelle's bed. Pillows had been shredded, their feathers spread across the room like snow. And someone had dragged a thick blade straight through the mattress, slicing it in half as if it were made of butter.

This place hadn't just been ransacked. Someone had left a message.

For me.

My breaths came hard and fast. Red crept into my vision, mingling with the dark mist of my shadows. A roar built in my throat, and it took all my restraint not to unleash it.

Think, Varius, I told myself. *Take a breath and think.*

In this moment, I needed to be like Clermont. I needed to think about this critically.

I inhaled deeply through my nose, then forced myself to exhale slowly. Three breaths later, I could see clearly again. The violent rage simmering in my blood had dulled, but it was still there, ready to be loosed.

I turned to find Enzira and Clermont standing at the door. Enzira was watching me, her face stricken with terror. Clermont surveyed the room, his lowered brows the only indication of his concern.

"When did you last see her?" I demanded, my gaze fixed on Enzira.

"I walked her to her chambers after we left the revel," Enzira said quickly. "I—she was upset. I tried to console her, but she—she wanted to be left alone." Her cheeks flushed, and her eyes shifted away from me. I sensed there was more she wasn't telling me, but I didn't press her.

"So, you left?" I asked.

"Yes. It seemed like she needed her privacy, and I assumed she would be going to sleep soon." Her voice trembled. "I—I did not know, Your Highness! Mother of Shade forgive me for my negligence." She fell to her knees, burying her face in her hands as she sobbed. "It is all my fault. I should not have left her."

My chest tightened at the sight of the maid so distraught over Sybelle's disappearance. "Please," I said in a strained voice. "Enzira, this is not your fault. I need your help to find her. You are the closest to her. Is there any place she might have gone?"

Enzira sniffed and wiped her nose, then looked up at me through tear-filled eyes. "I am not the closest to her. Ramia is."

Ramia. It took me a moment to place the name. Then I recalled the severe-looking human female who had accompanied Sybelle here. Her own personal maid.

Of course. Why hadn't I thought of it?

"Where is her room?" I asked, my voice full of urgency.

"I will show you." Enzira climbed to her feet and disappeared through the door. Clermont and I followed her down the hall, past half a dozen doors. At the end was one that was open, still beckoning me to the training yard. Enzira gestured to it with a helpless expression on her face.

I slammed this door shut, too, and took a deep breath. "Please," I begged the castle. "Please show me Ramia's room."

The handle underneath my fingers hummed in response, as if taunting me. Gritting my teeth, I said, "I just need to see Ramia. Just for a moment, and then I will go to the training yard. I swear I will heed your warnings. *Please.*"

I opened the door, and a darkened room awaited me on the other side. Soft snores filled the space.

I suddenly felt uncomfortable intruding on the maid's privacy. I cleared my throat and knocked loudly against the open door.

A grunt sounded, followed by a shrill shriek. A loud thump echoed, and a female swore loudly.

I frowned. That did not sound like Ramia.

I sent a tendril of my Lumen into the bedchamber to illuminate the space. The moon-like orb hovered high in the air, casting a soft glow on the room.

From the bed, Ramia was sitting up, clutching the sheets to her shoulders. Her face was paler than death.

And by the sofa, a figure lay sprawled on the floor, a blanket tangled around her legs. It only took me a moment to recognize her.

It was Sybelle.

She jumped to her feet, wrapping the blanket around her shoulders. Her eyes blazed as she stared at me, fury etched on her face.

"What the hell are you doing here?"

THE BEAUTY

MY HEART CAREENED VIOLENTLY IN MY CHEST AT THE SIGHT OF Varius standing in the doorway. Ramia quickly lit a lantern, illuminating his wild eyes and mussed hair. His wings were partially out, but he didn't seem to notice. He only strode toward me, eyes wide as they roved over me, assessing.

"Sybelle," he panted, his voice full of disbelief. "Are—Are you hurt?"

I blinked, some of my ire fading as I registered the panic in his eyes. "No," I said slowly. "No, I'm fine."

Clermont and Enzira appeared behind him. Enzira peered over Varius's shoulder, and when her eyes met mine, she let out a yelp of alarm. Shoving Varius aside—shoving the damn *king* out of her way—she stumbled toward me and squeezed me in a tight embrace.

"Mother bless me, I was so worried for you, my lady!" she sobbed. "I thought you had been abducted or killed, and it was all my fault! I'm so sorry, lady, so very sorry."

I drew back and pressed my hand to her cheek, catching her tears. "Enzira, why would you say that? What's wrong?" My gaze slid past her to meet Varius's. In my language, I said, "What happened?" In this moment, I didn't care that I'd just revealed to everyone that I could speak Agnarrish. It didn't matter.

Varius took a step toward me, his eyebrows lowering. His

expression turned thunderous. "Someone broke into your rooms and ransacked them."

My blood chilled. "*What?*"

Varius quickly filled me in on the state of my room. With each word he spoke, my insides turned hollow.

The mattress sliced in two.

Furniture splintered and broken.

Drawers overturned.

Everything in my room had been searched.

I thought of the pouch of gemstones still tucked into my cloak pocket. I didn't dare glance at them, worried someone might notice. At least I'd had the foresight to take the jewels with me before leaving with Azure.

I folded my arms over my chest, shuddering at the thought of how close I'd been to confronting the thief. It had to have been Warwick, or someone working for him. Who else could it have been?

"Do you have any way of discovering who did it?" I asked. "Some kind of magical means? Maybe whoever was in my rooms left some... trace or aura behind?" I was reaching; I had no idea if such a magical detection process existed.

"Perhaps," said Varius. "I can have Tislora look over everything tomorrow."

I pressed my lips together, saying nothing. Somehow I doubted Tislora would want to help me.

"Where did you go?" Varius asked. "You weren't in your rooms, so we thought..." He ran a hand through his hair and heaved a breath. "If you weren't in there when the intruder was going through your things, then where were you?"

I exchanged a quick glance with Ramia, whose face paled. She knew. She knew I'd been out with Azure. My eyes flared wide, and she nodded slightly, her gaze resolute and determined.

She would keep my secret. Her expression said as much.

Realizing Varius was waiting for an answer, I said quickly, "I came to stay here with Ramia. I didn't feel safe in my rooms."

This was all true. Although, if Varius asked me where I'd gone directly after the revel, I wouldn't be able to lie to him.

Varius cleared his throat and nodded. "Yes. Well. I'm glad you decided to do that."

I stared at him, vividly remembering how Enzira had confirmed the human brides had been mistreated during past revels. "Did you know?" I said sharply.

Varius froze, eyeing me warily. "Did I know what?"

"Did you know what they did to the human brides at revels?"

The room fell deadly quiet. Next to me, Enzira uttered a soft gasp, her hand going to her mouth. I squeezed her free hand, hoping she knew I wouldn't betray her trust. I would never tell Varius it was Enzira who confirmed this information for me.

"If you're talking about what that bastard Warwick said..." Varius growled.

"*Fae cannot lie,*" I snarled. "It doesn't matter *why* he said it. It's the truth. So answer the damn question."

Clermont cleared his throat and drew forward, his expression stern. Varius lifted a hand to stop him, his dark gaze fixed on me.

"Leave us," he said quietly. "Please." He looked at me, but his command was clear.

Clermont and Enzira obeyed, although the latter gripped my hand tightly, her face still covered in tears.

Ramia drew closer to me, her chin lifted. "I will not leave unless my lady commands it."

I shot a grateful look at her. For a moment, I was tempted to ask her to stay.

But Varius had been forthcoming in our previous discussions. Well, partially forthcoming. And last time he had confided in me, I'd stormed off before allowing him to explain.

Somehow, I doubted he would be as amenable to answering my questions if Ramia were here.

"It's all right." I patted Ramia's hand and nodded at her. "Let me speak with him alone."

Her lips thinned as she glanced between us. Then, with a sniff, she grabbed her shawl and bustled out of the room. I noticed she left the door cracked open, but I didn't object.

I crossed my arms and stared expectantly at the king. "Well?" I knew I was being rude, but I didn't care. This was too important.

Varius closed his eyes, inhaling deeply before replying. "When my father was king, he did… many things I did not agree with. When I opposed him, he had me whipped. Or threw me in the dungeon for days at a time. After a decade of this, I learned to mind my own business.

"I did not pay much attention to what went on when the human bride arrived. I did not like how the other fae treated her. But I knew if I spoke out about it, Father would punish me. Or worse, punish the *human* just to spite me. He had done this to me before. I knew how his mind worked.

"There was… talk of the goings-on at the revels. I tried not to pay attention to it. And I never attended revels when my father was present because of his abhorrent behavior. I wanted nothing to do with it."

Varius's frame slumped, his expression turning dejected. "I have many regrets, Sybelle. Too many to count. And one of them was not standing up to my father when it mattered the most." When he met my gaze, a haunted look took over his face. His eyes were full of torment. "I am sorry. I do not know for sure what happened to the human brides, particularly during revels. But I went out of my way to ignore the horrors I suspected were going on in my home. And for that, I am sorry."

I stared at him, torn between revulsion for the sake of my people and hatred toward Varius's father. My breaths came in sharp spurts, and I suddenly found it hard to stand. Slowly, I sank to the edge of the sofa where I'd been sleeping, my hands shaking as I tucked them into my lap.

My insides felt numb. Nausea churned within me, and my eyes closed against the grief and agony coursing through me.

Several moments of silence passed between us. I sensed Varius watching me, but I couldn't look at him. All I could do was sit there and count my breaths, trying to make sense of all this.

At long last, I whispered, "You said to me I was the only human foolish enough to attend a revel." My gaze finally met his. "You lied?"

"I cannot lie. And… I said you were the only human to attend a revel as an *invited guest.*" He grimaced apologetically.

My eyes narrowed. "How convenient. I suppose that's the last time I'll trust what comes out of your mouth."

He bared his teeth at me. "I *did not lie.*"

"No, you just twisted your words, like all fae do." I angrily waved my hand in the air.

"What did you want me to say, Sybelle? That I suspected your ancestors had been raped and tortured by my father? Would that have made you feel better?"

I jumped to my feet, my face on fire as I glared at him. "It's not about making me *feel* better, Varius. It's about disclosing the truth to me. *That* is what I value."

"Even when the truth is disgusting and horrific?"

"Especially then! Because if you are honest with me about the terrible truths, then I know you'll be honest with me about *everything.*"

Varius fell silent at that. His face was still hard and unyielding. Our gazes locked, and neither of us looked away.

But he did not argue. I waited for him to defend or excuse his actions again, but he didn't.

To my utter shock, he said quietly, "All right. I can do that."

I blinked, stunned. "You—what?"

"I said, I can do that."

My mouth opened and closed.

He sighed. "I will be completely honest and forthcoming with you from now on, Sybelle. Or at least, as honest as I can manage. Is that sufficient for you?"

I swallowed, an unexpected warmth creeping up my throat. "Um. Yes. I think so."

"Good. I'll start right now. I believe the castle has been warning us from the beginning. Do you remember when we ended up in the training yard?"

"Yes. That was when Warwick threatened me."

A low growl rumbled from Varius's throat. "He did *what*?"

I quickly told him about my first interaction with Warwick. Varius's nostrils flared, and his dark shadows spilled over the floor, creeping toward me. I knew by now that they weren't dangerous, but I still edged away from them.

"That bastard," Varius hissed. "I'll snap his neck. I'll rip his arms clean off."

"As delightful as your threats are," I said, "I need to know what else he said to you at the revel."

Varius heaved a deep breath, then shook his head as if to clear his thoughts. "I can… only tell you part of it. The magic of this land prevents me from speaking about certain things." He gritted his teeth as if he were physically held back from saying more.

I bit down on my irritation, knowing it was not his fault. "All right."

"He has information for me about—about—" He broke off with a curse, and I recalled how he'd said there were certain things he could not utter because of magic that had bound him. "About how to stop the Necro Shadows," he finally said. "And he told me he does not belong to this court. He is not under my jurisdiction."

I gasped, raising a hand to cover my mouth. Warwick did not belong to the Shadow Court? Then, where the hell was he from?

The look of confusion and frustration on Varius's face told me he had no idea either.

"So, he is blackmailing you?" I asked.

"Essentially, yes."

"And you think the castle was leading us to the training yard to warn us about him?"

"Yes. In fact, when I was searching for you, every open door revealed the training yard. Even now, in the dead of night."

I glanced at the window, which showed the early rays of dawn.

"Or rather, the early hours of the morning," Varius amended, following my gaze.

Stones, we both had been up most of the night. And yet, the adrenaline coursing through my body made it impossible for me to sleep.

"But it doesn't make sense," Varius continued, rubbing the back of his neck. "Warwick is in the dungeons, so why would the castle send us to the training yard again?"

I straightened, leveling a determined look at Varius. "I suppose there's only one way to find out. Let's go to the training yard."

Varius's eyebrows lowered. "Absolutely not. You will stay with Enzira and Ramia, and you will rest here. I will investigate on my own."

I scoffed. "You will not. This concerns me as well as you. Warwick threatened *me*. He ransacked *my* room. Besides, I am not helpless. I know my way around a blade."

To my annoyance, Varius laughed. "Human training means nothing when you are faced with an unseelie fae."

I scowled at him. "If you leave this room, I will only follow after you. I'll open doors and go wherever the castle leads me."

Varius's eyes flashed with anger. "Sybelle."

"Varius."

He exhaled, uttering a low sound in his throat. "You are impossible."

I smiled sweetly at him.

He rubbed his temples and said, "Fine. You will accompany me. But you must remain by my side at all times."

My smile widened. "I can do that."

THE BEAUTY

Varius gave me a moment to don my cloak and boots. I discreetly tucked Wraith Killer inside one boot for good measure.

Ramia was waiting for us in the hall. I quickly explained where the king and I were going, and she insisted on coming with us.

"It isn't safe," she hissed, her gaze darting to Varius and back to me. He stood a few paces away. He could most certainly hear our whispered conversation, but he was polite enough to pretend he couldn't. "It's still dark out, and I don't feel comfortable with you being outside the castle. Not with those shadows nearby."

"I'll be safe," I said quietly. "Varius won't let anything happen to me."

Her lips thinned as if she doubted this.

I wasn't sure why I was so certain of this statement. But something about the manic fury I witnessed from him earlier—when he thought something had happened to me—told me he would do anything to keep me safe.

"We won't be long," I assured her.

Varius drew closer and glanced between us both. "Are you ready, Sybelle?"

I nodded. Ramia crossed her arms and gave the king a stern look.

"Your Highness, I trust you'll make my lady's safety your top priority?" she asked.

I raised my eyebrows at the demand in her tone. I had to admit, Ramia was bold. Though Varius towered over her like a giant, she didn't even flinch. She met his steely gaze with her own, unafraid of the terrifying unseelie king.

Varius bared his teeth, revealing his lower set of fangs. Behind him, his wings twitched, flicking outward to cast a shadow along the hall. "There aren't many creatures who are foolish enough to cross me. I will protect her with my life."

Ramia nodded stiffly, and heat spread through me at the conviction in Varius's voice. He couldn't lie... so I knew he meant it.

A mixture of warmth and shock suddenly made it difficult to breathe. Over and over, those words repeated in my mind.

I will protect her with my life.

How had this happened? How had we reached the point where the Shadow King would *die* for me?

And... would I do the same for him? If his life were on the line, would I risk mine to save him? I wasn't so sure, and that knowledge filled me with a shame so potent that it blotted out any sign of warmth in my chest. All at once, I felt cold and hollow inside.

I felt like a monster.

He would die for me.

But I would not be so quick to do the same for him.

Varius extended his elbow to me, and I gave him an odd look. He shrugged one shoulder as if to say, *Why not?* I chuckled —the sound halfhearted as the conflicted emotions continued to war within me—then laced my arm through his. It seemed oddly formal, given that, only hours earlier, I'd been sitting on his lap and writhing against his body.

My face flushed from the reminder. Stones, that damned diamond tiara had made me behave with such reckless indecency. Just the thought of the things I'd said and done made me want to crawl in a hole and hide my face for a week.

Varius seemed to notice the stiffness of my arm in his. He cast a quick glance at me. "Are you well?"

I wanted to say, *I'm fine*, but that would have been a lie. Instead, I said, "It's been a long night."

He nodded as if this made sense. He guided me down the hall to the next available door. When he pulled it open, the darkened training yard greeted us. I suppressed a shiver, remembering Warwick's threats when I encountered him here.

"Are you sure about this?" I muttered.

"Not at all," he said before steering us over the threshold.

The cool early morning air nipped at my skin. With my free hand, I tugged my cloak tighter around myself. Varius pulled me closer to him.

I glanced at him, noting the tunic open at the chest, and the short sleeves along his muscled arms. "Does your skin provide its own heat?"

He smirked. "No. But my body runs warmer than most."

I could tell as much. Through the fabric of my cloak, I could feel that warmth seeping from his arm to mine. It was quite pleasant. A bolder side of me yearned to wrap both my arms around him so the left half of my body could enjoy the heat, too.

Ridiculous, I chided myself. *You are sleep deprived, and your brain is addled.*

That, and I couldn't shove the memories of the revel from my mind. His shadows driving into me. The way he hardened under my touch. The way his hips met mine as we'd danced.

That dark and heady look in his eyes when he'd stared at me...

I swallowed hard, shoving the thoughts away.

"Your pulse is racing," Varius noted. "Are you afraid?"

"No." My voice was a bit breathless. Changing the subject, I said, "What exactly are we looking for?"

"I'm not sure," he admitted, scanning the massive training yard. We weren't far from the spot where the castle had deposited us before. I wondered if that was significant.

I squinted, trying to make out the details from far away. The castle entrance doors were up the hill. I remembered racing toward those after my encounter with Warwick. A quick glance over my shoulder told me there was a forest nearby.

I frowned as I looked over the trees. "What's in those woods?" I asked.

Varius followed my gaze. "That's the Noxen Forest."

My insides jolted with recognition, and I sucked in a breath. Had it really been right here this whole time? Somewhere within those woods was the enchanted rose I'd been looking for. I was only *steps* away.

"What is it?" Varius asked.

Damn. He could likely sense my pulse spiking again. I wasn't exactly subtle in my reactions.

"I—I think I've been in those woods before," I said vaguely.

"When?" His voice was sharp. "You shouldn't go in there. There is dangerous magic in those woods."

"Of course," I said at once, then looked back toward the castle. "When do the soldiers begin their training?"

Varius continued to stare at me, his eyes practically drilling holes into my skull. *Please let the subject drop,* I begged. *Please...*

If he asked me directly about the rose, I would have to tell the truth. Guilt wriggled through me. I was such a hypocrite. I had just shouted at him for concealing the truth from me, and now I was doing the same to him.

After a long moment, Varius cleared his throat. "At daybreak. It won't be long now."

"And Warwick won't be there because he's in the dungeons," I mused aloud.

"Right." Varius rubbed the back of his neck with a sigh. "So, what does the castle want us to see? Why take us here before dawn?"

"Maybe we should ask the library," I said, half joking.

He shot me a bewildered look. "What?"

My smile faded. "The... library? It gives you books based on what you request." When he only gaped at me, I said uncertainly, "Does it not do the same for you?"

Half his mouth quirked in a surprised smile. "No, it doesn't. The fact that it does for *you* is an anomaly indeed."

My face heated. I wasn't sure why that felt like a compliment.

A bell in the distance started chiming, the sound echoing across the yard. I jumped, and Varius stiffened, squinting toward something to the west. From far away, voices rang out.

"Damn," Varius muttered.

"Alarm bells?" I asked in a whisper.

"No. Just the morning bell to signal the start of training. The soldiers will be here any moment. Let's return to the castle. We can try to come back later."

A wild and reckless idea came to mind, and I snatched his arm before he could turn away. "What if the castle sent us here to witness something important?" I asked, my hushed words coming out in a rush.

Varius's eyes searched mine. I instinctively knew he was following my train of thought.

If the castle *only* wanted to warn us about Warwick, it had already done that. Which meant there was something *else* it wanted us to know.

The voices grew closer.

"Sybelle," Varius said in a low voice. "You cannot be seen here."

I kept one hand on his arm while the other sifted through

the pocket of my cloak. The pouch of gemstones rattled, and I held my breath, thinking quickly.

This plan was dangerous. It required the use of one of my gems. Could I trust Varius?

I didn't have to explain about my magic. I could just imply the jewels were magical and came from my kingdom.

Or I could claim the same thing he had about the shadows, and say I was bound by secrecy.

Either way, I resolved then and there to *not* tell him about my fae magic.

Once more, that same tendril of guilt worked its way through me. I was keeping secrets, too.

But this was different. My magic did not affect Varius's safety at all.

The thought did nothing to ease the tense knots in my stomach.

"Neither of us will be seen," I said to Varius. "But I need you to trust me. Can you do that?"

Varius's brows knitted together, and he stared intently at me for a long moment. "Yes," he said at last. "I trust you, Sybelle."

The conviction in his voice sent another surge of warmth through my chest, followed by a twinge of regret.

Because I did *not* trust him.

More guilt. More lies. More deception.

It would never end.

"Come with me." My fingers interlaced with his as I tugged him toward the forest.

At first, he resisted. "Sybelle..."

"We won't go *in* the woods," I promised. "But we need some-thing behind us to provide camouflage."

After a moment, Varius relented, and he let me lead him toward the forest. When we were a few paces away from the darkened wood, I crouched low to the grass, the morning dew leaving wet patches on my trousers and cloak. As discreetly as possible, I tugged open the scaled pouch, making sure to keep it hidden in my pocket. Going by touch, I ran my fingers over each one, searching for the topaz stone. Its edges were slightly smoother than the others, and it was a rectangular shape.

There. As soon as my fingers closed over it, I felt the magic sweep over me. My other hand remained tightly enclosed in Varius's. An icy tickling sensation crept from the top of my head and inched down my spine. Beside me, Varius drew in a sharp breath, and I knew he was feeling it, too.

"What is that?" he hissed.

"Be quiet, or they'll hear you," I whispered.

I kept one hand firmly on the stone and the other tucked in Varius's palm. A few seconds later, the first of the soldiers emerged from the barracks. Some were jogging down the hill, while others ambled at a leisurely pace. One tall, wiry figure shoved another and laughed at something he said.

A low hiss emitted from Varius's lips, and I followed his gaze, my stomach hollowing.

Warwick was here.

"How the hell did he escape his cell?" Varius breathed, his chest rumbling with a growl.

I shook my head, warring between terror and anger. I couldn't tear my gaze away from Warwick. He was the tallest soldier, his bulky frame impressive compared to his peers. He strode downhill with a confident swagger that made my blood boil.

Bastard.

When over two dozen men were crowded at the bottom of the hill, Warwick clapped his hands together.

"All right, soldiers, you know what to do. Start with twenty laps. The one in last place has to take my spot in the dungeons tonight and relieve poor Rylen."

Laughter and howls met his words, and Warwick grinned in response.

Varius was rigid beside me. I turned to look at him, and his eyes were dark with fury.

"They broke him out," he whispered. "And left a decoy in his place. They… *defied* me. For him."

His dark brows were knitted together in confusion. Something akin to hurt and shame filled his features.

He had been betrayed by his own men. I couldn't imagine the pain this was causing him.

"Why is Warwick giving orders?" I asked quietly, changing the subject.

"Because Murvo is dead," he said softly. "And Warwick is the First Lieutenant."

My blood chilled. Murvo was dead? What the hell had happened? I scanned Varius's expression again, but his face had transformed into a hard mask, giving nothing away.

"But none of that should matter because Warwick should be in the *dungeons*," Varius seethed. "These soldiers shouldn't be running drills with him *at all*. Why are they acting as if everything is normal?"

Black shadows crept along the ground in front of us. I dug my fingernails into the back of Varius's hand.

"Stop that," I snapped. "I can't camouflage your shadows."

Varius's gaze jerked to me. "How *are* you camouflaging us, exactly? I thought humans didn't have magic."

I bit down on my lower lip, considering how to respond. If I dodged the question, he would assume I had magic of my own.

I made a calculated decision and withdrew my hand from my pocket, showing him the topaz stone. "With this. It has magical properties. I found it in a cavern near my castle."

Varius's eyes sharpened as he looked over the stone. He reached for it, but I tucked it back into my pocket.

"If I let go, the magic stops," I said by way of explanation, hoping he wouldn't press further.

I returned my gaze to the soldiers, who had begun running

laps around the length of the yard. Their strides were lengthy; at least twice as fast as I could ever run.

And Warwick was in the lead.

I felt Varius's gaze on me. I hoped he didn't notice how my palm began to sweat.

To distract him, I asked, "What does it mean that Warwick is in charge? Will all the soldiers follow him now? If so, that would explain why he seems so confident he won't go back to that prison cell."

"There's a captain for every squadron," Varius explained. "Until I appoint Murvo's replacement, Warwick would have been in charge of this one. The others are commanded by different fae."

I nodded, chewing on my lip. Just because *these* soldiers were loyal to Warwick didn't necessarily mean they all were.

But was there a chance Warwick could persuade the entire regiment of soldiers to follow him instead of Varius?

No, I thought at once. *Varius is their king. Surely he inspires more loyalty than some arrogant prick of a soldier.*

Even so, doubt crept into my mind. I didn't know anything about this court or its politics. For all I knew, the Necro Shadows looming nearby had caused the citizens to lose faith in their king.

And if Warwick claimed to know of a solution to the shadows, he could easily exacerbate the issue.

Varius and I remained silent as we watched the men run laps. It took them half an hour before Warwick stopped them. Panting, the men crowded together once more.

"Fallon is sleeping in the dungeons tonight," shouted a soldier, and several others laughed.

"Shut up," said the soldier who had to be Fallon.

"All right, all right," Warwick said, raising his hands to silence everyone. That same cocky smirk was back on his face. I wanted to punch it right off.

I hadn't noticed my fingers had clenched around Varius's until he whispered, "Easy. He can't hurt you here."

"I'm not afraid. I'm furious. I want to claw out his eyeballs."

Varius looked at me in surprise. Then, he chuckled. "You're a violent little creature, aren't you?"

I shot him a glare. "I'm not little."

"To me, you are."

I rolled my eyes. "Well, by human standards—or rather, *female* human standards—I'm taller and thicker than the ideal wife. Father always said it was a good thing I'd be married to *you* instead of a human prince or noble. Nobody else would want a body like mine to warm their bed."

I wasn't sure why I was saying this. But the more I spoke, the more my anger dissipated. The rambling had a strange way of calming me.

At least, until a low hiss expelled from Varius's mouth, and his shadows started swelling again. At first, I thought Warwick had done something.

Then, I realized the king was looking at me with venom in his eyes.

"Your bastard father actually said that to you?" he said through clenched teeth.

My lips parted as I realized he was enraged on *my* behalf. I snorted. "Don't worry, I didn't take it to heart. It's not the worst thing my father's said to me."

"Well, he's wrong," Varius bit out.

I blinked up at him. "About what?"

"About your body being undesirable."

My face flushed, and something hot coiled low in my belly at the intense way he held my gaze. "Is he?" My voice was slightly breathless.

Varius leaned closer until his mouth was mere inches from mine. "Do you not recall the way my body responded to yours at the revel?" His voice was low and sultry and made my blood heat. "That should be answer enough."

My eyelashes fluttered, but I didn't want to look away from him. I didn't want to break this moment.

"No!" shouted one of the soldiers, jolting Varius and me from our heated moment. "Warwick, it's too soon. We *can't*."

Shit. We had missed something important. Cursing myself for being such a fool, I loosened my grip on Varius's hand and shifted slightly away from the alluring warmth of his body.

The Shadow King was far too distracting.

Other soldiers were shouting now, their protests melding together until Warwick stuck his fingers in his mouth and whistled loudly. The crowd fell silent.

"I know you're all concerned," Warwick said loudly. "But with Murvo dead, our timeline has to be adjusted."

Beside me, Varius went perfectly still.

"We need to rally whatever forces we have," Warwick continued. "We still have the element of surprise on our side."

"What if your contact isn't ready?" asked a soldier.

"He's been ready," Warwick said. "I'm in direct communication with him. As of yesterday, he had a thousand men ready to march on the Shadow Court's doorstep."

My breath hitched, and my blood turned to ice in my veins.

Shit, shit, *shit*.

But which court was planning to invade? How could Warwick have rallied so many allies willing to attack Varius?

And who was his contact?

Warwick's voice lowered, so I had to strain to hear what he said next. "In three days' time, we'll rendezvous at Chesser Road. I'll give the signal for the all clear. And from there, we can make our move."

Horror pooled in my gut, churning so violently I thought I might be ill. Varius sensed it and looked at me with a question in his eyes.

I couldn't speak. If I did, I was certain I would be sick.

"What?" Varius whispered. "What is it?"

At long last, I found my voice. "Chesser Road… is the road that leads directly out of Terrona Castle," I said in a shaky voice. Slowly, I looked up at him with grief and regret swelling in my chest. "*My* castle. The kingdom that's invading is the Earthen Court."

The Beast

Thunder roared in my ears as I stared hard at Sybelle, trying to discern if she was lying to me. Her face was ghostly pale, her lips thin and her eyes flaring wide. She was shaking.

The scent of fear on her was pungent. It was so foreign, coming from her. I'd frequently anticipated her fear before, but she had always surprised me.

Right now, with her stunned gaze pinned on Warwick, it was as potent as ever.

A million questions raced through my mind. I wanted to yell. To smash things.

I couldn't do any of that here. Already, my shadows were oozing forward of their own accord, drawn out by my rage.

"Varius," Sybelle whispered, her breath a mere plea.

I closed my eyes, trying to reel my shadows in. "We need to leave. Now."

"We *can't*," she hissed. "If we move, the camouflage breaks. The stone doesn't turn us completely invisible, and these are trained soldiers. They will notice."

Damn it. She was right. I shot a glance behind us and swore under my breath.

It was the only way. My shadows were rippling, moving across the grass. Any second now, the soldiers would notice.

I gripped Sybelle by the arm. "Follow me."

Carefully, we inched backward, moving in the direction of the forest. Sybelle inhaled sharply when she realized where I was taking her.

"But you said—"

"I know," I said shortly. "It's either the woods or Warwick. Which would you prefer?"

Her mouth clamped shut.

The Noxen Forest was the last place I wanted to be. Especially with Sybelle. It was the home of all the reminders of my curse.

And it was dangerous. The sorceress's magic still lived in these woods.

A few steps more, and we would be under the cover of the trees. I cast a wary glance toward the crooked tree branches that looked like jagged teeth waiting to devour us.

"You command those soldiers," Sybelle said. "Can't you simply say you were... observing their training?"

"With you there?" I raised an eyebrow at her. "Not a chance. Warwick would see right through it. He was already suspicious of you being in the training yard once. And now we know this squadron is loyal to him and not me."

She shook her head, her breath shuddering. "What does he want with me?"

My anger flared again. "You tell me. He's from *your* court."

Her eyes narrowed. "He's fae."

Gritting my teeth, I shook my head at her naïveté. Humans could be so dim. Never seeing what was right in front of them. I opened my mouth to argue, but a sudden burst of my shadows rushed forward, spearing into the open air.

One of the soldiers shouted something, clearly noticing my magic.

Shit.

I tugged on Sybelle's sleeve and all but shoved her into the forest before jumping in after her. If we disappeared quickly enough, hopefully the soldiers would attribute my shadows to someone else's magic. In the Shadow Court, wayward shadows were not entirely unheard of.

Sybelle and I collided on the earthy ground, elbows and shoulders knocking together. She cried out in pain, but I clamped my hand over her mouth to silence her.

"The forest hears everything," I whispered. "Hold your tongue, human."

She jerked her head away from my hand and said under her breath, "So it's back to *human*, now that you think I'm a traitor?"

"I'll call you human when you act like one," I growled. "Short-sighted, narrow-minded, and downright ignorant to everything around you."

Her nostrils flared. "Should I call you beast, then? The brutal unseelie king who thinks all humans are scum, regardless of how innocent they might be."

"Innocent?" I wanted to shake her. How could she be so blind?

A harsh ringing sound split the air. Sybelle and I both groaned, clapping our hands over our ears.

Mother of Shade. The magic had found us.

"What is that?" Sybelle mouthed, her voice inaudible over the noise.

My ears throbbed as the sound only intensified. It wouldn't take long for my ears to start bleeding. After that, my brain matter would begin to deteriorate.

"This way!" I mouthed back, keeping my ears covered as I lumbered deeper into the forest.

Sybelle said something, but I couldn't make out the words. I glanced behind me and found her sprinting to keep up with my long strides.

The piercing chime reverberated through every bone of my body. My jaw clenched as I struggled to focus on the path ahead of me. It had to be close.

Unless I'd gone in the wrong direction. It had been years since I'd taken this route.

Behind me, Sybelle let out a harsh retching noise. I turned and found her on all fours, coughing up blood.

"Sybelle!"

If she didn't cover her ears, the enchanted tone would melt her brain.

She wheezed, and more blood splattered on the ground.

"Shit." I rushed to her side, dropping my hands so I could scoop her against my chest. The ringing blared against my skull, drilling harder and faster. The pulse hammered ruthlessly like an axe burrowing deeper and deeper into my flesh. I bit down hard enough to taste blood. The warm liquid trickling from my ears told me I was bleeding there, too.

Almost there, I told myself. *It has to be close.*

Sybelle's head slumped against my chest. She had lost consciousness. I shouted at her, but I couldn't hear my own voice against the ringing. My steps quickened, but my vision blurred. Blood trickled from my nose.

The thick oak tree ahead looked familiar. That had to be it.

I stumbled, nearly falling. My ankle rolled, and I groaned, leaning against the nearest tree for support. I took a breath and moved forward, edging around the oak until I saw what I'd been searching for.

A door.

I shifted my weight, lifting Sybelle with one arm so I could use my fingers to tug on the handle. The door flew open, and I lunged, not caring where it took us, just knowing we needed to escape.

I groaned as my body met the hard stone floor of my chambers. With my boot, I shoved the door closed, then let my head fall backward. My eyes shut tight against the agony quivering through me. The ringing had stopped, but it still echoed in my brain, blaring on and on. It would never stop.

I cradled Sybelle against my body. Blood coated her jawline from where her ears had bled. Her eyelids fluttered open as she gazed blearily at me.

"Varius," she mumbled, her voice sleepy.

"I'm here. You're safe." My voice was gravelly. Just speaking made my skull ache.

Both of us had blood dripping down our faces. Thankfully, we were close enough to my writing desk for me to grab a handkerchief and use it to mop up the blood on her face. When I finished, I folded it over and used the clean side to dab at my own wounds.

"What… happened?" Sybelle lifted a hand to rub her forehead and winced. "How did we get here?"

I crumpled up the bloodied handkerchief and set it on the floor. "When we discovered the dangerous magic lurking in the Noxen Forest, I had a doorframe built into the thickest oak tree. I hoped that using the same materials as the doors in this castle would allow its magic to extend to the woods." I offered a half smile. "It looks like I was right."

Sybelle's brows furrowed as clarity slowly crept into her gaze. "That horrible ringing sound… What was that?"

My gaze fixed on her, only just now realizing what this meant. "It's a protection spell that's meant to defend the magic of the wood."

"Defend against what? Intruders?"

"Defend against fae creatures." My voice was slow as I let the implication sink in.

She shook her head, frowning. "I don't—" She froze, then looked at me in horror. For a long, tense moment, we only stared at each other. My mouth set into a thin line at the guilt and fear that struck her expression.

"The sound only affects fae," I said. She had not been the only human bride foolish enough to enter those woods.

But she *had* been the only one struck down by the enchantment.

"Sybelle." My voice was low and dangerous. Every inch of me held perfectly still. I was aware of her body still sprawled on mine, but in this moment, I felt like a hunter who had caught his prey. "Are you fae?"

THE BEAST

I waited. Inside, my confusion and outrage roiled, but I remained frozen, staring at Sybelle while I waited for her to speak.

"Are. You. Fae?" I asked again, grounding out each word.

She inhaled a sharp and jagged breath, her face turning ashen. The fear emanating from her body was potent enough to taste. My hands tightened around her waist, keeping her pinned to my chest.

Neither of us moved.

Sybelle wet her lips, her breath shuddering. "Varius—"

"It's a simple question. Are you fae? Yes, or no?"

Her eyes closed. "You have to let me explain."

"*Yes or no?*" I bellowed.

"Yes!" she squeaked. "Yes, I am fae. *Half* fae. But—"

I slid her off me, depositing her on the stone floor while I lunged to my feet. An anguished sound built in my throat. I spread my arms wide, my wings flaring out, and unleashed a roar of fury. Shadows burst around me like puffs of ash, clouding the air and thickening until I could see nothing but darkness.

Sybelle was fae. My supposed *human bride* was fae.

She was a liar. Her entire family, they were liars.

I had been deceived.

And the curse… Mother of Shade, the *curse*—

I whirled to find her cowering on the floor, her small frame trembling. She stared at me with horror and dread, her eyes wide as saucers.

This was how she should have seen me from the beginning. When I had first shown myself to her, it had been this very emotion I had expected.

She was afraid for her life. She thought I would kill her.

I wanted to. I wanted to wrap my hands around her throat and choke the life out of her. My entire kingdom was at stake. Tens of thousands of fae were endangered by the Necro Shadows every day. And Sybelle and her family thought this was all a joke. They thought they could simply substitute a fae for a human and no one would notice.

I was a bloody *fool*. How had I not seen it? I knew what fae creatures were like. The way they talked, to avoid uttering untruths… Sybelle spoke this way, too. I should have *known*.

"Varius," Sybelle said in a broken voice.

"Don't talk to me," I growled. If she exacerbated my anger, I didn't know what my shadows would do. It was a miracle they hadn't suffocated her already. "I don't want to hear another word out of that lying mouth of yours."

"I didn't lie!" She climbed to her feet. "I *can't* lie. My fae blood prohibits it."

My lip curled with my sneer. "You preached to me about *twisting my words*. That's exactly what you've done this whole time, isn't it?"

"No!" she cried. "I was born with fae blood, but I was raised by humans. Every part of my life has been human. It's all I've ever known."

I shook my head, baring my fangs at her. I couldn't believe anything she said. How was I to know if half fae could lie or not? Perhaps they could, and this was another deception.

"Get out," I snarled, jerking my finger toward the door.

"No." She lifted her chin, her eyes flashing. "Not until you let me explain."

"Get out of my damn room!"

"*No!*"

I turned away from her, my fingers flexing as I let out another terrible roar. The walls shook, and the window pane rattled. When I turned to glare at her, she was staring at me, unflinching. Her fear had vanished.

Only stubborn determination remained.

I was tempted to throw her over my shoulder and toss her from the room. But I was afraid if I touched her, my claws would cut her to ribbons. I had very little control over myself and my body right now.

"Talk," I seethed.

She sucked in a breath, as if she hadn't expected me to let her speak. After a moment, she said in a rush, "My father wanted to produce an heir with fae gifts to defend against your kind. He trained me from birth to be the perfect wife, but it was all meant to deceive you."

A rumbling growl poured from my lips, but she raised a hand.

"I don't *intend* to deceive you," she said in an even voice. "If I did, would I be telling you all of this? Would I be betraying my father's trust and exposing his lies?"

I had no response to that. This was all under the assumption that she couldn't lie. I nodded, indicating she should continue. But I hadn't yet decided if I believed her.

She exhaled before going on. "My human bloodline protects us from violating the terms of our treaty. Technically, the Earthen Court still provided a human bride. But she was only half human." When I snarled at her, she quickly added, "This was how my father saw it."

"Oh yes, and you are completely blameless in all this," I sneered.

Her gaze sharpened. "This is what I was born to do, Varius. For my entire life, my father and my kingdom preached to me about the evils of the unseelie fae. How the Wraith King stole human brides to feast on them like a creature of the night."

I scoffed, but I knew there was truth to her words. Even in my own kingdom, villagers whispered about the horrible Wraith King. Those who did not know me thought I was a phantom who haunted the realm.

Was it really so outlandish that humans thought the same, if even my own people were saying such things?

"So, what then?" I asked, my voice carefully level. "You came here to kill me?"

She grimaced, her expression twisting with unease.

I barked out a laugh. "Who, *you*?" I gestured to her figure, which looked so small compared to mine. Especially with my wings out. "This slight, pathetic creature was meant to kill me?"

Her face flushed. "You have no idea what I'm capable of."

"You're right. I don't. Because you've been deceiving me from the day we met."

"So have you!" she cried, waving a hand toward me. "You've lied to everyone about the whole reason behind the human brides! We've *both* kept secrets, Varius. I am not the only one to blame."

My nostrils flared. "*Your* kingdom is the one plotting against me, Sybelle. That's pretty damning."

She shook her head. "Father would never invade. He's too afraid of your shadows. And with me here, his plan is still in play. None of this makes sense."

"It makes *perfect* sense. You are fae. So is Warwick. Clearly, your kind don't mind mingling with the fae if it suits their own purposes."

"*No*," she said firmly. "There are *no* fae in my court. I swear it. Father only had one fae concubine, and he killed her shortly after my birth. He despises the fae." Her eyes turned dark. "He despises *me*."

I refused to pity this lying creature before me, no matter how much her dejected expression tugged at something within my chest. "Then, what is your explanation for all this?"

She chewed on her lower lip. "I don't know." She paused, her gaze dropping to her hands as she wrung them together. "It—It is *possible*… that my father would invade, if he believed I was unsuccessful in my mission."

My eyes narrowed. She wouldn't look me in the eye. "Is it, now?" My voice was low and dangerous.

She finally met my gaze with guilt and fear swirling in her eyes. "But he would *never* ally himself with fae. *That* is what doesn't make sense. Even if my father is sending an army to invade, I know for a fact your forces can overpower him. And it still doesn't explain how he is connected to Warwick. If there are fae involved, this changes things."

I rubbed my chin, unsure if I believed her or not. I heaved a sigh, frustrated that I wasn't getting the answers I needed. My gaze suddenly snapped to hers, and I frowned. "What is your fae power?"

Sybelle blushed again, her mouth tightening. I was certain she wouldn't tell me.

But, to my shock, she said, "Gemstones."

I blinked. "I beg your pardon?"

She reached into her cloak and pulled out a small topaz stone. "This was how we were camouflaged earlier. It isn't a magical stone. It produces magic only when *I* touch it."

I frowned at the small jewel tucked in her hand. "Do all stones perform the same function?"

"No."

I waited for her to elaborate, but she didn't. I couldn't entirely blame her. She had already been more forthcoming than I'd anticipated. Certainly more forthcoming than I would have been if our roles were reversed.

Assuming she wasn't lying.

I crossed my arms. "Can you show me?"

Her brows lowered. "You want me to prove I'm telling the truth? Fine." She wrapped her fingers around the topaz and closed her eyes. She slowly backed up until she was up against the stone wall.

The air around her rippled, and in an instant, her coloring had changed. I could still make out the shape of her against the wall, but she matched the stone precisely. It looked as if she were shrouded in a cloak made of stone.

My arms dropped, and my mouth fell open in surprise.

Sybelle stepped forward and broke the enchantment. She tossed the topaz at me. I caught it easily, then turned it over in my hands.

It was a simple stone. No magic emanated from it. That much I could tell.

"Satisfied?" she asked.

I ground my teeth together, incensed at the accusation in her tone. She had no right to be irritated with *me* right now. She was lucky I didn't toss her in the dungeon for lying to her king.

"You never answered my question," I said slowly. "Did you come here to kill me?"

She was silent for a long moment. When she spoke, her voice was quiet. "I came here to infiltrate the Shadow Court and locate the source of the toxic shadows that are threatening my people. But, as I've come to learn, it isn't quite that simple. My court was under the impression *you* controlled all the shadows. Now I understand that's not true."

"You think I would simply allow my shadows to poison your people?" I growled.

"Yes!" she shouted, waving her hands in the air. "Because

you've told us *nothing*, Varius. What other conclusion are we supposed to draw? You are the king of shadows, and shadows are attacking my court."

"And you didn't think to *ask* me or my court?"

She snorted and crossed her arms. "When were we supposed to ask? Between giving you human brides and fending off attacks from your soldiers, we were a bit too busy."

My nostrils flared. "Your people haven't been welcoming toward my kind, either, Sybelle. Unseelie fae are hunted by human soldiers daily because of their prejudices."

She let her hands fall against her thighs. "I suppose both kingdoms are to blame for this, then."

"I suppose so."

A tense silence fell between us. Sybelle chewed on her lip, her gaze dropping to the floor. My wings curled inward, and my shadows thinned. Gradually, my anger ebbed, though irritation still prickled through me.

"For what it's worth," she said softly, "I'm sorry. For deceiving you. For not telling you the truth. I—I should have told you."

I stared at her. She blinked back at me, her wide eyes full of sorrow and regret.

I swallowed hard. "Thank you. I apologize as well. You're right; we both are to blame."

She nodded, her mouth forming a thin line.

More silence followed, but this time it wasn't as tense as before. I sensed something shift between us. Something that made it easier to breathe. Easier to look at her without anger.

"Do you still need my blood?" she asked suddenly.

I hesitated. "Yes."

"Even though it contains fae blood as well?"

"Yes. I may need more of it to dilute the fae blood. But it should still work."

She stepped closer to me. "And you still can't tell me what you'll do with this blood?"

"Tislora will make an elixir."

"Yes, you mentioned that before. But can you tell me *anything* else? What is causing these Necro Shadows? If it's not you behind it, who is it?"

The words rose to my lips, eager to burst free after all these years. But my mouth clamped shut of its own accord, controlled by the magic of that damned sorceress.

"All right." Sybelle raised her hands in surrender. "Can you nod or shake your head? Is that allowed?"

Slowly, I nodded.

She exhaled in relief. "Good. Is someone else controlling the Necro Shadows?"

Mother of Shade, how was I supposed to answer this? After a moment, I nodded.

"Do you know who is controlling them?"

Another nod.

"Do you know where they are?"

I shook my head.

She started to pace, one arm curled against her chest and the other raised so she could chew on her thumbnail. "Do you know how to find them?"

Again, I shook my head.

"Hmm." She walked the length of my bedchamber, her eyes distant as she worked over the information. Then, she stiffened and turned to face me. "Is this person dead?"

I nodded.

"Shit."

I chuckled without humor. "Shit indeed."

She laughed, then ran a hand through her hair. I was momentarily distracted by the way the chestnut tresses fell around her head in tousled waves, wild and free.

She looked stunning, despite the pallor of her face and the tangles in her hair from running through the Noxen Forest.

"Everything I've read about fae magic says it cannot supersede the fae's lifespan," she said. "So it doesn't make sense that someone can conjure magic and then *die*, and that magic lives on."

I said nothing. Even if I could speak, I wasn't sure what to say. The sorceress had possessed untold power, unparalleled by anyone my court had ever seen before. It was very likely she'd been strong enough to maintain this spell even beyond the grave.

And it was also quite possible the books Sybelle had read from were untrue.

Sybelle's wide eyes fixed on me. "Was this person fae?"

My mouth pressed together, forming a thin line. It had been nearly a thousand years since the spell was cast. The clans of witches had died out since then. Technically, they had fae blood in them, but it had been a distant line. Distant enough for there to be a division between our species.

I looked at Sybelle and shook my head.

Her lips parted in surprise. "*Not fae,*" she whispered to herself.

I cocked my head at her, fascinated by her process. She began pacing again. I noticed she chewed on her fingernails or her lip when she was concentrating. That faraway look in her eyes was identical to how she looked when something piqued her curiosity.

"You hesitated," she said, pointing to me as she paced. "Which means there might have been a reason to say *yes*, this person was fae. If this happened long ago, it wouldn't be too far-fetched to say the bloodlines mingled later on. So..." She gasped and whirled to face me once more.

"A witch," she said with a triumphant smile. "The person who cast the spell was a witch, wasn't she?"

Damn. My eyebrows lifted, and I gazed at her, impressed and awestruck. She was much more brilliant than I gave her credit for. "Well done, human. I'm not sure that this helps you, though."

"Oh, it does." Her grin widened. "It gives me *answers*. It gives me context. I can do a lot with this information." She rolled up the sleeve of her cloak, exposing her pale wrist to me. "Starting with giving you my blood."

THE BEAUTY

I nodded, my arm still stretched out toward him. "Yes. Now."

His mouth opened and closed. He gestured to the closed door. "I should fetch Tislora."

Before he could move, I said, "No. Not Tislora. I don't trust her."

He froze, going rigid as his gaze swept over me. I knew he read the underlying meaning behind my words.

I *did* trust him. But no one else.

He swallowed, his throat bobbing. "I'm… not sure I can do it properly."

My eyebrows lifted. "What, draw blood?"

He rolled his eyes. "Human, I can slice open your thin flesh faster than you can blink. I just don't know how much volume of blood Tislora will need for the spell, if it's diluted by fae blood."

"You can't tell her I'm fae," I blurted.

Varius frowned.

"You can't tell *anyone* that I'm fae," I said. "The secret is too dangerous. It risks my safety, and the safety of my people."

"Sybelle—"

"You were about to rip out my throat not ten minutes ago!" I argued.

"That was because of the deception!"

"Yes, and what will your people say when they learn about this deception?"

He had nothing to say to that. He sighed. "I do not keep secrets from Tislora."

I scoffed. "She's your subject."

"She's… much more than that."

I stilled, then scrutinized him. His mouth was drawn, and a muscle feathered in his jaw. His eyes were full of something soft and molten.

My chest cinched so tightly I couldn't breathe.

Oh, Stones. *Stones.*

She'd been his lover. She likely still was.

My throat was thick with emotion. "I see." The words came out strained.

Varius stepped toward me. "Sybelle."

I raised a hand to stop him, then drew back a step to put a healthy distance between us. "Kings are allowed their consorts, are they not? It's none of my business."

"*Sybelle,*" he growled. "It's not like that."

I snorted. "You don't need to give me details, Varius. We both knew this marriage was unwanted on both sides. You can seek your pleasures however you wish, and I'll do the same."

Varius stiffened, and his eyes narrowed. "What does that mean?"

How the hell did he have the right to be jealous right now?

"We never vowed to reserve our bodies only for each other," I said. "So neither of us would be breaking a vow if we were to take other lovers."

His nostrils flared, and black shadows spread across the floor. "I do not have any lovers. I forsook them all the moment you arrived."

The statement should have been comforting. But all I could envision was Varius wrapped in Tislora's embrace right up until the moment my carriage entered his kingdom. I pictured their naked bodies intertwined as a servant burst in on them to announce the human bride had arrived.

I had come between them. Even if they had parted ways, they still worked closely with one another. And he just told me he did not keep secrets from her.

Not even the secrets of his wife.

I hadn't seen Tislora at the revel. But if she had been there, would it have been *her* on Varius's lap instead of me? Would she have elicited those reactions from him?

Would he have given in and taken her against the wall? Would it have been her moaning with pleasure while he reached up her skirt?

Stop it, I told myself. Nausea swirled in my gut.

This was an awful mistake. More than anything, I yearned to take back the last hour, to erase from Varius's mind the secrets he had learned about me.

The secrets I had willingly given him.

My eyes closed, and despair coiled in my chest. I was such a fool.

"Sybelle," Varius said again, his tone gentler now.

My eyes snapped open, and I glared at him. The last thing I wanted was his pity. In an icy voice, I said, "You're welcome to keep warming her bed, Varius, if that's what you wish. Don't stop on my account. But don't tell her I'm fae. I won't give you my blood unless you swear to keep my secrets."

His exhale was long and slow. He gave a terse nod. "Very well. I swear it."

"Say the words," I snapped.

His eyes darkened. "I swear to keep your damn secrets, human. From everyone."

"Good. Now take my blood, please. I've had a long night and would like to return to my rooms to rest."

Varius's gaze sharpened. "You'll do no such thing. If you'll recall, your room has been ransacked. Not only that, but you aren't safe there. I must insist you stay in my room."

I barked out a harsh laugh. "Hell no. We just established a mutual desire *not* to share a bed with one another. You're lusting after the sorceress downstairs. I am *not* sharing a room with you. Not tonight. Not ever. I'll go and stay in Ramia's room again. Or Enzira's."

His shadows thickened and swirled, darkening the room with his rage. "Stop making assumptions about me. I am only concerned for your safety right now. And you are my *wife*. You are staying with me."

"I am not!"

"If you stay with your maid, what will happen if Warwick finds you? Will you be able to stop him? Will Ramia? Are you willing to risk her life? Would you have her die to protect you?"

Rage surged within me, and I took a step toward him, my blood boiling. "Stop that," I hissed. "You know I would never—I could never—" I blinked, my eyes hot at the thought of Ramia stepping in the path of Warwick's sword.

She would do it. I knew for a fact she would.

Enzira would, too.

A knot of emotion welled in my throat, and I swallowed hard. I could handle a blade, but not against a trained fae soldier. Perhaps with Wraith Killer, my diamond blade...

But Ramia and Enzira? Even with Enzira's fae abilities, I didn't think she could handle Warwick. And what if he wasn't alone? What if he had other soldiers with him? Earlier today, he seemed quite friendly with some of them. I had no doubt many would pledge their loyalty to him, even if it meant attacking the king's wife while she slept.

"Are you really going to let your jealousy of my relationship with Tislora get in the way of your maid's safety?" Varius asked.

"Shut up!" I snarled. "You don't know what the hell you're talking about."

"Don't I? Tell me you're not at all jealous. Say the words."

"I—I'm not—" I bit back a scream of frustration. I wanted to smack the smug expression right off Varius's face. I cleared my throat. "I will stay in your room," I said through clenched teeth. "But I'm taking the damn bed. You can have the sofa."

He chuckled. "Very well."

Seething, all I could do was glare at him while he looked as smug as ever. It was another game for him. Another round he'd won.

My irritation faded as an idea came to mind. A smile tugged at my lips. "Oh, and you wouldn't mind if I bring one of those soldiers into bed with me for a bit of fun, would you? I've been aching for a good shag with someone strong and capable, and the way those soldiers *moved* during training..."

Darkness exploded around me, smothering the lights and shrouding me in a massive black void. My taunting voice died in my throat as I was swallowed by shadows. I could see nothing. I raised my hands and wiggled my fingers.

Not even that could pierce through the darkness.

Somewhere in front of me, Varius was breathing heavily, as if he had sprinted up a staircase. He was making deep, guttural noises, like a feral animal.

"Varius?" I asked uncertainly.

After a moment, the shadows receded. I blinked, my eyes readjusting to the lightened room, then stiffened in alarm.

Varius's eyes were all black, as if his shadows had leeched away the whites of his eyeballs. I gaped at him in shock, unsure of how to respond to this. Was there a threat nearby? Were we in danger? I glanced around the room quickly, searching for an assailant. But we were alone.

Varius was still short of breath, his arms rigid at his sides. Behind him, his wings had flared, and his claws seemed even longer than before.

"Varius," I said again.

He shook his head, and his eyes cleared, returning to normal. They were still black, but with the whites, I could tell where he was looking.

And he was staring daggers at me.

"Don't ever do that again," he hissed, stepping toward me.

My head reared back. "Do what?"

"Joke about bringing another male into *my bed* with you."

I scoffed. "But it's fine for *you* to tease me about being jealous?"

"I was teasing you for your *unwarranted* jealousy! There is nothing romantic between me and Tislora."

"Well, there is nothing romantic between me and any of those soldiers!" I shouted. "It's the same thing, Varius. You wanted me to admit I was jealous? All right, I was. But so were you."

His nostrils flared. When he said nothing, I raised my eyebrows expectantly.

"Well? Aren't you going to admit it?" I planted my hands on my hips. "Or am I going to have to draw out your shadows again to prove it?"

"Fine!" he barked. "Yes. I was jealous."

"Then, we're even."

He bared his teeth at me, showing his fangs. And I glared right back at him.

I wasn't afraid of him. He was a spoiled king, and he needed someone to tell him *no* every once in a while.

We continued staring at each other, neither of us willing to concede first. And as my anger faded, I realized how ridiculous we were both being.

We were married. This fae male was my husband. And we had just fought over our previous lovers.

All so we could prove the other was jealous.

Stones, why were we both so *petty*? It was embarrassing.

I sighed, rubbing my forehead. There were far more serious matters to be concerned with. We were both being absurd.

"What are we going to do about Warwick?" I asked.

"We?" Varius repeated, eyebrows raised.

"Yes, *we*. He poses a problem for both of us."

Varius rubbed his chin. "I need to have him killed."

I stiffened, though the statement shouldn't have been surprising. Warwick was too dangerous. And I would certainly sleep better knowing he was dead. "How?"

"I know a skilled mercenary who can handle brutes like Warwick. I just have to ensure it's done quietly, so the soldiers don't revolt." His gaze darkened, his brows drawing together. A muscle feathered in his jaw, and I knew he was thinking of how his own men had betrayed him. How many more were working with Warwick? Would Varius have a civil war on his hands?

"And what about… Chesser Road?" I asked quietly.

"I'll have guards watching the area in case Warwick's contact shows up. But, hopefully, with him dead, the plan will not move forward. If his contact suspects Warwick was caught, it will throw a wrench in their plans."

"That's a lot of assumptions," I muttered.

Varius spread his hands. "There is not much else I can do, unless you can provide me with answers as to why your kingdom is working with the fae."

I grimaced. "I still don't know the answer to that."

A tense silence fell between us. Varius watched me, but there was no accusation in his gaze. Instead there was something softer. Something that made my stomach churn.

"Are you going to take my blood now?" I asked, trying to ignore my racing heart. "I'd really like to get some sleep."

Varius made a gruff sound before stepping toward a small desk in the corner. From one of the drawers, he withdrew an empty vial, then approached me. The anger brimming in his gaze told me it would not be a good time to tell another joke.

So, I remained silent, drawing up the sleeve of my cloak once again.

Varius held my gaze, his eyes never leaving mine as he drew closer to me. My pulse thrummed at his nearness. I was keenly aware of the wings still spread behind him, partially blocking the light from the sconces.

"Do your wings expand only when you're angry?" The words left my lips before I could stop them.

Varius's eyes narrowed. "Why?"

I shrugged. Once I'd started, I couldn't stop. "I was just curious if it was only anger that drew them out, or... other emotions."

Stones, what the hell was I doing? The adrenaline from our argument and my lack of sleep must have addled my brain.

To my surprise, half of Varius's mouth quirked upward. "If you want to know what my body can do while in the throes of passion, wife, all you have to do is ask."

My face flushed, but I forced myself to hold his stare, refusing to back down.

He stared right back, his eyes glinting with a hungry heat that stirred something low in my belly.

"Did you know that some fae can smell arousal?" Varius asked, his voice low and sultry. The sound made my insides coil tightly.

I forced myself to adopt a calm and apathetic expression. I lifted an eyebrow. "Really? Well, then you must have smelled positively filthy at the revel."

His eyes flared wide for a brief moment, and then he barked out a surprised laugh. It was such a loud and boisterous sound that it caught me off guard. I couldn't help but grin right back at him. There was something endearing about the way his eyes crinkled at the edges. The look of delight on his face made him seem youthful and full of life. So unlike the brooding king I'd grown accustomed to.

"You are full of surprises, *dannahla*." He grasped my arm, then drew a small dagger from his belt.

"You won't use your claws?"

He snorted. "Would you use a butter knife for sharp, precise cuts?"

"Are you comparing your fearsome claws to the dull ends of butter knives?"

He chuckled again. "No. But my claws are for ripping large chunks of flesh, like wild game."

"And enemies."

His face sobered. "Yes. That, too. Unless you want your arm to be cut to ribbons, I would recommend this." He waved the dagger before bringing it to my wrist—the same spot where Tislora had extracted blood from me before the wedding.

"Are you ready?" he asked.

I nodded. The blade pressed into my flesh. A pinprick of pain, and then the blood began flowing. Varius immediately brought the vial to catch each drop of blood. When it was full, he ripped off a piece of fabric from the bottom of his tunic and held it to the wound.

"Unfortunately, I lack Tislora's skills in healing," Varius said with a grimace. "So you'll have to have this bandaged."

I tilted my head at him and smirked. "It's only a small cut. How fragile do you think I am? I just have to apply pressure until the bleeding stops, and it'll be fine. It probably won't even scar."

Varius frowned and gazed down at my forearm, as if this information perplexed him.

I couldn't help myself. "Perhaps *my* body will surprise you with what it can do, too."

His eyes snapped to mine, and they seemed to burn right through me, scorching my blood. Heat pooled between my legs, and I knew he could sense it.

But I didn't care.

"You make bold statements, wife." His voice took on that low and husky sound again. I could have sworn he was doing it on purpose, as if he knew exactly what it did to me.

"Does it bother you?"

"Not at all. In fact, it does quite the opposite." He leaned closer.

My mind was spinning. What would the opposite of *bothered* be? Excited? Amused?

Aroused?

All thoughts fled my mind when his gaze dipped to my mouth. My breath hitched, and a deep sound rumbled from his throat, a cross between a growl and a groan. He lifted a hand, his forefinger hooking under my chin. The claw of his thumb tugged at my bottom lip, prying my mouth open. I held perfectly still as that claw traveled downward, dragging gently down my chin. I suppressed a shiver as my awareness homed in on that singular sensation of the sharpened tip pressing against my flesh.

But I was not afraid.

"Aren't you worried I'll cut you?" His voice was a murmur, his breath tickling my face.

"No," I whispered.

"Why not?"

"You wouldn't be a very competent king if you couldn't control your claws."

He huffed a soft laugh at that. "So, my beastly form does not frighten you?"

"No. It never has."

He hummed, the sound vibrating through his chest and warming my body. He withdrew a step, putting distance between us. I couldn't help the crushing disappointment that swept over me at the absence of his heat.

"Perhaps it should." He corked the vial and turned away from me.

I deflated, my shoulders sagging. Still, my pulse continued to race, and I knew my face was flushed again.

"I'll see that Tislora gets this for her elixir." Before he reached the door, he turned to look at me, his face a mask I couldn't read. "I can't promise she won't discern your fae bloodline. It's possible that, when she inspects the blood, she'll know."

"She's taken my blood before. And, if what you say is true and you don't keep secrets from each other, then she would have told you by now."

His lips thinned. "I should not have said that earlier. Tislora and I are… friends. We work together. But you are my wife, and my loyalty is to you. There was a time when I did not keep secrets from her. But that time has passed."

A knot formed in my throat, and I wasn't sure how to respond to that.

"I'll give you some privacy to dress before bed," Varius said. "I won't be long. But I'll make sure a soldier I trust is guarding the door."

My response was stuck in my throat. I couldn't form a reply before he opened the door and disappeared from view, leaving me alone in his chambers.

THE BEAUTY

STILL DAZED FROM MY CONFUSING INTERACTION WITH VARIUS, I strode into the bathing chamber and began to disrobe. When my cloak fell to the stone floor, a heavy *chink* sound echoed in the room.

My heart seized. *The gemstones.* I'd forgotten they were still in my cloak pocket.

I knelt to the floor and grabbed the pouch. I was about to tuck it back inside my cloak when I recalled what Azure had said. The strange black stone had emitted the same ringing sound as the gleaming red-jeweled rose in the Noxen Forest.

But they were clearly different stones. The black stone was quite different from the ruby-like features of the rose buried in the earth.

If I pulled out the dark stone, would the ringing noise return? Would other fae nearby hear it?

I certainly *was* feeling bold tonight. Despite the warnings blaring in my mind, I overturned the bag, dumping my gems onto the cold stone floor.

It called to me at once. The black jewel gleamed in the low light of the bathing chamber.

And once my eyes locked onto it, the searing ringing sound split the air.

With a yelp, I snatched the stone on instinct. I didn't know why I did it; all I knew was I had to silence it.

As soon as my fingers closed around it, the ringing stopped. The jewel began to warm my palm, sending heat up my arm and into my chest. I gasped from the intensity of it, prepared to drop it to the floor again.

But I didn't want that sound to return. I was sure Varius or Clermont or someone would come bursting in at any moment, demanding to know what was going on.

"She agreed," said a soft voice.

I jumped, whirling around. My hand went behind my back in an attempt to hide the stone from whoever was here.

But the bathing chamber was empty.

Heart racing, I looked around, wondering if someone was using magic to hide themselves.

"Are you serious?" asked another voice, this one female.

"See for yourself," said the first voice.

I wet my lips, my frantic pulse fluttering. The voices sounded *so close*. Once more, I surveyed the room, and my eyes snagged on the large oval mirror hanging on the wall.

It wasn't a mirror, but a *window*. I peered into it and made out two familiar figures: Varius and Tislora. He was holding out the vial to her.

Tislora's silvery eyes darted up to meet his. I quickly ducked to the side, worried she would see me.

But she didn't even glance my way.

With a frown, I glanced around the bathing chamber a third time, trying to figure out *why* Varius would have a looking glass in here.

But... it had been a mirror before. I was almost certain.

My breaths came in short spurts as I slowly lifted my free hand and waved it around my head, trying to get Tislora's attention.

She didn't even blink.

She couldn't see me at all.

I sucked in a sharp breath, unsure if I was hallucinating or if this was some strange magic I didn't know about.

Then, my gaze fell to the stone in my hand.

Holy shit. Was that its power? It allowed me to see through mirrors?

"How did you convince her?" Tislora asked. My gaze snapped to the mirror, my attention fixing on the scene before me.

"She offered it willingly," Varius said.

Tislora took the vial from him, uncorked it, and sniffed its contents. I held my breath, waiting for her to recognize the scent of my fae blood.

But she only wrinkled her nose. "Human blood is so foul. I don't know how you stand being in the same room as her."

Anger and shame washed over me, boiling my blood and cinching my chest. What a bitch.

"I hadn't noticed," Varius said.

Tislora snorted before pouring the contents of the vial into the cauldron in front of her. "Is she making you soft, Varius? I thought you hated humans."

"I only hate the ones who inflict harm on my people," Varius said. "And that does not include Sybelle."

Tislora laughed without humor as she stirred the liquid bubbling in the cauldron. "You really think she's much better, just because she's not on the front lines? She was raised to despise us, Varius. She believes us to be monsters."

"No, she doesn't."

"If you believe that, then you are a fool."

Varius growled, the sound low and threatening. "Watch yourself, Lor."

"She will murder you in your sleep," Tislora snapped. "That vile human brat is charming you, waiting for you to let your guard down. And when you do, she'll shatter the fragile remains of our kingdom."

Varius's black wings flared wide, his claws extending as a roar burst from his lips. "She is *my wife*, Tislora," he snarled. "You will show her the respect she deserves or I will slice open your throat."

Tislora's silver eyes flashed as she pinned him with a glare. "I'd like to see you try, oh great king."

"My lady?"

I yelped and dropped the black stone. It clattered loudly to the floor. In an instant, the scene in the mirror vanished. Heart pounding, I turned to find Enzira poised at the doorway of the bathing chamber, a small frown on her face.

Had she seen? Had she witnessed the magic in the mirror?

I pressed a hand to my chest, trying to calm my breathing. I carefully angled my body so I was blocking her view of the gemstones on the floor. "You scared me," I said breathlessly.

"Forgive me." She pressed a fist to her chest. "I thought you might need assistance."

I swallowed around the fear knotting in my throat. "I—I have had quite a rough night. I was going to bathe and get some sleep."

Enzira nodded with a hesitant smile. "I'll ready your sleeping gown."

She turned to leave, but I stopped her. "Enzira?"

She paused, not quite meeting my gaze. "Yes, my lady?"

"I'm sorry for my behavior toward you after the revel. I should not have yelled at you like that. I—I know none of this is your fault, and you have been nothing but kind to me. Please forgive me."

"All is forgiven, my lady. I do not harbor any ill will toward you." She met my gaze at last, her eyes guarded and full of despair.

My mouth opened to ask her what was wrong, but she left

the chamber before I could. I heard the door to the bedroom creak open as she no doubt went to fetch my clothes from the queen's suite.

Assuming they were still there and the thief hadn't ripped them to shreds.

When I was sure she was gone, I crouched to the floor, hastily sweeping the gems into the scaled pouch and drawing the strings tightly. Then I tucked it into the pocket of my cloak, which I folded and slid under a pile of fresh linens in the corner of the bathing room.

When Enzira returned, I had already undressed and lowered myself into the gaping hole that contained the hot spring below. The steam coiled around my bare skin, making me shudder. When I eased into the steaming water, I let out a groan of satisfaction.

"I'll never get used to this," I told Enzira as I leaned my head against the black stone behind me.

"You have a letter, my lady," she said.

I looked up and found Enzira with a strangely solemn look on her face, holding up a sealed envelope. I recognized the blue insignia of the Winter Court.

It was a letter from Eira.

My heart lifted, and I grinned. "Oh, thank you! Can you place it on the desk, please?" I was eager to see what Eira had to say.

Enzira nodded and smiled, but it didn't quite reach her eyes. She moved toward the bedchamber, but I stopped her.

"Enzira?" I straightened and looked up at her. "What's wrong?"

She sniffed and looked away. "Do not worry about me, my lady."

"Enzira."

"I—I will be fine." Her voice trembled.

"Are you still upset with me?" I asked. "Stones, I'm so sorry. You have every right to be angry with me. I—"

"No, no, it isn't that," Enzira assured me. When she finally met my gaze, her eyes sparkled with tears. "I—I *failed* you, my lady." Her voice cracked. "My duty was to remain by your side, to protect you during the revel, and I failed. I—I should be reassigned. It isn't right for me to keep serving you."

"Enzira, *no*." With a splash, I tried to climb out of the spring so I could reach her. But she waved her hands at me.

"Do not trouble yourself, my lady," she said quickly. "Please, tend to your needs. As I said, I will be fine."

"Enzira, you did *not* fail me. Would you say that Varius also failed me?"

She flinched. "Of course not."

"Well, he couldn't protect me, either. So please do not blame yourself. It isn't *you* who threatened me or ransacked my room. None of that is your fault. No one can possibly predict where our enemies will turn up. I couldn't, and neither could you. I do not blame you for any of it. I swear."

She pressed her lips together, and a tear raced down her cheek. "Those are kind words, my lady. But they do not ease my guilt."

"I understand. But please don't leave my service. I consider you a dear friend, and it would be devastating to lose you."

Her eyes shone, and she sniffed again. "Thank you, my lady. I do love our conversations."

I grinned. "So do I."

Her smile was genuine this time, and I relaxed in the springs once more.

I heard her bustling around the bathing chamber for a few minutes. Then, she went into the bedchamber to place my letter on the desk. With a sigh of contentment, I leaned my head against the stone and closed my eyes as the hot water bubbled around me.

I must have dozed off. Someone cleared their throat loudly, and I jerked awake, sitting up so quickly my head started spinning.

Varius stood in the doorway of the bathing chamber, leaning casually against the wall with an amused smile on his face. "Enjoying the springs?"

My face heated as I struggled to come up with a response. My brain felt like sludge, and I couldn't even form a coherent thought. "I—uh—"

"It's been an hour. I thought that would be long enough for you to dress for bed, but clearly, I was wrong." He sounded like he was trying not to laugh.

I rubbed my head. An *hour*? Stones… What the hell was wrong with me? "Sorry," I muttered. "It was just so comfortable."

Varius chuckled. "No need to apologize. I've done it myself a handful of times. I'll give you a moment."

He retreated into the room, and I loosed a breath, still mortified. After ensuring he was gone, I climbed out of the bathing hole and grabbed a folded towel Enzira had left nearby before wrapping it around myself. My sopping wet hair clung to my body, and I quickly wrung it out so it wouldn't drip so much. Already I was shivering, yearning to return to the heat of the springs.

I glanced around the chamber, frowning when I didn't see my nightgown anywhere. My eyes shifted to the doorway leading to the room.

Ordinarily, Enzira would lay my clothes out on the bed. She likely had done that here as well. I scowled, unsure if the mistake had been innocent, or if Enzira had known I would have to traipse naked through the room with Varius here.

With a deep breath, I lifted my chin and strode into the bedchamber as if I belonged there. I kept my gaze firmly fixed on the bed, noting the lacy, translucent undergarment waiting for me.

Irritation prickled through me. Oh, Enzira had *definitely* done this on purpose. This was the most scandalous garment I owned. It was about as modest as the red dress I wore to the revel.

A strangled sound came from the desk where Varius was sitting. I didn't glance at him as I snatched the undergarment and turned back to the bathing chamber.

"You—I—" Varius cleared his throat. "Should I leave again?"

I finally looked at him. He was rubbing the back of his neck, his gaze fixed on the floor. If I didn't know any better, I would've said he was *blushing*.

I couldn't help myself. I grinned at him. "Varius, you have seen me in much more revealing clothing than this." I gestured to the towel around my body.

He coughed. "It was dark at the revel."

My eyes narrowed. "You have fae sight."

"I—I simply wasn't expecting you. Like this." He waved a hand at me, still not meeting my gaze.

Reminders of how he had taunted me before rose to my thoughts. I smiled and inched toward him, noting the way his body went rigid in his chair.

"I am your wife, you know," I said. "It wouldn't be totally inappropriate for me to walk naked through the room."

His eyes darkened as he glared at me. "We haven't consummated."

"That didn't stop you from pulling me onto your lap and stroking me with your shadows."

"And *you* stroked *me* when we danced."

I leaned closer, my face hovering over his. "But you liked it, didn't you?"

A deep sound rumbled in his throat, like a moan mixed with

a growl. He gritted his teeth, his nostrils flaring, and I remembered what he said about scenting arousal.

Could he smell it on me now?

"Are you going to change?" he bit out. "Or will you continue to torment me?"

Quoting his words to me from a few days ago, I said with a laugh, "You make it so easy, *dannahla*."

I turned and strode into the bathing chamber. Perhaps I let my towel drop just before I disappeared from view.

Perhaps I heard Varius's sharp intake of breath as he no doubt saw my exposed backside.

As I slipped on my nightgown, I thought of the scene I had witnessed through the mirror. Had it been real? I had watched Varius give Tislora the vial of my blood. After leaving me, it would make sense for him to have gone straight to the apothecary so Tislora could make the elixir.

What other explanation was there? That scene *had* to have been real.

Varius had defended me in front of Tislora. He had threatened to kill her for insulting me.

I wasn't sure how that conversation had ended, but I was achingly curious. Had Tislora submitted? Or had Varius stormed from her chambers, fuming? He hadn't seemed upset when he'd shown up in the bathing chamber... Then again, finding me asleep in the hot springs might have lightened his mood.

I cringed as I braided my wet hair into a long plait down my back. Stones, I was an embarrassment. I thought of Tislora and her dark and elegant grace. I could see why Varius had been attracted to her.

But me? Compared to the unseelie, I was pale and frail and bland.

I was *nothing*.

A hollow feeling settled in my chest. Varius might be

attracted to me in some way or another. But he could never love me. Too much deception had come between us, and I could hardly compete with someone as stunning as Tislora. He had only defended me out of duty because we were married.

That was all.

Besides, I still had to track down the rose jewel. Now that I knew that grasping the black stone had silenced the ringing, perhaps I could do the same thing with the rose.

And maybe it held the key to ending the Necro Shadows.

But what if destroying the Necro Shadows means Varius dies? If I destroy the source of his magic... could it possibly kill him, too? I couldn't stop these questions from rising in my thoughts.

I shoved them aside. His shadows were different from the Necro Shadows. Surely, there would be a way to destroy one without the other.

But I knew one thing for certain: however I managed to vanquish the shadows would require me to betray Varius.

Because either I would have to kill him or destroy his magic completely—neither of which would be forgivable.

There could be no future for us at all.

It would be best if I pushed that fantasy from my mind entirely.

THE BEAST

I was poring over a letter from one of my captains when Sybelle finally emerged from the bathing chamber. I cut a quick glance her way, then looked away immediately, my face heating.

The scrap of fabric she wore covered even less of her body than that damned towel.

The quill I gripped in my hand snapped in two. This human was tormenting me. Ruthlessly.

She started climbing into the bed—*my bed*. She froze when she noticed a letter on the comforter. "What is this?"

"It was on my desk," I said, struggling to keep my voice even. "I assumed it was for you."

She lifted the letter and turned it over, her eyes narrowing slightly. "Did you read it?"

I stiffened at the accusation in her voice. "As you can see, the seal is *unbroken*. But I appreciate your demonstration of trust."

"Sorry," she muttered quickly. After looking over the letter once more, she stuffed it under her pillow. I frowned but said nothing, though I was deeply curious as to *who* the letter was from. The insignia did not belong to the Earthen Court. Who could she be writing to?

Hot anger flooded me as I envisioned her penning letters to a lover from another court. But I quickly shoved the thought away before it drove me mad.

Sybelle eased into bed, shifting to make herself comfortable. Her movements caused the lace fabric of her gown to ride up, revealing an alarming amount of alabaster skin. When it hitched up again, this time rising high up her thighs, I averted my gaze, gritting my teeth.

I tried not to think of her rolling around in my sheets. Of how they would smell like her now. Her skin. Her hair.

She's right, I told myself. *She's your wife. There is nothing wrong with this.*

But that wasn't true. There *was* something wrong with me lusting after a human whom I was using to break my curse. She was a means to an end, and there was no future for us. No matter how aroused she made me, or I her, this would only end in pain for both of us.

Because, in order to break the curse, she had to die.

It was the only way.

I cleared my throat and focused on my letter, re-reading the same paragraph three times without retaining any information.

"If you need to, you can go to the library to work on that."

I looked up. Sybelle was tucked under the covers, and she watched me with an unusually somber expression. All amusement from her earlier teasing was gone.

"I insist on staying here with you," I said. "Even with a guard stationed outside the door, I would… feel more comfortable if I remained here. Just in case."

She nodded, as if she expected this answer. She bit down on her lower lip, her eyes going unfocused.

I frowned. "Will it bother you if I'm sitting here?"

"No!" she said quickly. Too quickly. Then, she huffed a laugh, her cheeks going pink. "Actually, it would… do the opposite."

She was quoting my own words at me. Again. I stared at her, and she stared back, unabashed. Bold as ever.

Heat coiled low in my belly at the look she was giving me. Mother of Shade, this woman would be the death of me.

For just a moment, I indulged the thought of prowling over to the bed, holding her gaze as I made my way to her. I would climb on the bed, my large body hovering over hers.

How far would she take this little game between us? Would she let my hands roam over her bare flesh? Would she let me ease my fingers between her thighs to see just how wet she was?

When would she tell me to stop? When would that inevitable look of horror cross her features at the thought of *truly* bedding a monster like me?

I didn't want to find out. It would be best to cut this off now.

"I will be focused on my work here," I said in slow, measured words. Even so, my voice still came out a bit strained. "I'm sorry if it will be a distraction. But you fell asleep just fine in the hot springs. I'm sure you'll rest eventually." I smirked at the way her cheeks reddened before returning to my work.

I distinctly heard her mutter the word *ass* as she turned over in the bed, draping the covers over herself. I chuckled under my breath, grateful our game had halted.

For now.

I responded to a few letters before the exhaustion of last night finally caught up to me. After conferring with Clermont in the hall to ensure certain tasks were taken care of, I dimmed the lights and curled up on the sofa to rest for a while, hoping it would only take an hour or two before I was alert enough to tackle the next item on my agenda.

My dreams were plagued by shadow storms and the screams of my people—of the people I couldn't save, no matter how hard I tried.

The dream shifted, and I saw my father laughing at me for my weaknesses, taunting me for my growing feelings for Sybelle.

"A *human*," he spat. "They are nothing more than the dirt beneath our feet."

I tried to shout at him, to claim this wasn't true, but my mouth had been sealed shut. My scream drowned in my throat.

"Varius," whispered a voice that sliced through my dreams.

I stirred, and the vision of my father drifted away.

"Oh, *Varius*," the voice said, louder this time.

My eyes snapped open. The darkened room greeted me, and the auburn glow of the setting sun glinted from the windows. Slowly, I sat up, scanning the room. I was certain I'd heard someone call my name.

"Please don't stop," said the voice.

I froze, my skin prickling. It was Sybelle. But I'd never heard her voice like this before. It had a strange echo to it, ringing as if she were shouting in a massive cathedral.

With slow and silent movements, I slid off the couch and crept over to the bed. Sybelle was still tucked tightly under the covers, half her face pressed into the feathery pillow. Her chestnut hair was strewn around her like a lion's mane.

Aside from her soft, slow breathing, she made no sounds. She did not speak at all.

"Varius," said the voice again.

I turned and found a strange shimmering light gleaming from the bathing chamber.

I swallowed, glancing down at Sybelle once again. This felt like a trap. Clearly whoever was in the bathing chamber was *not* Sybelle. What if someone was trying to lure me away from her side so they could attack her?

"Varius, please." Sybelle's voice was a strained moan now, and my entire body stiffened at the note of pleasure in her voice.

She sounded like...

Mother of Shade. Was this real? Surely, I was still dreaming. I flicked one of my claws over my forearm and felt a sharp lance of pain. Black blood bloomed from the wound, and I sniffed it. The tangy metallic scent was familiar to me.

This was real.

I looked at Sybelle again, who turned her head slightly and let out a soft sigh. More moans echoed from the bathing chamber.

My curiosity got the better of me. Telling myself I would only peer into the chamber without actually losing sight of Sybelle, I inched closer to the bathing room. The glow intensified, forming a strange orange light that flared as if it had its own rhythm. In and out. Brighter and dimmer.

"Can I touch it?" Sybelle asked breathlessly, her voice bouncing off the chamber walls. Her breath hitched, and a surprised laugh rang out.

The light sharpened, and I squinted against its brilliance. When it faded once more, I pinpointed its source: a pile of towels.

I frowned. This had to be someone's idea of a prank.

I wouldn't at all be surprised if Warwick was behind this. It sounded like something he would do to drive me mad.

"Varius, I *need* you," Sybelle crooned.

The glow flashed, then faded, and I cocked my head, brow furrowing. There was a small bundle stashed under the pile of towels. Whatever it was partially blocked the glow.

I crept into the bathing chamber, each step slow and methodic as I waited for an assailant to jump out at me. When I reached the towels, I crouched to the floor before carefully easing them off the bundle.

I recognized Sybelle's cloak immediately. After sifting through the layers of fabric, I found a pouch made of some kind of rough material. The flash of light glowing from within nearly blinded me. Hissing against the blazing intensity, I pulled on the strings, fumbling with the small, round objects contained inside before I found the one that was glowing. When my fingers clamped around it, the glow disappeared, and I heard Sybelle's voice in my head as if she were crouched right next to me.

"Stones, Varius, it's so big," she breathed. *"Will it hurt me?"*

My mouth fell open in shock. I looked over my shoulder, half expecting to find Sybelle there, uttering these things. But I was alone in the chamber.

She was panting now. *"Please,"* she rasped. *"Please, I can't wait any longer."*

The object felt like a small rock. I pulled it completely out of the pouch, trying to blot out her loud moans from my mind.

It was a gemstone. The brownish-gold color matched the glow that had been beckoning me earlier. My eyes narrowed as I realized the gem looked familiar.

It was nearly identical to the one Sybelle wore around her neck every day.

Shock rippled through me. She said her fae magic was tethered to gemstones. Was this her magic at work? Was she summoning me to her in a dream?

My throat tightened. I didn't have to guess what she was dreaming about.

Me. And her.

Naked.

Sybelle cried out, and I jumped to my feet in alarm. Her shout tapered off into a moan of delight.

Whatever was happening in her dream had just escalated.

I looked down at the pouch on the floor, then glanced toward the bedchamber, unsure of what to do. Discard the gem and run to wake her? Or keep the gem in my hand in case the strange glow reappeared?

What did this magic *mean*? Was she trying to communicate with me? Was she in trouble? Or was this entirely accidental?

I clenched the stone so tightly in my fist that it formed small grooves in my palm. Gritting my teeth, I strode out of the bathing chamber just as another cry of ecstasy flooded my mind. Those sounds were driving me mad. She whispered my name, her breaths becoming more frantic and wild.

A building heat pressed in on me, making me hard for her, the aching need almost unbearable. It felt ridiculously unfair that Dream Varius was engaging in these acts with Sybelle while I was here, doing nothing.

And here I was, jealous of *myself*. It was ludicrous.

But I could guarantee that whatever she was envisioning in her dream was nothing compared to the pleasure I could give her.

I moved to the bed, noting the way she squirmed under the sheets. She murmured something incoherent, then sighed again, her body arching.

Oh, yes, she was definitely dreaming about something scandalous.

"Oh!" she cried out, the sound echoing both in my mind and from the sleeping figure before me. Her hips bucked, and she thrashed against the blanket.

My black shadows exploded from the bed, spearing in every direction and climbing the walls. I let out a shout of panic, trying to reel them in before they hurt Sybelle.

Then, I faltered. These shadows were different. They had a strange blue tint to them, and they were more translucent than my own.

My pulse skittered as I stared down at Sybelle, who still writhed against the blankets. Tendrils of that bluish-black smoke oozed from her fingertips.

My shadows.

"Sybelle," I said urgently, leaning down to shake her shoulders.

She hummed a soft sound, her eyebrows lifting. But she didn't wake.

"*Sybelle!*" I bellowed, shaking her more roughly.

With a strangled gasp, her eyes flew open, her pupils dilated.

Her body sank down into the mattress, suddenly going limp. Gasping for breath, she looked around in a daze until her gaze landed on me.

"Varius," she breathed. "What—"

Her eyes went from the stone in my hand to the shadows still climbing up the walls. Her face paled. "What the hell happened?"

THE BEAUTY

Varius's large body pins me to the bed, his strangled gasps tickling my ear. He buries his face in my neck, his incisors gliding up the column of my throat, scraping my flesh without breaking skin.

"You smell divine," he groans.

I arch against him, eager to have his hands on me. In me.

"Please," I gasp. "Please, I can't wait any longer."

"Patience, dannahla. First I want to make you so wet you'll soak these sheets."

I tremble from the promise of his words before he brings his mouth to mine. His tongue is long and smooth and plunges deep inside, exploring every part of my mouth. I kiss him back, hungry for more. My tongue brushes his sharp fangs, but I am not afraid. If anything, the point of contact sends shivers of awareness skittering across my body.

His hand moves between my legs, and my cry is part shout, part moan. He lightly drags one claw along my center, and I lose my breath, unable to even think clearly. One of his knuckles slides inside, and I shudder, my body taut with awareness.

"Mmm," he purrs. "So wet. But not wet enough."

He adds another knuckle. Somehow, he manages to stroke me without piercing me with his talons, his hand curling inward so his claws are angled toward himself. I remember his claim that he had perfect control over his claws.

Was this what he referred to?

I cry out again as his fingers pump in and out, gaining speed. My body writhes against him, urging him onward. My panting grows louder.

With his other hand, Varius cups my breast, pressing his thumb against my nipple. Stars burst in my vision, and I bite back a scream. My hips buck as I ride his fingers, desperate for release. I'm so close to the edge. So close to tumbling over.

Varius leans over me, capturing my nipple in his mouth. When his fangs drag along the peaked tip, my climax shatters through my body, breaking me completely. A strangled scream bursts from me, and I thrash against him, chasing that feeling over the cliff. Varius groans in my ear, his voice low and deep. I thread my fingers through his hair.

"Sybelle!" he says urgently.

I blink and stare at him. Something about his voice doesn't sound right.

I jerk violently, and Varius vanishes, his heavy weight and warmth disappearing. The vision before me fades, and I am yanked back to reality.

I startled awake, gasping, my pulse still racing from the events of my dream. Varius's hands gripped my shoulders, his eyes full of panic.

"Varius, what—" I froze as I noticed a gemstone in his hand. The shade of amber was unmistakable.

Horror tightened in my chest as I noted the dark shadows streaking along the walls. "What the hell happened?"

Varius lifted the glowing stone, his eyes sharp and full of accusation. "You tell me."

My brows knitted together. "Tell you what? I've been asleep! Why are you holding one of my gemstones?"

"It… called to me." His voice sounded uncertain.

"Called to you," I repeated. "How?"

For some reason, he averted his gaze from me, his lips pressing into a thin line. "I—I heard your voice, Sybelle. It was coming from this stone."

I sat up, clutching the blankets against my chest. I was achingly aware of my rather revealing nightgown, especially considering the wildly inappropriate dream I'd been having. The space between my thighs was wet and hot, and I prayed to every god I could think of that Varius couldn't scent my arousal.

"I followed the sound into the bathing chamber," Varius went on, still not meeting my gaze. "The stone was glowing. Only when I touched it did the light vanish. Then, I heard your voice in my head."

My mouth went dry. Shit… What did this mean? The amber stone was used to communicate with Azure.

So, why was Varius hearing me speaking to *him*? Azure could only talk to me when we were both touching the stone.

My hand flew to the necklace at my throat. Normally, I could only hear Azure's voice in my head when my *fingers* were touching the stone. I was never entirely sure why it worked that way—Azure didn't need to touch it with her claws. As long as she wore the jeweled collar around her throat, it worked just fine for her.

I could access magic from other gems by touching them with other parts of my body. The diamond tiara, for instance.

Was it possible the amber stone *could* be used to communicate with others, even if my fingers weren't touching it?

"Sybelle," Varius said, startling me from my thoughts. "Can you explain this?"

I licked my lips, and his eyes darted to my mouth. That unbearable heat between my legs only intensified as I realized we were both sitting very close to one another on the bed.

I scooted backward, trying to keep my movements subtle. Clearing my throat, I said carefully, "The amber stone allows me to… communicate with others. Mentally."

Varius frowned, then glanced at the necklace. "Who have you been communicating with?" His voice was laced with suspicion.

I flinched. *Stones, what do I do?* If I avoided the question, he would assume I was feeding information to the Earthen Court.

But I couldn't tell him about Azure.

Or could I? He already knew about my gemstone magic.

No, I thought firmly. *Azure is not my secret to tell. I can't betray her trust. I can't tell Varius about her unless she gives me permission to do so.*

I had to think quickly. Varius's eyes were narrowing with distrust.

"I wear this necklace for sentimental reasons," I said. "It brings me comfort when I'm alone or afraid. In the Earthen Court, I used it to speak with my best friend."

"Does this *friend* also have an amber stone?"

"Yes. But the magic doesn't work from this far away. I'm not able to communicate with anyone in the Earthen Court."

Varius stared at me, his expression hard. I stared right back, fully aware that everything I uttered was the truth.

"Sybelle?" asked a voice.

I almost yelped in surprise, then quickly let go of my necklace. If the amber stones were somehow working on Varius, I couldn't risk him intercepting any communication with my dragon.

I had no idea if anything Azure said to me would be overheard by Varius with *his* stone.

Varius cocked his head at me, his eyes sweeping over my form. "Your heart is racing."

"Can you blame me? You shook me awake like the castle was on fire. Was this all just because the stone was glowing?"

"No," Varius said in a tight voice. "You also summoned shadows."

I blinked. "I... summoned shadows?"

"Yes. They were not mine."

"How can you be sure?"

He gave me a flat look. "I *know* my magic, Sybelle. These shadows were thinner and bluer than mine. I had no control over them."

I snorted. "You already have no control over your own shadows, Varius."

"I have *some* control," he said defensively.

I shook my head. "I don't understand. How did *I* summon shadows? Are you sure it was me? There are lots of other fae in this castle who might have access to that kind of magic."

Varius stroked his chin, considering this. "You could be right."

But none of this explained how Varius could hear my voice calling him through a stone in another room.

"When you heard my voice," I said slowly, "what was I saying? Are you absolutely sure it was me?"

"Yes," he answered quickly. *Too* quickly.

I looked at him, but his gaze was fixed on the sheets as he fisted them in his hand.

"Varius," I said.

Slowly, he met my gaze, his eyes guarded.

"What was I saying?" I repeated.

He swallowed, and his throat bobbed. "You—You were dreaming. I think."

My stomach hollowed. *Oh, shit.*

"You said my name," he said.

My eyes closed. *No, no, no.*

"I—" Varius coughed, then shifted his weight on the bed. "I'm fairly certain… you were dreaming about me… and…"

"Stop." My voice came out strained. "Don't—Don't say any more." My face was on fire. Stones, I wanted to disappear. I wanted to sink into the covers and bury my face until I died of shame.

"Sybelle." His voice was gentle.

I winced. "Please don't." I couldn't bear to look at him.

His warm hand pressed against mine, and I drew in a sharp breath.

"I had a similar dream," Varius said quietly. "After the revel."

My eyes snapped open at that. "You did?"

He nodded, half his mouth quirking up. "You made quite an impression. That dress…" He made a low humming sound that only reminded me of my dream. My legs clenched together. "The things you did to me, sitting on my lap like that…" He exhaled, long and slow.

When his eyes met mine again, they were molten. Fire churned in my belly as his thumb brushed along my knuckle.

Then he murmured, "We can't control our dreams."

My heart twisted, and the heat within me turned to ice. I hadn't expected him to say that. "Right." My voice was shaky.

"It's nothing to be ashamed of. It doesn't mean anything."

"Okay." My voice sounded numb.

He was giving excuses for both of us. He was assuring me that we both had these dreams, and they meant nothing.

But mine had certainly meant something. It wasn't just a random dream. It was a manifestation of all the pent-up tension that had been building between us.

And it killed me to know that *his* dream hadn't been the same thing. *His* dream really had been nothing.

I felt his eyes on me, probing. I took a deep breath before meeting his gaze, then forced a smile. "Thank you for under-standing." I pulled my hand away from his.

A wrinkle formed between his brows, as if he could sense the falseness behind my voice.

I needed to change the subject. "Any news about Warwick?"

His eyes darkened. "I've dispatched my hired hand to take care of him. His name is Tavish, and he's very skilled. Warwick should be dead by tomorrow."

I heaved a shaky breath and nodded, trying to be reassured by this.

"Once Tislora has finished inspecting your chambers, it should give us the evidence we need to convict him publicly. Hopefully, that will turn the soldiers against him, and they won't revolt when they realize he's dead."

I cringed inwardly at the sound of Tislora's name. Varius's gaze snapped to mine, missing nothing. "What is it?"

I blew air through my lips. "I don't really think Tislora is all that concerned for my safety."

Varius said nothing for a long moment. Then, he sighed. "She doesn't trust humans. But… I know her. She'll perform her task to the best of her ability, regardless of who benefits from it. She excels at magic, and she would never intentionally hold back her abilities. She loves her spells too much for that."

There was a fondness in his voice that made my chest tighten so painfully that I couldn't breathe.

Without warning, I pushed up from the bed, needing some space between Varius and me. My eyes fixed on the window, which boasted a glowing pink and orange sky from the setting sun.

"Dusk already?" I forced a laugh. "At this rate, I'll be nocturnal before long. I should probably dress and eat."

To my disappointment, Varius stood, too. "You shouldn't roam the castle alone. I'll go with you."

"No." My voice was sharper than I intended. In a softer tone, I said, "You can't guard me every hour of the day. With Warwick and a possible army approaching, I'm sure there are important things you need to do to prepare."

Varius's face hardened. He looked at me with a conflicted expression.

"I'll take Enzira with me," I added.

He sighed. "Very well. But I'll find you later." He speared me with a stern gaze.

I snorted. "That sounds like a threat."

He gave me a feral grin. "Maybe it is."

My stomach fluttered, but I forced away the warm tingly feeling that blossomed inside me when he flirted with me. I pointed to the bathing chamber. "Right. Well, I'll just go get dressed, then."

Before I could embarrass myself any further, I strode into the bathing room, eager to put as much distance between Varius and me as possible.

THE BEAUTY

As soon as Varius left, I pulled on a tunic and trousers, donned my boots, and grabbed my cloak. A sharp clinking sound alerted me to the gemstones that had spilled from my pouch.

It took me a moment to recall that Varius had been digging through them to locate the amber stone.

Because I had been calling to him.

No, *moaning* his name.

While I dreamt of him plunging his fingers inside me.

Horror and humiliation washed over me as my cheeks burned anew. "Not now, Sybelle," I whispered to myself. Varius wasn't even here, and I was still overcome with embarrassment.

I quickly thrust the gemstones back into the pouch, then paused when I reached the mysterious black stone. Frowning, I wrapped my fingers around it and looked up at the mirror. The contents swirled like smoke, and my heart seized in fear. For a moment, it looked like Necro Shadows.

But then the mist cleared to reveal Varius striding down the hall. He approached Clermont and asked, "Is everything ready?"

Clermont's mouth formed a thin line. "Tavish has located Warwick. The plan is in place. He should be dead within the hour."

Varius gave a curt nod. "Good. We can't risk leaving him alive. This needs to be done quickly and quietly."

"You know how efficient Tavish is. I'm certain the task will be fulfilled to your liking."

Varius's eyes narrowed slightly. "You disapprove."

Clermont heaved a sigh. "I have always disapproved of Tavish's methods, my lord. I find them to be barbaric."

Varius spread his hands. "What would you have me do? Imprison him, only to let him escape once more? Kill him myself, and risk losing the loyalty of my soldiers? Let him roam free, so he can threaten my wife again?" The last words came out as a low growl.

Clermont said nothing, but a muscle worked in his jaw, betraying his discomfort.

Varius rubbed a hand down his face. "What news from the spy network?"

"No sight of any approaching army. All is quiet on Chesser Road."

Varius nodded, his eyes distant. "They must be waiting on word from Warwick. If so, it means that, when he dies, the plan falls apart."

"That is the hope, my lord."

"Keep me apprised of any new information you hear."

Clermont pressed a fist to his chest. "Of course, my lord."

Varius strode away, and the glass in the mirror swirled with smoke once again.

My chest tightened with unease. This still didn't feel right. Even if Warwick died and whoever his contact was decided not to advance, it didn't explain why my father would be working alongside a fae like Warwick.

I rubbed my thumb over the smooth surface and murmured, "Show me my father. Show me King Maddox of the Earthen Court."

I looked up at the mirror. The smoky contents continued

churning. I waited for the image to clear, but it never did. Nothing but gray nothingness.

Frowning, I tried again. "Show me my sister, Orla, Princess of the Earthen Court."

More churning smoke. Just when I was about to conclude that the stone was only connected to Varius, the mist faded to reveal my sister sitting in the dining hall, wearing a vibrant peach gown and a gaudy tiara with amethysts bigger than my fist. She was tucking into a plate of roast meat and seasoned potatoes. But she was alone at the table. Father wasn't with her.

Perhaps he was traveling. Or sleeping. Maybe that was why the mirror couldn't show him to me.

I dropped the stone into the scaled pouch with the others. Immediately, the scene in the mirror vanished. I marveled at what this meant. If I could command the stone to show me anyone in the realm, the possibilities were endless.

After securing the pouch, I slid Wraith Killer in my hilt, donned my cloak, and stepped onto the balcony. A fierce wind rippled around my face, and I glanced up at the darkening sky. My hand went to my amber necklace.

"Azure?"

"I'm here, Sybelle."

"I'm in Varius's rooms. Can you meet me?"

"I'm on my way."

While I waited, I quickly snatched Eira's letter from underneath my pillow and tore open the seal. I scanned the contents, making sure Eira hadn't written anything incriminating in case the intruder who had torn apart my rooms decided to snoop in here as well.

My dearest Sibby,

· · ·

What diverting and alarming news you provide! I have many questions... But first and foremost, I am desperate to know if a dutiful wife such as yourself will tend to the carnal needs of such a cranky curmudgeon. And, if so, I'm afraid I must beg you for details.

I suppressed a snort as the beating of Azure's wings drew closer, drawing my attention to the window. I stuffed the letter back under the pillow, vowing to read it thoroughly later. A dark shape took form against the auburn sky, and I smiled at the sight of my dragon. I drew back to the doors to give her enough room to land. She gracefully planted herself in the middle of the balcony.

"*What happened earlier?*" she asked. "*I heard you speaking to me. Something sounded... wrong.*"

I quickly filled her in on everything she had missed: Warwick in the training yard, running through the Noxen Forest with Varius, him finding out about my fae abilities, and then the incident with the amber stone. I told her everything except the sordid details of my scandalous dream. She didn't need to know that.

Azure was silent for a long time. Then, she said, "*Have you used the amber stones to communicate with anyone besides me?*"

"No," I admitted. As soon as I discovered this secret way to communicate with my dragon, it became something special that only we shared. To tell someone else about it, even Gerard, seemed like I was betraying that secret side of me that no one else knew about.

"*Then, I suppose we don't have a lot of information to go off of,*" she said.

Silence fell between us as we both considered this. I wondered if I could use the amber stone on others, like Enzira or Ramia.

"For the record," Azure said, startling me from my musings, *"you can tell him about me. If you wish."*

My gaze snapped to hers. "Really? You are comfortable with that?"

"I trust you, Sybelle. And you clearly trust him, if you told him about your fae magic. If you believe he poses no threat to me, then I will believe it, too."

A mixture of warmth and unease spread through my chest, making it hard to breathe. I swallowed hard, unsure of how to respond to this.

"There's something else on your mind, isn't there?"

Grateful for the subject change, I looked at Azure, who was still scrutinizing me. She could always read my emotions.

"I found out what the black stone can do."

Her eyes sparked with interest. *"Tell me."*

I explained how the mirror showed me things upon my request. Except, apparently, my father.

"Fascinating," she said, her voice bright with excitement. *"Can you show me?"*

I swallowed hard. "I will. But right now, I need you to take me to see the rose jewel."

A low growl rumbled in her throat. *"You want to endure that agonizing pain again?"*

"I think I know how to stop the ringing," I said quickly. "But, if you prefer, you can drop me off at the edge of the woods so you don't have to hear that again. I know your hearing is much sharper than mine. I don't want you getting hurt."

A thoughtful humming sound resonated in her chest. *"It is true that my hearing is* far *superior to yours, small human."*

I snorted.

"But I can't let you wander into those woods alone. If you believe you have a way to stop the sound from attacking us, then I will trust you. But if it doesn't work, I reserve the right to grab you and flee as quickly as possible."

I nodded. "That's fair." I was painfully relieved at her insistence to stay with me. If she had decided to wait outside the forest, I would have respected that. But I didn't realize until now how terrified I was of entering those woods alone.

"Why do you need to go back there? What is so important about that gem? Could you sense its magic?"

"No, but I think it's connected to the Necro Shadows and how to stop them. If it is, it means I can put an end to this for good."

Azure sank to her knees, allowing me to climb on her back. My legs tightened around her, and her sharp scales dug into my trousers.

Without warning, she leapt off the balcony ledge.

My scream died in my throat as my stomach bottomed out, making me feel weightless in the most terrifying way. Wind whipped at me, making my hair fly around me. My eyes burned and my cheeks stung.

Azure's wings flared out, slowing our descent with a violent jerk that made me yelp. I lunged forward to wrap my arms around her neck as I slid precariously. Her scales shimmered as they shifted to match the same dark blue as the sky.

"Very funny," I muttered. Even without touching the amber stone, I knew she could sense my ire. I felt her rumbling laugh underneath me.

As we arced over the training yard, I ducked down, keeping my body tucked close to Azure's. She might be able to camouflage herself, but I didn't have such an advantage.

I peered around her scales, trying to discern if there were soldiers below us—and if Warwick was there. Had Varius's assassin taken care of him already? But with dusk's approach, it was too dark for me to see.

Azure swooped low, keeping close to the tree line. She crossed to the other side of the Noxen Forest so we could avoid the training yard.

I couldn't risk Warwick seeing me. Varius was right—he had already caught me near the training yard once.

Azure glided gracefully toward the earth, her claws landing in the soil with the barest of thuds. When she'd come to a halt, I slid off her back, then withdrew the opal stone for light. Before entering the woods, I turned to look at her and pressed a finger to my amber stone.

"You can still wait out here, if you prefer."

Azure grumbled her displeasure. *"I'm with you, Sybelle."*

I smiled, then turned and strode into the forest. I remembered the path fairly well, but I still paused occasionally to check with Azure. She would hum if I was going the right way or nudge me with her snout if I wasn't.

"Do you hear the ringing?" I whispered, my hand on my necklace.

"Not yet."

I frowned, wondering why the ringing didn't assault us right away like it had when I was with Varius. The last time Azure and I were here, she had heard it almost immediately.

I shot a quizzical look toward my dragon, prepared to ask her about it, but her voice was already in my head.

"I believe the enchantment here is more sensitive to full-blooded fae," she said. *"When you were here before, I think it recognized Varius immediately, which was why it attacked you right away. But you and I are foreign, and we are taking care not to trigger it. From what I can gather, this enchantment is... fickle. It's like it's alive. Like it has a mind of its own."*

I shuddered, then swallowed hard, ensuring each step was as silent and careful as possible. The idea that a living, sentient spell was nearby made my skin prickle with unease.

It didn't take us long to find the spot where the glowing rose was buried. The earth was still overturned from when I had last been here. Already, I could see the crimson glow of the gemstone beckoning me closer.

Knowing the ringing sound would attack me soon, I didn't waste any time. I sank to my knees and dug my fingers into the earth.

As soon as my fingertips met the rich soil, the blaring noise assaulted my ears. I cried out, gritting my teeth against the shrill sound that drilled into my skull. But I kept digging, pressing further into the soil until I unearthed more of the glowing rose. Behind me, Azure whined, her breathing sharp and ragged.

I didn't have much time now.

When I had uncovered enough of the rose, I took a deep breath and pressed my fingers to the jeweled petals.

The ringing abruptly stopped, though an echo of the sound still resonated in my mind. The crimson glow intensified, burning against my eyes. I hissed, trying to draw back, but my hands were cemented to the rose petals.

Something within my stomach lurched, and I found myself tumbling forward, my yell drowned out by a roaring sound that surrounded me. I tried to find Azure, to call for help, but she had vanished.

I landed in a heap on the leafy ground, my head throbbing and my bones aching. With a groan, I climbed to my feet, the jeweled rose still clutched in my hands.

It was daylight, and I no longer stood in the forest, but on the steps of the castle. It looked different, though—there weren't as many turrets and towers, and the forest behind the castle was more lush than I remembered.

Before me stood a fae with brown skin and long black hair. Were it not for his pointed ears, I might have assumed he was human. His dark eyes and strong chin were so familiar.

He turned, and I bit back a gasp. His features reminded me of Varius. But this fae had a wider nose and a permanent scowl that made him look far older than the king I was accustomed to.

My breath caught in my throat as I staggered backward, waiting for this strange fae to attack me.

"King Ragnus," said a voice.

I whirled and found another fae standing just behind me. He had pale skin and a mop of red hair atop his head.

"The witch is here," he said, pressing a fist to his chest.

Ragnus sneered. "Bring her forward."

My heart seized in my chest, but neither of the fae seemed to notice me at all. They didn't even glance my way.

Several soldiers dragged out a figure in rags, her wild gray hair a tangled mess around her. Blood and soot covered her face and hands, and she groaned when they tossed her to the ground before the king.

My eyes grew wide, and I found it difficult to breathe. I gazed down at the gleaming rose in my hands, suddenly realizing what it was.

It was a keeper of memories. This, right here, was a memory.

This king must have been Varius's ancestor. And the figure in rags… was the witch who had cast the spell, plaguing the land with Necro Shadows.

But why did everyone look so different? None of these fae looked unseelie like Varius's court.

Tentatively, I lifted my hand and waved it before me. No one blinked or even looked my way, just like with the vision in the mirror.

"Can you hear me?" I shouted, my voice ringing in the courtyard.

Still no response.

Relief settled in my chest. I was not in immediate danger. I drew forward to get a closer look at the witch. She had vibrant green eyes and sallow skin. But when she looked up at the king, her eyes were full of venom.

"What will you do with me, oh great king?" she spat, her voice dripping with rage. "Will you kill me to fulfill your barbaric mission to obliterate an entire race?"

King Ragnus bared his teeth at her. "Your magic has been a

blight on this land! Should I stand here and do nothing, after all the suffering you have caused us?"

"We were only acting in defense!" she bellowed. "Your soldiers were slaughtering my sisters!"

"Lies," Ragnus hissed.

"I cannot lie!" the witch cried. "I have fae blood, just like you."

"You are nothing like the fae, foul witch," said the king. "And your unholy magic dies today." He looked up at the red-haired fae. "Bring the shadowstone."

From within his cloak, the fae produced a familiar black stone. My pulse quickened as I realized it was identical to the stone that allowed me to conjure images in the mirror.

Shadowstone. Did that mean the gem was native to this court? If so, why did I find it buried in the caves of the Earthen Court?

The fae servant laid the shadowstone on the steps at the king's feet. Shadows poured from Ragnus's hands and coiled around the shadowstone, which began to glow. It was no longer black—now it was slate gray, and it thrummed with power.

"From the magic of this stone, I call forth your power, witch," said Ragnus, his voice resonating around the square. "I draw your magic and pull it into me for the good of this people and this kingdom. Let your strength flow with mine, forever joining the magic of shadows."

The witch's back arched and she shrieked in agony, her face crumpling. I instinctively reached for her, even knowing I could do nothing to help.

Tendrils of green smoke pooled from the witch's form and funneled toward the shadowstone. The king was siphoning her magic. He was stealing it for himself.

Ragnus's shadows intensified. A billowing wind howled, and lightning forked across the sky.

"From the magic of this stone!" Ragnus bellowed, repeating his words. "I call forth your power—"

"*No!*" roared the witch, climbing to her feet. Her emerald eyes glowed, blotting out the whites of her eyes. Her hair flew around her face as she murmured, "*By my blood, I curse this land and this people forevermore.*" Her voice rang out, echoing as if a thousand witches were speaking alongside her. Chills erupted along my arms, and I had the eerie sense that the spirits of the fallen witches were here, witnessing this final act.

"*As long as your kingdom lives, may your shadows turn poisonous, seeking to destroy the lives you swear to protect,*" the witch said. "*May your bodies be cursed to remain trapped in their beastly forms as a symbol of the monsters you are. May you never speak of the events of today. By the stone of shadow and blood, I make this vow: Until one of my kind gives up her life for yours, this curse will live on, even as my line lives on. And the blood of my sisters will poison this land until every last one of you is rendered to dust like unto us.*"

My jaw dropped, and my blood turned to ice in my veins. The shadowstone rattled and hummed, now glowing an iridescent white. The witch screamed, her back bowing as something loud cracked from within her, the sound piercing the air. As she crumpled, the shadows and the glow vanished. The wind died, and nothing but a deadly silence filled the square.

Then, a new scream erupted. The red-haired fae fell to his knees, hunching over as his body shook with violent tremors. A long, serpentine tail stretched from his backside, and his skin shifted from pale ivory to olive green. His red hair lengthened, spreading down his back like a mane.

Others in the courtyard cried out as they, too, transformed. Even the king. He groaned, falling to the ground as his skin darkened to the same crimson flesh as Varius. The fae around him shifted to their unseelie forms, growing horns and wings and fangs.

When every fae had transformed, they looked at one another in shock. Ragnus was panting, his eyes wide and his mouth open in horror. Then, he stiffened, his nostrils flaring. "Where is she?"

I turned to where the witch had been moments ago. Nothing remained but a pile of ash. Even the shadowstone had vanished. Now, a familiar gleaming crimson stone rested in its place.

I recognized it. It was the jeweled rose—the same stone I'd used to access this memory.

The green-skinned fae stumbled forward, clearly adjusting to his new form. His face twisted in disgust as he drew closer to the ashes, as if her essence alone could harm him. Slowly, he bent over and sniffed. "This smells like her magic." He looked up at Ragnus. "The power of the shadowstone must have disintegrated her."

Despite the effects of the curse, Ragnus smirked in satisfaction. "Then, it is done. The witches are all dead, and they will no longer terrorize our lands."

Cheers sounded as the fae rejoiced, but I couldn't pull my gaze from that pile of ash—all that remained of a powerful line of witches. My eyes swam with tears at the sight of it. My throat was full of emotion, and I could barely breathe. A roaring sound filled my ears, and my body was jerked violently forward. The air rushed around me, and I fell forward into the dirt once more.

It was nighttime, and I was back in the Noxen Forest. On all fours, I gasped for breath, trying to get more oxygen into my lungs. Tears swam in my eyes, streaming down my face.

Behind me, Azure moaned and nudged me with her snout, clearly concerned. I choked and sputtered, afraid I might vomit. My eyes closed against the sickening sensation that swirled within me.

Too much. It was all too much.

When I had finally caught my breath, I staggered to my feet, then inspected the jeweled rose in my hand. The sharp briars gleamed in the moonlight.

With my other hand, I touched my amber necklace. Immediately, Azure's panicked voice filled my head.

"Where were you? What happened? Are you hurt? Do you have any idea how frightened I was for you?"

"I'm sorry," I said in a strangled voice. "The gem—it took me into a memory." Blinking tears from my eyes, I looked at my dragon. "I know how the Necro Shadows began."

"Excellent," said a voice. "Now, be a good girl and hand over the gemstone."

I spun around with a gasp and found Warwick emerging from behind a large oak tree, a triumphant smile on his face.

THE BEAST

MY HEAD WAS STILL REELING FROM WHAT HAD HAPPENED WITH Sybelle in the bedchamber when I made my way to Tislora's apothecary.

Sybelle had been acting so strangely when she dismissed me. I couldn't tell if it was from embarrassment over her dream or shock from what had transpired with the gem and the shadows.

Or perhaps she had been acting odd because there was more she wasn't telling me.

I clenched my teeth. She wasn't the only one who was keeping secrets.

I still hadn't told her that breaking the curse would claim her life.

"Back so soon?" Tislora asked in a bored voice. She was lounging in an armchair by the window, reading with her legs propped up. Her thin eyebrows shot up at my entrance.

"Do you live in this room?" I asked, glancing around. A woolen blanket at her feet implied she often curled up in that very chair to sleep.

"When I have a grouchy king constantly barking orders at me to make more elixirs, then yes." She swung her legs down and straightened. "I'm assuming that's why you're here?"

"No." I paused. In truth, I was here to ensure the enchantments around the castle were in place, in case of an attack from the Earthen Court.

But unbidden, Murvo's words rang in my mind. *Find the original script of the curse.* Despite my searching, I still hadn't found any record of the sorceress's spell.

"Do you have any records from past sorceresses?" I asked.

Tislora went very still. The hairs on my arms stood on end at the almost predatory way she seemed to freeze. Like she was waiting to strike down her prey.

"Why are you asking me that?" Her voice was quiet, but lethal.

I hadn't told her about Murvo yet. There hadn't been an opportunity. I didn't know much about her background as a sorceress; all I knew was she had faced much persecution because of her magical heritage, and that trauma was still fresh.

To bring this up would likely reopen those wounds.

But this was of utmost importance. After all, she was bound by the curse as well.

After a deep breath, I filled her in on what Murvo had told me. Her mouth formed a thin line, her eyes darkening as she listened.

When I finished, she said, "I could possibly cast a spell on your blood, since your bloodline is entangled with the curse. It may bring forth the original terms of the enchantment. But… it would be extremely painful. And, with centuries between you and the curse, there's no guarantee it will work."

I nodded without hesitation. "Let's do that. Do whatever you need to prepare."

"Very well."

When I continued to stand there, unmoving, she cocked her head at me. "Was there… something else you needed?"

"I need to ensure our magical wards are intact. There may be a threat approaching."

Her expression sobered. "What kind of threat?"

Recalling our earlier argument, I hesitated. If I said *a human army*, she would scoff and blame my human wife.

So, instead, I said, "There's a spy among my soldiers, feeding information to another kingdom. Word has it he's planning to draw them out, and I need to make sure we are properly protected."

Her brows lowered. "My wards are *always* intact."

"Go check them anyway."

She glared at me. "Is that an order, oh great king?"

"Yes," I bit out.

She exhaled in exasperation and rose to her feet. "Really, Varius, is it going to be this way?"

"If you continue to insult my wife and accuse her of treason, then yes."

"Weren't *you* speculating about her duplicity mere moments before she arrived in this kingdom? It's hardly fair you would pass judgment on me for thinking the same thing."

"Things are different now. We have taken our vows. She is my *wife*. And... I trust her." I surprised myself by uttering those words. But they were true. I wouldn't be able to say them if they weren't.

Tislora blinked, clearly just as stunned as I was. "Wife or not, she has not been coronated. She holds no authority over this court or me."

I bared my teeth at her. "Why are you doing this?"

She drew closer to me, her silver eyes sharpening. "To *protect* you. You are blind when it comes to her, Varius. If you won't see clearly, then someone else has to."

My shadows coiled at my feet as anger bubbled within me. "Just check the damn wards," I said through gritted teeth.

Before Tislora could respond, someone knocked at the open door, and we both turned. Clermont stood at the doorway, panting, his eyes wide.

"What is it?" I demanded, my body tensing.

"Warwick," Clermont said. "He's—He's escaped. He killed Tavish."

My blood chilled. Tavish was the fiercest fighter I knew. How the hell had Warwick overpowered him?

"Shit." I ran a hand through my hair. "Where was he last sighted?"

"Just outside the training yard."

"Your trousers are glowing," Tislora said.

Clermont and I cast her matching looks of bewilderment. When she gestured to my thigh, I followed her gaze. Sure enough, a warm glow shone from inside my pocket. As silence fell, a muffled voice filled the air.

"You don't want to do this," said the voice.

My blood chilled. It was Sybelle speaking to me through the amber stone. I'd forgotten it was in my pocket.

I withdrew the gemstone and lifted it to my ear. The glow vanished, and her voice rang in my mind.

"Warwick, think about this. If you hurt me, Varius will kill you."

A menacing growl rumbled in my chest. "Warwick," I snarled. "He's with Sybelle."

"Where?" Tislora asked.

I shook my head, uncertain. I clutched the amber so tightly that the edges dug into my palm. "Sybelle, where are you?" I asked, not sure if she could hear me or not. Perhaps the amber stone worked both ways. She had mentioned she'd used it to communicate with a friend.

"What are you even doing out here in these woods?" Sybelle asked. *"Aren't there supposed to be enchantments to keep fae out?"*

I bit back a roar of rage. "She's in the Noxen Forest." What the hell was she doing there?

I was moving to the door when Tislora stopped me.

"I'm coming with you."

"The hell you are," I barked.

"You have no idea how many soldiers he has with him," she

said, already drawing her black cloak around her shoulders. "If the human's life is at stake, you could use my power."

I whirled to her, fangs bared. "And how can I trust you won't aim that power at my wife?"

She leveled a cold look at me. "I swear on my fae blood that I won't. Is that good enough for you?"

"Varius," Clermont said before I snarled at Tislora. "If Sybelle is in the Noxen Forest, you'll need powerful magic to help you."

I resisted the urge to ram my fist into the wall. Clermont was right. The moment the defensive enchantments of the Noxen Forest were activated, I would be unable to help Sybelle. The shrill ringing sound would render me helpless.

"Fine," I growled. "I don't have time to argue. I hope you're up for flying."

Tislora gave me a sinister smile. "I always am."

The Beauty

I stared at Warwick, my heart thudding loudly in my chest. One hand was pressed to my amber necklace. I hoped it looked like I was clutching at my chest in fear.

And, inexplicably, I heard *Varius's* voice inside my head. Just like with Azure. He must have kept the amber stone from earlier.

"Sybelle, where are you?" Varius asked.

I couldn't outright say, *I'm in the Noxen Forest,* or Warwick would get suspicious. I also didn't know if Varius could hear my thoughts, or if he could only hear what I spoke vocally, like Azure.

So, I said loudly, "What are you even doing out here in these woods? Aren't there supposed to be enchantments to keep fae out?"

My other hand was still holding the gleaming rose jewel. I knew if I dropped it, the horrible ringing sound would return. It would incapacitate Warwick… but it would affect me, as well.

I had to time this right.

"Yes, there are. But it looks like you have conveniently suppressed them. For now." Warwick inched closer, and I drew a step back.

If he attacked, I wouldn't be ready for him. I had to let go of the amber necklace and pray Varius had heard my response.

I didn't know where Azure had vanished to. But it was good she remained hidden. Warwick could *not* find out about her.

Slowly, I lowered my hand and discreetly moved it behind my cloak. I needed to withdraw my diamond dagger from the folds of my cloak, which was quite difficult to do without Warwick noticing. My sheath was strapped to my thigh—I had to grab the blade from behind so he wouldn't notice.

Warwick's eyes sharpened, his gaze following the movement of my hand.

I lifted the rose jewel to distract him. "Why do you want this? How did you even know about it?"

He smirked. "There is *so much* I know, tiny human. It would rattle your fragile little mind."

I lifted my chin. "Try me." I needed to buy more time. My fingers parted the fabric of my cloak and reached my trousers.

"While I would love to stick around and chat about my vast amount of knowledge, I'm afraid I'll need to take that jewel from you before the enchantments of this wood start attacking me."

My heart jolted at that. Did he not know that holding the jewel was how I had silenced the ringing?

And was the enchantment only silenced when *I* held the jewel? If Warwick held it, would it do the same thing?

Or was it because of my fae magic?

Either way, it was an advantage I could use. Clearly, Warwick didn't know as much as he claimed.

"I'm not just going to hand this over to you," I said. My forefinger brushed against the strap holding Wraith Killer. But I was already stretching as far as I could go without twisting. If I moved too much, Warwick would notice.

"You will if you know what's good for you." Warwick drew closer. "If I can kill Varius's pitiful assassin in a manner of minutes, just imagine how quickly I can dispose of *you*."

Fear chilled me to the bone, but I was determined not to

show it. "How are you connected to the Earthen Court?" I asked, my voice rising. Even knowing he wouldn't tell me, I still had to ask.

Warwick froze, his eyes flaring wide for a moment before that smirk returned. "You're cleverer than you look, human. I'll give you that."

"You're *fae*," I said. I stepped back again and pretended to trip over a root. My body twisted, as if to move out of the way, and I wrapped my fingers around the dagger's hilt as I staggered backward.

"Another astute observation," he mocked. "You'd be surprised what fae can do with a little glamour. In fact, you'd be shocked to discover *just how many* members of your so-called human court are actually fae in disguise."

My blood chilled as his gaze swept over me, cold and calculating.

Shit. Did he know I was fae? He had to, if he ascertained that I was the one who had silenced the enchanted ringing.

But... how many others in the Earthen Court were actually fae but masquerading as humans?

Warwick chuckled at the look of horror on my face. "Ah, did I break the little human's brain? You are *so* fragile."

No, he couldn't possibly know I was fae. He kept calling me *human*.

Swallowing around the lump of terror in my throat, I said, "What do you want with me? I'm no threat to you." My hand scrambled to pull the dagger from its sheath.

"You are a means to an end." His eyes dipped to the rose jewel. "I only needed you to procure *that* for me. Now that you have, I can dispose of you so you don't disrupt any more of my plans."

What plans? What is he plotting?

I didn't have time to ask. Without warning, he lunged for me. In that split second, I released the rose jewel and pulled out

Wraith Killer. Instantly, the shrill, piercing sound erupted all around us. Warwick sank to his knees, crying out as he clapped his hands over his ears. I gritted my teeth, pushing myself through the pain, and swiped the dagger. He jerked backward, but not quickly enough. The blade cut through his tunic and drew blood.

Hissing, he pressed a hand to his chest, glaring at the smear of black blood.

Over the ringing noise, he shouted, "You'll pay for that, you little bitch!"

He dived for me, but I swung again, my dagger slicing into his arm. It didn't stop him, though. One arm wrapped around my legs and tugged, bringing me crashing to the forest floor. I yelped, my fingers tightening around the hilt of my dagger. A surge of strength flooded me, and I snarled at him. I kicked and bucked, managing to free myself from his grip. Then I rolled before climbing to my knees and driving the blade straight into his abdomen.

He howled in agony, clutching at his side, but I wasn't finished. I elbowed him directly in his wound, then turned and smashed my head backward against him. Something made a sickening *crunch*—his nose, most likely—and I jabbed my elbow backward into his chest for good measure.

I turned, prepared to drag my blade across his throat and be done with it. But his arms wrapped around my chest, trapping me against him. I struggled and writhed, but his body was so much larger than mine. I tried slamming my head backward again, but he ducked, his face peering over my shoulder to whisper in my ear.

"I was going to kill you quickly," he rasped. "But now, I'll have my way with you first. You've brought this on yourself, you pathetic human."

He leaned in and bit down hard on my shoulder. I screamed as his fangs pierced my flesh, dragging through it and drawing blood. The ringing sound intensified, as if spurred on by our fight. I felt blood dripping from my ears, and my skull throbbed.

A roar echoed nearby, and something huge tackled Warwick, pulling him away from me. Blood soaked my tunic and cloak, but I forced myself upright as a flash of blue scales sparkled in the moonlight.

"No!" I cried. "Az, *don't!*"

But it was too late. Warwick stared at her, eyes bulging as she pinned him to the earth. Her talons dug into his chest, which was already covered in his blood. She roared again, then clamped her jaws over his shoulder—the same spot where he'd just bitten me.

Warwick screeched, his body thrashing as Azure tore into him.

I stumbled forward, falling to my knees as the piercing in my skull made my vision swim.

The pain was too much… too much…

Sudden silence covered the wood, and my head jerked upward in alarm. I searched for the rose jewel and found it still resting in the dirt where I'd dropped it.

But the ringing had stopped. Why?

Azure made a snarling sound, jerking my attention back to Warwick. Coming to my senses, I hurried over with Wraith Killer in hand. Before I could sever his head from his neck, he managed to kick Azure in the stomach. She groaned, her body coiling from the blow. Warwick wrapped his legs around her, then rolled so she was underneath him, her teeth still buried in his shoulder.

"A dragon," he hissed. "A *gods-damned dragon.* How you managed to find one, little human, I don't know. But I'm taking this one with me."

He wrapped his hands around Azure's throat, undeterred despite her ripping out a chunk of his shoulder.

I cried out and rushed him, driving my dagger between his

shoulder blades. He grunted but kept his hands on Azure's neck, as if getting impaled by my magical weapon was a minor inconvenience for him.

How the hell was he still conscious? I had stabbed him multiple times with an enchanted blade, and Azure was about to tear off his arm.

My dragon was growing weaker. Her eyes went unfocused, and she slumped over.

I elbowed Warwick in the face, then slammed the hilt of my blade against his skull. His head whipped sideways, his hands loosening for a moment. I managed to push him off Azure, then slammed my boot into his chest to keep him down.

I pressed my dagger into his neck. Black blood bloomed from the wound. I drove it deeper, but his fist struck my stomach, knocking the breath out of me. I slid sideways. Warwick shoved me fully off him, then climbed atop me, his knees pinning my body down.

"If that's how you want it," he growled, "then fine." His hips ground into mine.

I screamed and wriggled, trying to free my arms, but I was trapped. His hand clamped down on my wrist before he wrenched Wraith Killer from my grasp. With a snarl, he tossed the blade well out of reach.

In an instant, my strength left me, and the intensity of my wounds pulsed with fresh awareness. My limbs groaned, and spots danced in my vision.

Without Wraith Killer, I wouldn't last much longer.

A howl pierced the night air, and heavy, thundering footfalls approached. Warwick's head whipped up, his eyes flashing. Shadows spilled through the forest, blotting out the moonlight and drowning us in darkness.

But I was not afraid.

My husband had arrived.

THE BEAST

Rage fueled my movements, my wings stretching wide as I glided across the training yard. I sensed Tislora flying somewhere behind me, but I didn't bother to look.

All I knew was the unchecked fury that coursed through me. Shadows swirled around me, floating in the air like bats following their master.

I soared over the treetops, following the scent of blood. Both fae and human.

Warwick had hurt her. And I would destroy him for it.

When I landed hard, the ringing sound burrowed into my skull. I cried out, shaking my head, when Tislora grabbed my arm.

"I'll stop it!" she said, her voice rising over the sound. "You go!"

I nodded once, taking off toward the smell of blood. The shrill sound of the forest's magic continued to assault me, hammering against my skull and piercing my brain. Mother of Shade, it was unbearable.

Then, it stopped. Tislora's handiwork, no doubt.

Vowing to thank her for it later, I quickened my pace, not bothering for stealth. It was far too late for that. My wings were still outstretched, lifting me in the air as I leapt off the occasional tree stump for a burst of speed.

I heard Sybelle's scream. I had never heard her sound like that—terrified and angry. Helpless.

Black shadows spilled forth, engulfing the forest. A feral sound escaped me, a cross between a roar and a howl.

Their scent was almost upon me. I lurched upward, my wings carrying me, until I caught sight of two figures grappling on the ground. Warwick was on top of Sybelle, pinning her body to the forest floor.

A roar of fury burst from me as I slammed into Warwick. He shouted in surprise. My hands wrapped around his throat, my claws digging through flesh. His elbow caught my jaw, and he managed to kick me in the shin. But still I pressed, ready to remove his head entirely.

A streak of blue shot past me, and my head whipped up. Was someone else here with Warwick?

But when I looked around, nothing was there.

The distraction cost me. Something sharp pierced my side, and I hissed as hot blood gushed. Warwick had stabbed me. His hips jerked, and we rolled, but I never released his throat. He would lose consciousness soon, and then he would stop fighting.

Then, this would end.

"Varius!" Sybelle shrieked.

I managed to block Warwick just before he drove his dagger into my side again. But now, with only one hand on his throat, he was able to maneuver out of my grasp.

He rolled again, but I followed, baring my teeth.

Warwick had the gall to grin at me. "You'll find I'm quite difficult to kill," he said, his voice hoarse. "Just ask your assassin."

I tilted my head at him, nostrils flaring. My shadows spilled along the forest floor, creeping toward him. If I could keep him talking, then my shadows could sneak up on him.

Once I blinded him with my darkness, he would be mine.

"How did you do it?" I asked. "How did you kill him?" Tavish had been one of my strongest and most agile soldiers. No one had bested him in combat before.

Warwick's grin turned feral. "See if you can guess."

My eyes roved over his figure once more, taking in the wounds still bleeding freely, likely from Sybelle's dagger. A quick inhale told me there was even more blood that I couldn't see.

He was wounded. So wounded, in fact, that he should have lost consciousness by now.

"Endurance," I guessed. "That's your fae gift. You can push through the pain of your injuries for longer than an ordinary fae."

Warwick's smile was mocking as he inclined his head. "Excellent observation, Shadow King."

He was cocky and arrogant. I could use that to my advantage. My shadows continued coating the ground until the leaves and roots were swallowed up in the darkness.

I forced a solemn expression on my face. "Perhaps I cannot beat you."

Warwick chuckled. "It's too late for surrenders, Varius. You won't be leaving this forest alive." He jabbed a finger toward Sybelle, who was watching the exchange with wide, horrified eyes. "And neither is she."

A roar burst from me, and I unleashed everything on him. Shadows exploded around us, thickening and coiling around Warwick.

"You think this changes anything?" he spat. "Your shadows don't frighten me. I'm well acquainted with the darkness."

"Not my darkness," I growled, then flicked my fingers. Tendrils of smoke wrapped around his ankles and wrists, tying them together.

Warwick's eyes bulged as he struggled against my shadows. But they held him tighter, cinching until he yelped in pain.

"You didn't know I could do that, did you?" I cocked my head at him, giving him a savage grin. "Underestimating the Shadow King will be the last thing you ever do."

I picked up the dagger he'd dropped and raised it to his throat.

"If you… kill me…" he choked out, still straining against my shadows. "You'll never… break your… curse."

I bared my teeth at him. "I'll take my chances." With a swift motion, I dragged the dagger across his throat once. Twice. Three times.

If ordinary injuries wouldn't faze him, then I had to be sure he was good and dead.

Rivulets of black blood poured from his neck. With a third slice, his head fell from his body and dropped onto the forest floor with a sickening squelch.

"Let's see you recover from that," I hissed.

I was panting hard, my body still hot with fury. Slowly, my shadows released Warwick's body and retreated back toward me. But they didn't vanish completely. I was still too enraged for them to leave.

A small hand grasped mine, and I whirled with a snarl.

Sybelle kept her fingers wrapped around me, undeterred by my blind rage. "You're hurt," she whispered, gesturing to the wound in my side.

I stared at her. Thick red blood matted her shoulder, and the jagged teeth marks embedded in her flesh made me see red again.

"He bit you," I seethed, my voice hoarse and rabid. I didn't sound like myself at all.

"It will heal," she assured me. "We need to get you to a healer. You're losing too much blood." She tugged on my arm, trying to drag me away.

Only then did I notice the fear and exhaustion in her eyes.

How long she had fought with Warwick before my arrival, I did not know.

But she had fought.

"Sybelle." My voice was gentler now but still raspy.

She turned to look up at me, eyes wide. Her hair was full of twigs and leaves, and her cloak was ripped in several places.

But Mother of Shade, she had never looked so beautiful to me. She was a warrior. A goddess.

My wife.

My arm encircled her waist, drawing her chest to mine. She was breathing just as heavily as I was, her hands coming to my chest, her pulse racing. She stared up at me, eyes wild and frenzied. The heat of battle still roared in my blood, blotting out all sense of reason and logic.

All I knew was this feral *need* coursing through me. I gazed down at Sybelle, waiting for her to object or push me away.

She didn't. She stood on her toes and leaned up, her face angled toward mine.

I bent down, my mouth claiming hers. We were covered in dirt and blood and sweat, but I did not care. She had almost died, and I refused to live another moment without tasting her. My mouth opened, my tongue gliding along the seam of her lips. She trembled in my grip, uttering a soft sound that I swallowed hungrily. Her lips parted, and her tongue met mine in a clash of desire. Hers was smaller and smoother than mine, and the taste of it, the friction as I licked her again and again, was enough to undo me completely.

Her fingers fisted my tunic, drawing me closer. Her back arched as she met my fervent kisses with a desperation of her own, as if she were just as manic and hungry as I was. She pulled away only to draw in a gasp before plunging back in. Her lips moved faster and faster, devouring me as I devoured her. Her tongue slid over my fangs, my incisors, but she did not recoil. She did not shy away from them. If anything, her tongue and lips lingered as if she wanted to explore them further. As if she wanted to claim them for her own.

I moaned into her mouth, wrapping my arms more tightly around her waist until my hips were aligned with hers. She writhed against me, sensing my hardness, and a soft sigh escaped her.

Mother of Shade, I could pin her to a tree and take her right here, injuries be damned.

Someone cleared their throat behind me, and Sybelle went rigid. She withdrew, fear spiking within her.

I tightened my grip on her, breathless from our kiss. "It's just Tislora," I murmured. I didn't even have to turn around to check; I knew her scent.

This did not abate Sybelle's terror. "Is she—"

"She came with me. She stopped the forest's magic from attacking… me."

I'd been about to say *us* until I remembered my vow to Sybelle. Tislora did not know she was fae. I would not violate my wife's trust. I needed her to understand that.

Sybelle was gazing up at me, her eyes shining. "You really need to get that stitched up." She gestured to the bleeding wound in my side. It was dripping but not gushing, which was a good sign. I'd certainly had far worse injuries.

"I'll be fine," I assured her, then glanced over my shoulder at Tislora. "Are the woods clear?"

"Yes," she said. "Warwick acted alone." She eyed me, her expression a mixture of amusement and irritation. "I can't hold off the magic here much longer. We should go."

I nodded tersely, then turned back to Sybelle. She had knelt to the earth and grabbed something from the ground before shoving it into her cloak pocket. I watched as she glanced around the forest as if searching for something. Her hand went to the amber necklace at her throat.

"Sybelle?"

She jumped, then looked at me with wide eyes. "Are—Are you safe?"

I frowned at her, not understanding her question. "Yes. We are both safe right now." I gestured to her. "May I carry you?" I asked.

Sybelle exhaled, her expression oddly relieved. She nodded, dropping her gaze, a sudden blush blooming across her face. My movements were gentle as I gathered her against my chest, one arm braced under her legs. She gasped, arms flying around my neck, then stared at me in surprise.

"Did I hurt you?" I asked.

"No, no. It's just… You made that look so easy." She huffed a laugh.

I offered her a half smile. "It's easy to hold you, *dannahla*."

Her cheeks turned a darker shade of red. She drew a finger along my lip, pausing at my incisors as she dragged a fingertip over the sharpened edges.

I held perfectly still, jolts of awareness shooting through my body from that singular touch. Heat coiled low in my belly, and I had the insane desire to kiss her again.

But that was a bad idea. Not only because we were both injured but because it would lead nowhere. Thanks to the curse, it would be impossible for us to indulge these feelings. Whatever passed between us was temporary.

Nothing more.

I forced myself to look away from her heated gaze and faced forward. Behind me, my wings stretched wide, prepared to glide us out of these wretched woods.

"Hold on," I warned her before I took off into the forest.

The Beauty

"Are you safe?" I had asked Azure.

"*Yes,*" was her immediate response. *"I got away, and I am hiding near the stables."*

As soon as I knew my dragon was all right, I could breathe more easily.

Well, perhaps not *quite* so easily. My pulse was still racing from Varius's kiss. I wasn't sure what had happened. We had both been full of adrenaline and fury and fear. In spite of the danger, in spite of our injuries… nothing had felt more right in that moment.

Numbness and fatigue spread through my body, making it easy for me to lean into his chest while he carried me. I felt his powerful muscles straining as his wings kept us afloat, soaring over the treetops. I marveled that his wings never flapped like Azure's did. He had leapt into a tree, then used that momentum to propel us forward, wings spread as we glided with the wind.

Azure had fled the moment Varius had arrived. I saw her vanish into the trees, using the distraction of Varius's appearance to escape from Warwick's sight. But I didn't know for sure that she was safe until I heard her voice in my head.

I would never forget the sight of Warwick's hands wrapped around her throat, her eyes going dim…

I suppressed a shudder, pushing the image away from my mind.

Tislora was behind us somewhere. But in Varius's arms, I felt safe. My eyes closed as I buried my face into his chest, inhaling that familiar smell of dark spice and heavy rainfall.

He smelled like home.

And he had come for me.

Warwick had nearly killed me. But Varius had come for me.

I didn't realize my hand was curled against my amber stone until Azure's voice rang in my mind.

"I saw what happened. You are lucky to have a powerful king like that on your side."

"Are you all right?" I murmured without thinking. Warwick had nearly killed her.

"Yes," Azure said. *"It's nothing a night of rest won't fix. You saved my life, Sybelle."*

My eyes grew hot with emotion. I had almost lost her today, all because I'd been so foolish to enter these woods again.

"The wound isn't too deep," Varius said, clearly thinking I was speaking to him. His chest rumbled with his voice. "It will heal just fine. I'm more concerned with *your* injuries. Human flesh is more…" He paused.

I smirked. "Fragile?"

He chuckled. "That was *not* what I was going to say."

"If you weren't fae, I would call you a liar."

He laughed again. "I was going to say more *prone to infection.*"

"Well, that's also true." With my finger, I absently traced a line of muscle between his pectorals. He shuddered underneath my touch. "Thank you," I whispered. "For coming for me."

He was silent for so long that I thought he hadn't heard me. I stared up at him, but his gaze was fixed ahead, no doubt to ensure we didn't crash into a tree or something. In a solemn voice, he murmured, "I will always come for you, *dannahla.*"

I wasn't sure why, but the words sounded almost sorrowful. His brows were drawn together, his mouth turned down, and I wondered what he was thinking about that made him so somber.

Did he know about the rose jewel? Was he concerned that Warwick had found out about it? Just before Varius had lifted me into his arms, I had grabbed it from the ground. Now it was tucked into my cloak pocket, and I kept one hand firmly wrapped around the hard, smooth petals. The contact of my skin was likely keeping the enchantment from attacking us.

Perhaps Varius had noticed I'd taken the jewel, and he was upset I hadn't told him about it.

But there was plenty *he* hadn't told *me*. The witch's words still echoed in my mind, along with her screams of agony. So much about that vision still haunted me.

I would talk to Varius about it soon. But I had to process it all first.

And I needed to do some research in the library to see what more I could learn about the spell.

I must have fallen asleep in Varius's arms. When I awoke, I was surrounded by fluffy pillows and wrapped in a thick woolen blanket. I opened my eyes to find a darkened room. When I shifted, I realized I was lying in a massive bed.

Alone.

"Varius?" I croaked sleepily.

No answer.

With a frown, I slid out from under the covers, only to find I was dressed in a simple cotton shift. My wounds had been cleaned and bandaged, and someone had bathed me as well. Enzira, no doubt. Or Ramia.

How had I slept through it all? Either someone had used

magic to keep me asleep—Tislora, perhaps—or I'd been in worse shape than I'd thought.

My shoulder still throbbed from Warwick's bite. Wincing from the pain, I eased out of bed and lit the lantern.

In the armchair by my bed dozed a familiar figure. It was Ramia, her head cradled in her arm as she snored softly. I smiled. It had felt like ages since I'd last seen her.

I glanced around the room. It was definitely Varius's chambers, but he wasn't here. It was just me and Ramia.

My gaze flicked toward the door, my throat knotting. I supposed, with Warwick dead, there was no longer a need for my husband to guard me every hour of the day.

Perhaps Varius was busy. There were certainly more important things to do than sit by my bedside and wait for me to wake up.

I draped a shawl around my shoulders and strode toward Varius's desk. I found a spare bit of parchment and a quill and immediately began writing down every detail I could recall from the memory the rose jewel had shown me. The shadowstone. King Ragnus draining the witch's power. And finally, the words of her curse.

When I was finished, I set the quill down and folded up the parchment, then searched for my cloak. With a start, I patted my sides, my heart seizing with dread.

The rose jewel was gone.

Shit, shit, *shit*.

I hurried to the bathing chamber and searched under piles of towels and other linens. But there was no sign of my cloak or my pouch of gemstones.

"No," I breathed, my mind spiraling with panic. Where were they?

I returned to the bedchamber and gently shook Ramia's shoulders. I hated to rouse her... but she would want to know I was awake.

"Ramia," I whispered.

She mumbled something, then turned her head. One eye cracked open and surveyed me. Then, she stiffened and sat up straight.

"My lady! You're awake! Oh, thank the gods. I was so worried for you. When they brought you in here looking like *that*—"

"Ramia." I squeezed her arm to silence her. "I'm all right. But I need to know where my gemstones are."

She blinked, her brow furrowing. "Oh! You mean that blue pouch? It was with your cloak. I think Enzira sent it to be washed."

Dread coiled in my chest. *Damn it.* "And the rose?"

She frowned. "What rose?"

"There was a red jewel shaped like a rose. Did you see it?"

She considered this for a moment before shaking her head. "No. I didn't see anything like that."

I ran my hands through my hair, biting back a curse.

A knock sounded at the door, and Ramia stood to open it. I straightened, my pulse racing at the thought of seeing Varius. Perhaps he could tell me what happened to my gems.

My heart sank when Enzira entered. But I forced a smile as she beamed at me.

"So glad you're awake, my lady," she said before drawing the curtains. Midday sun spilled into the room, illuminating the darkened space. I flinched against the brightness, waiting until she was finished with the curtains before speaking.

"Where is the king?"

Enzira didn't meet my gaze. "In the dining hall."

I supposed I should be eating anyway. "Very well. I'll dress and meet him for lunch."

"He has asked not to be disturbed. He had your food sent up to you." Enzira gestured behind her, where a tray of sliced meat, fresh cheese, and toasted bread awaited.

My stomach sank, and I looked questioningly at Enzira. She finally met my gaze, her lips thinning.

Cold realization settled into my bones. "I see." My voice was strained.

He did not want to see me.

Perhaps he knew about the rose jewel and was angry with me.

Perhaps he regretted kissing me and didn't want to give me the wrong idea.

"What is it?" Ramia asked, glancing between us.

In Terrish, I explained that the king was too busy to see me today.

"He's the king," Ramia said with the wave of her hand. "He has a busy schedule, my lady. Think nothing of it."

I nodded, but something told me it was more than that. "Where are my clothes from yesterday? I need my cloak."

"I sent them to be washed," said Enzira.

"What about the items in my pockets?" I didn't mind if Enzira knew about the gemstones, but now didn't seem the time to explain it all to her. Especially not with Ramia present.

Enzira frowned, then strode over to the armoire. After pulling open a few drawers, she withdrew a familiar pouch and lifted it so I could see. "Is this what you're looking for?"

Ramia made a surprised sound, then covered her mouth. She must have been sleeping when Enzira had put the pouch there.

A relieved exhale whooshed from me. I hurried to Enzira's side and accepted the pouch from her, pressing my fingers against the rough material to ensure the stones were inside. "Thank you," I breathed. "*Thank you.*"

Enzira gave me a knowing smile that made me wonder just how much she knew. "I understand how precious that is to you."

I swallowed hard. "They are gemstones."

"I know. I've seen you with that one around your neck." She gestured to the amber stone at my throat. I brushed my fingers over it, grateful that she hadn't removed it while bathing me.

She *did* seem to perceive more than I realized.

I opened my mouth to say more, but Enzira lifted a hand to stop me. "You do not owe me an explanation, my lady."

"But I want you to know."

Her smile turned soft. "Then tell me your tale another time. I would love to hear it. For now, I must ensure you are dressed for the day before attending to other duties. The king has asked me to carefully inspect your chambers alongside the sorceress Tislora to see if any clues were left behind."

I frowned. "But Warwick is dead."

"Yes. But we do not know who else was working with him. Anything we find could lead us to his co-conspirators."

"What is she saying?" Ramia asked.

In Terrish, I said darkly, "We are talking of Warwick and who might have been working with him."

"It's a pity that scumbag died before I could get my hands on him," Ramia muttered as she rearranged the sheets on the bed.

I ignored her, knowing full well she would have been *no* match for Warwick. But perhaps Enzira and Tislora would find out how he was connected to the Earthen Court.

It still made no sense to me.

I needed to look more closely into my own court. I needed to use the shadowstone.

Just the idea of touching that cursed stone made me want to retch. It had been the tool that had brought about the witch's demise. It had glowed white with her curse.

It felt like a bad omen to use such a jewel.

But what choice did I have? I needed to figure out what was happening in my kingdom.

I itched to open my gemstone bag and ensure the rose jewel was safely inside, but I didn't want to tinker with the stones around Ramia and Enzira. The rose jewel and the shadowstone were powerful, and I didn't want to risk injuring either of them. Or drawing them into another memory from the rose jewel.

Enzira helped me into a satin turquoise gown that hugged my body like a second skin. The long skirt fell to my toes, and elegant tapered sleeves extended just past my elbows.

It covered far more of my skin than I was accustomed to. Since I'd arrived in the Shadow Court, most of my dresses had been borderline scandalous by Earthen standards.

"It's quite lovely," Ramia said with an approving smile.

I arched an eyebrow at Enzira. "Where did this dress come from?"

"A gift from the king." Her mouth pinched as if she were trying to hide a smirk.

I inspected the sleeves and the skirt with fresh eyes. It was certainly a beautiful gown.

I snorted. "So his plan is to avoid me and dress me in gowns that cover as much of my body as possible?"

The corners of Enzira's mouth twitched. "It appears so." She quickly added, "Perhaps he doesn't want to repeat what happened at the revel."

I knew Enzira was referring to Warwick and his threats. But her comment reminded me of *other* things that had happened that night.

Things between Varius and me.

Warmth coiled in my chest at the reminder. The way his body had responded to mine. The heat of his hands on my skin. His shadows plunging into me over and over.

That was what he was trying to avoid.

My stomach twisted. He was pushing me away.

I huffed in exasperation, then strode to the armoire. "No. He can hide from me all he wants, but I refuse to sit by and let him dress me how he likes as if I were some porcelain doll with no say in the matter." I sifted through several gowns before I found a black one that caught my eye.

I smiled. "This will do nicely."

Enzira approached me and hummed in agreement. "I think it suits you perfectly, my lady." Her eyes sparkled.

Ramia made a soft choking sound. "It's quite… revealing."

"Which means it will fit in perfectly with the fashions of this court," I said in Terrish.

Enzira helped me into it with ease, since there was no corset or petticoat. The bodice was made of sheer black lace that exposed every curve of my chest, the intricate floral design barely concealing my nipples. The skirt flowed outward, with sparkling silver leaves sewn in that shimmered with each movement. A long slit ran all the way up my right thigh, baring my leg with each step I took.

"Is there anything else I can help you with, my lady?" Enzira asked after she had pinned up half my hair, leaving the rest loose down my back.

"No, thank you, Enzira. You've been tremendously helpful."

She beamed and pressed a fist to her chest. Before she left, I called out to her.

"Enzira? If you see my husband, will you tell him I'll be in the library? Assuming he isn't too much of a coward to face me."

Enzira's face flushed. "I'm not sure I should repeat those *exact* words, my lady."

"Please do. Tell him I threatened you with excessive force if you did not relay the message to him word for word." I grinned, showing my teeth.

Enzira snorted, then covered her mouth. She cleared her throat. "I—I will do my best, my lady." After bringing her fist to her heart once more, she turned and left the room.

THE BEAUTY

After Enzira left, I asked Ramia to fetch me some ginger tea and motherwort to alleviate the pains from my monthly cycle. My cycle wasn't due for another week at least, but Ramia did not ask for confirmation, which meant I didn't have to lie.

It still felt dishonest, though.

But I needed to use the shadowstone. And, for Ramia's own protection, it was safer if she didn't know about it.

Once she was gone, I didn't waste any time. I dug through my pouch of gemstones and found the shadowstone.

The jeweled rose was nowhere to be found. But I would have to solve that mystery later.

For now, I needed to know for sure that the Earthen Court armies would not attack the Shadow Court. Not with Warwick dead.

I hurried to the bathing chamber and squeezed the dark stone in my hand. "Show me my father."

The mirror swirled with gray smoke, but all it did was churn and roil.

"Show me King Maddox of the Earthen Court," I said, my voice loud and firm.

Still nothing but smoke.

Unease spread through me. What was going on? Where was my father?

Perhaps he had some kind of protective amulet that prevented magic from locating him. That sounded like something paranoid my father would do.

I tried something else. "Show me Gerard, Captain of the Earthen Court."

If my father's armies were preparing to march on the Shadow Court, Gerard would be involved.

The smoke swirled, then faded to reveal the courtyard of the Terrona Castle. Gerard stood there in full armor, arguing with another soldier. The captain's face was ruddy with anger, his eyes dark and enraged. The soldier before him looked young; a new recruit who had neglected his duties, most likely.

Gerard was clearly in the Earthen Court. Relief settled over me, but doubt still crept into my thoughts.

Warwick had mentioned meeting the armies at Chesser Road in three days' time. That was today. Was there any chance at all the armies would still show up? Even without Gerard leading them?

I shook my head. "Show me Chesser Road."

I wasn't sure if it would work. But, sure enough, the vision changed and revealed a familiar cobbled road. It was covered in the roiling mist of the Necro Shadows.

Shit... My home, my kingdom. The shadows were on their doorstep now.

Chesser Road was only a mile from the castle. In no time at all, the shadows would breach the castle walls.

But there were no armies. How could there be, with the shadows so close?

I knew this was good news—it meant there was no army approaching. But it still didn't make any sense. Why would Warwick have a meeting in the thick of Necro Shadows? What was I missing?

Leaning forward, I peered more closely into the mirror's

depths, trying to make out any figures within the shadows. But they were too thick.

I placed the shadowstone back in the pouch, frustrated that I hadn't solved this yet. Was it possible that someone's fae magic allowed them to move through the shadows unaffected? Could someone be there, waiting for Warwick right now, concealed by the Necro Shadows?

I brought a hand to my amber stone. "Azure?"

It took her a moment to respond. When she did, her voice sounded sleepy. *"Yes?"*

"Never mind. Go back to sleep."

"I'm awake, Sybelle. What is it?"

"You need your strength."

"You silly humans always underestimate us. Just tell me what you need from me."

"I need you to fly over Chesser Road and tell me if anything is amiss."

Azure was silent for a moment. *"Chesser Road is too far for us to communicate."*

"I know. But this is important. You're the only one who can get there quickly enough. Warwick said he would rendezvous with his allies at Chesser Road today. I need to know if anyone is there."

Azure hesitated. *"I don't like leaving you."*

"Varius will protect me." Even as I said it, my stomach knotted again. He was avoiding me.

Regardless, I knew he would ensure my safety. He had made that much clear last night when he'd saved my life.

Azure sighed. *"Very well. But I won't linger for very long. I'll return before sundown."*

"Thank you. Please be safe."

"You too, Sybelle."

I knew how worried she was because she called me by my

name instead of *human*. I prayed I was making the right choice in sending her away.

I left the bedchamber in search of the library. But when I opened the door, I found myself in an unfamiliar hallway. Frowning, I made my way down the hall, searching for landmarks I recognized.

I froze when echoing voices drew closer, followed by soft footsteps. My instincts told me to return to the bedchamber, until I heard a child's wailing cry.

My heart jolted in my chest, and I hurried forward without thinking. When I rounded the corner, I froze, eyes wide.

Clermont was leading a large crowd of fae through the hall. Upon seeing me, he stopped and went rigid.

My eyes roved over the crowd of fae behind him. They certainly weren't nobles. Their faces were smeared with dirt, and their clothes were ragged and torn. And…

They were families. Several adult males and females, some with younger fae standing alongside them.

A few of the female fae were clutching small children in their arms. My eyes fell on one, a child with purple skin and cat-like eyes, who was writhing in his mother's grip. She was attempting to shush him to no avail. His screech bounced off the walls.

"My lady." Clermont stepped in front of me, drawing my attention to him. "Can I help you with something?"

"I'm just—" I was going to say I was looking for the library, but my gaze was fixed on the screaming child. "Clermont, what is going on?"

"These are refugees from the Pern District. Their homes were destroyed by the shadows, and they need a place to stay until the village can be rebuilt."

My heart twisted with horror and pain. I stared at the faces of the fae before me, seeing them in a new light.

Their homes were gone. Their lives uprooted. They were in a foreign place, and they were frightened.

In this moment, I had never felt so helpless. The fear in their eyes was so potent it stole my breath.

I inhaled shakily and approached the fae with the screaming child. Clermont uttered a protest, but I ignored him, drawing closer to the child with slow and careful steps.

The mother's eyes widened at my approach, and she tried to clutch the child more tightly to her, but he thrashed even harder.

Hesitantly, I spread my hands. "May I help?" I asked in Agnarrish.

The woman stilled, clearly surprised by my use of her language. She said nothing, so I didn't try to come any closer.

Raising my voice over the child's crying, I said, "Do you want to see something funny?"

The child's cries faded, but only slightly. He still maintained a halfhearted wail, but his eyes were fixed on me.

I held up my hands directly in front of my face, extending one finger on each. "Watch. My eyes will follow both fingers. Do you think I can do it?"

The child fell silent, staring at me with interest.

I lifted my hands so my extended fingers were directly in front of each eye. "You'll have to watch carefully to see," I said. "Are you ready?"

The child nodded.

I slowly brought my hands together until my fingertips were touching. When they met, my eyes were fully crossed, and I stuck out my tongue.

The child burst out laughing, the peals echoing in the hall. Around us, a few of the fae chuckled with amusement. Even the child's mother offered a small smile.

I dropped my hands with a grin and then said, "You are very brave. Do you think you can be brave for a few more moments?"

The child sobered and nodded again.

My smile widened. "Thank you." I nodded at the mother, who gave a warm look of gratitude.

I turned and moved back down the hall, where Clermont stood, watching me uneasily. He glanced from me to the child and back again.

"That was... impressive," he said. "Thank you for helping him."

"I wish I could do more," I said, wringing my hands together.

Clermont sighed. "So do I, my lady. Do you need my assistance with anything?"

"Where is the library?"

Clermont gestured behind him. "Just around that corner. I believe the door is already open, so you won't have to worry about exploring more areas of the castle." He offered a wry smile.

"Thank you."

He pressed a fist to his chest, then continued down the hall. The crowd of fae followed after, some shooting me curious looks. The child waved happily, then rested his head on his mother's shoulder.

For a long moment, I watched them make their way down the hall, my heart clenching painfully in my chest.

If I figure out how to break the curse, I can help them.

Resolve filled me, and I turned and made my way to the library.

Just as Clermont said, the door was already open. I stepped inside, scanning the room for Varius.

But he wasn't there.

I wasn't sure why I was surprised. It was clear he did not

want to see me. Whatever lust we felt between us was not something he intended to pursue.

I told myself it was fine. We had both entered into this marriage presuming that no feelings would be involved.

But the more I told myself the lie, the less I believed it.

No matter. I didn't need him to help me research. Now that I knew a witch was behind the Necro Shadows, I knew what to look for. Unfortunately, the sentient library was unable to provide me with any texts on the history of the Shadow Court witches. I gathered this was intentional; the witch must have included a clause in her spell that prevented people like me from asking too many questions. It was also why Varius was unable to speak directly of the curse.

However, I knew there were books about the witches of the Earthen Court. And, as the neighboring kingdom of the Shadow Court, surely there had to be similarities.

After Tislora all but admitted she was aware there had once been Earthen witches, I was intrigued. Was it possible there had been survivors after King Ragnus had killed the witches? Had any of them had children that had possibly lived on after the slaughter? Tislora herself was a sorceress. Where had she come from?

"Castle, can you give me the red volume from before—the one about the Earthen Court witches?" I asked.

The shelves rattled, and a heavy book dropped to the floor next to me. I picked it up, finding the place where I had left off before and re-reading the passage with greater interest.

The most powerful witch enchantments were anchored to an object or person, which fueled its power, allowing it to survive as long as the object or person remained healthy and intact. Trinkets, coins, heirlooms, and gemstones were commonly used. The rarest of spells were able to harness the power of a witch's lineage in order to fuel the magic.

I froze.

A witch's lineage...

I had told Varius that fae magic could not outlive the one who cast the spell. But, according to this passage, a rare spell *could* live beyond a witch's death… through her lineage.

Was I right? Had there been survivors?

What if the witch who cast this spell had had a child? A child that Ragnus did not know about?

I pulled out the scrap of parchment I had tucked into the bodice of my dress. On it were my notes from the rose jewel's vision.

I scanned the parchment, searching for my hasty scribblings of the witch's spell. I had only recalled bits and pieces, but it was better than nothing. If that damned jewel hadn't mysteriously vanished, perhaps I could jump back into the memory and recount the events myself.

I glanced over my recollection of the witch's curse.

…shadows turn poisonous, destroying lives...

...bodies cursed to beastly forms...

...never speak of today's events...

...stone of shadow and blood...

...one of my kind gives up a life...

...curse will live on as my line lives on...

...blood of witches will poison the land...

I chewed on my fingernail as I studied the words. My blood ran cold when I found what I was looking for. *The curse will live on as my line lives on.*

"Holy shit," I breathed, my hand shaking as I covered my mouth. "Holy *shit.*"

This meant at least one of the Shadow Court witches was still alive.

The Beast

I spent most of the day poring over letters from my spy network that Clermont had delivered earlier today. No whispers of any approaching army.

However, the soldiers who had been loyal to Warwick had been arrested and interrogated. And they were not giving up any information as to who in the Earthen Court they had been working for.

It was clear they were willing to die with their secrets.

I sighed, rubbing my eyes. I had spent the night here in the study, and the firm cushions of the sofa were not nearly as comfortable as the one in my chambers.

But I couldn't bear to share the space with Sybelle. Not again. Not after our kiss.

If I did, I might cross a line I could never come back from.

Things would end so much more painfully if we let this continue. The curse would either claim my life or hers.

Or both.

Each of the human brides had died from giving too much blood to the ravenous shadows.

And, soon after, the kings had died, too.

It was best to put a stop to any romantic attachment now, before anyone got hurt.

I was already hiding too much from her. She would never

forgive me when she found out the only way to break the curse was for her to die.

"Varius."

I looked up to find Tislora at the open doorway, her face unusually grim. "What is it?"

"I've finished sweeping the queen's chambers. I found something that might interest you." She lifted a wrinkled and half-burned piece of parchment.

"Did you find any traces of magic? Anything Warwick left behind?"

"There was a fae scent I didn't recognize. But no traces of magic."

I bit back a growl of frustration and fury. A fae had been in Sybelle's rooms. A fae who *wasn't* Warwick.

Which meant I had more than one traitor lurking in my court.

"Varius," Tislora said again.

I blinked. "What?"

"I found this in her room. You need to read it." She strode into the room, then handed me the parchment. Her mouth was set in a hard line, her jaw tight with concern.

I had never seen her so solemn before. With dread pulsing in my gut, I accepted the parchment and read over the words. It was written in Terrish, but I understood it well enough. With each line I read, anger boiled in my veins. Shadows spread along the floor, covering the carpet in inky smoke.

My Lady,

I yearn for you. Every moment since you've left has been torture for me. Please send word that you are safe. I am going mad not knowing. I miss having you to hold in my arms. I miss the way our bodies fit together.

There is no one like you. And there never will be.

But that is not the only reason I write to you. I must also ask if the endeavor we discussed previously has been accomplished yet. If it has, please send word immediately. Our armies intend to cross the border and invade the kingdom if it's clear you have been unsuccessful.

I am risking my life by sending this to you, but I would never forgive myself if something happened to you because I did not warn you. I am in love with you, my darling, and I would give anything to have you in my arms once more.

Please write back quickly. If you are close to achieving your goal, I can send word and delay the army.

All my love,

G

I read over the letter twice, and a growl vibrated through me.

"Where is she?" I bit out. I couldn't look at Tislora. I didn't want to see the smug satisfaction on her face.

She had warned me about this. And I hadn't listened.

"The library," Tislora said, her voice betraying nothing.

I crumpled the parchment in my hands, then stuffed it into my pocket. As much as I wanted to shred it to pieces with my claws, I needed it as evidence in case Sybelle tried to deny my accusations.

I stormed toward the door, shadows billowing behind me. The roaring in my ears only intensified when I reached the hall. I threw open the first door I reached. Perhaps the castle was on my side today, because it sent me directly to the library.

A fire was burning in the hearth, and my Lumen orbs cast faint glows along the shelves of books.

In the wing-backed chair—*my* chair—sat Sybelle, poring over a thick leather tome. On the table next to her was a massive stack of books waiting to be read.

Shadows burst forward, reaching for her. A snarl rumbled within me, and I stepped into the room, letting the door slam shut behind me.

Sybelle yelped and looked up, eyes wide. "Varius?" She frowned, clearly surprised to see me here.

My fingers curled into shaking fists, and I gritted my teeth so hard my temples throbbed. Slowly, I prowled toward her like a predator who didn't want to startle his prey. Dark clouds churned behind me as my shadows intensified.

Sybelle's face paled, and she jumped to her feet, her eyes fixed on the swirling shadows behind me.

I froze, only then noticing what she was wearing. It was certainly not the silky dress I had sent to her.

No, this was… this was quite different.

Thin black lace barely covered her bosom, forming intricate designs that only faintly concealed her breasts. So much was on display that I had to work around a lump in my throat to find my voice at all.

"What… are you wearing?" I rasped.

She gave a short exhale. "A *dress*."

"Why are you wearing *that* one?"

She placed her hands on her hips. "Because I want to. Is that a problem?"

"I—you—" I grumbled a stream of curses and ran my hand through my hair. This was *not* why I was here. "Tell me you have not been colluding with the Earthen Court to attack my kingdom."

Her jaw slackened, and she stared at me in horror. "*What?* No, I haven't! Why would you think that?"

"For starters, you are from the Earthen Court." I drew closer to her and slammed the parchment onto the table between us, making it rattle. "And then, there's this."

Her eyes dropped to the crumpled letter. With a small frown, she approached it and picked it up. As she unfolded it, her hands began to shake.

Her face turned ashen.

The guilt in her expression was the most damning evidence of all.

A roar climbed up my throat, and I turned away from her before I succumbed to the urge to wrap my hands around her throat. "Our arrangement is over. I'll have my soldiers escort you to a dungeon cell while I figure out what to do with you."

"Varius, wait—"

I was almost to the door. "Goodbye, Sybelle."

"Damn it, will you let me explain?"

"Explain *what?*" I snarled, whirling to face her. Shadows spilled along the floor and up the walls, creeping forward until they blotted out the light from my Lumen. Only the fire remained, bathing everything in a hazy orange glow. "How you are corresponding with your Earthen Court lover? How you had a *plan* with him to destroy my kingdom? Or how you knew the Earthen Court was sending an army to invade my lands?"

"None of that is true!" she shouted, surging toward me, her face full of panic. "I did not expect him to write to me, Varius. Things between us were over the moment I left my kingdom. And I already *told* you what my plan was: to locate the source of the Necro Shadows and destroy it."

"So you did *not* intend to kill me?" I asked, my voice full of doubt.

Her lips thinned. And it was all the answer I needed.

Rage coursed through me with violent fervor. If I didn't leave this room soon, I would tear it to shreds.

I would tear *her* to shreds.

I turned away, but she cried out again, stopping me.

"I did not know you then, Varius! All I knew was the stories that had been told to me of the terrible Wraith King and the poisonous shadows he used to attack my people. Everything I had been taught about you was a lie. I did not realize that until I came here."

I shook my head, unconvinced. "And the armies?"

She took another step toward me. "I wrote back to Gerard. I told him I was close, and to persuade my father to hold off on the armies. I thought he had listened! I thought I had bought us more time!"

Gerard. Hearing the bastard's name on her lips made me want to shove my fist through a wall.

And she wrote back to him… What else had she said in that letter? How much she yearned for him, too?

"I told you before, and I will say it again," she said, drawing even closer. "I have taken no lovers since we were wed. Not even through correspondence."

I sneered at her. "You think that's what I'm worried about? This pathetic human lover? I'm concerned for my *people*, Sybelle. Take whatever damn fool you want to your bed."

The words tasted like ash in my mouth. Just the idea of another man in her bed filled my blood with fire.

But I forced myself to say, "How long did you know about the armies?"

She sucked in a breath. A beat of silence passed before she answered in a timid voice. "I received the letter a few days after the wedding."

A rumbling snarl worked up my throat. "And you decided to keep this information to yourself?"

"I was still searching for the source of the shadows! You weren't telling me anything! If you had just been honest with me—"

"Oh, so this is *my* doing? I was supposed to share my deepest secrets with the human I had just met?"

"No, but you could have damn well told me why I was here in the first place!"

"You know I couldn't!" I roared, the firelight flickering as my shadows thickened. "I could not tell you *any* of it, Sybelle!"

She stepped closer to me. "You could have told me you needed me to protect your people from the shadows. You could have told me you needed *human blood*. You could have given me *some* information, Varius. But you've been lying from the beginning. Ever since that contract between our kingdoms was created."

"I didn't write the contract."

"No, but you carried it on. You kept up the ruse. I may have deceived you, but you deceived me, too."

She had closed the distance between us, our bodies now only inches apart as she glared up at me. I knew I needed to step back before I lashed out and hurt her.

Before I could move, however, she said, "Cut me, and I will swear it."

I blinked. "What?"

"Use my dagger to cut my hand. I will swear on my fae blood that I'm not lying. That I'm no longer loyal to my court. I am loyal to *you*, Varius."

I could only stare at her, shocked by her words. A vow with fae blood was sacred and unbreakable. Even if she could lie as a human, she would not be able to fabricate something like that.

As if to prove how serious she was, she reached to her thigh and unsheathed the dagger hidden there. She pressed it into my hand.

"You—You would swear such things?" I whispered.

"Yes."

Her gaze was steady as she held mine. She did not flinch. She did not waver.

"I will not cut you." I thrust the hilt of the dagger back into her grasp.

Her lips thinned. "Fine. Then I'll do it."

"Sybelle—"

But she had already pressed the tip of her blade into her palm. Crimson blood beaded from the wound. She lifted her hand, her expression fierce, and said, "I, Sybelle of the Earthen Court, swear by my fae blood that I am no longer loyal to the Earthen Court, but to my husband and the Shadow Court. I swear that I did not collude with the Earthen Court to invade the Shadow Court."

My breath caught in my throat as the air hummed with power, proof that her vow was magically binding.

Mother of Shade, she'd actually done it.

She was loyal to me. To my people.

Except...

"What of your human lover?" I spat the words before I could stop myself.

Her eyes shuttered, and she drew back a step. Her nostrils flared. "This again? I'm tired of this, Varius. Just tell me you want me all to yourself and let's be done with it."

I bared my teeth at her. "That is *not*—"

"How dare you? First, you ignore me as if our kiss never happened. Then, you command me to wear a dress of your choosing as if I'm your pet. And now, you're accusing me of harboring secret lovers." She laughed without humor as she returned her dagger to the sheath at her thigh. "Make up your damn mind. Will you claim me as your wife in earnest? Or will you continue to hide from this like a coward, only to be brought out by your petty jealousy at the thought of me seeking affection elsewhere?"

I growled, the sound low and feral, as I strode toward her until I was towering over her slight form. Despite our height difference, she still stared up at me with anger and determination, unfazed by my intimidating stature.

"I am the King of Shadows," I said. "And I claim what's mine."

"Prove it," she said. "Make me yours, Varius."

I stared down at her, conflict roiling within me. I couldn't see clearly; the rage and lust and heat churning in my body were too intense to sift through. All I knew was the pounding need that flooded my body, the desire quaking in my bones.

I bent over her, framing her face in my hands and drawing her closer. "You are mine, Sybelle."

My shadows danced around us as I brought her mouth to mine.

THE BEAUTY

My blood still simmered with a mixture of anger and fear, and when Varius loomed over me, his eyes dark and his fangs bared, I felt an unexpected bolt of desire.

His mouth was on mine, and I gripped the fabric of his tunic to pull him closer. His mouth captured mine with hungry fervor, a groan building in his throat and vibrating through his chest. Stones, it was the most delicious sound.

I waited for him to pull away, to withdraw from me like he had after our last kiss. Instead, his hands found my waist, and he spun us both around until my back was against the closed door, his chest caging me in.

"Do you really want this?" he murmured against my lips. "Every monstrous side of me?"

I stood on my toes to wrap my arms around his neck, my fingers tangling in his curls. "I want all of you, Varius. No part of you will frighten me."

His lips quirked upward. "Are you sure about that?"

I gasped as a cool mist wrapped around my fingers. I lowered my arms and found tendrils of his shadows snaking along my hands, caressing my skin like a whispering wind. The soft contact made me shiver.

I recalled how he had used his shadows to restrain Warwick

in the Noxen Forest. *You didn't know I could do that, did you?* he'd asked. I wondered if this was a special ability he didn't often use—corporeal shadows that could touch and pull as if they were as solid as his own hands.

I knew from experience just how solid those shadows could feel as they moved inside me.

Varius seemed amused by my reaction. His shadows wound tighter, pulling against my wrists and jerking them upward until my arms were pinned above my head. I uttered a noise of surprise, but he silenced me with another kiss, this one forceful and bruising. His hard mouth pressed against mine, his rough tongue scraping along my lips.

I moaned into his mouth, meeting his tongue with mine. I tried to move my hands so I could touch him, but his restraints would not budge.

"This is who I am," he growled. "I am a monster, Sybelle. I will not be gentle with you."

I leaned up and bit down on his lower lip. A rumbling sound resonated in his throat. "I know," I whispered. "I don't want you to be."

He exhaled shakily, dragging his sharp incisors along my lip and chin, then lowering to my throat. "You are part human." His breath tickled the skin of my neck. "I might break you."

I found it hard to breathe as he pressed that long tongue against my throat, gliding up and down in torturously slow movements.

"I—I can handle it," I gasped, my eyelids fluttering shut. "With my—my dagger."

Varius froze, then withdrew to stare down at me. "Your dagger?"

I nodded, still dazed. "It's a diamond-studded dagger. It gives me supernatural strength."

"How?"

"I have to be holding it in my hand. Diamonds make me bolder, but when I'm holding them in my hand, they grant me speed and endurance."

He arched an eyebrow, his lips curling upward. "Endurance, you say? And it's on your thigh?"

My legs clenched from the dark, sultry tone of his voice. Slowly, I nodded.

He glanced down to my legs, then dragged his gaze back up to mine. Shadows swelled around me, and the cuffs around my wrists tightened. "Last chance to turn away, *dannahla*," he breathed. "I told you I wouldn't touch you until you begged."

I leaned closer to him. "I'm not begging. I'm demanding."

His pupils flared. With inhuman speed, he dragged over a small table, the wooden legs groaning against the floor. He slid the table under me until it was against the door, then hoisted me on top so we were at eye level. My legs wrapped around him, drawing him closer. His fingers pushed up my skirt, exposing my thighs and my sheathed dagger.

I waited for him to draw the blade, but his fingers lingered on my thighs, inching upward. His hands were calloused and warm, and each touch sent fire coursing through my veins. His claws slid up and up, the sharpened points bringing a flood of awareness shooting through my body.

My head rolled back against the door, my eyes closing as an onslaught of sensations seared through me.

Varius leaned in, his breath hot against my throat, then pressed his teeth right in that space between my shoulder and my neck. He didn't push hard enough to break skin, but a line of fire exploded along my skin as he dragged his teeth up and down my throat.

"Stones," I whispered, my hips bucking against him.

"You trust me not to pierce your skin?" he murmured.

"Yes," I rasped. "I trust you, Varius."

He hummed against my throat, then swirled his tongue in circles over my flesh. My skin pebbled, and I let out a low moan.

His left hand slid up my thigh, then drew my dagger. In a swift movement, he placed the hilt in my hand. I clasped it tightly and felt a surge of energy. My hands jerked, pulling against his shadow cuffs. One hand worked free, and I used it to grip one of his horns.

He let out a feral sound, something between a growl and a snarl, his body going perfectly still.

"You *are* stronger," he hissed, his eyes fiery as he stared me down.

I tugged on his horn, dragging his face back to mine before plunging my tongue between his lips. His fangs brushed along my tongue. Cool mist tickled my hands as his shadows tugged on my wrist once again, dragging my hand to where the other one was still tied. I kept the dagger hilt clenched tightly between my fingers.

"Will you keep me tied up the entire time?" I asked.

He smirked. "I suppose you'll have to wait and see." He sank to his knees, then spread my legs open wide, baring me to him.

I froze. I wasn't expecting this. "What—What are you doing?"

"I want to taste you first, *dannahla*. I want to devour this sweet arousal of yours and see if it tastes as good as it smells."

My toes curled. Would he really… *lick* me there? Gerard had never done such a thing.

Varius sensed my hesitation. "Unless you don't want me to. I can stop, Sybelle." All amusement left his voice.

I shook my head, my insides quivering with anticipation. "No," I said breathlessly. "No, keep going. I want you to."

His eyes sparked with desire just before he buried his face between my thighs. I let out a sharp gasp, stunned by how his hair and nose tickled the most sensitive parts of my thighs.

And then his tongue met my center, and my world caved

inward. Sparks ignited in my blood, firing through my body. My hips jerked, and he flicked his tongue against me.

My head fell backward with a thud, and I moaned. He licked me, each stroke hard and unyielding. His tongue slid in deeper, thrusting further than I thought possible, hard enough for me to see stars. I gasped, unable to speak or even think as he ravaged me. The coarseness of his tongue against my slick core sent me reeling.

"So delicious," he growled, and his breath along my throbbing center made me cry out again.

His tongue drove deeper, tracing circles, moving faster and harder until the tension within me was coiled so tightly I thought I might die. I clung to my dagger, my palms covered in sweat. Without the strength of those diamonds, I might have passed out. It was too much. *Too much.*

"You are so close," he whispered. His hands spread me even wider, and he dragged his tongue along my inner walls, making me scream. My thighs clamped around him as I rode his tongue, urging him onward, demanding for release.

"Please, please," I choked out. *"Please."*

I didn't even know what I was begging for. All I knew was I had *never* felt anything like this before. My insides were wound up tight, ready to burst. Pressure mounted, climbing up my chest and knotting in my throat.

Varius pressed his thumb against my center, his claw bringing a twinge of pain without drawing blood.

It sent me over the edge. My body thrashed violently against him, my skin on fire and my blood roaring. Something inside me shattered, and I no longer knew who I was or why I was here. All I knew was the monumental tidal wave that crashed over me, carrying me away.

When my body settled, I was panting and sweaty, but I wasn't finished. Not even close.

"I want to see it," I said.

Varius stood and met my gaze, his lips slick with my moisture. "See what?"

My eyes dipped to his trousers, then back up. "I want to see it," I said, enunciating each word.

His eyebrows lifted. "Very well."

He tugged his tunic out of his trousers and pushed the sleeves down his arms. Then, he unfastened his buckle and let his trousers and tunic drop to his ankles.

My throat went bone dry at the sight of him. Holy Stones, he was magnificent.

And *huge*.

I licked my lips, letting my gaze roam over every glorious inch of him. That burgundy skin, those firm and muscular legs, the hard planes of his chest, his biceps and forearms.

My eyes kept returning to his arousal that twitched as if it sensed my stare. It was so thick and, just as he told me, covered in ridges and bumps.

"You said it's… barbed?" My voice came out strained.

"Only when I release them. And I won't. Not with you."

I nodded. "But—But you've released them before?"

He was quiet for so long that I finally stopped staring and jerked my gaze upward to meet his. His expression was solemn.

"It's more of a defense mechanism than anything," he said softly. "To protect against unwanted advances."

My blood chilled, and I immediately regretted asking. "I'm sorry," I said at once.

He shook his head. "Don't be. I want you to know everything about me, Sybelle. Even the dark and unpleasant parts."

"There are things I want to tell you, too," I said. I thought of Azure. He still didn't know about her. I was grateful she'd managed to escape during the fight with Warwick, but Varius needed to know. He needed to know *everything*.

"You will," he promised, leaning in to brush his mouth against mine. "Soon, we will bare all to each other, *dannahla*."

He pressed his fingers between my thighs again, but I stopped him with a fierce kiss, biting down hard enough on his lip to draw blood.

"No."

He hissed and jerked backward, eyes full of fire.

"It's my turn now," I told him.

THE BEAUTY

"I want to touch it. I want to lick you just as you licked me."

His breath hitched, and his throat bobbed as he swallowed. After a long moment, he said, "I suppose it's only fair."

His shadows loosened, and my arms fell at my sides, the blood rushing violently from the movement. It took a moment to orient myself and get the feeling back in my numb arms. Varius's hands came around my waist as he eased me off the table. I kept my dagger in one hand as I dropped to my knees. My fingers trailed up and down his gloriously muscled thighs. He hummed in satisfaction, his body taut under my touch.

When I reached his cock, I wrapped my hand around it, feeling the tough texture of those bumps against my fingers. His body jerked, and he made a sound like a choked-off groan.

"Tell me if I hurt you," I said.

"You won't," he growled.

I dragged my hand up, then down, my movements slow and measured. Another feral sound escaped him, and his hips thrust against me. I gazed up at him. His eyes were closed, his lips parted slightly.

With no warning, I wrapped my lips around him, taking him in my mouth.

He let out a long and strangled groan, and I felt him

"

twitching inside my mouth. Stones, the tough skin of him was delightful against my tongue. I licked his tip, and he roared before thrusting deeper into me. I took in more of him, letting my teeth scrape along his length. When he didn't flinch in pain, I clamped down harder on him, knowing my teeth were dull in comparison to his fangs.

And his cock was surrounded by toughened skin.

Sure enough, my bite drew out a ragged sound of pleasure from him, his whole body rumbling from it.

"Mother of Shade, Sybelle," he gasped.

I swirled my tongue around him again, then dragged my teeth up and down. He drove deeper, and I knew I wouldn't be able to take his entire length. Using my free hand, I wrapped my fingers all the way up to the shaft, massaging his skin and squeezing him.

He pumped harder and faster, and I let my tongue and teeth scrape and taste him over and over. Wild, animal-like sounds poured from his mouth, and he murmured something in Agnar-rish that I couldn't make out.

My chest swelled with satisfaction. *I* was eliciting these sounds. *I* was driving him mad with pleasure and need.

Me, his human bride.

His wife.

You are mine, Varius, I thought.

I am yours.

I stilled. His voice had resonated in my head as clearly as Azure's when I communicated with her. I looked up at him, but his eyes were still closed, his brows drawn together as he continued to writhe against me.

Perhaps I'd imagined it.

I pushed it from my thoughts, focusing instead on his pleasure. I clamped down my teeth, biting hard, knowing I wasn't strong enough to draw blood. My fingernails dug into him, then pushed up and down.

"Sybelle," he groaned. "*Sybelle.* I—I—"

Moisture beaded at the tip of his cock, and I ravenously licked it off him, eager for more.

"No."

He withdrew, pulling out of my mouth. In one abrupt movement, he pushed me down to the floor and pressed himself against me. With his arms braced on either side of me, he caged me right there on the cold stone floor, his body crowding mine.

His eyes were manic, his shadows swirling behind him. "I will not come until I'm so deep inside you that your bones quake and your blood cries out for me." He leaned in, pressing his nose into the base of my throat and inhaling deeply. "I will show you what it truly means to have someone worship your body, *dannahla.*"

I found myself trembling from the dark promise of his words. I let my fingers trail along the muscles of his broad chest, savoring the way his body seemed to quiver with a purr of satisfaction. My fingers traced delicately along the mark on his shoulder from the Necro Shadows.

"Am I allowed to touch you now?" I whispered. "Or will you tie me up again?"

He grinned, flashing his teeth. "Don't deny it. You loved being tied up."

My stomach fluttered, and my face heated. Because *yes*, I had loved it. It had been thrilling and dangerous. It had excited me in far too many ways.

"Besides," he murmured, leaning down and brushing his mouth against my collarbone. "You are wearing too many clothes. I must rectify this immediately."

His mouth moved lower, and he kissed the swell of my breast. My breath caught in my throat when he hooked his fangs through one of the lace embellishments of my bodice. He jerked his chin, and a ripping sound made me gasp. He dragged his teeth lower and lower, tearing the fabric in two until he reached my navel. As he worked his way up, his tongue danced over my skin, licking and caressing my stomach and abdomen.

I writhed under his touch, my body arching and my breaths ragged. With slow movements, he parted the two slices of fabric across my chest until the bodice fell off me completely.

My breasts heaved with my frantic breaths. I couldn't get enough air. I was gasping, the sounds so loud they echoed in the vast library.

But it didn't seem to bother him. If anything, it only aroused him further. He let out a strained sound of desire before palming one of my breasts and massaging it with his fingers.

"So beautiful," he murmured.

My head rolled back, a loud moan pouring from my lips. He continued kneading my breasts, and my body jerked when he captured my nipple between his lips. He flicked his tongue over it, sucking and nipping, before gently clamping those sharp incisors directly over the bud.

"Oh, *Stones*," I rasped, my hips grinding, desperate for more.

Varius continued to hold my nipple between his teeth, running his tongue over it until my moans turned into harsh, feral grunts.

"I can't—I can't—" I broke off with a guttural cry.

"Can't what?" he breathed against my nipple.

His breath, his tongue, his teeth... It was all too much. Sensation after sensation fired through my body with violent intensity.

His claws gently glided down the length of my arm. It wasn't until my eyes opened that I realized it wasn't his claws at all, but the barbs of his tail. The long, crimson appendage curled against my arm, the barbs poking but not hurting. The tail slid down me, then wrapped around my exposed thigh.

"Mmm, this dress," Varius growled. More ripping sounds followed, and the skirt fell to pieces around my legs, leaving me bare before him.

"That's better." His mouth worked down again, pausing just between my legs. I clenched my thighs in anticipation of feeling that tongue tracing circles inside me again.

"You've still got that dagger?" he asked.

I nodded, unable to speak. The hilt was still clasped in my sweaty palm, and I knew the moment I released it, my exhaustion would claim me.

I wasn't ready for this to be over yet.

Varius's hands gripped my thighs before parting them. He settled himself between them, and I held my breath, waiting for him to push inside me.

But he paused, his dark gaze fixed on me.

"I don't want to hurt you, Sybelle." All signs of his earlier amusement had vanished. He was dead serious now.

I leaned up, bringing the edge of my blade to his throat. "I like a little pain now and then." I spread my legs wider until they wrapped around his abdomen.

"Mother of Shade, you're so deliciously violent." He kissed me hard, his teeth skating over my lip.

I yelped when the cool whisper of his shadows wrapped around my wrists once more, tugging them backward until they were above my head again.

I huffed in exasperation, and he grinned in response. "Don't want you getting so wound up you accidentally slit my throat."

"You once laughed at the idea of me attacking you."

"Yes, and what a fool I was. For you alone hold the key to destroying me entirely."

My heart twisted at his words. Hot desire coursed through me like a river of lava. "Varius—"

He slid inside me, cutting off my words. The motion was slow and careful, as if he were afraid he might break me. I hissed out a breath at the sheer size of him pressing against me. Stones, he was so thick and hard and *everywhere*. My heels dug into his back, drawing him in.

"More," I demanded.

He slid in farther, and I cried out. Pain and pleasure mingled so fiercely I couldn't tell one from the other.

"Sybelle," he groaned.

He thrust again, driving deeper inside me. Stars burst in my vision, and all I could do was inhale sharply. Thoughts fled my mind. I was singularly focused on the feel of him filling me, stretching me to fit him.

"More," I whispered.

He pushed again, and I felt his rigid length brushing against my inner walls. My head was spinning. My throat went dry with my rasping shouts. My hips writhed, and he filled me more. Stones, I worried he would rip me in two. My body wasn't meant to fit someone his size.

But the diamond dagger granted me strength. The pain did not deter me. If anything, it filled me with a savage yearning for more.

I leaned up and kissed him, flicking my tongue against his lips. "More," I murmured into his mouth. "I want all of you, Varius."

He bared his teeth, his nostrils flaring. His hands came around my bare back, clenching tightly. I yelped as he rolled us both, settling me effortlessly on top of him. His shadows loosened, freeing my arms. My hands and the dagger now rested against his chest.

"Take me as deeply as you can," he said, his voice strained. I wondered if he was holding himself back for my sake.

I bent over and licked his chin. "You said you wouldn't be gentle with me, husband. I can handle it." I caught his chin between my teeth and bit down hard.

He growled something unintelligible, his chest thrumming with a barely restrained roar. With one brutal motion, he thrust upward, his hips jerking. I screamed as he entered me fully, the intensity shooting through me with violent fervor. I spread my thighs wider. He hitched my left leg up, shifting the angle as he drove into me again.

White-hot pleasure exploded within me, lighting up my veins like lightning. I rolled my hips, taking him in again.

"Grab my horns, Sybelle," he rasped, his voice strained. "I want you to hold them while you ride me."

I obeyed, keeping the hilt of my dagger tucked between two fingers while I wrapped the others around his long, black horns. I clenched them tightly, and he let out a strangled groan.

"That's it," he said. "Squeeze them hard."

My fingers clamped tightly around his horns, and his eyelids fluttered. I felt his cock pulse inside me.

"Sybelle." He thrust into me again.

Heat flooded my veins. I gasped, my blood sizzling with electricity.

"You're mine," he moaned with another thrust.

"Yours," I breathed, my insides turning molten.

"My wife." *Thrust.* "My queen." *Thrust.* "My goddess." *Thrust.*

I cried out, each brutal motion sending fire up and down my body. Hot moisture burned behind my eyes.

He set a harsh rhythm, pumping wildly as he rammed into me harder and harder. Each thrust was more violent, more unhinged.

His animalistic grunts matched our pace, becoming louder and more savage. Shadows caressed my arms and breasts, and a tendril of smoke glided down my belly. The cool mist was a refreshing respite from the heat of our bodies, the friction of our movements as we came apart together.

He pounded into me mercilessly. Relentlessly. And I knew he wasn't holding back anymore. I used my grip on his horns to anchor me, to keep me grounded; otherwise, his manic thrusts would send me flying. My throat was raw from my screams.

As he buried himself inside me again and again, something shattered within me, breaking who I once was. Together, Varius and I forged something new. A new version of myself that was perfectly aligned with him.

Not a human and a fae.

But a husband and a wife. A king and a queen.

Two sides of the same coin.

More shadows spilled around us, but these were different. They were thinner and the color of the midnight sky. I would have paused to study them, but my body was wholly consumed by Varius. Sweat trickled down his brow. His mouth was open, his eyes closed in rapture. His roars grew louder, and I knew he was close.

My pleasure mounted, churning faster and faster, ready to carry me into oblivion. But I welcomed it. I would dive off that cliff with Varius.

His eyes opened, and they were all black now, the darkness chasing away the white. I knew now it was a sign of him losing control.

And I wanted him to lose control.

"Varius," I moaned. "*Varius.*"

And then his voice was in my head. *"Gods, Sybelle, you ruin me. You destroy me. Mother of Shade, take me... Take me hard. Oh gods, I need more. Gods, you are everything. I can't hold it in. Damn it all, I want to come all over you. I want to taste you, to devour you. I want to go all night with you riding me like this. Harder. Harder. Yes, like that. Tell me you're mine. Take it. Take all of me. I'm yours, Sybelle. Oh, that's it. Yes, yes."*

Flames burst within me, singeing my blood and scorching my veins. I was on fire. My body was burning, but I didn't care.

Burn, I thought. *We will burn together.*

"*Yes, my love,*" came Varius's voice in my mind. "*Burn with me.*"

We both moaned, our voices mingling as our bodies crashed together. Release exploded through me, wrecking me, fracturing me into a thousand pieces. I was everywhere at once, my soul splintering across worlds and realms, carried away by pleasure I never knew was possible.

Varius spilled into me, but I couldn't contain him anymore. Hot liquid drenching my thighs, dripping onto the stone floor. His arms stretched out on either side of him, his palms smashing into the floor around us. The stone cracked as his claws sliced into it. He roared, making the walls tremble. He slammed into me, hips thrusting once, twice, and then a third time before he finally collapsed underneath me.

My hands shook, but I kept my hold on the dagger, knowing the instant I released it, I would feel nothing but pain. I certainly needed my healing moonstone to recover from this; otherwise, I wouldn't be walking for a week.

Shivers wracked my body, and I bent over, resting my head against his heaving chest. We both gasped for breath, our bodies sticky with sweat and other fluids.

I lay against him, eyes closed, focusing on the rapid thumping of his heart. I was too exhausted to speak, to move, to do anything at all. His arms settled around my bare back, holding me against him.

"You have destroyed me, dannahla.*"* His voice was in my mind again.

I licked my lips, finally able to focus on the strange sensation of hearing his thoughts. Was I hallucinating this? Was our lovemaking so violent that it had addled my brain?

"Really?" I thought in response. *"You seem perfectly fine to me."*

His chest shook with a wheezing laugh, and I froze, realizing he *had* heard me.

"You are my wife now in earnest," he said. *"And I would have you be the queen of this land. Reign by my side, Sybelle. As my equal."*

I drew back to stare at him, eyes wide and lips parted. "Varius," I whispered, my throat still raw. "Are you—did you—"

"Be my queen," he breathed. "Say yes, and I'll have you coronated tomorrow. Just be mine, Sybelle."

My mouth went completely dry, and I was at a loss for words. What *could* I say? I knew enough about the previous human brides to know none of them had ever been coronated. They were wives and nothing more. Not unseelie queens.

And certainly not equals.

Varius was offering me something that had never been offered before.

"So, you don't think I'm a traitor?" I asked.

He chuckled again, then leaned in and captured my lips with his. "Never," he murmured against my mouth. When he withdrew, there was a vulnerability in his gaze I had never seen before. It tugged at my heart, making it twist and lurch painfully in my chest.

He was offering not only himself but his entire kingdom to me.

And he was worried I would refuse him.

"Yes," I said quickly. "Yes, I accept."

He grinned broadly before kissing me again, his lips moving hungrily, urgently over mine. He framed my face between his large hands to kiss me harder and deeper. I laughed at his enthusiasm, kissing him with equal fervor.

"Varius," I gasped. "I—I need to tell you something. Well, lots of things." I absently traced my finger along the hard muscles of his chest.

We had just bared everything to one another.

Now, it was time for me to be completely honest with him. He deserved the truth from me.

"I have to tell you something, too," he murmured, stroking a lock of sweaty hair out of my face. "But you go first."

I cleared my throat, suddenly nervous. "I—I have a dragon."

He merely blinked at me. "A dragon?" His voice was full of doubt.

"Yes. She's a Blue Amethyst, and her name is Azure. She—She's my best friend."

His brows knitted together as he searched my face. Perhaps he thought I was joking. Then, his gaze dipped to the amber stone at my throat, and comprehension lit his features.

"She is who you communicate with through the stone."

I nodded.

He wet his lips, and his breathing became uneven. "You have a dragon? A real dragon?"

"Yes. She came with me from the Earthen Court to protect me. She's been hiding near the stables. But I swear she doesn't mean you any harm. I mean, as long as you don't hurt me..." I trailed off as I found Varius grinning. "What?"

"You have a gods-damned *dragon*." He choked on a laugh. "That's—That's *incredible*, Sybelle."

I found myself smiling, too. "You're not angry with me?"

"Why would I be angry? There's a *dragon* nearby! What is she like? I must admit, I've never seen one before."

My smile widened. "She's magnificent. Brilliant blue scales that can lighten or darken to help her blend in with her environment. And she can sense the magic around her and describe how powerful it is and where it came from. I can show her to you sometime. Maybe after a few days, though. She is likely a bit wary of strangers, and—"

Varius gently placed his fingers over my lips, silencing me. As he gazed at me, his eyes crinkled with warmth. "You can show her to me when you're ready, Sybelle. There is no rush. I trust you."

My chest cinched tightly from the affection burning in his eyes.

Would he still be looking at me like that after I shared my next secret?

He seemed to sense my hesitation. "What's wrong?"

"There's something else."

When I paused, he said, "Go on."

I took a shaky breath before I said, "I think the witch who cast your curse had a child in secret. And... I think it's Tislora."

THE BEAST

The euphoria from our lovemaking had not fully subsided when Sybelle uttered those words to me. They rang in my mind, circling over and over again until the elation died, and dread and anger took its place.

Sybelle stared at me with worry in her eyes. She chewed on her lower lip, and I could smell the fear wafting from her.

She thought I would be angry, just like when she'd told me of her dragon. She thought that I would deny her claim that Tislora was a traitor. That I might rescind the declaration I had spoken only moments earlier.

I wasn't sure how I could read all of this on her face. Ever since our bodies had come together, I could sense her thoughts. I wasn't sure why, but in this moment, it kept my anger at bay.

I swallowed hard. "Why do you think this?" My voice was low and rough, and I couldn't keep the rumbling anger from my tone. I had just told her how much I trusted her. I needed to prove that right now.

Besides, I was about to tell her the truth about the curse and what it would demand from her. The least I could do was hear her explanation.

She flinched, as if she had expected me to roar at her. I took a steadying breath. Perhaps she had a good reason for suggesting Tislora was a traitor. Surely, she would not base this off of petty jealousy alone.

Sybelle's words came out in a rush. "When Warwick found me in the Noxen Forest, I was looking for something. A glowing jeweled rose. When I touched it, it brought me to a memory of when the witch cast the curse."

I went rigid, my body taut with awareness. Slowly, I sat us both up so she was cradled against my bare chest. "You found the bloodstone?"

Her eyes grew wide. "That's what it's called?"

I nodded. "It was buried long ago by my ancestors who believed the stone itself was cursed. They thought that, in surrendering it to the earth, it gave our people a chance to conquer the curse on their own. Obviously, they were wrong."

Sybelle shook her head. "It's a *memory* stone. It holds the memories of that day."

I recalled Murvo's claim that there were other requirements to break the curse. Excitement quickened my pulse. "Do you remember the exact words of the spell?"

She glanced around, her hair whipping back and forth as she searched for something. With a grunt, she scooted away from me, crawling toward our shredded clothing, until she found a crumpled piece of parchment. She thrust it at me.

"This is what I remember from the memory. I wrote it all down."

My brows lowered as my eyes roved over Sybelle's hasty scribblings. Something knotted in my chest at the sight of those haunting words right in front of me. For centuries, this curse had lived on, and no one had documented it.

But here were the words, scrawled on this wrinkled parchment.

Emotion thickened in my throat, and I forced myself to read over the words three times. I had heard stories of that day, passed down from my father and his father before that.

They had destroyed the witch clans. Without trial. Without mercy.

And now, reading the words of the curse, my stomach plummeted with shame and regret so potent that my eyes stung with unshed tears.

"You were there?" I asked, my voice thick. "In the memory—you saw what happened?"

Sybelle nodded, her expression grim. "Varius, it was horrible. What King Ragnus did…" She shuddered.

"I know."

She stared at me. "You know?"

"I did not see it for myself, but my father told me the stories. I learned early on that Father only took pride in the most vicious and savage acts of destruction. The way he spoke of this slaughter, this execution… it was with a fondness that made me feel ill. I *always* knew that what my great-grandfather did to the witches was the gravest injustice."

Sybelle's eyes were moist with tears. "Well, I'm glad you know—that *someone* knows. I just wish something could be done to make it right."

My gaze dropped to the parchment with Sybelle's messy handwriting on it. Mother of Shade, I had been yearning to find the details of the curse. And this incredible woman had freely given it to me. I gave her a look of pure awe. "You have no idea what it means that you've shared this with me."

She offered a hesitant smile, her eyes turning guarded once more. "I was researching everything I could about enchantments and curses. I found an ancient text that stated a witch's spell can outlive her through her bloodline." She pointed to a phrase on the parchment. "*The curse will live on as my line lives on.* Do you see? I think one of the witches had a child no one knew about, and that child lives on. *That's* what's fueling the curse."

My heart lurched with recognition. Was this what Murvo had been trying to warn me about? If we discovered who this descendant was, ending their life would end my people's suffering.

"I still don't understand why you think it's Tislora," I said slowly.

"She has magic," Sybelle said shortly. "*Witch* magic. She's the only fae I've seen who casts spells like the witch in the memory did." She paused, then said, "And also, the bloodstone is missing. Enzira and Ramia didn't see it. But Tislora was with us when I lost consciousness. I think she might have taken it."

"Sybelle." I sighed. "I trust Tislora with my life. The things we have endured together..." I shook my head. "It cannot be her."

Sybelle bit her lip and dropped her gaze to the floor, wringing her hands together. "I was afraid you might say that."

I placed my large hand over hers to still her. With my other hand, I nudged my knuckle under her chin, tilting her face to meet mine. I leaned in, brushing my lips against hers in the softest of touches. She made a startled sound, then leaned into me, accepting my kiss. My arm came around her, pressing into her back and bringing her flush against my chest. A hum of contentment rumbled from me as the kiss hardened and deepened, our tongues clashing and breaths mingling.

When I pulled away, she was panting, her hands around my neck as if to pull me in for more.

I almost wanted her to.

"Whatever Tislora and I shared," I said breathlessly, "is *nothing* compared to what you and I shared here tonight. No other female has ever elicited such passion from me, Sybelle. It is you and only you. Do you understand?"

Her breath hitched, and she nodded, her eyes shining.

I inhaled deeply. "But, if you are concerned, I will speak to her about it. Right now, in fact. If she is loyal to me, as I believe she is, then she will not object to swearing an oath in her blood. She might despise me for it, but she will not refuse."

Sybelle's brows lifted, her lips parting. "You would do that?"

"Yes. I would."

Clearly, she had not expected me to agree to this. She gave me a broad smile, her eyes crinkling. Mother of Shade, she looked so devastatingly beautiful.

I carefully stroked strands of her hair out of her eyes, my mind snagging on something that had been burrowing within me for a long time. It wasn't until I had met Sybelle that the thoughts had grown stronger. More insistent.

"You said you wish something could be done for the witches," I said softly. I took her hand in mine. "Perhaps something can." When she only frowned, I said, "I have heard stories of persecuted witches in other kingdoms. Some have sought refuge in our lands, but because of the lingering hatred brewing between the unseelie and the witch clans, they always felt they were unwelcome."

Sybelle's brows drew together in concern as I continued, "Perhaps... I can change that. I can send decrees throughout the kingdom that witch refugees are to be welcomed. I can create a fund to help them start new lives here. It will take some time to undo hundreds of years of prejudice, but—but perhaps it's the change we need to move this kingdom in the right direction."

Fresh tears brimmed in her eyes. "Are you serious?"

I nodded solemnly. "I've wrestled with the guilt of my forefathers for my entire life. It's time I actually *did* something about it. I can't do anything for the witches who were killed, but perhaps I can help others."

Sybelle's breath hitched, and a tear raced down her cheek. "Varius, I—I don't know what to say. It's a beautiful idea. It's... *incredible*. It's..." She made a frustrated sound, clearly at a loss for words, then laughed as she leaned in and kissed me again. Her mouth moved hungrily over mine, claiming me again and again with fervor. Her fingers threaded through my hair, and her legs wrapped around me. I grew hard for her all over again from that singular movement. I growled in her mouth, devouring her fully, my hands gripping her thighs and spreading them wider.

I broke away from her before I thrust into her all over again. I knew she must already be hurting from our intimacy. To repeat those actions might cause permanent damage to her human body.

"If you don't stop," I murmured, "then I will rip apart more of this floor, and the whole castle will hear you screaming my name."

She exhaled a shaky laugh before sliding off my lap. I grumbled as she put more distance between us. Part of me had been hoping she would say, *Do it, Varius. Let the castle hear us.*

But the logical side of my brain knew there were more important matters at hand.

For starters, I needed to speak with Tislora. Sybelle was right. If Tislora had connections to witch magic, then she might know who this lost descendant was.

It couldn't be Tislora. It *couldn't* be.

But I had to find out for sure. I had to show Sybelle that I trusted her.

And once I did this, once I demonstrated my trust, then I would tell her the truth about the curse. I would tell her what the curse would demand of her.

Every human bride before Sybelle had given their blood to ward off the shadows, whether willingly or unwillingly.

After the first elixir of human blood, the Necro Shadows only grew hungrier and hungrier. They flooded the kingdom with violent rage, and nothing but the elixir containing both the king's blood and the human's blood would stop it.

Eventually, the demand for blood was so high that the human brides had died from loss of blood and malnutrition. The shadows had devoured them wholly.

Along with the king.

Generation after generation, the king and his human bride had given their lives to drive the shadows back. Some kings were strong enough to outlive a few brides—my father, for instance. But in the end, they always succumbed.

After such a sacrifice, the Necro Shadows were appeased for a few decades. But, then, the cycle continued when they grew hungry again.

I had to tell Sybelle all of this. She needed to know. But I was determined to find another way. Some way, somehow, we would be together. We would rule as king and queen.

Somehow, she would survive this. I would not let the curse take her.

"Well, there's no salvaging this," Sybelle said with a laugh, jolting me from my morose thoughts. With a smirk, she lifted up the shredded pieces of her dress. "Perhaps the castle will be merciful and take me straight to my rooms."

I offered a halfhearted chuckle. "Don't count on it. Making you traipse naked through the castle sounds like something it might do."

Sybelle gathered the ripped pieces of her massive skirt and held them to her chest, concealing those beautifully peaked nipples. She gazed up at the vaulted ceiling and said loudly, "Castle? I'd *really* appreciate if you could send me straight to my chambers. Or rather... *our* chambers." She cast a coy grin my way, sending heat flooding over every inch of my skin.

Our chambers.

We would share a room. A bed.

She was mine in earnest. My wife. My equal.

My chest felt so light I thought I might float away.

Sybelle inched over to the door closest to us. She slowly creaked it open, peering cautiously through the crack to the other side.

She exhaled in relief. "Thank you!" she called out, her gaze fixed on the ceiling. Over her shoulder, she shot me another grin.

Just before she stepped through the door, I told her, "I intend to bed you thoroughly tonight, wife."

Her cheeks flushed. "I would be quite disappointed if you didn't, husband."

I couldn't contain my smile as she stepped into our chambers, letting the door snap shut behind her.

I bathed and dressed before seeking out Tislora in the apothecary. For the first time, I found the room empty, though steam from the cauldron still filtered through the air. She clearly hadn't been gone for long because the contents within were churning and bubbling.

With a frown, I returned to the hall and placed my hand on the doorknob. I decided to try Sybelle's strategy of speaking directly to the enchantment surrounding me.

"Er, castle?" I asked, feeling ridiculous. "If you know where Tislora is, could you guide me to her?"

Mother of Shade, this was utterly stupid.

Exhaling in exasperation, I turned the handle and pulled open the door. I faced a dark, narrow hall. Metal clanging and loud voices echoed from within.

I stepped forward, immediately noting the smell of spiced herbs and charred meat.

This was the hall to the kitchens.

"All right, castle," I muttered under my breath. "Let's see what you want me to find here."

I strode forward, following the commotion of the kitchen staff. I paused at an open door to my left when a shuffling sound drew my attention.

The medicine room. The same place I had found Sybelle when she had been searching for birch root.

My brows furrowed as I realized why she'd needed it. She claimed it was a cure for headaches. I hadn't believed her at the time.

But now I knew: It must have been for her dragon.

"Damn it," hissed a familiar voice, jarring me from my thoughts.

I entered the medicine room and found Tislora with her wings tucked against her body as she tried to reach for a jar of forest green powder on one of the shelves. She cut a glance at me, her teeth bared.

"Damn this unseelie body," she growled. Glasses clinked as the talons on her wings nearly knocked several vials to the floor.

"Here." I stepped in and grabbed the jar she was reaching for. My wings folded more tightly than hers did, likely because mine weren't as strong.

"Thank you," she grumbled before taking the jar. "What are you doing here?" She inhaled deeply, then looked at me with narrowed eyes. "You smell different."

Shit. I'd been afraid of this. After such vigorous intercourse with Sybelle, it would be easy to scent the lingering arousal that likely still clung to my body. *Sybelle's* arousal. I had hoped that bathing in the hot springs would mask it.

Tislora uttered a sharp gasp, and I closed my eyes in defeat. Damn it all.

"You bedded her, didn't you?" she asked.

I heaved a sigh. Stalling for time, I turned and softly closed the door of the medicine room. It was quite cramped, but nothing could be done about it.

When I faced Tislora, she stared at me with a wrinkle between her brows, her eyes sparking with a mixture of anger and amusement.

"Yes," I said tightly. "We consummated."

She let out a harsh chuckle, shaking her head as if I were a child. "Oh, Varius. How could you be so foolish?"

I glared at her. "What the hell are you talking about? She is my wife."

"She's a traitor!"

Shadows pooled around us as I bared my fangs at her. "She is *not*. She swore it in blood."

Tislora didn't need to know that Sybelle had fae blood. Even humans could make blood vows with the fae, and it would bind them the same way.

"Did you tell her?"

I froze.

"Did you tell her that her life would be sacrificed to the curse, like all the other human brides?" Tislora asked in a hard voice.

I held my breath, my chest knotting so tightly I couldn't breathe.

"No," I said, my voice strained. "But I will tell her soon. And I *will* find another way."

I would save Sybelle from this fate. I would not lose her to the same dark magic that had already taken so many other lives.

"Damn it, Varius, the Necro Shadows are getting closer. You *know* the only thing that can hold them off is blood from your line and from hers. You need to feed them. Our time is running out."

I shook my head as raging thoughts clouded my mind. Thoughts of death and destruction. The image of the Pern District that had been devoured by the shadow storm appeared in my head.

"But perhaps consummation is the best thing right now," Tislora mused. "It will strengthen your bond with her and make the elixir more potent." She glanced at the jar in her hand, frowning at its contents. "Perhaps that will solve the problem.

Something is off with my supply of powdered hellebore leaves. I think it might be—"

"There will be no more elixirs," I growled. "I will not subject Sybelle to the same fate as the others."

Tislora blinked, then lowered the vial. "But you would doom your people to destruction at the hands of the Necro Shadows?" she shot back.

I ran a hand through my hair as my shadows thickened on the floor at our feet. This argument wasn't helping things.

"This isn't why I sought you out," I said.

"Then, why did you?"

I paused. The last thing I needed was for Tislora to find out Sybelle and I had consummated our marriage, only for me to turn around and accuse her of treachery... at Sybelle's suggestion.

I would need to word this carefully.

I cleared my throat. "I need to ask you something of a sensitive nature."

She placed the vial in her satchel and crossed her arms, her nostrils flaring. Already, I could sense her ire brewing. "What is it?"

"I need to know where you came from before you began working at Agnarr Castle." Even when I was a boy, Tislora had been here, working alongside my father. She had resided here even longer than I had.

I knew nothing of her background or her history. And now I realized just how alarming that was.

Tislora's eyes became tiny slits. "Why?"

"Something about the original sorceress's spell mentioned her bloodline living on," I said, trying to avoid mentioning Sybelle's involvement. "I just want to know if you knew any of the witches who lived here before—" I broke off with a wince.

"Before King Ragnus slaughtered them all?" she asked sharply.

"Yes." I met her gaze to show her that I knew just how abominable my ancestor had been. I did not condone his actions at all.

But I also did not condone the witch for cursing my people forever.

"I thought you couldn't access the language of the spell," she said, her tone full of accusation.

"I found a record of it," I said. Technically, not a lie, if Sybelle's wrinkled piece of parchment could be viewed as a *record*.

Tislora fixed a hard stare on me for a long, tense moment. I did not break eye contact. I would not betray Sybelle's trust.

Especially if it would make her a target of Tislora's wrath.

When I continued to hold her gaze, Tislora shifted her weight and crossed her arms over her chest. For a second, she looked strangely vulnerable. I had never seen her like this before. Tislora had always been strong and fiery.

"I grew up as an abandoned orphan," she said, avoiding my gaze. "There were other witch children with me, but I don't know what became of them."

I stilled, something within me tingling with this new information. "You grew up in an orphanage."

It was her turn to flinch. "Not exactly."

"Tislora, speak plainly. Please. This is important."

She rubbed her forehead with a long sigh. "Varius, you have to understand that among witches, vows of secrecy are taken very seriously."

"Don't lecture me about the gravity of sacred vows," I growled.

Her silvery eyes flared with anger. We stared each other down, neither of us relenting. Finally, she spoke. "I came from the same clan of witches that Ragnus killed."

I sucked in a sharp breath, my blood boiling in my veins. Shit, Sybelle had been right. She'd been *right*.

I took a step back, and Tislora raised her hands.

"Wait, please," she said quickly. "It's not like that. We were abandoned by them. Disowned. Raised by unseelie fae."

I gritted my teeth, my pulse roaring in my ears. Shadows flooded the cramped space, plunging us in darkness. "This whole time," I hissed. "This *whole time*, Lor?"

"I took a vow!" she argued.

"What about your vow to *me*?" I roared. "Your allegiance to your king? Instead, you chose to remain loyal to the witches who abandoned you?"

"Not them," Tislora spat. "My brothers and sisters. We vowed to one another that we would never share the true nature of our heritage."

"How many?" I bit out.

She swallowed. "There were four of us. Two were killed by witch hunters. After that, my brother and I parted ways, knowing that by remaining together, we put a target on our backs."

"Why did the witches abandon you?" I asked, my tone hard.

"We did not produce magic within our first year of life. Most witch offspring are able to manifest even small traces of magic by then. Males, in general, are unable to produce magic and are often abandoned, as was the case with my brothers. My magic, as it turned out, manifested much later in life, thanks to my unseelie blood." She offered me a cold smile. "Their loss."

"Is this a joke to you?" I bellowed. "Because of you and your lies, the curse lives on! If you and your so-called siblings had been destroyed, the curse would be broken!"

Tislora's face paled. "What the hell are you talking about?"

"Are you her daughter?" I asked. "The sorceress who cast the curse."

Her nostrils flared. "You mean Jessinda? No. My mother was a witch named Evangeline. She died before the spell was cast. My father was an unseelie fae soldier she met in passing."

My fingers curled into fists. "Tislora. I need you to swear to me in fae blood that you are not directly tethered to this curse."

Her wings twitched behind her, and she bared her fangs at me. "You dare ask me that? After everything I've done to prove my loyalty?"

"You mean after all the secrets you kept from me?" I barked. "Your demonstrations of loyalty mean *nothing* now, Lor. Swear with your fae blood, or I swear to the gods, you will be sentenced to death for treason. Hopefully your death will bring about the end of the curse."

Her head reared back, rage and hurt flashing across her face. Her eyes darkened, and she let out a low, menacing hiss.

I didn't even blink. I only continued to glare at her, unfazed by her anger.

She had no right to resent me for asking this of her. *No right.*

"Fine," she gritted out, drawing a small dagger from her belt. "You asshole." She dragged the blade along her palm, and black blood bloomed from the wound. "I, Tislora of the Shadow Court, swear by my fae blood that I am *not* tethered to the curse cast by Jessinda the witch, nor will my death bring about the freedom King Varius seeks for his people."

Energy hummed in the air, tingling across my skin.

Tislora shot me a hateful look. "Is that proof enough for you?"

"Did Jessinda have a child?"

Her eyes shuttered. "What?"

I repeated the words slowly. "Did Jessinda have a child?"

Her lips grew thin, her face turning a shade paler.

I stepped toward her, my hands gripping her shoulders tightly. I resisted the urge to shake her until she answered me plainly. "*Tell me*, Lor."

"Yes," she breathed, her voice shaky. "Yes, she had a son. But —But he has no magic. He poses no threat to the Shadow Court."

"He does if his mother included his bloodline in the language of her spell—as insurance that it would carry on after her death."

Tislora's face slackened in shock. "But I—how do you know that?"

"If Jessinda included this language in her curse, is it possible?"

She was muttering frantically now. "I didn't think… He had no *powers*, and… and I didn't know the terms of the original curse. There was no *record* of it—" She broke off, her lip trembling. "Shit." She covered her mouth with her hand, letting her dagger clatter to the floor. "*Shit*, how did I not see it? If the terms of Jessinda's curse allowed it, even a powerless heir could carry the magic of a curse like that."

"Yes," I said. "Especially if he produced a female heir who could continue the witch line."

She shook her head vigorously. "No. He did not marry or sire children. He returned to the home of our ancestors. The Earthen Court. For decades now, he has lived the life of a mortal."

I went still as death, something clicking into place in my mind. "What did you say?"

"The witches of our kingdom originally came from the Earthen Court. There are still witches there even now, living in hiding. My brother returned there and…" She faltered at the look of shock and horror on my face. "Did you not know this?"

Slowly, I shook my head, my breathing now sharp and ragged.

The witches came from the Earthen Court. *Sybelle's* court.

Sybelle.

I had to find her. *Now.*

THE BEAUTY

My body was still buzzing from my time in the library with Varius. I kept the jeweled dagger clutched in my palm, a lazy and contented smile on my face as I made my way back to our chambers. I found my pouch of gemstones in my cloak pocket and, one-handed, managed to wriggle out the moonstone.

Only then did I finally release Wraith Killer.

Exhaustion and throbbing agony coursed through my body, but it was quickly chased away by the heated warmth of the healing stone. I groaned, hunching over as the intense sensations fired through my body with relentless intensity. Flames boiled my blood and warmed my bones. I clenched my teeth from the force of it. A terrible ache pulsed between my legs, but the moonstone soothed the pain, healing every part of me.

When it was finished, I loosed a breath and gasped for air, dropping the moonstone back into the pouch. My head reeled from the overwhelming and nauseating array of magic that had crashed through me so violently.

As much as I longed to marinate in the hot springs for an hour or two, I only allowed myself a quick bath before hopping out and dressing in a simple aqua gown. I relished Varius's reaction to the seductive dress I had worn earlier, but it hadn't been entirely practical.

And, truth be told, I had worn it out of spite.

Another smile crept across my lips. Varius and I had consummated. Our marriage was *real*.

And he had promised to coronate me. I would officially become the queen of this court.

A giddy jolt of excitement rippled over me, and I could barely contain my squeal of glee.

I fastened the buttons of my dress, then made my way to Varius's desk to write a letter to Eira.

If she wanted a detailed explanation of how I satisfied my husband's carnal needs, I would have to find a clever way to convey them.

Dear RaRa,

Perhaps my husband is not as curmudgeonly as I had previously thought. In fact, I now see him in a new light. A light that makes him seem more like the fire dancer we encountered at the ball so many years ago.

I smirked at the memory of the muscular dancer Eira and I had fawned over at the ball in the Fire Court. As I paused to consider my next words, I absently tapped on my amber necklace.

"Sybelle!" My dragon's alarmed voice filled my mind.

I stiffened. "Azure?"

"Stones! I have been trying to reach you for over an hour. I made it to Chesser Road."

My blood chilled, and I set down my quill. "Did you find anything?"

"The road is covered in Necro Shadows. I couldn't even get close to it because the shadows are so thick."

Horror numbed my bones. That meant the shadows were even thicker than when I'd viewed the road with the shadowstone.

"Are you all right?" I asked, unable to hide the panic in my voice. "Azure, are you hurt?"

"No. The shadows don't affect me, remember?"

I closed my eyes, slumping against the back of the chair. My pulse quickened. "You didn't come across that ringing sound, did you? The one from the bloodstone?"

"Bloodstone?"

Oh, right. Azure didn't know. I quickly filled her in on what the bloodstone was and what Varius had told me about it.

"So, the bloodstone shows you memories?" she asked. *"And the shadowstone shows you visions? Perhaps the two are connected."*

I froze, my body going rigid. "Say that again," I said slowly.

"I said, perhaps the bloodstone and the shadowstone are connected. Are you a bit slow this morning, human? Should I speak in plainer words?"

I ignored her barb and scrambled for the wrinkled parchment tucked in a drawer in the desk. My heart slammed painfully against my chest as I read over the words of the witch's curse.

By stone of shadow and blood...

"Stones," I gasped. "Azure, I—I think this is it. I think I found it."

"Found what?"

My words came out in an excited rush. "When the witch cast her spell, she said *by stone of shadow and blood, I make this vow.* The shadowstone vanished, and the bloodstone appeared in its place. That can't be a coincidence. You're right. They *are* connected."

Azure was silent for a moment. *"Are you saying..."*

"I'm saying I think the two stones belong with each other." I dug through my pouch of gemstones, then impatiently dumped the contents on the desk with a loud clatter. Even knowing it wasn't there, I still had to check.

But no. The bloodstone was still missing.

"*Damn it,*" I roared, slamming my fist on the table and making the gems scatter. I exhaled sharply through my teeth. My gaze flicked to the shadowstone.

Maybe I could use it to find the bloodstone. Perhaps it would show me in the mirror.

I reached for it, and as soon as my fingers closed around it, the sharp ringing noise assaulted me.

I cried out, falling to my knees, my eardrums throbbing. The stone dropped from my grasp, and the sound immediately stopped.

"*Sybelle, what was that? Are you all right?*"

I shook my head, gasping for breath. "I—I don't know what happened. It was the ringing again. Why is it ringing? It didn't do this before." I stared at the shadowstone again, my mind working to connect the pieces. "Az. If the two are connected, maybe... maybe they are *calling* to each other. Could that be the true reason behind that horrible sound?"

Azure didn't respond.

"Az?"

"*I don't know, Sybelle.*" Her voice was solemn. "*You have to be careful with magic like this. Remember, you are not fully fae. You cannot heal like they can. If you endure this ringing sound for too long...*"

"I'll be fine," I promised. "And I will be careful. But Azure, I have to try. The fate of this entire kingdom is at stake." I thought of the crying child I had met in the hall. All those innocent fae without homes. "These are *my people* now."

Azure hesitated for a long moment. "*I understand. But keep your hand on the amber stone the entire time, understand?*"

I unclasped the necklace from my throat, perhaps for the first time in years. I wrapped the chain several times around my wrist, tucking the stone in my palm and closing my fingers around it. "There," I said. "Now you'll always hear me. I won't let go. I promise."

"Good. Tread carefully, Sybelle."

"I will."

With a deep breath, I grasped the shadowstone again. This time, I was ready for the shrill sound as it seemed to pierce my very skull. My eyes crammed shut, and I gritted my teeth. How was I supposed to use this sound to locate the other stone?

"Show me!" I shouted, clutching the stone tighter. When I had touched the bloodstone, the ringing had stopped.

But this was the opposite.

I turned back to the desk, wondering if I could utilize another gemstone to help me.

But as soon as I moved, the ringing changed in pitch, going even higher. I cried out, ducking my head, my eyes watering from the severity of it.

That was certainly different. And more painful.

I set the stone down on the desk, then rushed into the bathing chamber. A stack of clean washcloths sat next to the hot springs hole. I grabbed one, then ripped it into small pieces. After balling up two strips of cloth, I shoved one in each of my ears, then hurried back into the bedchamber.

When I picked up the shadowstone this time, the sound was loud and blaring, but it didn't sting nearly as much.

I exhaled in relief and turned in a slow circle, waiting for the pitch to change.

Only when I faced the door did the tone become shriller.

"You want me to go through the door?" I muttered. I stepped toward it, and the ringing intensified, causing me to wince.

"All right then," I breathed before throwing open the door.

I was staring at the empty dining hall, which was set for breakfast. Trays of hot rolls, pastries, and fruit awaited me. Though my mouth watered and my stomach growled as the delicious aromas filled my nose, I knew I was here for a different reason.

With cautious steps, I eased into the room. Again, the magic ringing pulsed louder. I strode deeper into the room, holding up the shadowstone and using the sounds to guide me. I had crossed the length of the room, reaching the end of the long table, when the ringing stopped abruptly.

I faltered, my mouth falling open. I glanced around, wondering what had changed. "Wha—"

A shadow appeared from across the table, and I tensed in alarm.

A man clad in full armor materialized, and in his hands was the gleaming bloodstone.

My chest seized, and I took a step back, shock and horror coursing through me. "*Gerard?*"

Gerard smirked, his eyes full of admiration. "I knew you would figure it out, Sybelle."

THE BEAST

I tore down the hallway, urgency flooding my veins, and threw open the first door I could find. Surely, in this moment of desperation, the castle would lead me to Sybelle.

But on the other side, I found the courtyard of the castle.

I faltered. Was Sybelle here? Or was the castle redirecting my path?

With a growl, I slammed the door shut. "Please," I pleaded. "Please, I need to find her."

I opened the door again and once more saw the courtyard. The afternoon sunlight gleamed along the polished stone steps.

Frustration built in me, so volatile I thought I might explode. Black shadows streamed around me. I almost flung the door shut hard enough to break it off the hinges… but something stopped me.

In the distance, an unfamiliar horn blew, echoing in the air.

I froze, my blood chilling.

Fae soldiers rushed into the courtyard, swords drawn. One paused to glance at me as I stood there, lingering in the doorway.

"What's going on?" I demanded.

"An army is advancing on the castle, Your Highness. We don't know where it came from; our sentries didn't see anything along the road."

An army.

But... how?

After Warwick's threats, I'd stationed sentries everywhere—beyond the castle, monitoring Chesser Road... There hadn't been a whisper of any soldiers.

At any rate, the shadow storm had completely overtaken Pern District. Any army would have to travel through the Necro Shadows to get to the castle.

I shook my head and stepped over the threshold. There wasn't time to think. I scanned the frantic soldiers flitting about, searching for a familiar face.

"My lord!"

I turned and found Clermont shuffling toward me. He was already dressed in armor, with a long sword strapped to his hip. In his left hand, he carried my breast plate.

"What the hell's going on?" I asked as he started fastening the breast plate to my chest.

"I don't know how they did it, Varius, but they are here," Clermont muttered, his nimble fingers moving quickly. He removed his sword, scabbard and all, and offered it to me.

I quickly fastened it around my hips and nodded my thanks. "Who is it? Where did the army come from?"

"They bear the flag of the Earthen Court."

I stared at him, horror sinking in my stomach. "That's... not possible. There was no one there! And the Necro Shadows..."

"I know. I don't understand it myself. Clearly, some kind of powerful magic is at play."

Magic? From a court full of humans? None of this was making sense.

"Can we keep them from breaching the palace?" I asked.

"They are already at the portcullis."

"Shit." I turned to race down the steps, then shouted over my shoulder. "Seal the castle doors and protect the staff, Clermont! That's an order."

"Yes, my lord."

As I hastened down the steps, I withdrew the amber stone from my pocket and held it up to my mouth. "Sybelle, if you can hear this, the Earthen Court army is here. It isn't safe. Stay in the castle with Enzira. I'll hold off the army to ensure they won't get to you."

No answer. Gritting my teeth, I shoved the stone back in my pocket just as I reached the portcullis. The sight made me go rigid with fear.

Hundreds—no, *thousands*—of human soldiers waited on the other side, the number so vast that they filled the road and even took up space in the forest surrounding the gate.

In front, sitting atop a large white mare, sat a woman with a gleaming silver crown on her head. She had dark blonde ringlets and icy blue eyes that seemed to pierce right through me. But there was something familiar about her heart-shaped face and the proud jut of her chin.

I spread my arms and bared my fangs. "What is this, human? Why have you come here?" I sensed soldiers assembling behind me, taking up a formation. But it wouldn't be nearly enough.

This army was ready to breach the gates. And we hadn't even assembled a single regiment yet.

"I am Queen Orla of the Earthen Court," the woman said, her voice loud and full of authority. "I have come to take your kingdom and end your deathly shadows for good."

My eyes narrowed. *Queen Orla?* "I have never heard of you before, *queen*," I spat. "Where is King Maddox?"

"My father is dead," Orla said without remorse.

I stilled. This was Sybelle's sister.

Sybelle had been adamant that her father *never* would have marched on my kingdom. Not when he had a plan in place already.

But... if he was dead, then his other daughter was free to do as she wished. Even if it meant invading my lands.

"I have an agreement with your court!" I shouted. "The contract has been honored for hundreds of years."

"I have signed no such contract, nor do I honor any agreement made by my foolish ancestors," Orla said coldly. "You have demanded brides from my kingdom and assaulted my people with your shadows for too long, Wraith King. It ends now." She drew her sword, wielding it with surprising finesse, given her minute stature. "Surrender now, or we will tear down these gates and burn your castle to the ground."

Hisses and snarls sounded behind me as my soldiers raised their own swords, prepared to fight to the death.

I knew they would. They would lay down their lives for our people and our kingdom.

But I couldn't sentence them to that fate. They would die in minutes. We had fae strength and magic on our side, but the humans had numbers. The mass of mortal soldiers was at least ten times as many as the soldiers defending the castle. I might have been able to obliterate them with my shadows, but most of my strength was being used to maintain the Lumen that protected our castle.

If I removed the Lumen, the Necro Shadows would descend. But those shadows did not know friend from foe. They would destroy both human and fae alike.

And those within the castle walls would be at the mercy of the deadly shadows, at least until sundown when the Umbra Mist reemerged.

"You try my patience, Wraith King!" Orla bellowed. "Give me your answer, or we will advance."

I swallowed hard. I was out of time. "Let us parlay," I offered. "We can discuss terms and come to a new arrangement. No blood needs to be shed today."

"It is too late for that," Orla sneered. "The moment your shadows breached our borders, our agreement was nullified.

Any promises you make of protection or peace will fall on deaf ears."

The shadows breached their borders? My blood chilled. The Necro Shadows had spread farther than I'd thought.

But if I tried to explain that I had no control over them, Orla would not believe me.

My fingers curled to fists at my sides. If I surrendered, my people would be at the mercy of these bloodthirsty humans. Judging by the enraged expressions on the soldiers standing behind Orla, they would not be benevolent.

We would likely lose this battle. My armies were spread throughout the kingdom and too far away to rally to our defense in time.

But perhaps we could hold off these humans until help could arrive. Tislora alone was powerful enough to fell dozens of soldiers with her magic. I had seen it on the battlefield before.

Did she know about the army? I had left her so abruptly...

The soldiers beside me shifted their stance, teeth bared as they prepared to fight. Orla lifted her sword in the air, a shout on her lips.

With a roar, I spread my arms, allowing my shadows to burst from me and engulf the courtyard. Screams erupted, but I pushed on, blanketing the square with black mist that spilled down the road, blinding the human soldiers.

With the humans shrouded in darkness, I drew my fingers to my lips and let out a shrill whistle. Loud, animalistic shrieks answered me, and the great beating of wings told me the alporas had heard my call.

My keen fae eyesight locating Zorben , my alpora, even in the darkness. He galloped toward me, and I swung atop him with ease.

"On me!" I bellowed, thrusting my sword in the air. Several soldiers mounted their alporas. Some cheered with battle cries, lifting their weapons toward me in unity.

As one, our alporas soared into the air, carrying us over the portcullis. Below us, the humans screamed, still blind thanks to my shadows.

I jabbed my sword toward the humans, the rage in my blood hungry for carnage. *"Attack!"*

THE BEAUTY

I stood, frozen, gaping at Gerard. In my mind, I couldn't reconcile his presence here. Nothing made sense.

Was he a vision? A hallucination? Was I under some sort of spell?

Answers, Sybelle, the logical side of my brain told me. *You need answers. You can panic later.*

"What are you doing here?" I asked carefully. My eyes darted to the bloodstone in Gerard's hands, but I pretended to ignore it. *He might not realize how much I know,* I reminded myself.

"I came for you, my darling," Gerard said, striding toward me. My muscles locked, and I had to fight the instinct to cringe away from him.

I shook my head. "I don't understand. Gerard, I'm *married* to the king."

"He won't be the king much longer. You will be free soon."

My blood turned to ice. "What—What are you talking about?"

Then, Varius's frantic voice filled my mind, summoned by the amber stone still gripped in my palm.

"Sybelle, if you can hear this, the Earthen Court army is here. It isn't safe. Stay in the castle with Enzira. I'll hold off the army to ensure they won't get to you."

My stomach dropped like lead. I fixed a horrified gaze on

Gerard. "What did you do?" My voice came out as a terrified whisper.

"She is relentless, and she will not stop until every fae is destroyed." Gerard reached for me, but I curled my arms behind my back, afraid he would notice the chain of my necklace wrapped around my left hand. "We can slip away during the battle. No one will notice. We can be free together, my love."

All I could do was shake my head like a fool. "*She?*"

"Your sister."

My skin tingled with unease. "Orla? What is she doing here? Where—Where is my father?"

Gerard's mouth formed a thin line, and my heart filled with dread.

"He's dead, isn't he?" My voice was hollow. Deep down, part of me suspected this. Why else wouldn't the shadowstone be able to show him to me when I asked?

Sorrow twisted in my chest. King Maddox had only seen me as a weapon to wield. But he was still my father and a beloved king. He had treated his people well.

My eyes narrowed. "Did you kill him?"

"No. Orla did. She insisted it was the only way."

"The only way for *what*? Speak plainly, Gerard! *Why are you here?*"

"To destroy the unseelie! To fulfill my mother's curse!"

I stilled, every muscle in my body taut with awareness. *My mother's curse.*

Holy Stones...

"You—You—"

"My mother was the sorceress Jessinda," Gerard said, his chin lifting with pride. "She died at the hands of these unseelie beasts. And I am here to avenge her."

My entire body was numb with dread. This couldn't be true. How could *Gerard* be the son of a sorceress?

Think, Sybelle! I told myself. *What do you know of sorceresses and witches?*

They possessed untold power. Even more power than the fae.

They were distantly related to fae and were said to possess fae blood, though not as much as the seelie and unseelie.

Male witches had no magic, but they could still produce female heirs and pass along the power through their bloodline.

Gerard has no magic, I realized.

He was staring at me, waiting for a response. I had to say something to buy myself more time. I needed a *plan.*

"What are you doing with that?" I blurted, gesturing to the gleaming rose jewel in his hands.

"This is the key to the curse," he said, cradling it in his hands, as if he knew just how precious it was. "I couldn't risk you bringing them together." His eyes fell on the shadowstone clutched in my right hand.

"What happens if they come together?" I asked slowly.

Gerard's eyes darkened with suspicion.

"I just want to be careful," I said quickly.

Not technically a lie.

"If they get too close, the stones will weld together on their own. And, once unified, if they are destroyed, a piece of the curse is broken. It was part of the language my mother built into the curse."

By the stone of shadow and blood, I make this vow. Those had been her words.

She had sworn *on* the stones themselves.

But, in the vision, the shadowstone had vanished after she'd cast the spell. Where had it gone?

"How do you know all this?" I asked. "You—You speak as if you were there."

He wasn't. That much, I knew.

"My mother told it to me."

My heart seized. "W-What? I—I thought the curse killed her."

He nodded gravely. "It did. But when she cast it, she used the last of her strength to travel back to me and give me that just before she died." He gestured to the shadowstone in my hand. "She entrusted me to hide it where the unseelie could not discover it." He chuckled. "I should have known you would find a way to dig it up."

I stared at the black stone in my shaking hand. *The shadowstone.* It had been buried in those caves in the Earthen Court all along... because *Gerard* had put it there.

"Why?" I asked in a hollow voice. "Why did you do all this? Why were you living in the Earthen Court this whole time?"

"My people came from there," Gerard said. "That horrible unseelie king thought he had obliterated the witch clans when he killed my mother." A slow smile spread across his face. "But he was wrong. Many of them fled to the Earthen Court and started new lives there. I couldn't join them, as I did not possess any magic. But I wanted to be closer to them and start my life anew. I made it my mission to ensure the division between the Earthen and Shadow Courts remained firm; otherwise, Mother's curse would have been for nothing. That's why I placed spies in the Shadow Court."

Spies? My gut wrenched as I realized what he meant.

Warwick. He had been one of Gerard's spies.

My mouth twisted in disgust. "You allied yourself with shit-holes like *Warwick?*"

Gerard blinked at me, stunned. "How do you know Warwick?"

"He attacked me!" I shouted. "He was utterly vile!"

Gerard gritted his teeth. "He *was* one of my spies, until he defected and tried to leverage his information for gold. His fae ability makes him impervious to nonfatal wounds. He thinks he's invincible, and he got reckless and cocky. I never should have recruited him."

My head roared, the chaos of my emotions and thoughts becoming a whirlwind I couldn't control. "You said *spies*... As in more than one?"

"Yes. I've been alive for a long time, Sybelle. Throughout the years, I've made allies who want to take down the Shadow Court as much as we do. They were willing to work alongside me. Some are fae; some are human. Some reside here, feeding me information. And others pose as nobles in the Earthen Court to sow seeds of discord between the two courts."

My heart jolted painfully as I processed his words. *Anyone* could have been working for Gerard. Members of the castle staff, soldiers in Varius's personal guard...

Even people I had grown up with in the Earthen Court.

"Who was in my rooms?" I asked in a hushed voice.

"That was one of mine. A skilled thief who works for me. I sent her to come fetch you when Orla's plans were in place. I didn't want you here when the army arrived. But my thief couldn't find you, so she took it upon herself to search for the shadowstone on her own." Gerard shook his head, his expression almost endearing, as if he were discussing a wayward toddler who was acting out. "Foolish fae. But, I shouldn't be surprised. It's in their blood to behave in such a way."

"Why are you working with them then?" I asked. "Don't you despise the fae?"

His eyes widened. "Of course not! I'm here for *you*, aren't I? Despite your blood, despite the magic in you, I am here, Sybelle."

I shook my head, resisting the urge to snarl at him. He preached as if he were some great magnanimous saint, deigning to grace me with his presence. Even though I was fae. Even though I was *tainted*.

Swallowing my revulsion, I said, "I just... don't understand why you did all this. I'm *here*, Gerard. Our entire plan was—was to take down the court from the inside! Did you not trust me? I wrote to you asking for more time!"

"I know." He sighed. "Most of my plans were mere precautions, just to ensure I had eyes and ears nearby. But Orla wanted to do more. I tried to hold her off for as long as I could. But... she doesn't trust you like I do. She didn't think you could do it."

Anger and indignation rose up inside me. Gerard lifted his hands, palms out, as if that gesture might calm me down.

Only then did I notice the gold ring gleaming on his finger.

I stiffened, then glanced up at him, reassessing. His hair was slicked back, and although he wore his usual armor, the sword at his hip wasn't his standard issue sword. This one had a ceremonial hilt and gleaming jewels decorating it.

It was *Father's* sword. The sword of the king.

"You married her?" I breathed. "You married my sister?"

He nodded, grimacing. "Yes. I'm sorry. It was the only way to get her to trust me. The only way I could get here, to *you*." He reached for me again, but I stepped back, revulsion churning in my gut.

This man seduced my sister and tricked her into marrying him all so he could rescue me as if I were some damsel in need of saving.

He wanted to destroy the Shadow Court. He wanted to murder thousands of innocent fae, all for a centuries-old vendetta.

Gerard was looking at me expectantly, and my mind worked quickly to formulate a plan. He was the enemy. He wanted to kill my husband.

But I also needed him to trust me.

Shaking my head, I said in a faint voice, "I—I just need a moment to process all this. Please."

Not a lie. It was a lot to absorb.

And I still didn't have a plan for getting rid of the army, escaping from Gerard, and somehow saving Varius.

"I know it's overwhelming. But we don't have time to hesitate. We need to leave before the army breaches the castle. I can't guarantee your safety once they enter these walls."

My fists were shaking. I could barely contain my fury. The shock of Gerard's revelations was wearing off, and in its place was unchecked rage.

For hundreds of years, he'd been plotting. Encouraging this division between the two courts. Hungry for *war*.

How many lives had been sacrificed for his efforts? The lives of both the unseelie and the humans... So much anguish and hatred, and Gerard was at the heart of it.

Would we have found peace if he hadn't been lurking within the Earthen Court with his spies? If Gerard had never settled in my kingdom, would we have enjoyed an alliance with the Shadow Court?

"What happens after?" I whispered. "After the castle is breached and... and Varius is dead, then what?"

A tender look crossed his features, and I realized he was misreading my fear. "You don't have to worry, Sybelle. I have a plan in place. While I get you to safety, Orla will ensure every last unseelie fae is killed. They will never be able to hurt you again."

Oh, Stones. My eyes closed, and in my mind, I pictured the sweet face of that fae child crying in the hall. His smile. His wide, doe-like eyes.

That child would be killed. *All* the fae children would be killed. Murdered by my sister. Murdered by *my own people*.

Gerard's revenge went much further than simply punishing the fae royals for what they had done to his mother. He wanted to obliterate an entire race.

Screams echoed in the distance, and an explosion shook the

ground, making the castle walls rumble. My eyes grew wide as I looked around, waiting for the palace to crumble around us.

"*Please*," Gerard hissed, grabbing my wrist. "We have to go. *Now*."

It took all my restraint not to jerk my arm out of his grasp, or to twist and break his wrist. Just his fingers on my skin made me want to retch.

"Gerard, I can't just *leave*," I argued, trying to buy myself more time.

"You can't stay here." He leveled a hard stare on me. "Don't you realize the Wraith King is dooming you to die?"

A tendril of icy dread curled in my chest. "What are you talking about?"

"Every human bride gave their lives to stop the deadly shadows."

I took a hesitant step away from him and shook my head. "No. That—That can't be right. The shadows only need a little blood."

He nodded slowly, as if I were daft for not putting the pieces together by now. "Yes. A little blood... *at first*. They feed on human blood and unseelie blood. And they demand more and more until the king and his bride are sucked dry and wither away into nothingness."

"No," I said again, shutting my eyes like I could block his words from reaching my brain.

"Think about it, Sybelle. Has he ever told you you're safe? Has he ever told you *how much blood* is required?"

I shuddered, hunching over as the truth of his words sank in.

Varius hadn't been able to promise me my life wasn't in danger by giving blood.

Because my life *was* in danger.

Once I gave blood, I wouldn't be able to stop... until I died.

Tonight, I only need a vial, Varius had said.

He had deceived me. Again.

I waited for the betrayal to hit me in full force, to slice through me and destroy the trust we had built together... but it never did.

Because if Varius had asked me if I would give my life to save this kingdom, I would have said yes. Right now, I was willing to bleed every drop of my blood to protect the Shadow Fae.

And that truth stunned me more than anything Gerard had told me.

My eyes snapped open and fixed on Gerard. "How do you know this?"

"I've been following the human brides to ensure the curse remains intact. It's why I didn't want to let you go to the Wraith King in the first place. I tried to stop you."

He said the words as if they made him a hero. A saint.

But he had known the truth the whole time and had never told me. He simply let me live my life, believing I could take down the Shadow Court on my own, when all the while he knew the truth: The curse was stronger. And it would claim my life.

He kept this from me. This whole time, he kept the truth from me.

"All those other brides... you just let them die?" My voice was weak, but I had to utter the words.

Gerard made a pained expression. "They weren't like you, Sybelle. They weren't strong-willed and determined. They weren't fierce and loyal. They weren't willing to fight the Wraith King or to die to protect their own people." He took both my hands in his, making my skin crawl. I swallowed down my disgust and forced myself to look him in the eye. "You *deserve* to live. You are the strongest woman I've met. Even with your fae blood, only *you* have captured my heart, Sybelle." He shook his head with a sigh. "I had to keep the truth from you. If you knew about the curse, I feared what the Wraith King would do to you."

I shook my head, nausea roiling within me. He had let my ancestors die, all because they weren't *strong* enough for his liking.

Stones, I was such a fool. How had I ever trusted this man? How had I ever believed the bullshit spewing from his lips?

"Sybelle, we're out of time. We have to leave."

I wanted to shove him away from me and flee for the door.

But he would only chase after me. He was faster and stronger. I had bested him while sparring before, but right now, he was heavily armed.

Besides, I still needed the bloodstone.

He had to believe he could still trust me.

I took a deep breath and looked up at him, forcing away my revulsion. Inside me, my anger still simmered, bubbling closer to the surface. I wouldn't be able to hold it off for much longer. "How do we get past the shadows?"

"I can travel us through them safely."

"Travel?" Unease momentarily blotted out my anger. "What do you mean?"

"I don't have magic, but my mother's blood protects me from the dark shadows. Not only that, but I can *travel* through them. Like portals. Anyone who travels alongside me has my blood as protection against the poisons in the shadows."

My mind worked furiously to keep up with everything I was absorbing. He could *teleport*?

From what I had read, most male witches did not possess any magic. But it seemed Gerard was an exception. He might not be able to cast spells like Tislora, but he could still use the magic in his blood.

Of course... Now, it all made sense.

Warwick had promised his allies would meet him on Chesser Road. But Azure had claimed the road was covered in Necro Shadows so thick that she couldn't even see through them.

Gerard had been *transporting* the soldiers through the shadows.

He could travel back and forth with ease. That was how the army had gotten here without detection. That was why Warwick was so certain Varius would be defeated.

Shit. That meant if I tried to run away from Gerard, he could easily find his way back to me through the Necro Shadows.

My eyes darted to the crimson stone in his hands. Now that it was so close to the shadowstone, the ringing had stopped, but an odd buzzing filled my ears. Like the stones *wanted* to be reunited.

I had to stop Gerard. Kill him, if necessary.

But, more importantly, I needed the bloodstone.

"If the king finds that…" I said, gesturing to the bloodstone. I tried to sound worried, as if the idea of Varius getting his hands on it was the worst possible scenario.

"He won't." Gerard tucked it into his pocket. "Besides, even if he does, he doesn't have the power to destroy it."

My skin prickled with awareness, and I stared at Gerard. The answer was so close. *So close.* "What do you mean?" I tried to sound innocent, like I was merely curious.

"The only thing powerful enough to destroy the stones is the same magic that created the curse. The dark shadows."

THE BEAUTY

"The dark shadows," I repeated.

"Yes. The most powerful concentrated area of the dark shadows would be the shadow storm itself."

Shadow storm? My thoughts were raging, my mind working frantically to stay one step ahead of Gerard.

But everything he was revealing to me shattered what I thought I knew. My confidence was broken.

Make a plan, I told myself. *Make a plan!*

An army was here, attacking the Shadow Court. Varius's people. *My people.*

But I knew how to break the curse. I could end this.

I needed to somehow take the bloodstone from Gerard. I had Wraith Killer on me, and I knew I could best Gerard in a fight. I had done it before.

But I didn't know if I could kill him. Not with an army about to burst through the doors.

And if I didn't kill him, he could just travel through the shadows. As soon as I stole the bloodstone from him, he would know what I was about to do. He would teleport to the shadow storm and stop me.

"We have to leave, Sybelle," Gerard was saying as he grabbed my wrist again. "We don't have much time now."

I nodded quickly. "I know." I had to get away from him. I

needed to talk to Azure, to form a plan with her, but I couldn't do that with him listening. "I just—I can't leave without Ramia."

Not a lie. I would never leave without her.

His lips thinned, and I knew he was about to suggest I leave her here.

"I will not abandon her to be slaughtered!" I shouted. Let him think I was referring to the brutal unseelie fae.

In truth, I feared what the Earthen soldiers would do to her.

Gerard sighed. "Fine. Let's go get her."

I shook my head. "You can't. The castle is enchanted. It will sense your ill intent and it won't let you pass through its doors."

Gerard's eyes narrowed.

"Trust me!" I pleaded. "It did the same thing to me when I first got here. When you open a door, it sends you wherever it thinks you need to go. But it trusts *me* now. I can get through. Let me go to my rooms and fetch her, and I'll return to you. I promise."

He held my gaze for a long moment. He knew I could not lie to him.

And I *would* be back. I had to return in order to get the bloodstone from him.

Somehow.

He nodded tersely. "Be quick. I will wait for you."

Relief filled my chest, and I gave him a quick smile and squeezed his hand in mine. Then, I took off toward the door, half expecting him to snatch my arm and stop me.

But he didn't.

Please, please, please, I thought, internally begging the castle to be on my side. When I opened the door, my own chambers awaited me.

The knots in my stomach loosened slightly as I cast one last reassuring smile over my shoulder. Gerard only offered me a grim nod in return.

I stepped over the threshold and eased the door shut.

Roaring filled my ears, but I kept my hand on the knob and held it there while I counted to ten. Inside, my pulse hammered with each panicked breath I took.

"Please keep him away from here," I whispered to the castle. "*Please* read his intentions. He wants to destroy this court. He wants to destroy my husband. *Please keep him away.*"

Slowly, I released the handle, and I could have sworn I heard the faint *click* of the locking mechanism engaging.

I blinked, eyes wide. I hadn't known the doors could lock. But perhaps I'd imagined it.

Another deep breath.

I turned and faced the room, searching for Ramia or Enzira. My heart sank when I realized the room was empty.

Well, shit.

Chewing on my lower lip, I thought quickly, then hurried over to my pouch of gemstones.

"Azure, are you there?" I asked, clutching the amber tightly in my palm.

"*Sybelle! Thank the gods. I've been trying to stay quiet so as not to distract you. Is that horrible captain gone? What in all the realms is he doing here? Where are you right now? An entire army of human soldiers appeared out of nowhere, and—*"

"I know. It's a bit of a long story." Azure had only been able to hear the words uttered from my lips, so I quickly filled her in on the most essential information I'd gleaned from Gerard. When I mentioned the death of my father—by Orla's hand—I faltered, my chest cinching painfully.

"*Holy gods. Sybelle, I—I'm so sorry.*"

I nodded. An unexpected lump of emotion tightened my throat. Father's death was no great loss to me. And yet... I hadn't gotten to say goodbye to him. Or utter the many things I'd kept buried inside for so many years.

Now, I would never get that chance.

Because of Orla.

I shook my head, pushing aside my emotions to focus on a plan that was forming. I grabbed my pouch of gemstones and shoved it in my bodice, wedging it between my breasts. I had no idea which ones I would need, so it seemed like a good idea to bring them all.

"Azure," I said. "Do you know where the shadow storm is?"

"Yes. I had to fly west to avoid getting sucked into it. It's like a massive tornado, tearing apart the lower towns of the kingdom."

I thought of the refugees—the fae families who had been escorted into the castle. They had likely fled such a storm.

Were they safe now? If the army breached the gates, all those innocent fae—the mothers, the children—would die.

I had to stop this.

"I—I think I might have a way to end all this." I took a shaky breath. "Are you with me?"

"Of course," she said at once. *"Sybelle, I am with you to the end. I trust you implicitly. Just tell me what you need me to do."*

Heat stung my eyes, and I blinked rapidly, finding it difficult to swallow. "Thank you, dear friend. For now, I need you to stay out of sight. Gerard doesn't know about you, and we need to keep it that way. I'll get him outside of the castle. Stay close by. And, when I say go, I need you to come get me." I paused and took a breath. "For this plan to work… you'll have to fly us into the heart of the shadow storm."

Azure only paused for a moment before she said, *"Very well. I'm assuming this has to do with breaking the curse?"*

"Yes. Are you able to do it?" If I wasn't certain the shadows couldn't harm her, I would have never asked her to do this.

"Of course."

"Thanks, Az." I glanced at the door, anxiety twisting my heart. Where were Ramia and Enzira? Had the Earthen soldiers made it inside the castle?

Were my two friends already dead?

And what about Varius? He was strong, yes, but even he wasn't indestructible. With a sizable army and the element of surprise, he could be overpowered.

Panic seized my chest, and I found it difficult to breathe.

I wouldn't get to tell him goodbye. I would never get to tell him how much he meant to me.

There wasn't time.

Because it had all finally come together in my mind.

Until one of my kind gives up her life for yours, this curse will live on.

The shadowstone and bloodstone were only *part* of the curse. Gerard's life was only *part* of it.

There was one last crucial step. Without it, the curse would live on.

My life had to be sacrificed. *I* was the last piece.

The witches came from the Earthen Court. *My* court. I had their blood running through my veins, even if it was diluted with hundreds of years of human blood.

Tislora had confirmed it. The texts I'd read had confirmed it.

I was descended from the same witches who had been slaughtered by Varius's ancestor.

By the stone of shadow and blood, I make this vow: Until one of my kind gives up her life for yours, this curse will live on, even as my line lives on.

Three pieces to the puzzle: stone of shadow and blood, a life willingly given, and Jessinda's bloodline.

When the stones were destroyed, Gerard had said only a *piece* of the curse would be broken.

Varius had thought only *one* of the three things was needed to break the curse. But in truth, *all three* had to be accomplished.

The stones had to be destroyed.

I had to willingly give up my life for Varius.

And Jessinda's heir needed to be killed.

Once I was dead—and the stones were destroyed with me—then all that was left was Gerard. And Jessinda's curse would finally end.

I had to do this. There was no other way.

THE BEAST

BETWEEN MY SHADOWS, THE ALPORAS, AND THE DULL SENSES OF the humans, we had the upper hand for far longer than I'd anticipated.

They clearly weren't expecting to be blinded by my darkness. And they weren't expecting us to be able to fly, either.

While those of us with alporas made our assault from over the gate, the rest of the soldiers snuck out the side entrances to converge on the human army on foot. This kept us from raising the portcullis.

We had to keep them from breaching the castle entrance.

I slashed my sword with relentless precision, cutting down human after human. Their foul blood coated my arms and splattered my face. Beneath me, Zorben roared, the sound mingling with the carnage and urging me onward.

More blood. More death. More rage.

Beside me, my fae comrades fought mercilessly, their blades tearing through the human flesh as if they were made of parchment.

After a few hours, we managed to push the humans farther down the road and away from the portcullis. The sun was dipping below the horizon. The fading lavender sky warned of nightfall. Exhaustion pulled at my body, and my shadows had grown thinner. I hoped the humans' eyesight was too weak to notice.

I wouldn't be able to keep this up much longer. In a few moments, I would have to pull my shadows inward or remove my Lumen.

I hadn't yet decided what I would do when I heard Orla shout the words I'd been longing for.

"Fall back! Retreat to the forest!"

Relief blossomed within me, bolstering me to sever the heads of a few more humans before they could escape. Several of my soldiers drew their alporas forward, chasing after the humans who were retreating to the cover of the woods—a fear tactic to ensure they would be cowering between the trees, buying us more time.

I kept my shadows in place, even after Orla and the army had vanished from view. I waited a moment more before reeling them in with a gasp, my body slumping over from the strain of it. Were it not for Zorben keeping me upright, I would have collapsed to the ground.

"To the courtyard," I urged the soldiers closest to me. "Let us regroup before they return."

A line of men formed in front of the portcullis, standing guard for the humans' inevitable retaliation. The rest of us made our way to the other side of the gate, either by flight or on foot.

I dismounted, my knees buckling the moment my feet touched the ground. Zorben leaned into me, catching me before I fell. I patted the side of his neck in gratitude, then scanned the nearest soldiers. "Where is General Vexon?"

"Here, my lord." Vexon appeared, his windswept red hair covered in dirt and blood.

"Any word on the rest of our forces?"

"We have one regiment here. Another will arrive within the hour."

I winced. That wouldn't even give us half the numbers the humans had. "And the others?"

"No word. It's likely they haven't even received our call for aid yet."

Shit. I ran a shaking hand through my hair. My magic was spent. All I had left was the strength in my body, and even that was failing.

"My lord?"

I blinked and found Vexon gesturing to the hand I had just used to run through my hair. "What is it?"

"Your claws."

I scrutinized the black talons of my fingers, and my heart seized.

The claws were *elongating*. They now stretched longer than each of my fingers.

"Mother of Shade," I hissed, glancing to my other hand. Those claws were lengthening as well.

This had never happened before. Well, except for...

I glanced up at the darkening sky. The sun was sinking into the horizon, and on the other side of the castle was the moon, growing clearer with every passing moment.

The *full* moon.

"No," I whispered. "No, this cannot be."

Tislora had been giving me elixirs. Sybelle had consented to using her blood. I had drunk the potions specifically to avoid this from happening!

I shook my head violently, hoping I could force the effects of the curse away from me. A riot of fear assaulted me, blaring in my mind, warning me I was doomed. Everyone would die because of me.

"My lord!" someone shouted. A sudden sharpness bit into my forearm, jolting me from my tortured thoughts.

I sucked in a breath and looked at Vexon. He had dug his

fingernails into my arm and was staring up at me with worry in his eyes.

"My lord, are you well?" he asked.

My gaze flicked to my claws, which had stopped growing. They still seemed much longer than before, but perhaps that was my imagination. It was very likely my waning strength was causing hallucinations.

But that wouldn't explain why Vexon had seen the claws.

I straightened to my full height. We were at war. And even if the curse's transformation was about to claim me, I could not abandon my people.

I still had time.

"Take whoever you can to defend the rear side of the castle," I said to Vexon. "We will fortify here."

Vexon nodded. Before he could turn away, I grabbed his elbow. "Send someone you trust to fetch Tislora. We need her." Worry wriggled in my gut, and I feared something had happened to her. Had the humans captured her already?

"Yes, my lord." Vexon and several of his soldiers hurried off to the other side of the castle.

It was then that Sybelle's voice suddenly echoed around me.

"Varius? Are you there?"

With a gasp, I glanced down at my trousers, which were glowing from the amber stone. I quickly withdrew it and clutched it tightly in my hand. *"Sybelle!"*

She uttered a half laugh, half sob. Relief burst in my chest. Thank the gods she was safe. *"Mother of Shade, I've been sick with worry!"* I directed my thoughts to her. *"Where are you? Are you safe?"*

"I'm inside the castle, and I'm fine. Varius, the Earthen army—"

"I know. I'm battling them right now."

Her voice turned panicked. *"You—what? Why the hell are you talking to me then?"*

I chuckled, casting a quick glance around the courtyard.

Soldiers were speaking to one another and tending to wounds. *"We've pushed them back, and we are regrouping. I have a moment, but not much more. Your sister is here."*

"I know," she said. *"And so is Gerard. Varius, he's Jessinda's son."*

Gerard. Her gods-damned human lover. Tislora had told me as much just before I bolted from the medicine room. With a heavy sigh, I said, *"I was afraid of that."*

"You knew?"

"I suspected Jessinda had an heir, but I didn't know for sure until today. Tislora confirmed it. Have you seen her?" I looked around the courtyard once more, hoping the sorceress had appeared. But she wasn't there.

"No, I haven't." Sybelle paused. *"Varius, I found a way to break the curse."*

I went rigid, clutching the amber stone so tightly that my fist trembled. *"How?"* I demanded, urgency flooding my veins.

"I have to combine the shadowstone and bloodstone and bring them into the shadow storm."

Cold horror washed over me. I swallowed hard, immediately shaking my head. *"To hell with that, Sybelle. We can fend off the Necro Shadows our own way. I don't want you going anywhere near that storm."*

"Varius, if we do this and kill Gerard, that army will have no way to retreat. Their entire purpose for fighting you will be nullified. And without your Lumen constantly shielding the castle, you'll have the strength to overpower them. We can win."

"But at what cost?" I argued. The panic cinched tightly in my chest, cutting off my breath. She was going to get herself *killed*.

All to free me.

To free our people.

Mother of Shade, I couldn't breathe at the thought of her dying. *"I cannot lose you, Sybelle. Do not make me choose between you and my people, because... because I will choose you."*

The words felt like they were ripped from me by force.

Because, until this moment, I hadn't realized they were true.

I would sacrifice *everything* to keep her safe. My own people. My own life.

All of it.

Sybelle's voice was shaking. *"You don't mean that."*

"I do mean it. I refuse to give you up. I want you to reign by my side for eternity, Sybelle. You are mine, dannahla. A thousand curses could not tear me away from you."

A tear streaked down my face as I held my breath, waiting for her response.

Her voice was thick with emotion when she finally replied. *"Stones, Varius, I—I have to do this. Please don't make this harder than it is."*

No. She couldn't do this. She *couldn't.* "Sybelle—"

She let out a broken sob. *"I have the shadowstone. I will find a way to take the bloodstone from Gerard. But I don't know if I can kill him. There isn't enough time. I have to end this,* now.*"*

"Sybelle, stop!" I roared. She had to listen to me. She had to see reason.

"Hold off the army as long as you can," she said, her voice louder than my objections. *"Then find Gerard and kill him. And this will all be over. I—I love you. Gods, I love you more than I ever thought possible."*

"Don't you dare." My pulse raced, my vision tinted red as horror surged through me.

Please, please, please.

I could not lose her. The entirety of my soul belonged to her. She was my lifeblood. My salvation. The light that beckoned me from the darkness.

If she died, I would be lost.

"You are my wife. My queen. Don't you dare leave me."

Another sob. *"I wish we had more time, my love."*

Hot tears ran down my cheeks, and I shook my head, desperate to cling to her for another moment. *"Please—"*

Something in my mind snapped shut, cutting off my connection with her. I blinked, my heart sinking like a stone in my chest.

"Sybelle?"

No answer.

"Sybelle!" I roared.

Still nothing. She must have dropped the amber stone.

Or found a way to cut off communication with me.

"Damn it, Sybelle," I growled, gripping the amber so tightly in my fist that my lengthened claws skewered my flesh, drawing droplets of black blood.

I glanced around the courtyard. Soldiers continued to rush about, donning more armor and weapons. Barricades had been formed on the entrance doors and windows of the castle.

I had no idea how much time we had before the humans advanced again. But I couldn't let Sybelle move forward with this plan of hers. I had to stop her. I had to *try*.

I dashed up the steps of the castle, making my way to the nearest door. One door was all it would take. Surely the castle would take me directly to her...

Before I could reach the entrance, a slice of agony burst in my chest. I stiffened, my back arching as pain bloomed along my chest and abdomen. A tortured cry tore from my lips, and I fell to my knees. My wings flared, then grew in size, the sharpened talons lengthening just as my claws had.

No. This couldn't be happening.

Fur sprouted along my chest and arms. My fangs extended far beyond my lips. A guttural howl poured from my mouth, piercing the air and echoing around the courtyard. The soldiers all fell silent as they gaped at me.

I had to leave. I had to get away, *now*, before I hurt someone.

My back bowed, and I hunched on all fours, my claws carving jagged grooves in the ground. My breaths became deeper and more feral. Saliva dripped from my lips.

My vision narrowed. I could no longer see faces or expressions—just shapes and colors. My awareness was slipping. There was something urgent pressing on my mind, but I couldn't recall it.

I couldn't even remember my own name.

"My lord?" A figure approached. Deep inside, I felt I should know him, but the beast had taken over.

All I saw was a threat.

A menacing growl rumbled up my throat, and the figure took an alarmed step back. Shouts rang out around me, and I hissed and spat at the commotion, the fresh fur on my body standing on end.

There were too many predators here. I either needed to escape or slaughter them all.

"My king!" Another figure drew closer, his face hovering near mine. I snarled and spat again, but he was undeterred. "King Varius, we need you!"

The note of panic in his voice only raised my hackles even more. I tried to back away from him, but there were more behind me, crowding me.

I was trapped.

Rage and bloodlust consumed me. I bared my teeth at the predator leering closest to me. I dug in my hind legs, my throat rumbling. My vision turned red, and I pounced.

THE BEAUTY

I was still weeping from my conversation with Varius. I wasn't sure if the amber stone would work, but I had to try. My heart yearned for him, to hear his voice one last time.

But Stones, it killed me to hear him beg. To hear his own voice breaking with sobs.

Tears streaked down my face, blurring my vision. I wiped them away impatiently. I had to keep moving forward.

I had a curse to break.

Clutching my amber stone, I opened a mental channel to Azure, wiping tears from my face. "Are you ready, Az?"

"Ready."

"Good. Let's—"

A fierce pounding sounded at the door. I went rigid, my blood running cold.

Shit. Gerard was coming for me. And I hadn't even found Ramia yet.

I hastily grabbed my cloak and fastened it around my shoulders.

More heavy knocking.

"Just a moment!" My voice was shrill and panicked.

"Sybelle, it's me."

I froze, alarm and confusion washing over me. The turmoil

of emotions from the last hour was enough to drag me under for a full minute before I registered who was calling for me.

It was Tislora.

I opened the door, my pulse skittering at the sight of her. Her hair was disheveled, her eyes wide and slightly crazed.

"Tislora?" I asked uncertainly. I had never seen her look so… unhinged.

"I need to speak with you," she said in a strained voice. "Urgently."

I swallowed hard, uneasy with the idea of being alone in my room with her. But time was of the essence. I had to return to Gerard soon.

"Make it quick," I said, stepping back to let her in.

She swept past me, one of her wings catching me in the shoulder and knocking me backward. I yelped, about to protest, when she spun to face me and held a jar up to my face.

"What does this smell like to you?"

I blinked, my brows furrowing. "What?"

"*Smell it,*" she hissed. "What does it smell like to you?"

I inspected the bright green powder within the jar, then lifted it to my nose and inhaled deeply. Then, I frowned. "It smells like… parsley." There was something familiar about it, though. It was parsley mingled with an earthy scent that reminded me of home.

"Take another whiff," Tislora urged.

I cast her an incredulous look but inhaled again. A sudden onslaught of memories filled my mind. Hot, fragrant tea from the kitchens of the castle I grew up in. My nursemaid used to drink this tea every single morning. The scent reminded me of her.

"That's Terrish tea. Or, rather…" I paused, inspecting the powder. "Ground Terrish leaves, I suppose. It comes from the Earthen Court." I handed the jar back to her. "Tislora, what is this about?"

Her face crumpled, and to my surprise, she grabbed the jar and hurled it against the stone wall. I shrieked as the glass shattered, spraying the floor with tiny shards.

"Everything—Everything has gone to *shit!*" she screeched, her wings flaring wide. I gasped and withdrew a step, startled by how *huge* they were. Larger than Varius's, they nearly filled the span of the room, black as death with sharpened talons at each peak.

"I don't understand," I whispered. "Why are you here? What's happened?"

"Someone has tampered with my store of hellebore leaves." She ran her hands through her hair, making it look even wilder than before. "Hellebore has a similar smell to whatever this tea leaf is. It's quite close. Close enough to deceive me."

I shook my head, not understanding. "What does that mean? What do you use hellebore for?"

Her silver eyes snapped to mine. "Varius's elixirs."

My stomach hollowed, and my hand flew to my throat. "No..."

She nodded, her eyes grim. "It's a key ingredient. Without it, the elixirs won't work."

Dread coiled tightly in my chest, so sharp I couldn't get enough air in my lungs. I sat down in the chair by the desk, my hands shaking. "So—So those potions you made, with my blood, with Varius's..."

"They did nothing." Her voice was filled with despair. "With your blood, they lessened Varius's symptoms, giving us the illusion of success. But it was a farce. The elixirs did not push the shadows back. And they did not delay his condition."

My head whipped up, and I stared at her in alarm. "What condition?"

"Every full moon, he transforms, his features becoming more monstrous with each cycle."

My heart seized in my chest. "*What?*"

"The wings and tails were the last to appear before the previous kings were lost to the beast within."

I felt the blood drain from my face. "What—What does that mean?"

"Every full moon, the king of the land becomes more of a vicious beast, losing all awareness of who he is. Varius's father died from the wounds of the transformation. His grandfather slaughtered an entire village before the soldiers managed to kill him." Tislora's mouth thinned, her silvery eyes looking haunted. "Varius is out of time."

My head was spinning, and my body felt icy with horror. My mouth went bone dry, and I couldn't swallow.

Varius was dying.

The elixirs had done *nothing*.

All of it had been for nothing.

I took a shuddering breath, trying to calm my raging pulse. "I can fix this." My voice was shaky.

Tislora looked at me incredulously. "What are you talking about?"

"I know how to break the curse."

She went rigid, then turned to face me fully, her eyes flashing with intensity. For the first time since she appeared at my door, she seemed like the sharp and cunning Tislora I was used to. "Tell me."

I explained about the two stones and how I needed the shadow storm to destroy them.

"Once they are destroyed, Varius will kill Gerard, and—"

"Gerard?" Tislora said sharply.

"The captain of the Earthen Court armies. Well, he's actually the Earthen King now, I suppose." My stomach twisted at the thought. "But he's Jessinda's son, and—"

Tislora's face twisted with rage, her eyes going dark. She curled a hand into a shaking fist and bared her fangs with a feral hiss.

I staggered back a step, taken aback by this reaction.

"Gerard," she seethed. "It was *him*. He must have tampered with my stores. Damn him!" She slashed her claws into the stone wall behind her, carving jagged grooves into the hard surface.

"How do you know him?" I demanded, my heartbeat quickening.

"We were raised together," Tislora said. "I once considered him my brother. We came from the same witch clan."

I sucked in a sharp breath, then pointed a trembling finger at her. "You—You are from *Jessinda's* clan? You're part of this?" I shook my head, gritting my teeth as rage blurred my vision. "I *knew* it. You're a traitor! You—"

"Silence, feeble human," Tislora barked. "I am no traitor. I already swore in blood my fealty to Varius. Gerard deceived me, too." She shook her head so violently that her dark hair swung around her. "No more. He has crossed a line he cannot come back from." Her sharp gaze slid to mine. "Can you take me to him?"

I hesitated. I still wasn't sure I trusted her. If she grew up with Gerard, how did I know she wouldn't betray me for him?

Tislora stepped toward me, then dragged a claw down her palm. Black blood welled from the wound. "I swear on my fae blood that I will end Gerard's life if you take me to him, Sybelle. Take me to him, and I will get you that bloodstone."

The air hummed with power that rattled my bones and made my blood sing. I knew she spoke true.

She was on my side.

I nodded once. "Fine. Here's the plan…"

After detailing our plan together, Tislora and I opened several doors before we found Enzira and Ramia huddled in the kitchens with the other castle staff. I grabbed Ramia, promising I would keep her safe. Before we could leave, Enzira rushed forward, insisting on coming, too. Both maids were pale and panic-stricken, but the fire in their eyes told me they needed a purpose.

They needed to fight. Even if they couldn't wield swords, they needed to retaliate somehow.

I understood that all too well.

So, I agreed.

The four of us headed down the spiral staircase that led to the dining hall. In an undertone, I told Ramia of our plan, while Tislora translated for Enzira. To her credit, Enzira only nodded, her mouth set in a grim line. But Ramia's grip on my arm tightened with each word I uttered.

When I mentioned the role Azure would play, Ramia's fingernails pinched my skin, making me wince. "Who is Azure?" she asked.

"Oh." I cleared my throat. "She's my dragon."

The two maids stopped short, causing Tislora to bark at us to hurry up. She'd only blinked once at me, her face devoid of emotion, when I'd revealed I had a dragon lurking nearby.

"I knew it," Ramia hissed, shaking her head at me as if I'd merely confessed to sneaking into her stash of sweets.

"You—You have a dragon?" Enzira whispered. "What is she like? Is she dangerous?"

"No. Well, not to me. She's serpentine with blue scales. If you see her, keep in mind she's on our side."

Enzira's mouth trembled, and she sucked in a shaky breath. I knew this was a lot for her to take in.

Her reaction reminded me of the awe and wonder on Varius's face when I'd told him of Azure. My chest *ached* to be with him. To show him my magnificent dragon.

I would never get to see the look on his face when he finally met her.

My amber stone was still clutched in my palm, and I ran my fingers over it before I reached out to him.

"Varius?"

No answer. Perhaps he'd lost the gem while fighting.

I didn't want to consider the possibility that he had been killed. Or that the curse had already claimed his life. He was too strong for that. And my heart couldn't bear it.

We reached the double doors to the dining hall, and I paused, wondering if the castle would take us to a different room.

It had to be on our side. If it understood what we were planning, it would know we were only trying to save the people of the Shadow Court.

"Please," I whispered before turning the handle and stepping inside.

Gerard was pacing the length of the hall, hands curled into fists and his hair disheveled as if he'd run his fingers through it repeatedly.

"Finally," he growled when I entered with Ramia. He faltered at the sight of Enzira behind me. As planned, Tislora waited in the hall behind the door, which had been left slightly ajar. "Who is this? I thought you just went to fetch Ramia."

"This is Enzira," I said, gesturing to her. "She was my hand maid during my stay here. I'd like to bring her, too. She doesn't deserve to be left behind to die."

I didn't mention that *none* of the unseelie fae deserved that fate. Such a statement would fall on deaf ears.

Gerard's face twisted with disgust. "She is *unseelie.*"

I lifted my chin. "I possess fae blood. Technically, so do you. She is innocent and has nothing to do with the politics here. If you want the king dead, then letting her live will not change that." It took every ounce of my strength to keep my voice level. "Bury your prejudice, Gerard. I'm not going with you unless you let me bring her, too."

Gerard made a disgusted sound and rubbed his forehead. "Fine. We don't have time for this. Come with me."

He grabbed my arm and steered me toward an open window on the opposite wall. Only then did I notice the rope dangling over the edge.

"What are you doing?" I asked.

"This is how I entered the castle. You were right about those enchanted doors. Every time I tried to open one, I found nothing but a stone wall." He shot me a sly grin. "But apparently, whatever magic enchants these doors does not apply to windows."

My heart sank with dread. I hadn't expected to be hauled out the window. I thought he would take me through the hall, where Tislora was waiting.

Gerard noticed my hesitation. "What's wrong?" He glanced around the room, eyes narrowing with suspicion.

"I just—how far down is it? Aren't we on the third floor?" I said quickly, not wanting him to investigate.

"Yes, but the rope is secure. Trust me, darling." He pulled on my arm, drawing me close and brushing his lips against my temple. I swallowed down bile and resisted the urge to recoil from his touch. His smell, his warmth—it was all so unfamiliar to me now.

And it only made me crave Varius's touch even more.

"I'll go down first, to ensure it's safe," he said. He shot an uncertain glance toward Enzira before climbing out the window and shimmying down the rope.

When he was out of earshot, I hissed to Enzira, "You'll come out last. Quickly, tell Tislora we'll be on the grounds by the western side of the castle."

Enzira nodded and hurried to the hall to relay the message while I climbed out the window after Gerard.

Dusk had fallen, and the gleaming full moon filled the sky. The Umbra Mist swirled like smoke around the castle. I suppressed a shiver from the cool night air. I slowly lowered myself down the rope, using my feet to propel my body against the stone wall of the palace.

When I finally reached the bottom, Gerard's arms came around me. I jerked away without thinking, and something like anger flashed in his eyes.

"Oh—I—you startled me," I said, pretending to be breathless from the climb. "Didn't you say we were in a hurry?"

His brows knitted together, and a muscle flexed in his jaw. He could sense something was off about me.

Unfortunately, he knew me too well.

Behind me, Ramia reached the ground, wiping sweat from her brow. Gray hairs came loose from her bun. A few moments later, Enzira hopped down with ease. Gerard eyed her tail with unease as it swished behind her body.

"To the stables?" I asked, my voice a touch sharper than was necessary. I wanted him to stop glaring at my friend.

"No," he said, meeting my gaze. "To the woods. There's a patch of dark shadows just beyond that we can travel through."

"All right. Lead the way."

He reached for my hand, but I pretended to fumble with the clasp of my cloak. With a sigh, he strode forward.

Then, I made my move.

I yelped loudly, and he stiffened, whirling to face me. My hands grasped his tunic as if I had tripped. Together, we slid sideways, crashing into the bed of flowers that lined the castle walls. My cloak tangled with his sword belt, and his armor clanged loudly as we rolled together in the soil.

"Shit!" I cried, twisting further as he tried to extricate himself. "Damn my clumsiness. Hold on, my fabric is bunched here."

Enzira rushed forward to help, but Gerard barked, "Get away from us!"

"Don't talk to her like that!" I snarled, shoving his chest hard. "She has been nothing but kind to me."

His nostrils flared, and he stared at me as if seeing me for the first time. "You have changed. I thought you hated the unseelie."

"I hate those who endanger my people," I said coldly. "That doesn't include Enzira."

I clambered to my feet and slid the bloodstone in the pocket of my cloak, praying he hadn't noticed I'd taken it. I brushed dirt and leaves from my clothes, then stepped out of the flower bed and onto the gravel path. "Shall we?"

Gerard said nothing, striding past me, then froze, his hand sifting through his pocket.

Damn it.

"Wait a moment." He whirled to face me, eyes blazing. "What did you do?"

Fear tightened my chest like a vise, but before I could reply, a voice bellowed, "Gerard!"

Gerard turned. Standing beyond the gravel path stood Tislora, her wings stretched wide and her icy silver eyes pinned on him. She offered him a cruel smile.

"It has been a while, hasn't it, brother?"

THE BEAUTY

Gerard went rigid at the sight of Tislora, his arms slackening at his sides. "Lora?" he asked, his voice full of disbelief.

"Don't play games with me," she snapped, striding toward him with lethal grace. "I know what you've done to my stores of hellebore."

I slowly backed away from the two of them, then gestured wildly for Enzira and Ramia to leave. "Run!" I whispered. "Remember the plan!"

They both nodded and retreated toward the opposite end of the castle. Enzira shot me one last look of regret before she vanished from view.

I knew they wanted to stay with me. But they were not fighters, and Gerard could easily use them as leverage against me.

Besides, they had explicit instructions to access the armory so they could distribute weapons to everyone in the castle. The Earthen soldiers would likely breach the entrance soon, and I wanted to ensure the staff had a means of defending themselves.

"Azure, are you close?" I breathed, squeezing my amber stone.

"Just say the word, and I'll grab you," she replied.

I retrieved the shadowstone from my other pocket, then held

it alongside the bloodstone. The air hummed, and the shrill ringing sound returned. I gritted my teeth, and Gerard whipped toward me.

"No!" he roared, reaching for me. "*Stop!*"

Tislora's wings flared, and she flew toward him, claws extended. I took several steps back, then slammed the two stones together.

An explosion of white light burst from the stones, powerful enough to send me flying into the stone wall behind me. I screamed, pain bursting behind my skull as the force of it nearly knocked me out. I heard Gerard's grunt and Tislora's screech and knew she was trying to keep him away from me. I didn't have much time.

My teeth rattled from the quivering stones in my hands. Heat burned into my palms, singeing my skin. I hissed at the scorching pain.

Then, voices echoed around me, ethereal and ghost-like. I made out the words from Jessinda's curse: "*By the stone of shadow and blood, I make this vow: Until one of my kind gives up her life for yours, this curse will live on, even as my line lives on.*"

The blinding light seared against my eyes, and even with my eyelids shut, it burned me until I thought my eyeballs might melt from it.

Slowly, the voices vanished and the lights faded. I opened my eyes, gasping, my body hunched over and trembling from pain. As my sight adjusted to the darkness of night, I made out two struggling figures before me. Gerard had his sword out, and it gleamed with Tislora's black blood. Her hands were wrapped around his throat, her talons drawing his own blood as they hissed and spat at each other.

I glanced down at the stones in my hand, only to find they had merged into one stone. It was a gleaming white gem, shaped just like a rose. It warmed my palm as I held it.

"You will doom us all!" Gerard bellowed, his eyes wild with

fury at the sight of me with the stone. He stormed toward me, but Tislora tackled him, pressing his face into the grass.

"*Go*, Sybelle!" Tislora shouted. "Now!"

I staggered to my feet and took off down the gravel path, circling around the palace. "Azure!" I cried as I ran. "I need you!"

The giant beating of wings drew nearer, and I yelped as something huge wrapped around me, lifting me in the air.

Azure gripped me between her talons, her icy claws wrapped around each of my arms. She didn't even pause to land.

I cried out, my legs dangling below me. My stomach dropped with each movement she made, and I couldn't shake the terrifying feeling of weightlessness, like at any moment I would free-fall and plummet to my death. My palms were covered in sweat, and I feared the stone would slip out of my grasp. "Do you know where the shadow storm is?" I asked.

"*Of course I do. It isn't far from here. Don't lose your nerve.*"

I rolled my eyes, knowing her teasing was keeping my fear at bay. It was likely why she kept it up.

My legs swung wildly as she arced left. I glanced to the right and made out the human soldiers, their swords clashing with the unseelie fae. My heart seized in my chest. Not only were the humans wearing armor that was much stronger, but there were more than twice as many humans as fae. The Earthen soldiers had pushed them all the way up to the portcullis. Several humans were climbing over the gate to reach the castle.

"Stones," I whispered. "They're losing. Badly."

"*It will be over soon, Sybelle.*"

A knot formed in my throat, and I nodded. This would not be for nothing. I would make sure of it.

Azure carried me over the treetops of the Noxen Forest. Once we passed the woods, a fierce wind rippled over us, and she had to beat her wings harder to continue forward. The howl of the storm filled the air, and my stomach fluttered with anxiety.

In front of us was a raging tornado, twisting and roaring like an enraged monster. Dark gray thunderclouds surrounded it, but at the heart of the storm was a pitch black void.

The very same void I would have to drop into.

Trees were uprooted, tossed about like rag dolls as the storm consumed them. The massive funnel cloud drew closer, the wind and dirt particles stinging my eyes.

My blood seemed to freeze over with icy fear. *Am I really going to do this?*

The foul stench of the Necro Shadows surrounded us. It wouldn't take long for the toxins to infect my body. My mouth went bone dry, and I had the sudden urge to retch. I was going to be sick.

"Are you still down there?" Azure asked. *"That wind is so intense I thought it might blow away your feeble human body."*

I had no response. My tongue was glued to the roof of my mouth. If I tried to speak, I would likely vomit.

"You can just drop it in," Azure reminded me. *"Just drop the stone into the storm, and I can carry you away."*

"No," I said, finding my voice at last. "No, it's not that simple. I—I have to fall in myself."

Her talons tightened around me. *"What are you talking about?"* Her voice was full of panic.

This was why I hadn't told her. She never would have agreed to this if she'd known.

Leaves and dust swirled around us as we drew closer. The wind burned, making my skin throb. I had to shout over the roaring wind to ensure Azure could hear me. "The spell mentions blood and shadow, which references the stones. But it also says someone from Jessinda's kind must offer up their life. I come from the Earthen Court, descended from the witches who once lived here. *I* am one of Jessinda's kind. And my sacrifice will end this curse."

Azure was silent for a long moment, but she kept flapping

her wings, maneuvering through the fierce winds. She did not stop.

"Tislora," she said at last. *"Tislora could have broken the curse. And she had no idea."*

"You're right," I agreed. "But I would never condemn anyone else to this fate. It is my responsibility. It is what I was always meant to do. All those generations of human brides were given to do *this exact thing*. And now, finally, hundreds of years later, it will be finished. The curse will end with me."

"Sybelle." Azure's voice was strained. *"Please."*

"There is no other way. Gerard must die. The stones must be destroyed. And I must give up my life. You know this. Otherwise you would have turned us around by now."

"Then I will die alongside you."

Tears streamed from my eyes, but the wind dashed them away before they reached my cheeks. "You can't! I need you to protect the Shadow Court. If the Earthen soldiers keep fighting even after Gerard is dead, you have to keep my people safe. Promise me, Az. Promise me you'll do that."

Azure said nothing. Would she refuse me this last wish? Was she so angry with my decision that she would deny my request?

At long last, she whispered, *"I swear it. I will protect your people."*

My people. Yes, the unseelie fae were my people. Not the humans. Even though I was part human, even though I had been raised in the Earthen Court... it was no longer my home.

I wasn't sure when this had changed for me. When had I no longer considered the humans *my people*? When had I decided that the lives of the shadow fae were more precious to me?

The wind was so intense that Azure was having trouble flying straight. The wind screamed and howled. The black void was upon us, the darkness so thick I couldn't even see my legs swinging below me.

"We are at the epicenter now," Azure said, her wingbeats slow-

ing. She teetered, bobbing up and down. *"I cannot fight the wind anymore."*

"Then drop me," I said, the storm raging around us. I could see nothing but the dark shadows. The toxins filled my nose and throat, making me choke.

Even if Azure retreated now, there was every likelihood I would still be poisoned.

No turning back now, I thought.

"Azure, drop me!" I cried. The longer she stayed here, the worse the wind would get. She might be immune to the Necro Shadows, but she wasn't immune to the storm.

"I love you, Sybelle."

Azure's talons loosened, and she released me.

I fell, the weightlessness rushing around me. My stomach flipped as my body careened with the wind. Tree branches and debris slammed into me, barreling me left and right. My body was battered as I slammed into something hard and unyielding. A choked scream built in my throat, but I couldn't find my voice. Darkness pressed in on me. Poison seeped into my veins, coursing through my body like fire. My bones melted. My blood burned.

And then my body shattered into nothingness.

THE BEAST

Screams and shouts echoed around me, but they were drowned out by the bloodlust burning in my veins. I was on all fours, paws hitting the earth hard as I pounced from one soldier to the next. I saw no faces. Only enemies.

I swiped my claws, then dug my fangs into the flesh of the enemy closest to me. My wings flared, lifting me upward to avoid the slash of his sword. With blood dripping down my chin, I broke away from the throng and howled at the full moon, my entire body quivering from the euphoria coursing through me.

It felt glorious to unleash the demon that had been festering inside me for so long. Years of pent-up rage had been mounting, and now, finally, I was free to let it all loose.

My roar split the air, and I took off at a run, the muscles of my legs pumping hard. I was a beast built for speed and death. And I embraced it fully.

"Varius?" A sudden voice echoed in my mind.

I faltered, my stride slowing as I homed in on that singular sound. The voice awakened something that was slumbering inside me. Something I wanted to keep buried deep.

Confusion clouded my mind, and I shook my head with a growl, ready to lose myself to the bloodlust again.

But that damned *voice*... It haunted my thoughts now. All I could hear was her. All I wanted was *her*.

Sybelle.

She consumed my mind. Her eyes, her smile, her laugh. Her scent, her taste, her moans... All of her surrounded me in echoes, taunting me.

My roar was halfhearted as a newfound lust took over.

I needed her. *Now.*

I bolted, my legs pushing furiously, giving me a burst of speed. I was unsure of where I was going, only that I needed to move quickly. The shapes before me became a blur, and I only paused once I was away from the crowd of enemies, lest their blood tempt and distract me from my mission.

I lifted my nose in the air, inhaling deeply.

There. I caught a whiff of her earthy scent and clung to it, my sharpened senses picking up on her trail. I sniffed the ground, following it, then broke into a run once more.

Sybelle, I am coming.

My paws pounded into the earth. Saliva dripped from my fangs, mingling with the blood still lingering there. I was so close now. *So close.*

I rounded the corner and froze. Shouts and grunts sounded nearby. Ahead of me, two creatures grappled with one another. One had wings and dark hair like me. The other had paler skin and...

My hackles rose. He smelled like her. He smelled like Sybelle.

Snarls ripped from my throat as I prowled toward the figure. I didn't care who he was. The scent of my wife was on him, and for that, he would die.

The male swiped his sword, drawing blood from the winged female. She fell backward, her face already covered in blood from a gash that oozed black droplets. One of her wings was torn, and her eyes were hooded.

The male advanced, his sword slick with her blood. He cradled his left arm as if it were broken, and fresh blood ran down his chin. He raised his sword, and I pounced, landing directly in his path.

He froze, eyes wide, his arm poised midair as he gaped at me.

"What—*What is this?*" he bellowed.

"This… is the king whose life you seek," the female said as she staggered to her feet.

I cocked my head toward her, recognition flashing in my mind. She nodded encouragingly.

"You know me, Varius."

I squinted, my vision coming in and out of focus. One moment, I knew who she was. And the next, I didn't.

I shook my head roughly, frustrated by the lack of clarity. With a low grumble, I slowly prowled toward the other figure— the one who smelled like Sybelle.

He lifted both hands, as if that might stop me from advancing.

"You can't do this," he said, his voice tinged with panic. "You can't kill me."

"Do it, Varius," said the female. "He's the one who brought the army. He's the one who's murdering your people."

The male's face twisted with rage, and he jabbed a finger at her. "*She's* the traitor, too! She never told you about the witches. She never told you about *me*."

I stilled at that, tilting my head with interest. Slowly, my gaze shifted from the male to the female.

Their scents had mingled. And, if I focused intently, I could smell Sybelle on the female, too.

She had touched my wife. What if she had hurt her? Kidnapped her?

Where was Sybelle?

Fangs bared, I shifted toward the female instead, creeping closer to her. Her eyes flared wide in alarm.

"Varius, don't," she whispered. "You *know* me. I did not hurt Sybelle." She pointed to the male. "But *he did*. If you kill him, you can end this. All of this." She spread her arms around her, indicating the castle and the soldiers fighting nearby.

With a keening moan, I shook my head again, burying my face underneath my paws. It was too much. I couldn't think. I couldn't *remember*.

"This is ridiculous," snarled the male, drawing closer to me and raising his sword.

Before he could bring it down on me, I lunged.

My paws hit him in the chest, slamming him into the ground. I bared my fangs at him, relishing the scent of fear that wafted from his trembling body.

My claws pierced his breastplate, carving straight through the steel. He screamed when they met his flesh.

"Kill him, Varius!" the female urged.

The male roared, his elbow jabbing upward until it slammed into my snout. With a whine, my head snapped sideways from the impact, pain shooting through me.

The male managed to kick me off him. I rolled, paws sliding in the ground to stop myself. He swung his sword, but his movements were clumsy from his injuries. I ducked, avoiding the blow. He swung again, and this time, I wasn't quick enough. The tip of his blade pierced my side, drawing blood. I howled in agony, swiping at the sword with my claws. The sharp sound of clashing metal rang out.

With a mighty shriek, the female launched herself forward, colliding with the male. He fell as she dragged him to the ground, wrenching the sword from his grip. Her claws skewered his arm, drawing blood. The male roared, the anguished sound echoing around us.

The scent of his blood drew out the ravenous beast within me. Saliva dripped from my fangs.

"*Now*, Varius!" the female cried. "End it!"

The male struggled, but she pinned him further into the ground. "No—Lora, *wait*—"

I silenced him, clamping his throat between my teeth and ripping at his flesh. His screams only urged me onward, and I dug deeper into him.

He managed to kick the female off him. She hit the ground hard with a pained grunt.

The male thrashed, his knee connecting with my jaw. My head reared back, and he wriggled out from under me. He grabbed his sword and clambered to his feet, but the river of blood gushing from his throat was too much. He swayed, his face paling. He drunkenly swung his weapon, and I nearly barked out a laugh.

As if that would stop me.

The hair on my back stood on end, and I growled, the sound low and menacing. We circled one another. He was losing color fast. He tried to lift his broken arm to stifle the bleeding in his throat, but he winced in pain, clearly too injured to manage.

He didn't have long now.

"You'll never have her," he choked out. More blood bubbled from his lips. "She will never be yours."

Bloodthirsty rage burned through me, tinting my vision red. My voice was deep and rough, the sound of the monster within, as I spat, "She already is."

I flew toward him, pinning him to the ground. My claws made quick work of shredding his throat, tearing through him until his head detached from his body and rolled into the flowerbed. Even after he was dead, I wasn't satisfied. I still hadn't found *her*. I still didn't know why this male smelled like her. My claws shredded the rest of his armor, his trousers, his arms and legs. He was nothing but a bloody pulp when I sensed another presence behind me.

With a snarl, I whirled, facing the winged female. She lifted a vial of a vibrant green liquid and extended it toward me.

"The choice is yours, my king," she said softly. "If you want to remain a beast, you can. But, if you hope to save her, you'll need to drink this."

I stared at the liquid, alarm ringing through my body with violent intensity. I did not want to lose my strength. My freedom. For decades, I had fought so hard to be the king my people needed. The king everyone expected me to be. Now, after only moments of losing those restraints, I needed to cage myself once more?

"She needs you, Varius," the female whispered.

In my mind, I heard Sybelle again. Her screams. Her cries for help.

A tortured cry poured from my lips, and I sank back on my hind legs, my back bowing in agony. I was being ripped apart. The anguish was too great. Too potent.

I could never escape it. I could never truly be free. Not now. Not ever.

But... I *could* be with her. I would not be free from burdens or responsibilities or expectations, but... I could have her by my side.

And perhaps that was enough.

The female waited expectantly for me to make my decision. The vial could easily contain poison. But somehow, I knew she could be trusted. I wasn't sure how, but I knew.

I reached forward, my paw awkwardly taking the vial from the female's grasp. My lips parted, and I downed the contents.

Immediately, shivers rippled over my body. I hunched over with a tortured groan, pain setting my blood on fire. My bones snapped and mended, my skin stretching and shrinking. The thick, coarse fur along my body vanished. My paws lengthened into fingers. My rumbling roar of agony melted into a bellowing howl. All I knew was fire. All I felt was pain. My body was breaking, one piece at a time, and reconstructing itself.

When it was over, I collapsed in a heap on the ground, my body trembling and covered in sweat and blood. I didn't know if it was mine or not. The memories of my time as a beast flooded my mind, making me weep.

How many had I killed? How many of my own soldiers had I attacked in this state?

An anguished wail poured from my lips. I slammed my fist into the ground as broken sobs overcame me.

I was a monster. A demon. I had killed my own people.

"Varius," Tislora whispered, her hand pressing into my bloodied shoulder.

I flinched away from her touch. I did not deserve to be comforted in this moment.

"She took the stones to the shadow storm," Tislora said.

I stiffened, my memories returning with frustrating sluggishness. It took several moments before comprehension dawned on me.

Sybelle. The bloodstone and shadowstone.

She was going to sacrifice herself for me. For the kingdom.

I stood, my arms and legs throbbing from fresh wounds. Dizziness clouded my vision, but I couldn't stop. I had to find her.

If there was one last thing I could do with my pitiful existence, it would be to save her. My kingdom deserved to be ruled by someone who loved them. Who gave their life for them.

That was Sybelle. Not me.

I would save her. And then I would leave this court, never to show my face here again. I was a murderer. I could not come back from the crimes I'd committed against them.

The ground rumbled, and energy rippled through the air. In the distance, an echoing *boom* sounded.

Heat tingled up and down my body. I hunched over, shuddering from the intensity of it as magic coursed through me in violent waves. Across from me, Tislora cried out in pain.

The earth continued to tremble. The castle walls quivered. Shouts and screams rang out, but I didn't know if it was from my people or Orla's.

In an instant, the earthquake stopped, and the magic receded from my body. I glanced over myself, expecting to find fur and paws again.

But nothing had changed.

Gasping for breath, I looked at Tislora, who seemed as stunned as I was.

"What the hell was that?" I asked.

She shook her head, her mouth opening and closing. She stared at her hands as if expecting them to transform. "I—I don't know. I've never felt magic like that before."

Heavy wingbeats approached. I glanced skyward, thinking it might be Zorben, my alpora.

Instead, a figure much larger than any alpora floated above us, its shimmering dark scales blending in with the midnight sky. It slammed into the earth before us, making the ground tremble.

I stumbled back in shock and fear.

It was a dragon. *Sybelle's dragon.*

I stared at the beast, my terror ebbing as I recalled how fondly Sybelle had spoken of it. Azure was her name.

I held perfectly still, allowing my gaze to rove over her huge form. Her body was long and serpentine, coiling in the grass. Before my eyes, her scales shifted from a navy blue to a brilliant cerulean. Her gleaming eyes fixed me with an intelligent stare that seemed to pierce through my very soul.

A voice resonated in my mind. *"Can you understand me, Fae King?"*

I yelped, turning to Tislora, my eyes wide with shock. But she only frowned in response.

"Did—Did you hear that?" I gasped.

"Hear what?"

I turned to look at the dragon again.

"Use the amber stone," said the voice.

My brow furrowed before I remembered the orange gem I had used to communicate with Sybelle. I fumbled over my tattered trousers until I found the stone lodged in my pocket, trapped inside several frayed threads. Miraculously, it was still here, even after my time as a beast.

I clutched the amber tightly in my fist. *Can you hear me?*

"Speak aloud," the dragon commanded. *"That is how it works."*

I cleared my throat, feeling ridiculous. "Can you hear me?"

A rumbling sound of contentment quivered through the dragon. *"Yes. Sybelle has broken your curse, but she is dying. You must come with me."*

I froze. She broke the curse?

Was that the cause of the earthquake? The spark of magic that rippled over my body?

Before I could process this, my mind snagged on Azure's last statement: *She is dying.*

Panic and terror blotted out all other thoughts. "Where is she?" I demanded.

"Just past the Noxen Forest. I didn't want to bring her body here amidst the bloody battle."

My blood ran cold. *Her body.*

She couldn't be... She wasn't...

"Climb on my back," Azure commanded.

"Lor." I turned to the sorceress, who was staring at the dragon with starstruck eyes. "Climb on with me." I would have asked her to fly behind us, but Gerard had managed to shred one of her wings.

I wished I could rip out his throat all over again.

"I can fly in my crow form," Tislora said.

I nodded as Azure sank to her knees and allowed me to climb on. Her scales were sharp and bumpy, and I shifted, trying to find a comfortable position. "Are there no reins?" I asked.

An indignant snort rippled through her. *I am no common mule.*

"How am I to hold on?"

You trust that I will not unseat you.

Before I could object to this illogical arrangement, Azure leapt into the sky.

THE BEAST

I bit back a cry of alarm as my stomach dropped, the wind whipping at my hair and face. Azure's great wings beat behind her, putting on a burst of speed. The muscles of her body moved with each powerful thrust, and I felt my body slipping from the jolting movements.

Just when I thought I would topple off her back, she angled herself to the left. Gravity brought me back down. She leveled out, wings stretched wide, and my stomach settled.

In a few moments, we had crossed the Noxen Forest. A horrified gasp escaped me at the sight that greeted us.

What had once been a bustling village was nothing more than a heap of rubble. Smashed buildings. Leveled forests. Cracked concrete. With the shadow storm gone, I could now see it all in terrible clarity. Tree branches and debris stretched on for miles, mingled with the broken remains of the buildings that had once stood here.

Tears stung my eyes, but as I surveyed the devastation, I realized it made a strange spiral shape. Rings of ash stretched wider and wider, expanding from the center outward as if marking where the storm had spread.

And in the center of the circles lay a motionless figure, her eyes closed and her chestnut hair fanned out behind her.

"*Sybelle!*" I roared. My body was desperate to get to Sybelle, to hold her in my arms once again.

Azure arced wide, then landed a few feet away from where Sybelle lay. I climbed off the dragon's back within seconds and rushed to my wife's side.

Even before I reached her, I knew she wasn't breathing.

I sensed Tislora's crow form landing behind me, and she shifted to her fae form.

"Lor!" I bellowed as I crouched beside Sybelle, cradling her against my chest. Her face was smeared with dirt and bruises. Bloody cuts and scrapes lined her neck and arms. It looked like the storm had completely battered her. "Lor, can you—can you do something?" I lifted Sybelle's body, bringing my ear to her chest.

There it was. The faintest of heartbeats.

But Tislora did not move.

I glared at her over my shoulder. "What are you doing? Help her!"

Her face paled, and she shook her head slowly. "I'm sorry, Varius. But… she is too far gone."

"She is *not gone*," I growled.

"*No, she is not,*" Azure agreed. "*I can still sense her. Her fae blood is keeping her alive. But she is fading. You must do something, Fae King.*"

"What am I supposed to do?" I hissed, my eyes burning as I stared at Sybelle. There had to be something. *Something* I could do to bring her back.

If Sybelle were here, what would she say?

Books, I thought at once. Sybelle would consult all the books in the library, searching for a method of healing. Ancient rituals, archaic spells, healing stones…

Stones. *Stones!*

I turned to Azure, whose somber gaze was fixed on Sybelle. Those magnificent blue eyes were moist with unshed tears. "Is there a gemstone that Sybelle used? Something that could bring someone back from the brink of death?"

Azure blinked slowly, as if reluctant to tear her gaze away from her beloved human. After a moment, she said, *"Yes. The moonstone. It would be in her pouch. I believe she had it somewhere on her person."*

With shaking hands, I fumbled with her bodice and skirts, searching for hidden pockets. There was nothing but her jeweled dagger strapped to her thigh. Gritting my teeth, I gingerly pressed my hand to her chest, then faltered. There *was* something lumpy there.

Cringing at this invasion of her privacy, I tugged on the neckline of her dress, peering down to see if anything was hidden there.

Yes. There was a small blue pouch tucked between her breasts. "Only you, Sybelle," I muttered in annoyance, trying to tenderly extract the pouch without fondling her. In ordinary circumstances, this would have felt highly inappropriate, never mind that I was her husband. She was unconscious—dying, even.

She would forgive me for this. In fact, I had no doubt she would tease me mercilessly for it later. I looked forward to it. Just the idea of that smirk on her lips made my heart lift.

She'll be all right, I told myself. *She will rise and taunt you, and you* will *see that smile again. You will see the way her eyes shine with curiosity and wonder. She will not die today.*

When the pouch slid free, I tugged on the strings and over-turned the contents on the ground. "Which one is it?" I asked, my gaze roving over the stones. They were of varying shades and colors, and I had no idea what a moonstone looked like.

"It is white and orb-like."

I found it nestled between two blue gems. As soon as my fingers wrapped around it, my blood hummed with awareness. I gasped, then dropped the stone. The humming stopped, and my body instantly felt cold.

My eyes met Azure's. "What was that?"

"You know what it was," she said.

Swallowing hard, I grasped the stone again. The air pulsed with energy, and power sizzled along my skin.

"Mother of Shade," Tislora whispered, drawing closer. "Even I can sense it. What magic is this, Varius?"

My mouth went dry, and my stomach roiled with unease. I had never felt anything like this before. It was certainly not *my* magic.

My gaze slid to Sybelle's. "It's hers. It's her power."

"That's not possible." Tislora's voice was full of doubt.

"How else can I communicate through the amber stone? How do you explain the shadows she conjured?" I turned to look at Tislora, whose eyes were wide. "We are sharing magic, Lor. It's the only explanation."

Her brows knitted together as she considered this. "The marriage bond is strongest when consummated," she mused. "I would also wager she is the only human bride who fell in love with her husband."

"And whose husband fell in love with her in turn," I whispered, gazing at Sybelle once more. "Azure, what do I do to heal her?"

"I have only seen her use it a handful of times," said the dragon. *"She held it in her hand, then pressed it to the one who was wounded. Then, somehow, their injuries were healed."*

I nodded. "All right." I kept the amber stone clutched firmly in one hand, feeling a sense of comfort knowing Azure was nearby if anything went wrong. With my free hand, I clutched the moonstone tightly, then pressed it against Sybelle's chest.

"Please," I whispered, my eyes cramming shut. *"Please,* gods, bring her back to me. Do not take her from me."

Power crackled in the air like lightning, and Tislora yelped from behind me. I held perfectly still, keeping the stone against Sybelle's body and trying not to think about how cold she felt.

"Come back to me, Sybelle," I breathed, my voice ragged. "Be my wife. My queen. My everything. *Please.*"

My chest felt as if it were splitting in two, like a jagged blade had carved straight through my rib cage.

I could not lose her. To lose her would be to lose my very soul.

Heat blossomed from my hand, and the moonstone began to vibrate against my skin. From beneath me, Sybelle's form trembled. Warmth spread from her chest, and I felt her start to move.

Holy gods. It was working. The stone was healing her.

My eyes flew open, my breaths sharp and painful as I dared to hope, dared to believe she had been healed.

"Sybelle?" My voice cracked, and a tear traced down my cheek.

She inhaled, a small wrinkle forming between her eyebrows. Her chest rose and fell, and then she coughed, the sound wet and hoarse. Blood dribbled from her lips, and I quickly leaned her forward so she wouldn't choke on it. Her matted hair fell, shielding her face like a curtain. I carefully drew it back, tucking it behind her ears.

Her eyelids fluttered, and she squinted, her incoherent gaze taking in Azure, Tislora, and me as we crowded around her.

"What—What happened?" she rasped. She sounded as if she hadn't spoken in days.

"By the gods," I sobbed before crushing her against my chest. Her frail hands clutched at my arms, bringing me closer. Her shoulders shook, and I couldn't tell if it was from laughter or tears. "You're alive. You're here. Mother of Shade, you're *here.*" Fresh tears flowed down my face, and I couldn't will them to stop. The devastation of almost losing her was still so fresh, so potent, that it hung over me like a dark cloud. I buried my face in her shoulder, clinging to her, afraid if I released her that the god of death would snatch her away from me.

"Varius," she murmured, her fingers digging into my arm.

I sniffed, realizing I was soaking her bodice with my snot and tears, then drew back to offer her an apologetic smile. "Forgive me, *dannahla*. You scared me half to death."

Her eyes warmed, and she pressed her palm to my cheek, catching my tears with her fingers. "It's all right. I'm here." Her mouth puckered in a slight frown. "But… I don't know how. I thought the curse could only be broken by my death."

"What were the exact words of the curse?" Tislora asked.

Sybelle's eyes grew distant as she no doubt recalled the words from her notes. "*Until one of my kind gives up her life for yours…*"

"It did not mention death at all?" Tislora prodded.

Sybelle hesitated, then shook her head. "No."

Tislora's thin lips curved into a satisfied smile. "That clever bitch."

I snorted, then shot her a look that was half amusement, half irritation.

"You *did* give up your life, Sybelle," Tislora said. "You had every intention of dying when you jumped into the storm. Your sacrifice was valid because you did not expect to return. But Jessinda never stated you had to die."

My gaze cut to hers, my face slackening in shock. "So it's true? The curse is broken?"

Tislora spread her arms. "Do you see the Necro Shadows anywhere?"

I glanced around. While it was utterly wasted and as grim as a graveyard, there wasn't a single shadow in sight. The moon was high in the sky, bathing the ruined village in pale light. The faint Umbra Mist that surrounded the castle still lingered nearby, but it was feeble compared to the thick, roiling Necro Shadows, which were nowhere to be found.

They were gone. Well and truly *gone*.

My heart lurched in my chest. "I—can you—Lor, can you shift?" My voice was weak because, once again, I did not dare to hope. Sybelle's survival was already a miracle I did not deserve. But for my people to be freed, too? It was too much. It couldn't possibly be true.

Tislora closed her eyes, and a flash of white light engulfed her. When it faded, she stood before me in her seelie form. Her wings had vanished, and she had shrunk a few inches. Her charcoal skin had lightened and warmed to a deep mahogany. She still wore her signature black robes, but her claws had shrunk to dulled fingernails, and her once-silver eyes were a muted gray. Only her pointed fae ears gave away her true nature.

"*Stones*," Sybelle breathed, her eyes wide as she took in Tislora's new form. "You look so... ordinary."

Tislora wrinkled her nose, glancing over herself. "You're right. This is terrible." Another flash of white light, and her unseelie form returned, wings and all. She sighed with contentment, her wings stretching wide behind her. "That's better."

I chuckled, then found Sybelle looking at me, that spark of curiosity gleaming in her eyes. "What about you?"

"I am content sitting here and holding you, *dannahla*."

She arched an eyebrow. "What if I asked you to show me? I want to know *all* the forms my husband can take." The dark and sensuous look in her eye made me growl with desire.

Tislora made a retching sound. "Spare me."

Azure uttered a soft rumbling noise, the sound suspiciously like laughter.

I carefully eased Sybelle off my lap, ensuring she could sit up on her own before I edged away from her. When she looked at me in confusion, I explained, "I don't know if the transition will hurt you."

She nodded, biting on her lower lip in anticipation. I closed my eyes and held my breath, searching within myself for that long-lost magic. It had seemed easy for Tislora, but she was accustomed to shifting to her crow form. She knew what the transformative magic felt like.

I did not. Never in my life had I shifted to a seelie form. Would my body even know how to do it?

As I dug deep within the well of power in my chest, I sensed a new presence. A gleaming white light beckoned me forward, and I grasped for it, reaching further and further into the recesses of my mind.

As soon as I made contact, the light exploded around me, and I felt my body shift. My skin stretched and shrank. My wings folded inward, disappearing into my shoulder blades. Pain split through me, so reminiscent of the curse's transformation that I almost cried out for Sybelle to take cover. I did not want to hurt her.

I hunched over with a groan, prepared to crouch on all fours and endure the pain like I had every full moon.

But, all too suddenly, it stopped. The white light faded.

And Sybelle gasped.

THE BEAUTY

There he stood, still *my* Varius, but... different. He was several inches shorter, though still taller than me. If I stood, I would likely come up to his nose. His broad frame and muscular figure were the same, but now his skin was a golden brown, perhaps a shade lighter than my chestnut hair. His curly hair remained jet black, as did his eyes. A short black beard lined his mouth and chin. His talons were now blunt fingernails, and his tail and wings were gone.

My jaw dropped as I took him in. He could have been a member of the Earthen Court. He could have been *human*, were it not for his pointed fae ears.

I drew closer to him, too stunned to speak. He appraised me, his eyes guarded. Vulnerability shone in his gaze.

He was nervous. Did he fear my reaction? Did he think I would despise his new form?

Ironic how, now that he could *appear* human, he feared this would disgust me.

I found myself laughing, then quickly covered my mouth. He blanched, his face paling.

"Shit, is it bad?" He glanced over himself in worry.

I laughed harder. "No, not at all! I—I just can't believe it. You —You look beautiful, Varius. But... I fell in love with your unseelie form. *That* is the Varius I know." I closed the distance between us, resting my palms against his chest. His tunic was ripped down the middle, exposing his muscled torso. I dragged my finger between his two pectorals, then looked up at him with a sly smile. He was *so close*. If I tilted my face up, our lips would meet.

Perhaps there were benefits to this form after all. I didn't have to stand on my tiptoes to reach his face, for one. He sighed with contentment and closed his eyes, bringing his forehead to mine. His warmth, his familiar scent, enveloped me. It felt like... *home*.

Unseelie or seelie, he was *mine*. My king. My everything.

"Stones, I love you," I whispered.

"I love you, too."

His mouth crashed into mine. I wrapped my arms around his neck, drawing him closer, allowing my fingers to thread through his soft hair. He groaned, gripping my waist and bringing me flush against him, his hips grinding along mine. His hands and arms still felt so strong, so sturdy. I felt *safe* in his grasp.

And he was mine. All mine.

Tislora cleared her throat loudly, and we broke apart. My face was on fire, but Varius was unperturbed as he smirked down at me. His fingers captured a lock of my hair, and he tucked it behind my ear. "We will have plenty of time to explore this new body of mine, *dannahla*."

Heat coiled low in my belly from the seductive promise of his words. I caught my lower lip between my teeth, and his eyes tracked the movement.

"For the love of Shade," Tislora snapped. "Are you two quite finished? Because we have an army to get back to."

Varius glanced upward, his brows lowering and a muscle feathering in his jaw. All heat fled from my body as I, too, remembered the army that had invaded our home. Was it still there? It was wishful thinking to believe the soldiers would simply turn around now that the Necro Shadows had vanished.

Azure pressed her claws further into the ground and rumbled something low in her throat. I ran to her side, wrapping my arms around her and nuzzling her neck. "I missed you," I whispered. "And I'm so sorry."

She moaned something I couldn't understand. I must have lost my amber necklace in the storm. But I could detect the sorrow in her voice and tightened my embrace.

She knelt, lowering herself so I could climb atop her. I looked at Varius, who faltered, his face full of grief and uncertainty.

"What's wrong?" I asked.

He took a step backward, his face pale as he shook his head. "I can't—I can't go back."

I frowned and slid off Azure's back. "What are you talking about? Of course you can."

"Sybelle, I—I killed so many people. *My own* people." His voice was full of anguish. His eyes crammed shut, his expression crumpling. "I cannot face them."

"That's bullshit, Varius," Tislora snapped. "You weren't in control."

"That doesn't matter!" he shouted. "A king should protect his people! Not tear them apart. I—I shouldn't have even been there with them. If I had hidden myself away, then perhaps..."

"Then perhaps those foolish humans would have taken the castle," Tislora said sharply.

My heart twisted at the devastation on his face. This was not something that could be argued away.

This would haunt Varius for the rest of his life. I was sure of it.

I strode toward him, grateful he was still in his seelie form so

I could easily clasp his face between my hands. I forced him to meet my gaze and fixed my most fearsome stare on him.

"You are a king, Varius. For good or ill. And the king I fell in love with did not run from his fears. He faced them head-on."

His eyes filled with tears, but his gaze stayed locked onto mine.

"You made mistakes," I went on. "*Terrible* mistakes. Nothing you can do will erase what you've done. But you *can* move forward from this. You can make amends as best you can. And you can become a better king for your people. *That* is what they deserve. Not a king who runs from his problems, but a king who will acknowledge his flaws and beg forgiveness. A king who will change for the better."

Tears streaked down his face, and he closed his eyes. "Sybelle..."

I drew closer to him, pressing my forehead to his. "It will not be easy. But I will be by your side the whole time. I will help you through it. I swear it."

A shattered moan poured from his lips, and his arms encircled my waist. His head dropped to my shoulder, his large body shaking with fresh sobs. "So much pain. So much loss."

I gently lifted his head and wiped the tears from his eyes. My throat knotted with emotion, and I blinked the moisture from my own eyes, determined to keep my composure for his sake. The sight of him like this broke me, but I needed to be strong right now.

For him.

"Let's make sure that loss was not in vain," I whispered. "One step at a time, husband. And right now, the first step is to face this army and stop a war. We can focus on the next steps later."

He inhaled deeply and nodded, drawing back to look me over. He stroked my cheek, his eyes warming despite the tears that still lingered. "How did you become such a mighty and courageous leader?"

Half my mouth quirked in a smile. "I've always been like that. It's just taken you a long time to see it."

He huffed a laugh at that, then allowed me to steer him toward Azure, who was still kneeling before us. I climbed on her back, and Varius followed suit. I glanced uncertainly at Tislora, noting her torn wing.

The sorceress rolled her eyes. "My crow's wings are still intact. I can fly behind you."

"Or I can heal you, if you prefer," I offered.

Her eyebrows lifted, and the irritation on her face melted away. "I—well, that would be much appreciated. Thank you… Sybelle."

I smiled at the usage of my name. Without her, none of this would have been possible. The curse would never have been broken. She had become… an unlikely ally, of sorts. And having her on my side had been an unexpected and pleasant surprise.

We weren't the closest of friends, but it was certainly a start.

A few minutes later, with Tislora freshly healed and flying behind us, Varius and I rode atop Azure as she flew us back to Agnarr Castle. With her great wings, Tislora managed to keep up easily with Azure's pace.

I held my breath when we passed the forest, expecting to see the clash of weapons between humans and fae.

Instead, I found the two armies facing off. Shouts and screams echoed below, but… no one was fighting.

Azure circled the crowd, then slammed into the ground next to both armies. Shrieks of alarm filled the square, and I found myself laughing. For so many years, I had been desperate to keep Azure's identity a secret.

Now, it seemed, it didn't really matter. In the kingdom of the unseelie, there were all kinds of beasts and creatures. Like me, it just felt as if Azure *belonged* here.

And it was time for her to make herself known.

I slid off her back and raced toward the road where the armies stood. In front, wearing a massive silver crown and a scowl worthy of our father, stood my sister, Orla. Her face was pale as she took in my dragon, but when her gaze fixed on me, she glared with venom.

"Orla," I panted when I reached her side. "What is this? Why are you doing this?" I gestured to the fae, then faltered when I realized *all* of them were in their seelie forms.

No wonder the humans had stopped fighting. When the curse broke and the fae realized they could shift forms, it had probably shocked everyone enough to halt the fighting.

For now.

"They are unseelie!" Orla snarled, jabbing a finger toward the row of fae soldiers in front. "They must die!"

"They are *my people*," I said firmly. "You would kill them all just because of your prejudice?"

"Their shadows have been attacking our people for years," Orla snapped, then pointed to Varius. "*His* shadows!"

"They were not mine," Varius said, drawing forward. His gaze flicked toward his soldiers, and the barest hint of agony crossed his features.

I slid closer to him and laced my fingers through his, giving his hand an encouraging squeeze.

Varius cleared his throat and continued speaking. "We were cursed, Orla. Your sister has now broken that curse. Don't you wonder why we are all suddenly able to change forms?" He spread his free hand toward his soldiers.

"It's a deception!" Orla cried, waving her sword at the people standing behind her. "Do not fall for their tricks! They mean to confuse us so they can slaughter us while we are unawares."

"We do not mean you any harm!" I shouted, my voice rising over my sister's. "The Shadow Fae *never* meant to harm humans. Their land was cursed by the poisonous shadows. That's why they needed human brides; only a human from the Earthen Court could break the curse."

Orla's nostrils flared. "How *convenient* that you just happened to break this alleged curse right when my army is upon your doorstep."

"It's not convenient at all to destroy the lives of my people based on false information," I hissed. "Ask Gerard. His *mother* was the one who cast the curse."

Orla opened her mouth to speak, but Varius interjected.

"Gerard is dead."

I stared at Varius. The darkness in his eyes told me what I needed to know: *He* had killed Gerard.

Deep down, I had known; the curse could not have been broken without Gerard's death.

Even so, the truth of that statement jolted through me. Varius uttering it made it all too real.

Gerard was dead.

Shocked murmurs rippled over the humans, and Orla's face turned ashen. "He—He's *dead?*" she whispered.

My stomach sank. Stones, had she truly cared for him? I assumed she had just married him as a slight to me, but the look of devastation on her face made me believe otherwise.

"He wanted to stop us from breaking the curse," I said as gently as I could. "He *wanted* war between our kingdoms. Orla, he wanted the Necro Shadows to get stronger."

Orla shook her head, her eyes squeezing shut. "Be silent. I don't want to hear any more of your lies."

"I *cannot* lie!"

"I don't believe you!" she roared, jabbing her sword at me. "You deserve to die along with them. You murdered my husband! And you will pay for it."

She advanced, teeth bared and hatred burning in her eyes. I stepped away from Varius and drew my dagger, which seemed pitiful in comparison to Orla's massive sword.

But if she wanted a fight, I would give it to her.

A low growl rumbled from my dragon, and she stomped toward Orla, placing her massive blue-scaled body between us.

"She says if you want to kill Sybelle, you will have to go through her first," Varius said. "And you will also have to go through *me*." His voice was lethal and deadly. When I glanced at him, his teeth were bared, and there was fire in his eyes.

All hesitation and anguish were gone. All that remained was a fierce king, willing to do anything to protect his people.

To protect *me*.

Suddenly, I registered something. Since when could Varius *communicate* with Azure? I shot a surprised look at him, and he offered me a half smile.

Orla staggered back a step, glancing between me and Azure. "That's not—you can't—"

"If the rest of you decide to leave peacefully, we will allow it," I shouted, my voice carrying over the soldiers. "But if you do not, my dragon will attack. And she will not show mercy."

To prove my point, Azure snarled, revealing her fangs. Her entire body seemed to rumble with a growl. She couldn't breathe fire—none of her kind could.

But the soldiers didn't need to know that.

Several of the humans whispered among themselves, backing slowly away from the dragon. When Orla noticed, she screeched, "Stop! You obey *my* command! And I order you to attack!"

No one moved.

"Attack!" Orla screamed, waving her sword wildly.

Still, her soldiers did not move. Many of them cast uncertain glances at Azure. Others outright glared at Orla, their faces full of distrust.

"I suggest you redirect your efforts to leading your own people," Varius said loudly, "before you decide to take over mine. It doesn't seem like your people are willing to follow you into battle, which, in my experience, is not the mark of a good ruler."

Orla glared at him. "That isn't your concern, Wraith King."

"It is when you invade *my home* and kill *my people*." Varius stepped closer to her, his arms rigid at his sides. He pointed to her soldiers. "Your men are refusing your command. So we will offer you one last opportunity to leave the Shadow Court. If you don't, I will take advantage of the instability of your army and slaughter anyone who remains here. I'll wager many of your soldiers would rather flee than face a dragon, wouldn't you?"

Orla's lips thinned, and she glanced at the soldiers. Already, several of them had started sprinting for the forest. "Shit," she hissed.

"Orla," I said, and she swung her head toward me, eyes flashing with fury. "The shadows are gone. You can see it for yourself. There is no reason to wage war."

"I'll be the judge of that," she spat, backing away from Varius and Azure. She reached her large white horse and grabbed the reins. "This is *not* over. Don't think that just because we share blood that I will forgive what you've done, Sybelle. You are still one of *them*." She jerked her sword toward the fae soldiers. "And it's because of you that he's dead." Her voice broke on the last word.

Emotion filled my throat. I had no answer for that, because she was right. Gerard had wanted the curse to live on, but he had also come for *me*. He had made that much clear.

All I could say was, "I'm sorry."

This only made Orla angrier. Her face twisted into something savage and unrecognizable. This was not my sister. This was a stranger.

She mounted her horse, then jerked on the reins before taking off toward the forest. Slowly, her soldiers followed after. Varius and I stood next to each other, watching as each human retreated. Only after their footsteps faded did we turn to look at each other.

"I could not have done this without you, Sybelle," he murmured.

"This isn't over," I said softly. "She will come back."

Varius nodded before wrapping his arms around me and cradling my head against his chest. "I know, *dannahla*. But we will be ready for her when she does."

THE BEAUTY

Enzira fussed over my lacy sleeves, then ensured my curls were pinned in place. When she stepped back to look me over, her eyes were moist with tears.

"How do I look?" I asked, my voice trembling from my nerves.

Enzira's lower lip wobbled, and she clapped a hand over her mouth, barely stifling a sob.

"She means you look like a queen," Ramia said, bringing her hand to my cheek. Her eyes were moist, too, but she managed to keep the tears from flowing. "I'm so proud of you, lady."

I offered her a breathless smile. "Thank you. Both of you. For *everything*." I repeated the words in Agnarrish, then took both of their hands in mine.

I would not be here were it not for them. I owed them everything.

They both beamed at me, and I took a moment to gaze lovingly at my dearest friends. Enzira was in her seelie form, standing a bit shorter than me, with dark brown skin and a multitude of thick black braids. With her wide grin, I almost found myself missing the familiar sight of her fangs.

But she was still utterly beautiful to me, no matter what form she took.

From outside our tent, a loud horn blew, and I tensed, my body quivering.

"It's time," Enzira said, pressing her fist to her chest. "We will be right outside… my queen."

Ramia curtsied, then followed Enzira out of the tent, leaving me completely alone. I stared at myself in the mirror. This was so very different from the marriage ceremony. For one thing, the ceremonial garb covered far more of my body than I was accustomed to. White lace reached up to my neck, the sleeves falling to my wrists. White roses were sewn into the skirt, and diamonds trimmed the hemline, making the fabric sparkle with each movement.

Despite the strength the diamonds gave me, I was still a puddle of anxiety.

This was the first time I would be facing my people. My kingdom.

Everyone.

The marriage ceremony had been a private affair. I knew now that it was because of the curse. The ritual only needed to be completed; it did not need to be publicly announced in any way.

Varius wanted to rectify that. So, with this coronation cere-mony, he created a celebratory event for everyone, regardless of their station, to attend. He wanted to announce me not only as their new queen but as the one who had broken the curse and saved his people.

To be honest, it made me deeply uncomfortable. I had not acted alone, and it felt wrong for me to take all of the credit.

But it made Varius so happy. From the moment he began planning this ceremony, the gleam in his eyes had only gotten brighter. I had never seen him so alight with joy.

I took a deep breath to steel myself before stepping through the flaps of the tent. An aisle of crimson fabric led the way from my tent to the courtyard in the center of town. It had been a few weeks since the Necro Shadows had vanished. Varius had sent a team to repair the Pern District so the civilians could return to their homes.

Now, the village was a bustling hub of activity. The homes had been rebuilt. New roads had been paved. Debris had been cleared away.

Cheers and applause rang from the square. I lifted my chin, gathered my skirts, and strode down the carpeted path.

A row of armored soldiers stood in front of the crowd. Each one drew their sword and pressed it to their chest as a symbol of honor and loyalty. I inclined my head to them before sweeping past, my fingers trembling at my sides.

On either side of the red carpet were thousands of fae. Some still maintained their unseelie forms; others chose to wear their seelie forms. My eyes roved over the crowd, taking in the purple and green skin tones, the wings and tails that had once frightened me. They mingled with the pale and brown skin tones of the seelie.

But to me, they all looked like one unified group of people. *My* people.

I found myself beaming at them, delighted to see them all here together. They cheered and applauded as I made my way down the aisle. Their grins of delight were infectious, and the sight eased the knots in my chest.

I climbed the steps to the dais and found Varius waiting for me, sitting on the throne that had been hauled to the village square. Next to him was a matching throne, this one unoccupied. *My* throne.

Varius wore his ceremonial jerkin, his tunic open at the chest. A silver crown was atop his head. And he, too, was in his unseelie form.

But I didn't mind it one bit. I let myself admire the great

wings stretched on either side of him, the barbed tail coiled beside him, and the glittering black claws extended from his fingers. He smiled down at me as I approached, his gaze heated and full of a love I did not deserve.

Stones, the heady look he was giving me… It was powerful enough to unravel me within seconds. My chest tightened, and I found I couldn't tear my eyes away from him. His lips parted, and fire burned in his gaze, hot enough to scorch me from the inside out.

Next to him stood Tislora, a gleaming silver crown in her hands. Like Varius, she was also in her unseelie form—wings, claws, and all. She rolled her eyes at the steaming tension brimming between me and Varius, then lifted her hand to quiet the crowd.

The people fell silent, watching with interest as Tislora drew closer to me. I obediently knelt before her, ready to accept my crown.

"Sybelle of the Earthen Court," she said, her voice ringing over the square. "Do you accept this crown that marks you as Queen of the Shadow Court?"

In a firm voice, I said, "I do."

"And do you vow to uphold the laws and oaths of this kingdom as its ruler?"

"I solemnly vow."

"Do you vow to protect your people at all costs, and put their needs above your own?"

"I solemnly vow."

"The ceremonial dagger, please," Tislora said.

From the side, Clermont appeared with the same jeweled dagger that had been used for the wedding ceremony. He was in his seelie form—tall and wiry, with white-blond hair and olive green eyes. He drew closer, his eyes questioning me. I nodded and raised my palm. With one smooth motion, he slid the blade along my hand, drawing blood. I clenched my teeth at the fleeting pain from the wound.

"Do you, Sybelle, swear on your blood to honor the vows you've made here today?" Tislora asked.

"I solemnly swear it on my blood." Heat burned from the wound as the power of my vow swept over me.

"Then, by the ancient magic flowing through my blood, and the powers of the earth at our feet, I hereby crown you as the rightful queen of the Shadow Court."

I closed my eyes as she lowered the crown onto my head. The cool metal weighed heavily on me. I drew in a gasp as magic crackled in the air, circling around me. Tislora offered a small smile before stepping off to the side with Clermont. I climbed to my feet, careful not to let the crown tip over in the process. Varius stretched his hand out to me, and I took it, gliding to the throne beside him before sinking onto it.

The people erupted in vibrant cheers, some jumping on their feet, others whooping with joy. I laughed at their enthusiasm, tears stinging my eyes. Varius squeezed my hand in his, then brought my knuckles to his lips.

"My queen," he murmured against my skin.

I grinned at him. "My king."

The people cried out with delight. From within the crowd, someone shouted, "All hail the King and Queen of the Shadow Court!" Several others roared their assent, raising their hands in the air to show their support.

Eira, my friend from the Winter Court, launched herself into my arms the moment we descended the dais. She had been standing in the front row alongside her father, a fae with gray hair and a warm smile. His bright blue eyes were identical to Eira's. Her raven black hair was pulled into a braid down her back, and she wore a cerulean dress that matched the color of her court.

"Sybelle!" she shrieked, squeezing me tightly against her chest. "You have no idea how thrilled I am for you." She withdrew to give me a huge smile that was all teeth. When her gaze slid to Varius looming behind me, her eyes rounded, and a faint blush crept into her cheeks. "Blood and ice, Sybelle..." She pressed a hand to her chest and swallowed. Then, she leaned in to mutter, "I don't know how you *ever* thought he was *curmudgeonly*."

I elbowed her hard, and we both burst into laughter, knowing full well Varius's fae hearing meant he had understood every word. I pressed a fist to my chest, inclining my head toward the king of the Winter Court. "Your Highness. I am honored that you are here."

King Judas bowed to me, his eyes crinkling with his smile. "We were thrilled to receive your invitation. And I know my daughter has been anxious to see you again."

"Anxious. Desperate. *Frantic.* Whatever you want to call it." Eira's laugh was infectious. I had always admired that about her.

Behind me, Varius cleared his throat, and I felt my face flush. I quickly stepped back and gestured to my husband. "This is King Varius of the Shadow Court."

Eira sank into an elegant curtsy, her eyes sparkling. "Your Highness."

King Judas bowed again, his eyes solemn. "King Varius. I had the pleasure of meeting your father once, long ago."

Varius stiffened. "My condolences."

Judas chuckled. "Yes, I can't say I was too fond of him. But I can already see how different you are from him. You have my congratulations for such a happy union. And for already demonstrating yourself to be a fine king to these people."

My chest warmed from his words, and I laced my fingers through Varius's. His arm was rigid, though, and he said nothing in exchange. Instead, he merely pressed a fist to his chest.

An awkward silence passed between us. Eira's shrewd gaze flicked from me to Varius and back again, missing nothing.

I widened my eyes meaningfully at her, hoping she would take the hint. She nodded, then looped her arm through her father's. "Let's grab some drinks, shall we, Father?"

Judas muttered a quick farewell before his daughter steered him away. I shot Eira a grateful look, vowing to catch up with her more thoroughly later. She had assured me they would remain in the Shadow Court for a few days, which would give us plenty of time.

I squeezed Varius's hand. "Are you all right?"

He looked down at me, his eyes full of warmth. "Yes, *dannahla*. I am more than all right." With his free hand, he cupped my chin and lowered his mouth to mine. I stood on my tiptoes and kissed him fully, wrapping my arms around his neck and relishing the heat of his body against mine.

Hours later, my cheeks hurt from smiling so much as we greeted one guest after another. The square had transformed into a place of merriment and revelry. Drinks and refreshments had been brought out. The people were dancing and laughing and drinking.

I was chatting with Enzira and a few of her friends when I caught sight of Varius. He stood off to the side, having withdrawn from the crowd a while ago. His arms were folded over his chest as he watched the celebration. Despair darkened his features, and I knew where his thoughts had turned.

He was still haunted by what he'd done as a beast. He had buried the fallen soldiers himself, had even visited the grieving families, offering to provide for their needs as long as necessary. My husband had worked tirelessly to make amends and serve his people as much as possible to atone for what he'd done.

But it would never be enough. It was a start, but nothing could erase the trauma of that night.

I squeezed Enzira's arm and bid her farewell as I crossed the square to where Varius stood. When he noticed me coming his way, his expression warmed, though his eyes still remained heavy with grief.

"Dance with me," I said.

His mouth quirked in a halfhearted smile. "Sybelle…"

"You are my husband, and I want to dance with you." I lifted my chin.

His eyes heated as he recognized those exact words from the revel. His smile widened, revealing his fangs. With a long-suffering sigh, he took my hand in his and escorted me toward the throng of dancers.

Our bodies moved together, matching the rhythm of the music. Varius's hands felt hot on my waist, and my chest was flush against his. The longer we danced, the more his body seemed to loosen, as if the weight of his thoughts and fears drifted away with each passing moment. He even managed to twirl me in his arms, eliciting a surprised laugh from me. My face flushed, my skin heating as I remembered our dance during the revel.

Stones, things had been so different back then.

Varius brought his mouth to my ear. "That crown looks magnificent on you."

I suppressed a shiver as his breath caressed my skin. My grip tightened on his arms as our bodies swayed together. "Perhaps I'll keep it on for every hour of the day." I looked up at him through my lashes. "Even in bed."

He growled, his fingers splaying along my back as his hips met mine. "You wear nothing but that crown tonight and I swear to worship every inch of your body. With my tongue."

Liquid heat pooled between my thighs. My voice was slightly strained as I said, "That does seem like a service fit for a queen."

His sultry gaze held mine, and my heartbeat quickened. He leaned in, and I arched upward to meet him as he kissed me.

His tongue collided with mine, and a moan escaped me as his fangs gently caught my lower lip. I gripped his tunic, drawing him closer as my hands roamed the hard planes of the exposed parts of his chest. Stones, I wanted him. I wanted *all* of him.

He broke the kiss with a gasp, then took my hand and steered me away from the square. I let out a soft yelp, glancing over my shoulder at the crowd. Eira was laughing alongside her father. She caught my eye and winked suggestively.

I couldn't even process a response because I was hurrying to match Varius's quick pace. He guided me toward an unfamiliar building. We stepped through the doors and made our way up a winding set of stairs that led to the roof.

"Varius, what—" I broke off with a startled cry as he scooped me into his arms, then started sprinting toward the edge of the roof. My heart jumped into my throat when he leapt over the edge. My stomach hollowed, and I crammed my eyes shut, waiting for us to plummet to the ground.

Varius's wings snapped open, and we glided, the momentum of his jump carrying us over the square.

My eyes flew open, and I uttered a soft gasp as we floated over the myriad buildings spread below us. It wasn't quite like flying with Azure—her massive wings could lift us as high as the clouds. Varius's were only meant for gliding. And, thankfully, the Pern District rested on a hilltop, allowing us to fly freely toward Agnarr Castle.

I held my crown in place, afraid it would fall and be lost forever. When I looked up at Varius, I found him smirking down at me.

"That was *terrifying*," I said, slapping his chest with my free hand. "You could have warned me."

"Ah, but where is the fun in that, *dannahla*?" He flashed a wicked grin at me.

We coasted in the air until the hill leveled out. Varius gracefully landed on the road that led past the Noxen Forest. To my surprise, he didn't lower me but kept me nestled in his arms.

"I can walk just fine," I protested.

"This is faster," he insisted, his grin downright feral as he broke into a run.

I squealed in surprise, huddling against his chest as he sprinted down the road and toward the castle. My laughter was breathless, and he chuckled along with me, not even winded when we reached the entrance doors. A pair of guards obediently pulled them open for us, and we made our way down the hall. Varius turned the handle of the first door he could find.

The castle led us straight to our bedchamber. Even after the curse was broken, the sentient castle remained, which led us to believe the walls had always held magic; it had merely come alive with Jessinda's spell.

It would also explain why the castle had refused to help Gerard, Jessinda's son. The castle had been on *our* side. Not his.

And that was how it always would be.

Varius kicked the door shut and carried me to the bed before gently depositing me on the soft mattress. I kicked off my shoes and sat up to tug at the row of buttons holding my dress together.

With an impatient growl, Varius slid his claws through the fabric and ripped it in half.

I scoffed. "Was that really necessary?"

"The offensive fabric was impeding my devout worship of your body," he said defensively, sliding the torn lace away from my arms and back. I slid off his tunic, which was far easier to remove, since it was already open at the chest. My impatient fingers wriggled underneath the band of his kilt before tugging it down to reveal his hard length. My throat went dry at the sight of it.

Stones, I would never tire of this. I would never tire of *him*.

I was still surrounded by piles of fabric, but Varius made

quick work of discarding the pieces of my dress on the floor, then hovering over me with a hungry look in his eyes.

"You'd better keep that crown on, too," I whispered.

His eyes darkened as they roved over me. A low rumbling sound resonated in his throat. "As you wish, my queen."

He brought his mouth to mine, his tongue sweeping over my lips. He moved his mouth to my cheek and jawline, then my throat, sucking and nipping at my neck. I moaned, arching into him, my fingers winding through his curls. Still, his tongue moved lower, slipping between my breasts. He captured one in his mouth, his fangs brushing against my hardened nipple. Heat flooded my veins, setting my blood on fire. My hips bucked, and I bit back a cry of ecstasy.

His hands were on my thighs, spreading them wide. He groaned at the moisture there, then dipped his head between my legs. With one long stroke of his tongue, I was completely undone. I jerked wildly, my eyes closing and my head rolling back.

"So delicious," he murmured. "I could feast on you all night, *dannahla*."

"Varius, please," I rasped, then cried out when his tongue met my core again. I writhed under him, urging him onward, and he obliged. He thrust deeper, his long tongue reaching farther than I thought possible. My head was spinning, pleasure coursing through me in violent waves. Tension mounted within me, coiling tighter and tighter until I thought I might explode.

"I—I need you," I panted. "Varius—"

"Mmm," he purred against me, then sucked on the tenderest parts of me. I let out a whimper, a plea. "So much to worship... I don't think I'm quite finished, my queen." His lips pressed into me, his tongue tracing circles as he licked and sucked.

When the edge of his fangs brushed against me, I shattered completely. My hips rolled, and I thrust against him. He continued to feast on me, chasing me over that edge, drawing out the sensations that fired through me.

He withdrew, his arms coming around me and sitting me atop his lap. He righted the crown, which had fallen sideways on my head. "Eyes on me, *dannahla*. I want to look at you when I come."

My eyelids fluttered open, my body molten from his efforts. I didn't have my diamond dagger this time, but we had conducted plenty of experiments in bed, both with and without the help of diamonds. It turned out my fae blood granted me more strength than I realized.

And my body was growing accustomed to fitting Varius's length inside me.

He spread my legs again, and I wrapped them around his middle, my heels digging into his back.

"Take me, Shadow King," I commanded.

He kissed me, hard and bruising, his fangs digging into my lip just before he plunged into me with a singular powerful thrust. I cried out, but he silenced me with his tongue, claiming my mouth again and again. He slid out, then drove back into me, harder this time. My fingernails dug into the skin of his back, and I buried my face in his shoulder.

"No," he growled. "*Look* at me."

I leaned back, my eyes fixed on him. His pupils flared as he thrust again, a deep and rasping groan tearing from his throat. He set a hard pace, pushing deeper and deeper, his hips lifting with each movement. Still, I held his gaze, watching the way his eyes grew wilder. Shadows poured around us, framing the bed like a curtain.

"Sybelle," he moaned, slamming into me. The bed creaked loudly from our frantic movements. The sound of his animal-istic grunts mingled with our skin slapping together. My legs tightened around him. He shifted, lifting me higher so he could bury himself at a sharper angle. My throat was raw from my guttural cries.

He filled me so completely. The friction of his skin grinding against mine was so potent, so intoxicating. Stars danced in my vision, and my own shadows exploded around us, tinting the darkness with midnight blue.

Our powers collided, and I cried out his name. His teeth scraped my bare shoulder, my throat, before he drew back to look at me again, to pin me with that feral gaze. I felt him everywhere. Our bodies were one.

He pounded into me, holding nothing back. I screamed again and again, unable to contain myself. With one more violent thrust, he spilled inside me, his cock quivering from the force of it. I followed soon after, my mind spiraling, my body dissolving from his touch. I was nowhere and everywhere. Nothing and everything.

Time stopped. The world ceased to exist.

It was only me and Varius and the thrashing intensity that burned between us.

Varius shuddered against me, leaning his head against my shoulder as we caught our breath. My legs were still wrapped around him, our bodies slick with sweat.

Slowly, he lowered us down until we were reclined on the bed, still entangled in one another. Our crowns fell against the pillows, and we both chuckled.

"Are you all right?" he whispered, leaning back to look at me, his eyes full of concern. "I didn't hurt you, did I?"

I smiled, tucking his sweaty hair behind his ear. "No. That was… perfection."

He kissed me, long and slow, so unlike the desperate and wild kisses from before. This one was deliberate, as if we had all the time in the world.

And perhaps we did.

"You deserve nothing less than perfection," he said against my lips. "My Shadow Queen."

He rolled us so I lay atop him, my arms around his neck as he kissed me fully. Our legs were still intertwined, the sheets bunching around us. My sighs mingled with his deep voice as he murmured promises of the eternity we would spend together.

An eternity with my husband. My king.

My beautiful, monstrous *dannahla*.

If you want more steamy fairy tales, read **Crown of Poison**, a Snow White retelling about Sybelle's friend, Princess Eira!

ACKNOWLEDGMENTS

There are so many people who helped to bring this story to life! None of this would have been possible without you.

Tori, Melissa, Kari, Jenni, and Sara, my beta readers, who critiqued the rough draft and helped me shape the story.

Kaylerin Arts, Mary Begletsova, Kalynne Art, and Samaiya Art for the stunning character art for the book.

Blue Raven Book Covers for the covers and formatting.

Allison Rose, my editor, for your incredible work in polishing up the story.

The Crown of Briars special editions are all thanks to the many Kickstarter backers who supported the project! Thank you to everyone who pledged. Without your contributions, the deluxe versions of this book wouldn't be possible! Thank you so much for your amazing support.

A huge thank you to my stellar ARC team for reading early copies of the book! Your enthusiasm for Varius and Sybelle's story warmed my heart, and your early reviews were monumental to the success of the book launch.

Thank you to my Tuesday Tribe, who patiently listened to me vent my frustrations and problems when the plot wasn't working, and helped talk me through the issues to get me through the writer's block. Without you, I might not have been able to finish!

Above all, a big, beautiful thank you to my devoted husband and children for your support and love, and for your patience and understanding while I struggled to meet deadlines and finish this book. Thank you for being my champions. You are my rock!

ABOUT THE AUTHOR

R.L. Perez is an author, wife, mother, reader, writer, and artist. She lives in Florida with her husband and three kids. On a regular basis, she can usually be found napping, reading, feverishly writing, revising, or watching an abundance of Netflix. More than anything, she loves spending time with her family. Her greatest joys are her children, nature, literature, and chocolate.

Subscribe to her newsletter for new releases, promotions, giveaways, and book recommendations! Get a FREE eBook when you sign up at subscribe.rlperez.com.